The Jungle Book

Retold by
Saviour Pirotta

Illustrated by
Alex Paterson

ARCTURUS

For Jode Paton—SP.

For Alexa and William—AP.

ARCTURUS

This edition published in 2018 by Arcturus Publishing Limited
26/27 Bickels Yard, 151–153 Bermondsey Street,
London SE1 3HA

Copyright © Arcturus Holdings Limited

All rights reserved. No part of this publication may be reproduced, stored in a retrieval system, or transmitted, in any form or by any means, electronic, mechanical, photocopying, recording or otherwise, without written permission in accordance with the provisions of the Copyright Act 1956 (as amended). Any person or persons who do any unauthorised act in relation to this publication may be liable to criminal prosecution and civil claims for damages.

Writer: Saviour Pirotta
Illustrator: Alex Paterson
Designer: Jeni Child
Editor: Sebastian Rydberg
Art Director: Jessica Crass

ISBN: 978-1-78828-691-6
CH006179NT
Supplier 24, Date 0618, Print run 7517

Printed in Malaysia

Contents

CHAPTER 1
Man Cub Joins the Pack 4

CHAPTER 2
Beware of the Monkeys 14

CHAPTER 3
The Scary City 24

CHAPTER 4
Fire! Fire! 34

CHAPTER 5
Mowgli in the Man Village 44

CHAPTER 6
The End of Shere Khan 54

CHAPTER 1
Man Cub Joins the Pack

It was late evening when Father Wolf woke up from his nap. He looked around the cave. His four cubs were playing happily. Mother Wolf was licking behind their ears as they tumbled in the dust.

Suddenly, there was a loud roar outside the cave. The wolf cubs stopped playing at once. Their eyes widened with fear.

"It's Shere Khan, the tiger," whispered Mother Wolf. "He sounds very angry."

"He must be hungry," said Father Wolf.

"Don't worry," Mother Wolf comforted the cubs. "We're safe in here. The entrance to our cave is too narrow for him."

A shadow appeared in the mouth of the cave. It was Tabaqui, the jackal.

"Father Wolf," he said. "Do you have anything to eat in there?"

"There are some bones at the back of the cave," replied Father Wolf. "But there's no meat on them."

"They'll do for an old starving jackal like me," said Tabaqui. He crunched noisily on the bones. "Did you hear the news about the terrible Shere Khan? He's moved to this part of the jungle. It's closer to the village, and that gives him a better chance of catching a man cub."

"He shouldn't be in this part of the jungle at all," growled Father Wolf. "Not without warning us first. The people from the village are sure to come looking for him. I don't want man hunters finding my family's cave."

"He's been chasing a man cub all day," said Tabaqui. "But he's lame, as you know, and the man cub got away. Shere Khan accidentally stepped in a fire chasing him. He's burned his paw. That's made him even more angry than usual."

There was another tiger roar outside, and something on two legs came tottering into the cave. It was a man cub and it looked frightened.

Shere Khan's angry face blocked the light at the mouth of the cave. "Is the man cub in there?" he roared.

"What if he is?" answered Mother Wolf bravely.

"I've been chasing that man cub and his parents all day," growled Shere Khan. "The parents got back to their village. But the boy ran the other way. He is in there, I know it. GIVE HIM TO ME."

Mother Wolf gently drew the man cub deeper into the cave. "We shall do no such thing, you brute. Pick on someone your own size."

"You'll never get the man cub, I promise you that," snapped Father Wolf.

Shere Khan tried to get into the cave, squirming his powerful shoulders. His enormous paws raked the air. But he knew it was no use. The entrance to the cave really was too narrow.

"This is not the end of the matter," he spat. "I WILL get my paws on the man cub."

"The man cub will learn the ways of the wolf," said Father Wolf. "And when he is a man, he will come and hunt you down. The jungle will be rid of Shere Khan forever."

"Now, go back to your own part of the jungle," added Mother Wolf. "And leave my family in peace."

Shere Khan limped away, howling with rage. When the coast was clear, Tabaqui left the cave, too. Mother Wolf licked the man cub's hair. He looked funny with fur only on his head. "He must get very cold at night," she said.

The man cub cuddled up to Mother Wolf for warmth. The four cubs licked his hair to be friendly. Soon, the man cub had forgotten all about Shere Khan. He tumbled around the cave with the cubs.

"What shall we call him?" wondered Father Wolf.

"He reminds me of a hairless frog," said Mother Wolf. "We'll call him Mowgli."

On the night of the full moon, Mother and Father Wolf took the four cubs to Council Rock. They took Mowgli with them, too, because now he was part of the family.

Council Rock was a hilltop in the jungle. Here, the wolves met to inspect the new cubs before they were allowed to join the pack.

Akela, the leader of the pack, was lying on top of Council Rock. He was a powerful wolf with amber eyes. Below him, some forty wolves sat in a circle. They were inspecting the cubs.

Father Wolf pushed his four cubs into the circle. The older wolves watched them closely as they played and chased each other. At last, one of them nodded. "They shall be proud members of our pack."

Mother Wolf nudged Mowgli forward.

He sat in the circle, playing with pebbles.

"The man cub has no right to be in a wolf pack," roared a voice behind the rock. "I chased him across the jungle. Hand him over to me."

It was Shere Khan. He'd been watching the meeting from behind a tree.

"But Mowgli has lived with us for over two weeks," said Mother Wolf. "He is part of our family."

"He might be part of your family," argued some of the other wolves. "But we don't want him in the pack. He doesn't even have any fur."

"Silence," called Akela. "You know the rules. If there are two here who are not part of his family but can speak for Mowgli, he can join the pack."

Mother Wolf looked around the hilltop. Who would speak for man son? A sleepy bear stepped forward. His name was Baloo. He taught the wolf cubs the laws of the jungle and was the only animal allowed to attend wolf meetings.

"Let him stay," he said. "I shall be his teacher."

"But we need another to speak for Mowgli," said Akela. "Who will it be?"

There was a rustle in the trees, and

Bagheera, the black panther, slunk out. "I have no right to be in this meeting," he purred. "But I couldn't help overhearing. To prevent a cub from joining your pack because he has no fur is a mistake. It is not his fault he is hairless. Accept him, and I shall be a teacher to him, too."

Mother and Father Wolf looked at each other and smiled. At last, Mowgli was part of the pack.

CHAPTER 2
Beware of the Monkeys

Time passed, and Mowgli grew into a strong, healthy boy. Father Wolf taught him how to recognize the sounds of the forest. Baloo showed him how to pick nuts and how to climb up trees for fruit.

When Mowgli wanted a treat, Baloo helped pick honey without disturbing the bees. Often, Mowgli would go fishing in the river. On sunny days, he swam in the cool water and slept on the rocks in the sunshine. Bagheera would tell him stories of the village where the people lived. Bagheera often went there at night, looking for hens to steal.

He didn't always come back with prey, but he learned a lot about how people behaved and what they did.

"I have to be very careful when I'm hunting," he said. "Man has a precious red flower that is hot to the touch. He calls it fire. It scares me."

The wolf pack grew to like Mowgli. When they had thorns in their paws, Mowgli would remove them with his nails.

Only one beast watched him with hate in his eyes. That was Shere Khan, the tiger.

One day, Mowgli would not sit still for his lessons. Baloo was trying to teach him how to hiss like a snake. Baloo got angry. He smacked Mowgli on the bottom.

"Ouch," said Bagheera, who had dropped by to watch the lesson. "The poor boy's black and blue. Leave him alone, Baloo. You're going to kill him."

"I just gave him a gentle bear pat," argued Baloo. "Mowgli has to learn how important bird calls are. Animal calls, too. One day, he might find himself in danger and need to make one of those calls."

"But I know them all already," groaned Mowgli, rubbing his bottom.

"Well, show me how a snake hisses, then," said Bagheera.

Mowgli stuck out his tongue and hissed very loudly. "Hissssssss! Hissssss!"

"My, that's very good," said the black panther. "I almost looked behind me, expecting to see a real snake."

"Now show Uncle Bagheera how you would call a kite."

A kite was a very large bird. It had a call that could be heard from far away. Mowgli cleared his throat and called out. "Twee-eek! Twee-eek."

"Ha," said Bagheera. "That sounds just like my old friend Rann. He's a wise kite. You're learning fast, Mowgli. Well done!"

"The monkeys think I'm clever, too," boasted Mowgli.

Baloo, who'd been resting against a tree, sat up. "You have been talking to the monkeys? They are not to be trusted."

"But they give me nuts and bananas!"

"They don't give you fruit because they're kind," warned Baloo. "They're always up to mischief. The monkeys don't obey the law of the jungle. That is why the other animals don't speak to them. Promise me you'll never to talk to them again."

Mowgli promised. The sun got hotter and Baloo, Bagheera, and Mowgli found a shady spot to sleep in. Soon, Baloo and Bagheera were snoring.

Mowgli heard chattering in the trees above him.

"Hee-hee-hee. These nuts are crunchy."

"Hee-hee-hee. Absolutely delicious."

It was the monkeys. Mowgli desperately wanted some nuts, but he had promised Baloo he would not talk to them. He closed his eyes and tried very hard to go to sleep.

"Hee-hee-hee," came a voice from the tree branches. "Man cub is fast asleep."

"Hee-hee-hee," tittered a second voice. "Let's get him. We need someone to show us how to weave wind breakers out of reeds. Man cub will do that. He weaves wind breakers for the wolves."

Suddenly, Mowgli felt furry paws all over his arms and legs. They hauled him up into the branches of the trees. "Help," he shouted. "I'm being kidnapped. Help!"

His shouting woke up Baloo and Bagheera. Bagheera growled fiercely and leaped up the tree. But the monkeys beat him down again. There were so many of them, Bagheera could not fight back.

Baloo watched helplessly as Mowgli's

feet disappeared into the tree canopy. He howled and beat his head against the tree trunk, making it shake.

"Mowgli! Kidnapped by vile monkeys!"

Up in the treetops, Mowgli was terribly frightened. The monkeys were hauling him from one tree to another. The treetops grew so close together, Mowgli couldn't see the forest below. But he knew it would be a long way down if he fell. He hoped the monkeys wouldn't let go of him.

"Hee-hee-hee," chattered one of the monkeys. "Aren't we clever? We managed to snatch man cub right from under Baloo and Bagheera's nose."

Mowgli tried to think. Where were these horrible monkeys taking him? What did they want from him? And how could he escape?

At last, the monkeys stopped to rest. They lay back on the tree branches and closed their eyes for a nap. Their tails swung back and forth as they snoozed.

Mowgli looked up at the sky. The sun was setting, and the clouds seemed to be on fire. And there, soaring high up in the air, was Rann, the kite—Bagheera's friend!

Suddenly, Mowgli knew what he had to do. He put his hands around his mouth and called out. "Twee-eek! Twee-eek!" It was the bird call Baloo had taught him.

Rann heard the call and answered. "Twee-eek! Twee-eek!" He spotted Mowgli far below and swooped down toward him.

"Why do you call, man cub?" he asked, settling down on a tree branch close to Mowgli.

"I've been kidnapped by the monkeys,"

whispered Mowgli. "Please find Baloo and Bagheera. Will you tell them where the monkeys are taking me? They might come to rescue me."

Rann flapped his wings to rise back up in the air. He watched from the skies as the monkeys pulled Mowgli back into the treetops. He followed at a distance as the monkeys made their way through the trees. And then, he set off to find Baloo and Bagheera.

CHAPTER 3

The Scary City

Baloo sat howling. "My poor man cub!"

"We need to think, not howl," said Bagheera, "or we might never see poor Mowgli again."

Just then, he spotted Rann swooping down out of the sky. "I have a message from Mowgli," said the kite. "He has been kidnapped by the monkeys."

"We know that," wailed Baloo. "But we don't know where they have taken him."

"I followed them," said Rann. "They're holding him prisoner in Cold Lairs."

Cold Lairs had once been a beautiful city. Kings and queens had lived there. They had received people from all over the world in it. But then, the royals moved away.

Now Cold Lairs was just a long-abandoned ruin—and haunted! No animal ever set foot in it except the monkeys, who were too stupid to be scared of ghosts.

"How can we get there?" asked Baloo.

"My friend Khaa, the python, will take us," said Bagheera. "He knows every inch of the jungle. And the monkeys are terrified of him. One look at his powerful coils, and they'll let Mowgli go."

In Cold Lairs, the monkeys set Mowgli down in a great courtyard. They danced in a circle around him. "Teach us how to make wind breakers out of reeds," they said, "or we'll feed you to the ghosts."

"I'll gladly teach you," said Mowgli. "But first, you must give me something to eat. I'm hungry."

The monkeys went away to fetch some nuts. There was a lot of chattering as they argued over who should pick them. In the end, no one did. The monkeys started fighting.

Mowgli set off to find some himself. He walked across the courtyard past a throne where the king used to sit. He peeped into a stable where once the queen's elephants were kept. At last, he came to a garden full of fruit trees.

"Look out!" shouted one of the monkeys. "The man cub is escaping."

The monkeys swarmed all over Mowgli and dragged him into the king's old summerhouse. There was a clang as the monkeys slammed the gate shut. One of them turned the key in a padlock.

Mowgli looked around him. The summerhouse was full of snakes, and they were all hissing and glaring at him.

Mowgli froze for a moment. The snakes were crawling toward him. Their tongues flickered. Then, Mowgli remembered the snake call Baloo had taught him.

"Hissssssss!"

The snakes stopped wagging their tongues.

"Hissssssssss!" went Mowgli again.

The snakes stopped crawling toward him. One of them raised his head and answered Mowgli's call. "Hisssss!"

Mowgli sighed with relief. The snakes knew he was a friend. They would not hurt him now.

It got dark. The monkeys fell asleep in the ruins. Some snored loudly. From the corner of his eye, Mowgli saw a shadow creep across the palace wall.

He recognized it at once. It was Bagheera. Rann had fetched him.

There was a loud roar as Bagheera started hitting out at the monkeys. The creatures woke up and fought back fiercely, crawling all over the panther. They pinched, poked, and bit his back.

But Bagheera had fought bigger enemies than monkeys. He roared again and lashed out with his terrible claws. The monkeys on his back went flying up in the air, howling and screeching.

The other monkeys fell back, muttering.

"I'm here to save you, man cub," shouted Bagheera. He'd spotted Mowgli in the summerhouse. "And I am not alone."

A moment later, the palace wall shook and came tumbling down. Baloo had arrived. He had knocked a hole in the wall to get into the garden.

Baloo grunted and started ripping monkeys off Bagheera's back. Their screeches drew more monkeys to the fight. They hurled themselves at Baloo from every corner. Mowgli could hardly see the poor bear under the sea of monkey fur. He wished he could break out of the summerhouse to help him.

For a while, it looked like Baloo would be finished. There were too many monkeys. But then, a terrible sound echoed across the garden. "Ssssssssssssssss!"

The monkeys stopped chattering at once and looked around them in alarm.

Through the trees came the dreaded shape of Khaa, the python. The moon shone on his scaly skin, and his eyes glimmered like two jewels. The monkeys backed away, their teeth chattering in panic.

Khaa swung his head from side to side. He fixed the monkeys with his deadly stare. "Sssstay you sssooo," he hissed.

The monkeys all froze like statues. They tried to move, but they couldn't. The python had hypnotized them.

He wrapped his coil around one monkey to make sure his powers had worked. The monkey didn't even flinch. It stood as stiff as a straw doll.

Khaa hissed at Baloo and Bagheera. "Get the man cub out of here while my spell lasts."

Baloo growled at Mowgli. "Stand aside, man cub." He threw himself at the enormous gate, and it came crashing down in the grass. "Come on," he said to Mowgli. "Let's get you home."

Mowgli turned to Khaa. "Thank you for your help! I would still be a prisoner if it were not for you."

"I admire your free spirit, man cub,"

said the python. "Perhaps you will come to my help one day."

"If you ever need me, come look for me," replied Mowgli. "I would be very happy to help you."

Khaa flicked his tongue and slid up to the monkeys. "You sssssshall dancccceeeee," he hissed. "And you will keep on dancing till the sun comes up."

As Bagheera carried Mowgli out of the garden on his back, the monkeys started moving. At first they, swayed slowly. Then, they began stomping and chattering.

And they went on dancing till the sun rose, and Mowgli and his friends had escaped.

CHAPTER 4

Fire! Fire!

Mowgli and Bagheera started spending a lot of time together. They explored the deepest parts of the jungle, where no one else had gone before.

Late one night, they sat together on a moonlit rock. "Remember I once told you about Man's red flower?" asked Bagheera.

Mowgli nodded. "Fire."

"You might need it soon—Akela is getting old," he explained. "Soon, he will not be able to lead the wolf pack anymore. There are younger wolves desperate to take his place. Some of them are friends with Shere Khan. They don't like you."

"I've never done any of them any harm," said Mowgli sadly. "The wolves all come to me when they have thorns in their paws."

"Man has a power that scares the jungle animals," said Bagheera. "Look into my eyes."

Mowgli stared into Bagheera's eyes. After a while, the panther hung his head. "All men and women have that power in their eyes. The wolves are scared of it. They hate you for it. One day, they will try to destroy you."

Bagheera lifted up his head, so that Mowgli could see his neck. "Look closely. What do you see?"

"A scar," replied Mowgli. "The fur around it has been rubbed away."

"I was once captured by menfolk," said Bagheera. "They kept me in chains because they were scared of me. I don't tell anyone in the jungle about it. It's my shameful secret. I got used to living in the man village, but deep in my heart I knew I would one day escape and come back. And I did. Do you know why? Because the jungle is my home. It's where I belong. And you belong in the man village, with the people who walk on two legs. One day, you must go back to them."

"But the jungle is my home," argued Mowgli.

Bagheera sighed. "The wolves are having a secret meeting soon. Go fetch the red flower before it's too late."

When it got dark, Mowgli crept to the man village. He watched carefully from the bushes as a family sat around the fire. They were sharing a meal. When they finished, the mother led them all indoors. Only one girl remained to look after the fire.

Mowgli crept up behind her. The moment her head was turned, he snatched the fire pot and raced back to the jungle.

The secret meeting at Council Rock took place on the next full moon. Akela was there. He looked old and tired.

Shere Khan slunk out of the trees.

"What are you doing here?" asked Akela.

"I come for the man cub," growled Shere Khan. "Surely, you must have grown tired of him. He is not really one of you."

"We accepted him as a member of the pack," replied Akela firmly.

Shere Khan's roar shook the trees. "Give me to him, or I shall hunt down every single animal in your part of the jungle. There will be nothing left for any of you to eat. You will all starve."

"Let him have the man cub, Akela," said the younger wolves. "The tiger is right. Mowgli is not a wolf like us."

Akela sighed wearily. "I shall make a deal with you, Tiger. You can become the leader of the pack instead of me—if you promise never to hurt the man cub."

The younger wolves gathered around Shere Khan, wagging their tails.

"Shere Khan for leader!" they cried. "With the mighty Shere Khan leading us, we shall hunt and kill as we please. We shall be the most feared animals in the entire jungle."

"No," shouted Mowgli, leaping out from behind a tree. "You are wolves. Your leader should be a wolf. Don't let the tiger fool you. He will eat you all one by one."

"Seize the boy!" roared Shere Khan.

"Don't be scared," Bagheera hissed at Mowgli. "Remember your secret weapon."

The growling wolves surrounded Mowgli. Their jaws snapped, and their eyes glowed like embers. But Mowgli knew what he had to do. He'd brought the pot of glowing charcoal with him. Now, he thrust a branch into it, setting it on fire. He swung the burning branch in a big circle around him.

The wolves backed away at once; their growling turned to whimpering.

"Red Flower," they whispered.

"Come on, Shere Khan," shouted Mowgli.

"I'm here for you to eat."

He lunged at the tiger and thrust the burning branch under his nose. Shere Khan's whiskers burst into flames. He leapt back, batting away at his whiskers with his paws. "I will kill you for this." And then, he turned tail and disappeared into the jungle. Most of the other wolves followed him. Only a few remained. They were the ones who had welcomed Mowgli into the pack.

Bagheera came out from the trees. Mowgli's wolf parents and his four brothers gathered around him.

"I shall go and live in the man village," said Mowgli. "It is not safe for me here anymore. But I'll be back one day, you'll see. And I promise you this: I will bring Shere Khan's tiger skin with me."

"Goodbye, my child," cried Mother Wolf, giving Mowgli a lick on the face. "Take care of yourself, and remember, you have grown up with wolves. You are as cunning as we are. I shall think of you every day."

"Goodbye, my son," said Father Wolf. "Always be brave like I have taught you."

"I shall come see you when I can slip out of the jungle unnoticed," said the eldest of the wolf cubs, who was called

Brother Wolf. "I shall bring you news of the jungle."

Mowgli felt strange drops of water running down his face.

"Bagheera," he gasped, "My eyes are leaking. I am dying."

"Those are only tears," said the black panther gently. "You are crying. All human beings do. Goodbye, man cub. Remember all the animal calls that Baloo and I taught you. You must never forget them."

Then, he turned and started walking slowly away.

CHAPTER 5
Mowgli in the Man Village

An old man was standing at the village gate when Mowgli arrived. Mowgli had not eaten for a long time. He was very hungry and thirsty. But he didn't know the man words for food and drink. He pointed to his mouth and opened it wide.

The old man did not understand. "Help! Wild animal! Wild animal!" he called. "This creature is going to eat me up."

Children and grown-ups came running. They crowded around Mowgli, staring at his shaggy hair and long nails. Someone poked him with a stick.

"The creature is dirty."

"Its fur is all matted."

The headman of the village came out

to see why the villagers were making so much noise. "Why, it's a human child."

A woman pushed through the crowds. She held out her arms to Mowgli. "I lost a boy in the jungle many years ago. A tiger took him. He would be this boy's age if he had survived. Perhaps this is my son."

She took Mowgli's hand. "Come, I will look after you. You shall be as a son to me."

Mowgli didn't understand a word Messua said, but she looked friendly. Her eyes were full of kindness, so he followed her.

Messua could tell Mowgli was very hungry. She gave him some milk to drink. Mowgli sniffed at it suspiciously. He had never tasted milk before.

"Drink," Messua encouraged him.

Mowgli drank. Messua gave him some flatbread to eat. Then, she took him down to the stream to wash. She cut his hair and combed it neatly.

While she combed, she taught Mowgli a few words. "Hello" and "Please" and "Thank you."

At bedtime, she laid out a clean sheet on a cot.

"Sleep. Rest."

Mowgli lay down, but he couldn't sleep.

He had never slept under a roof before. He felt closed in. It worried him that he could not see the stars twinkling in the sky.

When Messua was asleep, he carried the cot outside. The man village was very quiet. Mowgli missed the sounds of the night in the jungle. He missed his wolf family, and Bagheera and Baloo.

Mowgli felt tears running down his face again. But he knew he had to get used to living outside the jungle. The man village was his home now.

Life in the man village was very hard at first. There were a lot of things Mowgli had to learn, especially talking in man language.

Often, Mowgli would get his words wrong. The other children laughed at him. This made Mowgli very angry. In the jungle, no one laughed at anyone if they got something wrong the first time.

Sometimes, he got so angry, he was tempted to hit the other children. He was much stronger than they were. But Bagheera had taught him to control his temper. He would never show those children that they were hurting him.

On dark nights, Brother Wolf would slink into the village. He gave Mowgli news of his family.

"What about Shere Khan?" Mowgli would ask. "Has he been seen?"

"You hurt his pride," said Brother Wolf. "He is still in hiding. But some say he swore to come and get you."

Some evenings, one of the herdsmen in the village would tell stories. His name was Buldeo, and he loved telling scary ghost stories. One night, he told one about a ghost tiger that haunted the jungle.

"What nonsense this man talks," said Mowgli to himself. "He has no idea what kind of creatures live in the jungle. He's probably never been there. There is no such thing as a ghost tiger."

The village headman could tell that Mowgli often felt sad. "The boy is not used to playing children's games. He grew up in the jungle where he had to fend for himself," he said to the other men. "He is used to the open air and to hard work. Let him be a herdsman in the fields. He will be happier there than playing games with the children in the village.

The herdsmen took Mowgli under their wing. They taught him how to look after the cattle and the buffaloes. One of them carved Mowgli a herdsman's stick. He showed him how to use it to prod the cattle along.

Mowgli enjoyed working in the open air. He preferred being with animals than people, and they liked him, too. They would come at once when he called, and they never strayed on their way to the river. Mowgli liked riding on the back of Rama, the buffalo. It was like riding on Baloo or Bagheera, only slower.

Sometimes, he watched Messua working in the paddies with the other women. They sang beautiful songs as they sowed the rice. Then one afternoon, Brother Wolf brought urgent news.

Mowgli was asleep in the shade of a tree. He woke up when Brother Wolf licked his feet to let him know he'd had arrived.

"Shere Khan's whiskers have grown back again," said Brother Wolf. "He has come out of hiding, and he has sworn to kill you."

"But how will he lure me back into the jungle?" wondered Mowgli.

"He is not waiting for you to come back," replied Brother Wolf. "He is coming for you here, in the fields. It will show the wolves in the pack how brave he is."

"When is this going to happen?" asked Mowgli.

"Tomorrow," said Brother Wolf.

"Then, I must act fast," said Mowgli. "I must lay careful plans if I am to defeat Shere Khan once and for all. Will you help me, Brother Wolf?"

"I shall defend you for as long as I live," said Brother Wolf.

"And I am your leader," growled a voice in the long grass. "I, too, have come to help you."

The grass parted, and Akela ambled out. He looked very old and weak. He walked with a limp. But he had fire in his eyes, which filled the others with confidence. He was still a leader.

CHAPTER 6
The End of Shere Khan

Akela suggested a very clever plan. "You must split the herd in two, Mowgli," he said. "I'll lead one half, Brother Wolf the other."

When Shere Khan came out of the jungle, he spotted Mowgli alone, riding on Rama at the bottom of a ravine. Bare rocks rose up on either side of him like walls.

"I have come to get you, man cub," growled Shere Khan, his eyes blazing with anger. "Prepare to die."

He bounded at Mowgli and Rama. Mowgli simply raised one hand and shouted, "Now!"

The ground started to shake. Pebbles rattled down both sides of the ravine. A great cloud of dust rose in the sky.

Khan stopped dead in his tracks, seeing a herd of buffalo thundering down one side of the ravine. It was led by Brother Wolf.

Another herd was coming down the other side. It was led by Akela. Before he knew it, Shere Khan was surrounded by angry, mooing buffaloes. He was trampled under a hundred stamping hooves.

When the air cleared of dust, Shere Khan lay dead on the ground. He would scare man and beast no more.

The people in the village came out to see what the great noise was. They saw Mowgli skinning the tiger. There was no sign of Akela and Brother Wolf. They had slunk back into the trees; they didn't want to frighten the children. Mowgli had calmed the herd down. The buffaloes were all munching grass, swishing their tails calmly.

"Such a beautiful tiger skin," said Buldeo. "Sell it to me. I'll give you one rupee."

"No," replied Mowgli. "I killed the tiger. It's my tiger skin."

Buldeo frowned. He didn't like Mowgli. A boy like that, who could kill a tiger, might become the headman in the village one day. Buldeo was jealous.

"How could a small boy kill such a big tiger?" he said to the other people. "He must have used magic."

"He sleeps under the stars at night," cried one of the children. "He is a sorcerer."

"He will bring bad luck to the village," shouted an old woman.

Messua pushed her way through the crowd. "You should all be grateful to the boy. He has killed the mighty tiger." She turned to Mowgli and hugged him. "Go back to the jungle," she said gently. "You will be happier there."

"Yes," cried the villagers. "Go back to the jungle where you belong. We don't want strange people here."

Some of the children started throwing stones at Mowgli. One of them hit Rama, and the beast snorted angrily.

"See," said Buldeo. "He has put a magic spell on the cattle and the buffalo. They might run away if we are not careful."

"Go quickly before they hurt you, my child," said Messua. "Goodbye, and may you have a happy life."

Mowgli gave Messua one last hug. Then, he ran across the fields. Brother Wolf and Akela were waiting for him at the edge of the jungle. Together, they ran through the trees.

Mowgli sighed happily. It was good to be back home.

Mother Wolf came out of the cave to welcome him. "I knew you would return," she beamed happily.

Father Wolf stared at the tiger skin. "And you have kept your promise," he said. "Shere Khan will trouble us no more."

That night, there was a full moon. The wolves met at Council Rock. They'd heard that Shere Khan had gone in search of Mowgli. They were expecting him back to tell them he'd killed the man cub.

Akela climbed to the top of the rock. He was quiet, but the other wolves noticed that he had a powerful look in his eyes. In the moonlight, his fur looked sleek and shiny. He was more like the strong leader they once knew.

"Listen, everyone," called Akela. "I have great and important news."

The wolves all fell silent. A shadow floated out from among the trees. The wolves gasped in surprise. It was Mowgli, walking tall and proud. He was wearing a thick cloak over his shoulders. Shere Khan had not killed him after all. Mowgli climbed to the top of Council Rock to stand next to Akela.

"The tiger came to find me," he shouted. "But I have come back to the jungle. And I have kept my promise."

Then, he unfurled his cloak for all to see. The stripes shone in the moonlight.

"See, I have killed the mighty Khan."

The wolves all stared at the tiger skin in disbelief. Then, they looked up at Mowgli as he stood on Council Rock.

"The man cub has killed the tiger," one of them said. "He should be our new leader."

"Yes!" the other wolves agreed. "The man cub is a brave and terrible creature."

"Silence," yelled Mowgli. He looked at the wolves gathered at his feet. "You are wolves. Your leader should be a wolf like you. I do not belong with you."

"Besides, you only want me in the pack now that you think I am a hero. Most of you didn't want me when I was a helpless little man cub. Akela is your real leader. He might be old, but he is wise. Do not let his wisdom go to waste. Let him lead you. As for me, I shall say goodbye to all of you."

The wolves all turned to Akela. "Yes," they said. "The tiger convinced us that Akela was weak. But his wisdom makes him strong. He shall remain our leader."

Mowgli bowed to Akela and climbed down from Council Rock.

His wolf family gathered around him. "Is this really goodbye?" asked Brother Wolf.

"I do not belong in the village," said Mowgli. "And I do not belong in the wolf pack either. I must find my own way, my own home in a part of the jungle where no one else lives. I must learn to survive by my own rules and my own strengths.

"Oh, let us come with you!" begged Brother Wolf.

"Yes!" said Mowgli, "We'll hunt together in a new part of the jungle."

Baloo came to say goodbye as Mowgli prepared to leave. "Do not forget me, man cub," he said.

"Nor me," said Bagheera. He and Mother Wolf and Father Wolf watched as Mowgli led the four cubs away.

Mowgli lived happily in a new part of the jungle for many years. He hunted with his four brothers and slept in a new cave. It is said that when Mowgli grew up, he left the jungle and started a man family. But that is another story. The wolves in the jungle still tell of Mowgli, the little man cub, who defeated the terrible tiger and brought peace to the jungle.

Robin Hood

Retold by
Stewart Ross

Illustrated by
Alex Paterson

ARCTURUS

For Ruby Pietrasik, with much love—SR.

For Eva and Nate—AP.

ARCTURUS

This edition published in 2018 by Arcturus Publishing Limited
26/27 Bickels Yard, 151–153 Bermondsey Street,
London SE1 3HA

Copyright © Arcturus Holdings Limited

All rights reserved. No part of this publication may be reproduced, stored in a retrieval system, or transmitted, in any form or by any means, electronic, mechanical, photocopying, recording or otherwise, without written permission in accordance with the provisions of the Copyright Act 1956 (as amended). Any person or persons who do any unauthorised act in relation to this publication may be liable to criminal prosecution and civil claims for damages.

Writer: Stewart Ross
Illustrator: Alex Paterson
Designer: Jeni Child
Editor: Sebastian Rydberg
Art Director: Jessica Crass

ISBN: 978-1-78828-688-6
CH006282NT
Supplier 24, Date 0618, Print run 7514

Printed in Malaysia

Contents

CHAPTER 1
Robin Hood the Outlaw 4

CHAPTER 2
The Sheriff of Nottingham 14

CHAPTER 3
Justice for Richard Illbeast 24

CHAPTER 4
The Archery Contest 34

CHAPTER 5
Robin and King Richard 44

CHAPTER 6
The Last Arrow 54

CHAPTER 1
Robin Hood the Outlaw

Long ago, when the rich lived in stone castles and the poor in wooden huts, all was not well in England. Good King Richard had gone overseas to fight his enemies, and the kingdom was in the hands of his cruel brother, Prince John.

John had no interest in caring for his people. He allowed the powerful to bully the weak. He looked the other way as bishops and abbots grew richer, while peasants starved. Taxes went up, and misery spread through the land like a disease.

One man fought bravely against this evil. He robbed from the rich to give to the poor; he defended the weak; he challenged the bullies, breaking their greasy heads and bringing down their flinty castles.

The name of this man was Robin Hood.

Robin's real name was Robert of Locksley, a young, well-to-do farmer of rich lands. But the monks of the Abbey of St. Mary looked with greedy eyes on these lands. If Robert were declared an outlaw, they plotted, they could seize his farm.

Fortunately for them, Robert of Locksley played into the hands of the wicked monks. He made himself an outlaw.

Robert became an outlaw because he fought for justice. He returned from a long journey to find that the man who looked after the abbey lands, Sir Guy of Gisborne, was treating the families who lived there most cruelly. Gisborne threw peasants out of their houses, stole money and women, and killed those who disobeyed him.

When Robert heard what was happening, he was mad with anger. His fury became unstoppable when he learned that his friend, Will Scarlet, was chained in Gisborne's prison. "Enough is enough!" Robert cried. "Follow me to end the rule of this devil Gisborne!"

Commanded by Robert of Locksley, the villagers attacked Gisborne's soldiers and killed many of them with arrows.

When they burned Gisborne's house, he just managed to escape on horseback into the night.

After that, Robert of Locksley was known as Robin Hood, the outlaw. Now that he had broken the law, he was outside the law's protection. He was a "wolf's head": Anyone was allowed to capture or kill him. But no one did.

Robin led his band of trusty followers deep into Sherwood Forest. There, safe from bullying lords and priests, they continued to fight beside Robin for generosity, fairness, and justice.

Robin Hood wished to marry his true love, the beautiful Maid Marian. She felt the same about him.
But her father was an earl, and marriage between ordinary people and nobles was frowned upon.

Robin had a rival for Marian's hand: the proud knight, Roger de Longchamp. *If Marian won't marry me for love,* Roger said to himself, *I'll capture her and marry her by force!*

So, when Marian came riding through Sherwood Forest one day, Roger ambushed her. "Come, my fair lady!" he mocked. "I'll find a priest to make you my wife."

Before the words left his mouth, a

humming echoed through the forest. It was an arrow, an arrow from the mighty bow of Robin Hood. Straight and true it flew, through the eyeholes in de Longchamp's helmet and into his head. He swayed, then fell from his horse. He was dead.

"Oh, Robin!" cried Marian, throwing her arms around him. "You have saved me from a monster. How can I thank you?"

"Marry me, and live with me in the forest," he replied with a merry smile.

"Alas, not until my father agrees," she said and went on her way with a heavy heart.

Those who wished to join Robin's outlaw band in Sherwood Forest had to promise to follow these rules:
1. Protect all women.
2. Protect all honest peasants.
3. Treat all unproud knights kindly.
4. Steal from rich priests, and give the money to the poor.

One man who accepted these rules was Alan de Tranmire, a young squire known to his friends as Alan-a-Dale. He met Robin when the outlaws were praying in church. Hob o' the Hill, one of Robin's tiny woodland friends, sneaked in and whispered a warning in Robin's ear. "Soldiers of your worst enemy, Sir Isenbart de Belame, have followed you!"

When the enemy attacked, Robin's men were ready for them. The furious fight was soon over, and all but one of de Belame's men lay dead. The one still living was Ivo le Ravener.

"Leave him to me," cried Alan-a-Dale. They fought long and hard, but in the end, the older knight tired, and Alan's sword pierced his heart. Thus were the merry men of Sherwood Forest joined by yet another brave and honest fighter, Alan-a-Dale.

Two days later, a second famous warrior joined Robin's band. His name was John o' the Stubbs—though the outlaws called him something different. Here's why.

Wandering through the forest, Robin and Alan-a-Dale found Grim Jake, a hated forester, bound up in front of his hut. When Jake said that he had been tied up for refusing to share his meal with a stranger, Robin cried, "I'd like to meet this admirable stranger!"

Not long afterward, he did.

Robin was crossing a broad, fast-flowing stream on a tree-trunk bridge when an enormous man appeared on the other bank. He was dressed like a peasant and carried a massive staff.

"Out of my way, little man, or I'll walk over you!" he roared, with a twinkle in his eye.

When Robin refused to step aside, the man sprang onto the oak bridge and attacked him with his staff. Thwack! Crack! The pair rained blows on each other, until, with a mighty swipe, the giant sent Robin spinning into the river.

"What a fighter!" laughed the soaking-wet Robin, as he dragged himself to the bank. "Join my outlaw band, mighty fellow."

He did—and they called him Little John.

CHAPTER 2
The Sheriff of Nottingham

By now, Robin Hood's reputation had spread far beyond Nottinghamshire. His men were also famous: Alan-a-Dale, Will Scarlet, and Little John.

Hob o' the Hill told of another brave man who ought to join them: Friar Tuck.

One spring morning, Robin met Peter the Doctor in the forest. Peter, who sold useless medicines, told Robin of his meeting with the hefty friar. The rogue had forced him to eat all his own medicines—and they had made him ill!

Robin roared with laughter. *I must meet this jolly rogue,* he thought. He found Tuck sitting beside a stream.

"Hey, holy man," Robin called, raising

his bow, "You look strong. Carry me across the water on your back!"

Tuck stood up slowly, waded over to Robin, and carried him back to the other side. Then, quick as an arrow, he grabbed Robin. "My turn now," he grinned. "Carry me across on your back!"

Robin saw the joke and carried the heavy friar to the other side. After that, they were best of friends, and Friar Tuck joined Robin's outlaws.

A few months later, Robin received a warning from his cousin, Master Gammell. "Ralph Murdach, Sheriff of Nottingham, is hatching a plot with Sir Guy of Gisborne," Gammell told him.

"They'll send spies dressed as beggars into the forest. Since you treat the poor well, they'll learn your secret hiding places. The soldiers will then attack."

Robin thanked his cousin warmly. Remembering the warning, he was suspicious when he met a sturdy beggar on a forest track. The fellow looked as if he were acting and his eyes moved shiftily from side to side.

Robin asked what he was doing. The so-called beggar became angry. Without warning, he swiped Robin over the head with his staff and ran off. Two outlaws gave chase and caught up with him.

Searching the villain, they found a money bag and a letter. As they were examining the letter, the villain reached inside his cloak, took out a bag of flour, and threw the dust in the outlaws' eyes. They were too blinded to follow, and he escaped once again.

"Sorry, Robin," they said when they returned to their camp, "but we got the money. And the letter might be interesting."

Robin's face turned grim as he read the letter. It came from Sir Guy of Gisborne and was addressed to the Sheriff of Nottingham. It read: "Richard Illbeast, the man bringing this letter, is a crafty devil who can lead us to the secret camp of that wolf's head, Robin Hood."

"Right, Sheriff," muttered Robin when he had finished reading the letter, "instead of you coming here, I'm going to pay you a visit."

The next day, Robin disguised himself as a potter and rode into Nottingham on a borrowed horse and cart. He sold his pots at such low prices that even the sheriff's wife bought some. To thank him for the bargain, she invited him to dine at the sheriff's table.

No one recognized the outlaw, and he enjoyed a hearty meal. When it was over, Richard Illbeast appeared. He had been set upon by a dozen outlaws in the forest, he lied. They had stolen his money and the letter he was bringing for the sheriff.

"Idiot!" sneered the sheriff. "Made a fool of by Robin Hood? Out of my house!"

Robin grinned at Illbeast's reception. Moments later, he grinned again: The sheriff was proposing an archery contest.

The sheriff looked surprised when Robin said he'd like to enter the competition. "Whoever heard of a potter with a bow and arrow?" he mocked. "But you can try your luck if you want."

"Thank you, sire," replied Robin politely.

The sheriff's men shot straight and true, but the potter shot straighter and truer. Those watching were astonished. By the third round, only two men were left in the competition: Robin and the sheriff's crack shot.

Robin won easily.

"Good heavens!" cried the sheriff, when he saw how well the potter handled his bow. "Where on earth did you learn to shoot like that?"

"Excuse me, sire," said Robin, "but I once shot with Robin Hood."

Murdach's face darkened. "Robin Hood, the wolf's head?" he asked suspiciously. "I hope you're not one of his band?"

"No, sire!" assured Robin, shaking his head. "I don't like that outlaw any more than you do. In fact, for a reward, I can lead you to his camp in the forest."

"Done!" growled Sheriff Murdach. "A hundred pounds for you, potter, if you will take me to that pesky Hood fellow."

"Nothing would give me greater pleasure," replied Robin, smiling calmly.

The following day dawned dark and damp. Sheriff Murdach took thirty armed soldiers and rode with the potter into Sherwood Forest. The farther they went, the gloomier it became.

Sinister howls and shrieks came from between the trees. "The forest spirits are coming," cried the soldiers and fled.

Soon, the potter was the sheriff's only companion. A horn rang out. As if by magic, twenty men with bows at the ready appeared on either side of the path.

"All well, potter?" grinned Little John.

"Fine, thank you!" replied Robin. "I've brought the sheriff along to have dinner with us." He turned to face his prisoner. "Well, Sheriff, I've kept my word, haven't I? You've now met Robin Hood!"

Murdach scowled as the forest echoed

to the outlaws' laughter.

A great feast was prepared. The main dish was venison from the forest deer that the sheriff and his foresters were paid to protect. Murdach ate with a sour face.

After the meal, the sheriff's money, arms, and other valuable possessions were taken from him. Little John then lifted him onto a pony, seated backward, and sent him on his way to Nottingham.

CHAPTER 3
Justice for Richard Illbeast

Of all Robin Hood's enemies, the most wicked was Sir Isenbart de Belame. Such terrible things were done in his castle that the peasants called it Evil Hold.

Alan-a-Dale had a special reason to hate the master of Evil Hold. He dearly wished to marry the young Lady Alice. Sir Isenbart de Belame had other ideas.

He threatened to take all the lands belonging to Alan's father, Sir Herbrand. The knight could keep them only if he gave Alice to Sir Ranulf de Greasby, one of de Belame's nasty old friends.

Eventually, Sir Herbrand agreed that Alice could marry the fifty-three-year-old Sir Ranulf. Maid Marian, poor Alice's dear friend, told Robin what was going on—and the outlaw sprang into action.

He disguised himself and led a band of his men to the church. The priest, who had been bullied into performing the ceremony, looked miserable. Alice was crying. Only Sir Ranulf looked pleased.

As the service began, Robin threw off his disguise and ordered the wedding to stop. Before Sir Ranulf could react, he fell dead with an arrow in his throat.

A tremendous battle began. Arrows flew and swords clashed, as the outlaws fought Sir Ranulf's soldiers and friends.

The fiercest fight was between Robin and Sir Ector de Malstane. The villain fought well, but Robin was more skilled. After killing him, Robin turned to see Sir Philip de Scrooby picking up Alice and carrying her off. Robin dashed to the rescue.

The outlaws caught Sir Philip before he got away. Free at last, Alice fell into the arms of Alan. Three weeks later, the couple were married by Friar Tuck beneath the trees of Sherwood Forest.

*

On the evening of the battle, Sir Isenbart de Belame had been at dinner in Evil Hold. With him were his foul friends: Sir Niger le Grym, Hamo de Mortain, and

Baldwin the Killer. They were waiting for Sir Ranulf and his bride to join them.

Suddenly, a black arrow thudded into the table in front of them. On it, written in blood, was a message:

These are dead—Roger de Longchamp, Ivo le Ravener, Sir Ranulf de Greasby, Sir Ector de Malstane, Sir Philip de Scrooby.

These shall die—Niger le Grym, Hamo de Mortain, Baldwin the Killer—and Sir Isenbart de Belame.

Sir Isenbart de Belame ranted and raged, but he never learned who shot the arrow into his table. Robin knew it was Hob o' the Hill, the only man able to sneak into Evil Hold unnoticed.

Meanwhile, the outlaws continued their struggle against wicked men. Robin collected money from the rich who passed through Sherwood Forest. Most of it he gave to the poor, but some he saved.

Sir Herbrand was in trouble again. The greedy monks of St. Mary's Abbey demanded four hundred pounds in rent for his lands.

"Pay within a year," cackled Abbot Robert, the head of the abbey, "or your lands will be ours." He knew that Sir Herbrand did not have the money.

The knight turned to Robin for help. The outlaw willingly lent him four hundred pounds, and Abbot Robert's plan failed. He was furious—but could do nothing.

Will Stuteley, one of Robin's most trusted followers, was also helping the poor and weak. One day in the forest, he met a little girl—Ruth. She was sobbing as she picked flowers to cheer herself up.

She led Will to her father, whose name was Ruben. "What has happened?" Will asked. "Why are you alone in the wild forest?"

Ruben explained how he and his people living in the city of York had been attacked. Their treasure had been stolen, their houses burned, and many killed.

"But why?" asked Will.

"Because we belong to the Jewish race," Ruben said sadly. "We did nothing wrong."

When Will heard who had led the attack on the Jewish people, his blood ran cold. It was that monster, Richard Illbeast, again!

Will asked how he could help. Ruben wondered whether the outlaw would go into Nottingham and tell the Jews there that he and Ruth were safe. Ruben didn't dare do this himself because Illbeast was in the city.

Without a moment's hesitation, Will agreed to do as Ruben asked. He disguised himself as a pilgrim and went into Nottingham. After delivering the message, he was resting at an inn, when one of the sheriff's soldiers seized him.

"Excellent!" he cried. "We've got one of Robin Hood's outlaws at last! My master will be delighted."

Sheriff Murdach was indeed delighted. "Hang him!" he ordered, when Will was brought before him. "Hang him in the square tomorrow!"

Will's friends hurried to Robin Hood with the dreadful news. When he heard it, Robin uttered just one word: "Rescue!"

At dawn, the sheriff's men brought Will into the main square. He looked at the wooden gallows and sighed. *Not even Robin Hood can save me now,* he thought.

He was wrong. The captain in charge of the hanging grinned cruelly and shouted, "Right, men! One, two …"

All at once, a stone whistled through the air and knocked the captain senseless, Little John cut Will free, and Robin's archers rained arrows onto the guards.

Sheriff Murdach was furious. "Bring more men from the castle," he screamed.

Before they arrived, Robin and his men had disappeared. Finding that the captain was none other than villainous Richard Illbeast, they had taken him with them.

On their way back through the forest, the outlaws found an important-looking man on horseback blocking their path. "Give me your prisoner!" he commanded.

Robin refused. "Who are you?"

"I am the King's Justice," he replied. "Illbeast is wanted for many foul crimes."

"In which case," suggested Robin, "shall we punish him together, now?"

The Justice agreed. A rope was slung over the bough of a tree. Moments later, Richard Illbeast, one of the nastiest criminals in all England, met his end.

CHAPTER 4

The Archery Contest

A year went by. While Robin Hood waited patiently to marry Maid Marian, he and the outlaws continued to rob the rich and give to the poor. But three wealthy bullies remained beyond their grasp: Isenbart de Belame, the Sheriff, and Abbot Robert.

One spring morning, things changed. As Robin was wondering when Sir Herbrand would repay his debt, Little John appeared with two fat prisoners. He had captured Abbot Robert and the monk who controlled the abbey larder.

Robin searched the saddlebags of his captives' horses, bringing out handfuls of coins. "My four hundred pounds! Thanks, good Abbot!"

The abbot fumed and swore and called Robin all kinds of awful names. The outlaws tied him to a tree and invited him to join their feast. He was too angry and embarrassed to eat much.

After the meal, Little John tied the abbot to his horse and sent him off. The larder monk walked beside him. Everyone they met, including the monks of the abbey, roared with laughter at the sight.

Abbot Robert never got over his shame, and the following spring he died.

The passing of Abbot Robert should have been good news for Robin Hood, but it wasn't. Sir Isenbart de Belame got his nephew, Robert de Longchamp, chosen as the new abbot. The two men plotted with Sir Guy of Gisborne and Sheriff Murdach to get rid of Robin and his outlaws once and for all.

The sheriff remembered the archery contest Robin had won when disguised as a potter. "I'm trying it again," he said with a sneer. "I'm offering first prize of a silver arrow tipped with pure gold."

"That wretched outlaw loves gold, and he's proud of his shooting. He's bound to turn up—and this time, we'll be waiting for him!"

He was right. Robin couldn't resist the idea of an archery contest. He suspected a plot, so he disguised himself as a vagabond. He told six other outlaw archers to enter the contest, with more to be in the crowd in case of trouble.

The day came, and eager spectators thronged the Nottingham meadows. Archers from all over the country had entered, all hoping to win the gold and silver arrow. The fine lords and ladies took their seats, a trumpet blared, and the contest began.

The first test was for each archer to fire three arrows at a target fifty yards away. Those who failed to get two arrows inside the bull had to drop out. The target was then moved farther back. More dropped out.

By the time the target was three hundred yards away, only twenty archers remained. The crowd became very excited when the large target was replaced by a thin wooden pole. Soon, there were only six archers left in the competition: Robin, Little John, Scadlock, Much the Miller's son, Reynold, and Luke the Red.

The shooting became even more difficult when the archers were not told the distance to the pole. Having worked it out for themselves, they had to select the right bow and arrow for that range.

After two more rounds, only Robin Hood and Luke the Red remained. Luke was the sheriff's man.

For the final round, Robin and Luke had just three seconds to raise their bow, fit an arrow, aim, and fire. Luke went first. The crowd held their breath … He missed!

Next came Robin, disguised as a tramp: one … two … three … The crowd gasped in astonishment. Robin's arrow had split the pole in two!

As the sheriff's wife presented Robin with the precious arrow, her husband peered closely at him. Suddenly, he cried out, "It's Robin Hood, the outlaw! Arrest him!"

Robin raised his horn and blew a clear blast. Immediately, thirty armed outlaws sprang to his side. Seeing this, the sheriff's herald blew his trumpet, and sixty of Murdach's men surrounded Robin and his band.

Though the fight was furious, the outnumbered outlaws eventually gained the upper hand. But before they could claim victory, a hundred more of the sheriff's soldiers came riding out of Nottingham Castle.

Robin ordered his men to fall back to a clump of trees. There, they would fight to the last. At that moment, a tiny figure appeared at Robin's side. It was Ket the Trow, the brother of Hob o' the Hill.

"Quick, Robin," panted Ket. "I come from Maid Marian's father, Sir Richard at the Lee. He offers you shelter in his castle nearby."

"But if he helps me, he will be declared an outlaw," said Robin.

"He cares not,'" replied Ket. "Come, follow me."

In the nick of time, Robin led his band to the safety of Verysdale Castle, where Sir Richard welcomed them most warmly.

Sir Richard told Robin that Maid Marian was staying with her aunt in Malaset Castle. "But she won't be safe now that Murdach is your enemy," cried Robin. "I'll go to her at once."

When he reached Malaset, his heart sank. Marian was gone.

"Sir Scrivel of Catsty has taken her away," explained a tearful maid. "He said that because Marian's father is an outlaw, he'll protect her by marrying her."

"Never!" cried Robin. "Sir Scrivel's a vile dog who wouldn't protect anyone!"

For days, he hunted for his dearest Marian. He searched in towns and in the countryside, in fields and in woods, but all in vain. He returned to Sherwood Forest to wait for news.

Three days later, Sheriff Murdach passed

nearby. He was escorting a prisoner—Sir Richard at the Lee. Without hesitation, Robin ambushed the soldiers and set Sir Richard free. "Now, Sheriff," said Robin grimly, "it is time to meet your end."

His swift arrow pierced the villain's chest plate and entered his heart.

Robin found Marian shortly afterward. She was happily asleep in the burrow home of Ket the Trow. "But how … ?"

Ket smiled. "Just be happy she's here."

CHAPTER 5

Robin and King Richard

Now that Sir Richard was also an outlaw, his daughter was free to marry her love. With her father's permission, Maid Marian said "yes" to Robin, and Friar Tuck married them beneath an oak tree.

Robin and Marian lived with their friends in the forest for several years. As before, they protected the poor and weak, and punished bullies and lawbreakers.

But good King Richard was still absent. At home, Prince John continued to govern England with a cruel and careless hand. The people longed for their king to return and restore justice to the land.

One evening, Will Scarlet ran up.

"Robin!" he cried. "Bad news! King Richard has been captured!"

"What?" frowned Robin. "By whom?"

Will said he didn't know, but that he was imprisoned in a castle far away. His captor said he would release him when England paid 100,000 pounds of silver as a ransom for setting the king free.

"Right," said Robin firmly, "we'll help raise the money, won't we, lads?"

The forest echoed to the cries of "Aye!"

Now that the outlaws had agreed to help King Richard, Robin collected half their store of money. They sold all the arms, fine clothes, and jewels they had stolen and added that money to the pile.

Robin sent the ransom money to London under strong guard. With it went a note written on the skin of a deer: *From Robin Hood and the honest men of Sherwood Forest. This is for their beloved King. They hope God will soon free him from his enemies abroad and at home.*

After this, Robin sent to London half of all the money he took. Thanks to such generosity, King Richard was quickly freed. He speedily returned to England.

Soon after he landed, the king began to hear stories of Robin Hood. Had a rich young lady given up her lands to live in Sherwood Forest with this outlaw? Was it true that he took the law into his own hands and punished those who did wrong? Did he really rob the rich to pay the poor?

When the answer to all these questions was yes, Richard decided he must go to Sherwood Forest and meet this extraordinary Robin Hood fellow.

King Richard did not hear only praise for Robin Hood. The brother of Sheriff Murdach said Robin was a murderer, and the monks called him a thief. The king was eager to learn the truth.

Wherever he went, he asked about Robin Hood and his men. The rich knew only that he lived in Sherwood Forest; the poor shrugged and said nothing. They would not betray their friend.

The king tried a new tactic. Having heard that Robin robbed rich monks, he dressed himself as an abbot. He put his companions in monks' clothes and set off through the forest.

The plan worked splendidly.

They had not gone far when Little John stepped out in front of them. "Stop!" he cried, raising his bow.

The monks obeyed. Robin Hood now appeared, saying, "Good Abbot, hand over your money, and we will let you continue in peace."

"I've only forty pounds," replied the king. "The rest I spent looking for the king. But I'll willingly hand over what I have."

"Well said!" cried Robin. "An honest abbot at last! And one who loves the king, too. I won't search your saddlebags, and I invite you to feast with us in the forest."

The friendly abbot—King Richard—accepted Robin Hood's invitation to feast with him. They ate deer killed by the outlaws (against the law!), and they drank wine stolen from monks and merchants.

The king said nothing. He was watching and listening, making up his own mind about Robin Hood and his band.

When the meal was over, Robin suggested an archery competition. Whoever missed the target would get their ears boxed by Robin. The men laughed and agreed to the idea.

Several missed the small tree at which they were aiming, and each one received a hit from their leader. But Robin grew careless, missing the target himself.

"Well," he grinned, "who's going to give me a blow?" He looked around. "Come on,

Abbot," he said cheerily, "what about you?'"

"All right," said the warrior king, getting to his feet. "This is not what abbots normally do—but take that!"

His huge fist smashed into Robin and sent him spinning to the ground.

At that moment, Sir Richard at the Lee and Marian arrived. The abbot's hood had slipped back on his head—the knight recognized him immediately. "Robin!" he cried. "Kneel! It's the king!"

Robin trembled at the feet of his king. How foolish he'd been not to recognize him! What fate now awaited them?

"I want the truth," said the king sternly.

"You shall have it, sire," answered Robin.

"Good. Then, tell me: Did you and your men kill Roger de Longchamp, Ivo le Ravener, Sir Ranulf de Greasby, Sir Ector de Malstane, Sir Philip de Scrooby, Sheriff Murdach, Sir Scrivel of Catsty, and others like them?"

"We did, my lord."

"Did you mock the Abbot of St. Mary's and steal his money?"

"We did, my lord."

"Did you give money to the poor and collect huge sums for my ransom?"

"We did, my lord."

King Richard smiled. "Then, stand up

Robin Hood and your merry men! You may have broken the law, but you acted for justice. I pardon you all."

At that, the outlaws cheered the king. He took aside Alan-a-Dale and Alice, and Robin Hood and Maid Marian. "You married without my permission," he said, "But I see you are made for each other. So, I have great pleasure in announcing that your marriages have my wholehearted approval!"

CHAPTER 6
The Last Arrow

On King Richard's command, Robin and Marian received back the Malaset lands that had been stolen from them. They lived as a lord and lady should live, treating all men and women with an even hand. In all the land, "Squire Robin" was known as a fair and honest man.

Meanwhile, many of the outlaws went with the king when he returned to France. There, some died, as did the king. Those who came home—Little John, Will the Bowman, Will Scarlet, and Much the Miller's son—settled on Robin's lands.

King Richard was killed before he could return to get rid of the nest of vipers near Sherwood Forest. From time to time, Sir

Isenbart de Belame, Sir Guy of Gisborne, Baldwin the Killer, and Sir Roger of Doncaster met to plot the downfall of the man they still called "wolf's head."

For long years, they schemed. Finally, sixteen years after King Richard's death, their chance came. Robin had left home to fight a band of robbers. When he returned, he found his castle half burned and many of those inside slain.

Fearing the worst, Robin ran to Marian's room. There she lay, her hands neatly folded on her lap—dead.

Sorrow swallowed up Robin like a great wave. For a long time, he knelt and prayed for the soul of his dead wife. Then, he stood and asked in a calm, cold voice, "Who did this terrible deed?"

"A fiend," replied a maid, red-eyed with weeping. "A fiend named Sir Isenbart de Belame of Evil Hold. He shot her even as she was talking with him."

"Thank you," said Robin. "That is all I need to know."

From all around, men came to his aid. Among them were Alan-a-Dale, Sir Herbrand, Ket the Trow, Hob o' the Hill, other surviving members of his outlaw band, and many more who loathed the very name of de Belame. All were willing to die to see justice done.

Robin led his army to the edge of the moat surrounding Evil Hold. "Come out and surrender, de Belame, you murderer!" he cried.

"Come and get me, wolf's head," sneered de Belame. "If you and your feeble rabble are strong enough."

"They are—and I promise we will," replied Robin.

Immediately, he gave orders for attacking the castle. The only way, he declared, was to cross the moat, hack down the drawbridge, and smash the portcullis.

Never was there such a siege as that of Evil Hold. It became the stuff of legends, and minstrels sang of it for many generations to come.

They told of how Robin's men, under a rain of arrows, crossed the moat on rafts and attacked the drawbridge with axes; of how the chains holding the drawbridge were cut, and a mighty oak brought as a battering ram; and how the portcullis was finally smashed open, and Robin's men poured into the castle.

No mercy was asked for, and no mercy shown. Some were cut down by swords; others were burned by boiling oil poured down from the battlements. The cobblestones of the castle courtyard ran red with the blood of battle.

In the midst of it all, Robin Hood and Little John fought together. Forward they went, cutting down their enemies on either hand. Their target was simple: Sir Isenbart de Belame, the murderer of the fair Maid Marian. Eventually, at the base of a tower, they cornered him.

"Wait!" called Robin, as Little John raised his great halberd above his head. "This villain must die as a criminal, not as a warrior. Bind him, and take him away!"

Two prisoners were taken during that terrible siege: Sir Isenbart de Belame and Baldwin the Killer. As they were led out in chains, the mob howled against them.

"Baldwin blinded my father!" cried one.

"De Belame was laughing when he killed Marian!" shouted another.

After a brief discussion, both men were hanged. Pitch and tar were then poured over Evil Hold, and the entire building was burned to the ground.

Robin could not face living in Malaset again. He gave the lands to a cousin and went to live in the forest once more. Here, with some of his old friends, he continued to help the weak and punish the wicked. Once again, the name of Robin Hood was on the lips of all who loved justice.

Of his foes, just two remained: Sir Roger of Doncaster and Sir Guy of Gisborne. Robin caught up with the latter one misty morning. It was a fair fight, and the better man won: Sir Guy of Gisborne finally got his just deserts from the point of Robin Hood's sword.

That left only Sir Roger of Doncaster. He was now an old man—but he still had a treacherous tongue.

Robin's deeds during his second spell in the forest would fill a whole new book. But time moved on. As the years passed, he grew weaker, and his eyes lost its sparkle.

All the while, Sir Roger of Doncaster waited. Every few months, he noticed, Robin called on his cousin, a nun in Kirklees Abbey. Slipping into the abbey at night, Sir Roger whispered in the ear of Dame Ursula, the abbess in charge: If Robin Hood should die, the abbey might receive thirty acres of good land …

Robin visited the abbey a week later. He told Dame Ursula that he felt unwell, and she invited him to rest. As was the treatment in those days, she opened a vein in his arm to let out some blood. But she did not close it up. As Robin slept, the blood continued to flow.

Fearing that something was wrong, Little John broke down the abbey door and rushed in. "Too late, dear John," whispered Robin. "I am gone. Pray, hand me my bow, and open the window."

With one final effort, Robin shot an arrow into the forest. "Where it has landed," he gasped, "dig my grave. There will I lie." And so it was done.

Treasure Island

Retold by
Stewart Ross

Illustrated by
Alex Paterson

ARCTURUS

For Ana Ross, with much love—SR.

For Martha and Molly—AP.

ARCTURUS

This edition published in 2018 by Arcturus Publishing Limited
26/27 Bickels Yard, 151–153 Bermondsey Street,
London SE1 3HA

Copyright © Arcturus Holdings Limited

All rights reserved. No part of this publication may be reproduced, stored in a retrieval system, or transmitted, in any form or by any means, electronic, mechanical, photocopying, recording or otherwise, without written permission in accordance with the provisions of the Copyright Act 1956 (as amended). Any person or persons who do any unauthorised act in relation to this publication may be liable to criminal prosecution and civil claims for damages.

Writer: Stewart Ross
Illustrator: Alex Paterson
Designer: Jeni Child
Editor: Sebastian Rydberg
Art Director: Jessica Crass

ISBN: 978-1-78828-695-4
CH006096NT
Supplier 24, Date 0618, Print run 7522

Printed in Malaysia

Contents

CHAPTER 1
The Captain's Map 4

CHAPTER 2
The *Hispaniola* 14

CHAPTER 3
Going Ashore 24

CHAPTER 4
Battle Begins 34

CHAPTER 5
My Sea Adventure 44

CHAPTER 6
Treasure 54

CHAPTER 1
The Captain's Map

My name is Jim Hawkins. My father and mother kept the Admiral Benbow Inn, high on the cliffs overlooking the sea. Our customers were mostly polite people from the nearby village. Occasionally, strangers stayed for a night or two, but never more.

All this changed when "Captain" Billy Bones moved in. His scrawny hands were a mass of scars and tattoos, his hair was tied back in a pigtail covered with tar, and his blue coat was patched and tattered.

The man's foul language and rough

ways horrified me. Mother and Father weren't too pleased, either. But he paid in gold, and we needed the money.

Every day, the old rogue kept a lookout on the clifftops. In the evenings, when he had drunk too much rum, he laid his cutlass before him on the table and sang an old sea song in a high, salty voice:

Fifteen men on the dead man's chest—
Yo-ho-ho, and a bottle of rum!

Captain Bones walked the cliffs to watch for a "seafaring man with one leg." He was obviously terrified of this one-legged sailor, and every month promised me a silver four-penny coin, if I kept an eye open for him. I did so, but he never paid me the money.

One day, the Captain had a visitor, a pale, scrawny sailor with two fingers missing from his left hand. "Black Dog!" the Captain gasped when he saw him.

For a while, the two men sat drinking rum and chatting. Gradually, their talk became angry, and they swore loudly at each other. When Black Dog asked a question, and the Captain shouted "No! No!" they began to fight.

Cutlasses clashed. The Captain lunged at Black Dog, who screamed and ran for the door. The Captain chased after him.

He aimed a mighty blow at Black Dog's head, but his cutlass hit the inn sign, and the rogue escaped.

The sudden exercise was too much for the Captain, and he collapsed to the floor. His life was saved by Dr. Livesey, who had called to treat my sick father. Nevertheless, the Captain knew that Black Dog would return, and next time he would not be alone.

Dr. Livesey told Captain Bones that if he went on drinking rum he would die. "Billy Bones," as Black Dog had called him, took no notice. After forcing me to bring him a tot of rum, he explained what was happening.

He had been the first mate on Captain Flint's ship. This Flint was one of the most cruel, greedy, and rich pirates who ever sailed the seas. As he lay dying, he gave Bones a map. It showed where he'd buried his gold and money on Treasure Island.

The crew of Flint's ship knew about the map. They knew Billy Bones had it, too. That's why he was hiding in our inn and keeping a daily watch from the cliffs. He was looking out for the pirates who wanted his precious map of Treasure Island.

Now Black Dog had found him, Bones was terrified. It wasn't Black Dog who scared him—it was the mysterious sailor with one leg.

*

Yes, I was alarmed by these bloodthirsty stories of pirates and treasure. But at the time, I had other things on my mind: shortly after Black Dog's visit, my father died.

Mother and I were now alone—and the murderous pirates were closing in.

The afternoon after my father's funeral, a blind man came tap-tapping along the road to our inn. He wore a huge cape and a hood over his head. When I approached him, he grabbed me with fingers of steel.

"Take me to the Captain!" he ordered.

"I dare not," I replied.

"Do it—or I'll break your arm!" he sneered.

I had to obey. I led the blind man to Billy Bones. When the two of them met, he handed over a piece of paper. That done, he spun round and disappeared up the road.

Bones looked at the paper. "The Black Spot warning!" he groaned. "I have six hours to hand over the map—or else!"

The shock was too much for him. He swayed and fell to the floor. Dead.

Cruel and harsh though Bones had been, I couldn't help crying. When my mother heard the noise and came downstairs, I told her all I knew. I told her about Captain Flint and his buried treasure, about the secret map that Flint had given to Billy Bones, and about the blind man and the Black Spot warning.

"The pirates will be here in six hours!" I cried. "What shall we do?"

Mother and I hurried to the village and begged for help. The people were too frightened to go back with us, but they did send for the police officers.

It was dark when we returned to the Admiral Benbow. Billy Bones hadn't paid us for months, and mother needed the money. We discovered the key of his sea chest and unlocked it. Inside were a bag of coins and a waterproof packet.

As mother counted the coins, a low whistle sounded—the attack signal! "They're coming!" I whispered.

Mother grabbed the coins, I took the packet, and we hurried outside.

We hid under a bridge and listened as the pirates smashed open the inn door and searched the place. They were furious when they realized the map was missing. Shouting and swearing, they ran into the road.

At that moment, the police galloped up, and the pirates scattered into the darkness. While friends looked after mother, I went with the police to find Dr. Livesey. I met him with his friend, Squire Trelawney, and together, we unwrapped the waterproof packet. Inside was a map—the map of Treasure Island.

CHAPTER 2
The *Hispaniola*

Dr. Livesey and Squire Trelawney decided to sail to Treasure Island and take me with them. We would find Captain Flint's buried treasure and be as rich as kings!

The Squire rode to Bristol to buy a ship. A few weeks later, he sent a letter saying he had bought a fine ship, the *Hispaniola*, and got an excellent crew to sail it.

The Squire's letter was exciting, but it worried me. He had told all Bristol about our voyage. What if wicked people—pirates even—heard about our map of Treasure Island? They might try to steal it.

I was also worried about a man the Squire had met. He said he was a brave old sailor who would be our ship's cook. He had helped the Squire choose the *Hispaniola*'s crew, too. His name was Long John Silver—and he had one leg.

Captain Bones had warned me about a "seafaring man with one leg." I hoped Mr. Silver was not him.

The next day, I said goodbye to my mother and set out for Bristol. Squire Trelawney was at the docks to meet me.

"We sail tomorrow!" he said.

After breakfast, the Squire gave me a note for Long John Silver. I'd find him at the Spyglass Inn, he said.

I found the inn easily enough— and there stood a "seafaring man with one leg." He was tall and strong, with a smiling face as big as a ham. As his left leg had been cut off at the hip, he walked very deftly with the help of a crutch.

On his shoulder sat a green-and-red parrot.

"Pieces of eight! Pieces of eight!" it squawked, the pirates' name for their cherished silver coins.

Long John Silver greeted me warmly.

As I was deciding he wasn't the man Billy Bones had feared, I noticed a familiar figure sneaking out of the inn door.

"It's Black Dog!" I cried. "Stop him!"

Silver sent one of the guests chasing after Black Dog because he hadn't paid his bill. The guest never returned—Black Dog had run away.

Meanwhile, Silver chatted merrily. He seemed a most amiable fellow. A little later, we walked together to find the Squire and Dr. Livesey. When Silver left us, we all agreed he was the ideal man for our voyage to Treasure Island.

I loved the *Hispaniola*. Her tall masts were hung with a spider's web of ropes and rigging, and her broad sails spread like huge handkerchiefs in the wind. On board, all was sparkling clean and shipshape.

I was less pleased with Captain Smollett. He was a fine sailor, I was told. But he complained crossly about the crew that the Squire and Long John Silver had chosen.

He also grumbled that the voyage was meant to be secret—yet, every crew member knew they were sailing for treasure. He blamed the Squire for this, which made him very angry.

Dr. Livesey calmed things down. There were seven men we could trust, he said: himself, the Squire, the Captain, me, and four other honest men. We would sleep at the back of the ship, above the storage of gunpowder and guns.

If the crew attacked us, we could defend our position like a little fort.

When Silver saw what was going on, he looked surprised. But when he heard it was the Captain's orders, he saluted and cried, "Aye, aye, sir!"

"What a good man he is," said Doctor Livesey.

"Maybe," replied the Captain, grimly.

The *Hispaniola* sailed smoothly across the Atlantic Ocean like a huge seabird. The weather was calm, and we made good progress. Our only problem was the ship's mate.

As the captain's right-hand man, the mate passed on orders to the crew and made sure they were obeyed. He was an officer, not one of the men.

But our mate, Mister Arrow, was always laughing and joking with the crew, who didn't respect him. Worse still, he had a blurry look in his eye, staggered about, and spoke as if he had a stone in his mouth. In short, he seemed drunk.

As the days went by, the crew laughed at Arrow more and more. Captain Smollett was furious and refused to let him have any rum. But Arrow still managed to find a bottle somewhere.

Then, one dark night, when Arrow was on lookout duty, he disappeared.

Everyone said he had fallen overboard. Now that I know more about our crew, I think they were lying. Silver didn't trust Arrow. I reckon he'd given him rum and pushed him overboard.

Arrow was never seen again.

Why do I think Silver tipped Mister Arrow into the sea? Listen carefully, and I'll tell you.

We kept a barrel of apples on deck. One evening, toward the end of our voyage, I felt like some fresh fruit and went to get an apple. As there were only a few left at the bottom of the barrel, I climbed inside. There, rocked by the movement of the ship, I fell asleep.

I woke to hear voices. Silver was telling the crew horrible tales of Captain Flint, murder, and piracy. I curled up in the bottom of the barrel, praying no one wanted an apple. If they found me, they would surely kill me.

My blood ran cold. Long John Silver was the "seafaring man with one leg" who had terrified Billy Bones. He had sailed with Captain Flint and knew all about the treasure map. Nearly all our crew were pirates!

Silver was planning to wait until we had dug up the treasure and got it safely on board the *Hispaniola*. Then he would murder me and all the honest men—and sail off with the treasure.

I was saved by a shout from the lookout: "Land ahoy!" We had reached Treasure Island.

CHAPTER 3

Going Ashore

Amid the excitement of seeing Treasure Island, I climbed out of the apple barrel unnoticed. I found Dr. Livesey and told him I had important news. Shortly afterward, he called me to the cabin to talk to himself, the Captain, and the Squire.

I told them what I had heard. Nearly all the crew were pirates, and Long John

Silver was their leader. They had sailed with us to steal the treasure—and they planned to murder every one of us.

It was a desperate situation. Nineteen pirates against us four, plus four loyal men: Hunter, Joyce, Gray, and Redruth. But we had one big advantage: We had the map marked with the spot where the treasure had been buried.

The Captain was worried that the pirates might try to get the map by attacking us. So, the next morning, he gave permission for the crew to go ashore. Thirteen went, rowing in two of the smaller boats.

I now did something very foolish. It was hot and stuffy on board, and the island looked green and exciting. Without telling anyone, I crept into one of the boats going ashore.

As soon as my boat ran into the sandy beach, I leaped out and ran off into the trees. I heard Silver calling after me, "Jim! Come back, Jim!" but I took no notice.

I ran until exhausted, then stopped and looked round. Wow! I had never been out of England before, and the sights, sounds, and scents of the island amazed me. There were trees rich with fruits and nuts, birds with bright feathers, and snakes slithering around my feet.

A rocky hill loomed over the whole island. Silver, who had been here before, had called it the Spyglass. I tried to remember Captain Flint's map and the place where the treasure was buried.

Just then, I heard voices coming toward me, and I dived for cover beneath some leafy bushes.

Moments later, two men came into sight. One was Long John Silver. The other was Tom, one of the few honest members of the crew. I listened carefully. Silver was trying to persuade him to join his gang, but Tom would have none of it.

Their conversation was interrupted by voices farther off. A shout of anger was followed by a long, horrible scream.

Tom turned pale when he heard the scream. "What's that?" he gasped.

Long John Silver remained as cool as a sea breeze. He said that the scream had come from Alan, another crew member who had refused to join his gang. Would Tom now change his mind?

"You've killed Alan," the man said grimly. "Kill me, too, if you can. I won't join you."

With that, he turned and walked off. Quick as a blink, Silver whipped his crutch from beneath his arm and flung it, point first, at Tom's back. It hit him between his shoulder blades, and he fell forward onto the ground.

Silver, knife drawn, was on him in a second. Two quick stabs, and it was all over.

The scene had been so cruel, so bloodthirsty, that I fainted. When I came to, I was terrified that I'd be Silver's next victim. Heart pounding, I sprinted into the woods.

Pausing beneath some spreading oaks to catch my breath, I saw a figure leaping between the trees. Surely this shaggy beast wasn't a man? A bear, perhaps? Or a monkey? Whatever it was, I was trapped between it and the pirates behind me.

Running away won't do me any good, I thought. I plucked up courage and walked toward the strange creature.

He was a man! His hair and beard hung down to his shoulders, his skin was baked black by the sun, and his clothes were rags. Hesitating, he edged forward and knelt at my feet.

"Who are you?" I asked.

"My name is Ben Gunn," he answered in a croaky voice, "and you are the first person I have spoken to for three years." He looked up anxiously. "Is that Flint's ship I saw at anchor? Is there a man with one leg on board?"

I told him Flint was dead, but many of his men—including the one-legged sailor—were the crew of the *Hispaniola*.

I asked Mr. Gunn how he knew about Captain Flint and Long John Silver. In reply, he told me his sad story.

Along with Long John Silver and Billy Bones, Ben Gunn had been a sailor on Captain Flint's ship. One day, the Captain had anchored off Treasure Island and gone ashore with his loot and six men. He returned alone, empty-handed, and without the six men. He'd killed them all after they'd helped him bury his treasure.

Later, Benn Gunn sailed back to Treasure Island on another ship. When he told two friends there was treasure ashore, all three went looking for it. They found nothing. Ben's friends were so angry that they left him on Treasure Island—and he had been there ever since.

Living alone for so long had made Ben a little odd. But he was also charming and friendly, and we were soon good friends.

"I can help you, Jim," he said with a pleasing smile.

"What do you mean?" I asked.

He winked at me and said, "Wait and see. But if I help you, you must help me."

"Fair enough," I replied. "What can I do for you?"

"Take me with you off this horrible island!" he cried. "Please!"

It seemed a good bargain. While we were talking, we heard gunfire. I now feared that my friends were in danger. We set off—I needed to join them as quickly as possible.

We were walking over some high rocks, when Ben Gunn stopped and pointed. I couldn't believe it. There, sticking up among the trees was a flagpole. On it, waving in the breeze, was a Union Jack!

CHAPTER 4
Battle Begins

After I had left the *Hispaniola*, my friends on board grew restless. It was now steaming hot, and they were worried what the pirates were up to.

Dr. Livesey decided to take our last small boat and go ashore. Hunter, a loyal servant, agreed to go with him. They would explore the island, look for me, and spy on Silver and his gang.

The two men landed on the shore and walked up a small hill. There, they discovered a fort built by Captain Flint's crew. A tall wooden fence surrounded a stout log cabin. The entrance to the cabin was open, and instead of windows it had holes for firing shots. Dr. Livesey thought the place was perfect for fighting off attackers.

He and Hunter went back to the *Hispaniola* and told the others what they had found. The Captain decided they should leave the ship and set up camp in the fort.

One man kept an eye on the pirates still on board, while the others went back and forth to the fort with supplies. However, on the last trip, no one was left to guard the pirates—who were then seen loading the *Hispaniola*'s cannon.

Boom! The cannon fired at the boat, which was carrying supplies to the fort. The Squire shot back with his musket.

Boom! The cannon fired again.

This was the gunfire I had heard when I was with Ben Gunn.

The cannonballs hit the sea near the boat. Since it was very full, the waves washed over its sides, and it sank. My friends snatched what supplies they could and waded ashore.

Meanwhile, on the island, Silver and his pirates heard the cannon's roar. They ran down to the beach and saw the Doctor leading the others toward the fort.

We now fought our first battle. One of our men, Redruth, was shot dead, but the others climbed the fence and got safely inside the fort. Several pirates were hit by our shots, so there were fewer of them now.

The battle had stopped by the time I reached the fort. I said goodbye to Ben Gunn, scrambled over the fence, and ran into the cabin. Everyone was relieved to see me, but their faces were deadly serious.

There we were, thousands of miles from home, on a desert island with food for just ten days, surrounded by murderous pirates.

Things looked very grim.

When I was safe inside the cabin, I told the others about Ben Gunn. He said he'd help us if we needed him. Only later did we understand what he meant.

I also mentioned that I'd seen the pirate camp. Then, they had been gathered around a roaring fire, singing, arguing, and drinking rum. Though they were twice our numbers, they wouldn't be much good at fighting for a while.

Captain Smollett kept our spirits up. He gave us all a position and a job to do. Mine was to carry loaded guns to the men shooting out through the round holes—"loopholes" the Captain called them.

Early the next morning, we had a surprise visit. Long John Silver and a man carrying a white flag on a stick approached the fort. Silver wanted to make a deal.

"If you hand over the map showing where the treasure is," he said, "we'll split the money between us. Then, we'll all sail home together. If that worries you, stay here with your half of the treasure. I'll send a ship to pick you up. That's a promise."

"Your promises," said the Captain angrily, "are not worth a bucket of seawater! Leave us!"

We had all left our positions while the Captain was talking with Silver. After he had gone, the Captain was furious. "To your positions!" he roared.

Three hours later, the attack began. The enemy swarmed up the fence like monkeys. We fired back through the loopholes and the cabin was soon full of smoke.

Our shooting was accurate, but the pirates were brave and determined. Four of them got over the fence and ran toward the cabin. One of them seized Hunter's gun and knocked him out. Another shot Joyce through the head.

"Attack!" commanded the Captain.

"Outside with cutlasses!"

We each grabbed a curved sword and ran into the open space between the cabin and the fence. I came face-to-face with Anderson, one of the pirate leaders. He yelled and swung his sword at me. As I dodged, I tripped and rolled over in the sand.

By the time I got up, the pirates were fleeing back over the fence. We had won!

We had slain six pirates, leaving just eight. But victory had its price. Joyce was dead, and the Captain was very badly wounded. That left just five of us: the Squire, the Doctor, Hunter, Gray, and myself, the cabin boy.

After the attack, we were unable to relax in case the pirates returned. What could we do? We knew where the treasure was, but we didn't dare go and get it.

Dr. Livesey decided to go and talk with Benn Gun, and he went to meet him. I had a secret plan of my own.

The most important thing in the whole adventure was the *Hispaniola*. She had brought us here, and only she could take us home again. But the ship was now in the hands of the pirates.

My idea was to sail out to her, cut her anchor rope, and let her drift onto the shore. The pirates would then have no way of leaving—even if they found the treasure.

I remembered Ben Gunn telling me about a little boat he had made from goat skin stretched over a wooden frame. He called it a "coracle," and I knew where it was hidden …

That evening, I took some sea biscuits and a pair of pistols, and sneaked out of the fort. I soon found the coracle and carried it down to the sea. The *Hispaniola* was riding at anchor only a short distance away.

CHAPTER 5

My Sea Adventure

I waited until dark, then slipped the coracle into the water. It wobbled crazily, nearly tipping me into the sea. But after a time, it settled down, and I started to paddle.

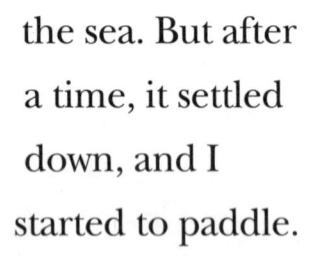

I now had another problem. Because the coracle was round, my paddling made it spin in circles! Luckily, the tide was flowing toward the ship, and I finally got close enough to grab the thick anchor rope. Opening my knife with my teeth, I began to cut through it.

From the open cabin window above me, I heard two angry voices.

I recognized one as Israel Hands, Captain Flint's gunner. The other belonged to a man I'd seen in a red nightcap. By the sound of their shouting and swearing, they were both drunk.

Silver had left these two men to look after the *Hispaniola* while the other pirates were ashore. Huh! I thought. They're not doing a very good job!

With a final effort, I sliced through the last strands of rope. Immediately, the *Hispaniola* swung around in the current. The ship's heavy bows swept toward my little coracle. If we collided, it would be smashed to pieces, and I would surely drown.

I fought like a fiend to save my little craft. Inch by inch, I pushed it along the hull to the back—or "stern"—of the *Hispaniola*. In the starlight, I spied a rope hanging down from above the cabin from where the voices were coming.

As you know, I sometimes act without thinking. That's what I did now. For some reason, seeing the rope, I grabbed hold of it. Up I went, hand over hand, to see what was going on in the cabin.

One glance was enough. Israel Hands and the red nightcap man were wrestling furiously. Each man had a hand on the other's throat. It looked like a fight to the death.

I dropped back down into the coracle and drifted slowly away from the *Hispaniola*. On the beach to my left, I could see the pirates gathered around their bonfire. Sparks flew high into the night sky, and the sound of singing floated across the calm, dark sea:

"Fifteen men on the dead man's chest—
Yo-ho-ho, and a bottle of rum!"

The words reminded me of my mother and the happy times we had spent together at the Admiral Benbow. How I longed to be back there!

Lulled by the rocking of my little boat, I fell into a deep sleep. When I awoke, it was broad daylight. I looked around.

During the night, I had drifted to a part of the island I didn't know. To my dismay, a strong current was pulling me farther from the shore. The sea was getting rougher, too. Waves splashed over the sides of the coracle, and I had to stop paddling to bail out the water. I was terrified the craft would sink.

I looked up. Impossible! Only a short distance away, I saw the *Hispaniola* drifting out of control. I paddled furiously toward her, and managed to grab a rope and pull myself aboard just as the coracle sank.

I found the two seamen flat out on the deck. The red nightcap man was dead; Israel Hands looked badly wounded.

"Right," I said, "I'm the captain of this ship now. If you tell me how to sail her, Mr. Hands, I'll tend your wounds and bring you something to drink."

Hands agreed, and I soon had the *Hispaniola* under control. But the pirate was not as ill as he looked. Worse, I knew he had a knife hidden inside his jacket.

We guided the *Hispaniola* into a cove known as the North Anchorage. I planned to steer her safely aground on soft sand.

I was concentrating so hard, I didn't notice Hands standing up. Suddenly, he was lurching toward me. In his right hand, he held a gleaming knife.

I grasped one of my pistols and fired. There was a dull click. The gunpowder was damp, and the gun didn't go off.

At that moment, the *Hispaniola* struck a sandbank. She tipped to one side, throwing Hands and myself to the deck. I recovered quickly and climbed up the rigging beside the mast.

Slowly and painfully, Hands came after me, holding the knife between his teeth. I quickly reloaded my guns with dry powder.

When the pirate was a few feet below

me, I pointed my pistols at him.

"Not another step, Mr. Hands," I cried.

I'm not sure what happened next. Hands whipped the knife from his mouth and flung it at me. It hit my shoulder, pinning me to the mast. At the same time, I fired both pistols. The guns fell out of my hands and tumbled, together with Israel Hands, into the clear blue sea.

Hands's knife had nailed me to the mast by my jacket. Luckily, the blade had only grazed my shoulder. I set myself free and cut down the mainsail, so that the vessel wouldn't move with the wind. I then tidied up the rest of the ship. By early evening, the *Hispaniola* was secure and in good order.

I was eager to tell my friends what I had done. Using Spyglass Hill to discover my position, I worked out that the fort was quite near. I decided to go there immediately.

I dived off the ship and swam ashore. Though it was dark by the time I got there, the fort was easy to find. That's strange, I thought, as I climbed the fence. No one on guard? The Captain will be furious.

I tiptoed through the door and listened to the men's snores. I smiled.

Instead of waking them, I'd sleep on the floor—they'd get such a surprise finding me there in the morning!

But the surprise was all mine. The silence of the night was suddenly broken by a harsh cry: "Pieces of eight! Piece of eight!"

It was Long John Silver's parrot. The pirates had captured the fort!

CHAPTER 6
Treasure

When I realized I was in a nest of pirates, I dashed for the door. A strong arm grabbed me and brought me back.

The villains fingered their daggers and gave me murderous looks. They wanted to kill me! "Let me live," I argued, "and I'll defend you in the law courts back in England." Five of the men sneered, saying that I couldn't be trusted.

But not Long John Silver. He said he'd save my life now, if I saved his in England.

At this, the men muttered angrily. They handed Silver a Black Spot warning, written on a page torn from a Bible: He was no longer their leader.

"Not your leader?" he laughed. "So,

you don't want this?" From his pocket, he pulled Billy Bones's map showing where the treasure was buried.

We were astonished! How had Silver found the map, we asked.

He grinned and said that Dr. Livesey had given it to him. The two of them had come to a kind of agreement. I also learned the pirates were in the fort because my friends had abandoned it when they discovered the *Hispaniola* was missing.

I was now utterly confused.

I was even more confused when Dr. Livesey appeared at the fort. He had come, he said, to treat the wounded pirates. It was his duty as a doctor to heal the sick and injured, whoever they were.

This was very brave of him. I feared that the pirates, like savage dogs, might turn on him at any moment. I asked Silver if I might speak to the Doctor in private.

He agreed, if I gave him my word that I would not try to escape.

I promised.

At first, the Doctor was angry with me for running away and getting captured by Silver. But he soon changed. He was delighted when I told him how I had taken the *Hispaniola* from the pirates and hidden it in the North Anchorage. I had saved the honest men yet again!

"So, come on!" he urged. "Jump over the fence with me, and leave these dreadful people!"

"I'd love to," I said, "but I have given my word. If I broke my promise, I'd be no better than a pirate, would I?"

The Doctor nodded sadly and departed. Once again, I was alone and at the mercy of Long John Silver.

After the Doctor left, we left to find the treasure. Silver, map in hand, led the way. I was attached to him by a rope, like a dog on a leash. The other five pirates trailed along behind.

At first, we trudged slowly through the marshy jungle. The ground was drier on the slopes of Spyglass Hill, where Flint's treasure lay, and Silver hobbled quicker. He was eager to reach his goal.

In a clearing, we found the skeleton of one of the pirates Captain Flint had killed. It was propped up against a tree, its arms pointing toward the treasure.

The sight gave the pirates the jitters. As they were wondering whether Flint's ghost was nearby, a weird voice began singing his old song:

"Fifteen men on the dead man's chest—
Yo-ho-ho, and a bottle of rum!"

The pirates were scared out of their wits, until Silver cried, "It's Ben Gunn; the old fool marooned here. Nobody minds Ben Gunn!"

The pirates agreed. Much relieved, they hurried on toward the long-awaited treasure trove.

"Hurrah!" they yelled, as they reached the spot marked with an X on the map. "We're rich …"

They stopped. Before them lay a deep pit, a deep, *empty* pit.

The treasure had gone.

In the pit lay a broken shovel and some empty boxes. Before we had arrived, someone had dug up Flint's treasure and carried it off.

The five pirates were furious and swore at Silver. George Merry, the angriest of them, said the one-legged seaman had swindled them. "We'll kill you, Silver," he yelled, "and that wretched boy too!"

At that moment, there was a crackle of gunfire from the bushes nearby. Merry tumbled over headlong into the pit, another one of his mates collapsed to the ground, the other three ran for their lives.

Then, all at once, Dr. Livesey, Gray, and Ben Gunn came out of hiding, guns smoking. Long John Silver—the crafty devil!—reminded the Doctor that he had saved my life. He was one of the Squire's team now, he said.

The Doctor explained it all to me. During his three years on the island, Ben Gunn had dug up the treasure and moved it to a secret cave high on Spyglass Hill. He then explained this to Dr. Livesey. That's why the Doctor had been happy to give Billy Bones's map to Silver—the X no longer marked the spot where Flint's treasure was hidden.

The treasure of Treasure Island—seven hundred thousand pounds—was ours!

*

The rest of my tale is swiftly told. Ben Gunn showed us the cave in which he'd hidden Flint's treasure. The Squire and the Captain were keeping guard.

We found the *Hispaniola* safe and sound in the North Anchorage. Carefully, we carried on board the bars of gold and bags of precious coins. When we were ready to leave, we had to decide what to do with the pirates.

Long John Silver and Ben Gunn could come with us. We chose to leave behind the three men who had run away. To help them in their lonely life, we left them gunpowder, food, medicine, tools, clothes, tobacco, and a few other useful bits and pieces.

As we were sailing away, they stood on the shore gesturing to us, begging us to take them with us. What could we do? Back in England, they would be hanged for piracy. We sailed on.

I have one more thing to report. After sailing for some time, we stopped in South America to stock up on supplies. After returning to the ship, we found that Long John Silver had stolen a sack of gold coins and disappeared. We were all glad to be rid of him.

At last, as I entered the Admiral Benbow Inn and threw myself into my mother's arms, my Treasure Island adventure was finally over.

Black Beauty

Retold by
Jo Franklin

Illustrated by
Joëlle Dreidemy

ARCTURUS

For Eleanor and Cedric—JF.

To Willow and Rowan, with love—JD.

ARCTURUS

This edition published in 2018 by Arcturus Publishing Limited
26/27 Bickels Yard, 151–153 Bermondsey Street,
London SE1 3HA

Copyright © Arcturus Holdings Limited

All rights reserved. No part of this publication may be reproduced, stored in a retrieval system, or transmitted, in any form or by any means, electronic, mechanical, photocopying, recording or otherwise, without written permission in accordance with the provisions of the Copyright Act 1956 (as amended). Any person or persons who do any unauthorised act in relation to this publication may be liable to criminal prosecution and civil claims for damages.

Writer: Jo Franklin
Illustrator: Joelle Dreidemy
Designer: Jeni Child
Editor: Sebastian Rydberg
Art Director: Jessica Crass

ISBN: 978-1-78828-683-1
CH006277NT
Supplier 24, Date 0618, Print run 7509

Printed in Malaysia

Contents

CHAPTER 1
My Early Life 4

CHAPTER 2
A Very Happy Family 16

CHAPTER 3
A Midnight Emergency 26

CHAPTER 4
Problems at Earlshall 38

CHAPTER 5
A Change of Fortune 48

CHAPTER 6
Another Life 56

CHAPTER 1
My Early Life

When I was a foal, I lived with my mother in a beautiful meadow with a pond of clear water in the corner. During the day, I ran by my mother's side, and at night,

I lay close by her. When it was hot, we stood under the trees in the shade, and when it was cold, we had a snug stable to keep us warm and dry.

My mother's name was Duchess. Our master had many animals, but he loved her best of all. Every day that he came to see us, he petted her as if she were his own child. She was gentle and wise, and he loved her for it. So did I.

In the field next to us lived six young colts. They were older than me, but I had great fun galloping around the field with them. Sometimes, the game got a little rough, and the colts kicked out as they played and tried to nip each other's necks. One day, when our game became too lively, my mother whinnied for me to come to her.

"You must listen to me carefully, my young son. The colts are good colts, but they are carthorse colts, and they have no manners. You have been well born. Your father was a cup winner at the races, and you have never seen me kick or bite." She nudged my neck with her soft muzzle to make sure I was listening properly. "I hope you will grow up gentle and good like your parents. You must work hard with a good will, whoever your master is. Pick your feet up well when you trot, and never bite or kick when you are playing."

"Yes, Mother," I bowed my head with shame. "I won't play rough with the colts again."

My mother nudged my ear, which was her way of saying she trusted me to keep my word. I promised myself that I would always try to be a good horse like her.

When I was four years old, I was ready to be broken in. This was the training I needed to become an adult horse. I'd always worn a soft head collar and was used to being led, but now I had to learn to wear a leather bridle and a saddle, so that anyone could ride me.

At first, I didn't like the cold steel bit that was pushed into my mouth, but my master spoke softly to me, which made me less scared. I didn't like the feel of the hard saddle, either, but after a few weeks, I was proud to wear a saddle and carry my master.

Before I could go out onto the road, I had to have shoes to protect my feet from the hard stones. Master took me to the blacksmith, who made iron shoes that fitted my feet perfectly. My feet felt stiff and heavy at first, but before long, I was used to them and picked my feet up smartly as my mother had told me to do.

One day, my master took me to a nearby farmer. I was turned out into a field on my own. I didn't know why I had been sent there, but the grass was tasty, so I was happy enough. Suddenly, a thundering monster hurtled out of nowhere and roared alongside the hedge. Smoke belched from the funnel on the back of its head. Instead of legs, the monster had wheels that sped around faster than any cart.

I'd never seen anything like it, and I ran to the far corner of the field in case the monster leaped over the hedge and gobbled me up. But the iron monster sped into the distance without even looking at me.

Many monsters passed the field. Some were slow and lumbering. Others screeched their whistles as they passed by. None of the monsters even glanced in my direction, and I realized that a train on a track was absolutely nothing to fear.

*

The best part of my training was when my master drove me in a double harness with my mother. She showed me how to behave and gave me instructions as we worked together.

"A horse never knows who may buy them," she said, as we trotted along. "But you must always be the best you can be whoever your master or mistress should be."

Once my training was complete, I was taken to my new home at Squire Gordon's stables. The stables were airy and clean, and I felt very privileged to be led into a large box stall where I didn't need to be tied up.

The sides were topped with iron rails that were low enough for me to see through.

In the next stall stood a fat, dappled pony with a thick mane and tail.

"How do you do?" I asked politely through the rails. "What is your name?"

The pony turned to look at me through the bars, holding his head up high. "My name is Merrylegs, and I carry the young ladies on my back because

I am so handsome. Are you going to live next to me?"

"Yes, I think so." I felt a little shy because I was new, and he was so confident.

"Well, I hope you are better tempered than the other one." Merrylegs tossed his head toward the stall on the other side to me. "That one bites."

Just then, another horse looked over from the stall behind me. She was a tall, chestnut-brown mare, with a white blaze down the middle of her face.

"So, you are the one who has taken my box."

"I beg your pardon," I said politely but stepping back, so that the chestnut horse couldn't bite me. "I have not taken anything. The man put me in here, and I wish to live in peace with you all."

The grumpy horse snorted and moved over to the other side of her box.

"Don't mind her," Merrylegs said. "Ginger is always bad-tempered. She was badly treated before she came here. But this is a good place for a horse. John is the best groom, and James, the stable boy, treats us very well."

Before I could answer, my stable door was opened, and John, the groom, led me out into the yard where the squire and Mrs. Gordon were waiting.

"Well, what do you think?" the squire asked his wife.

"He's wonderful!" Mrs. Gordon said, as she ran her hand along my back.

I could feel how kind she was by her gentle touch. Merrylegs was right. This was a good home.

"I know the perfect name for him." She leaned in close and pushed her face to my ear just like my mother had done. "Black Beauty," she spoke softly. "I hope you like that name."

I whinnied softly in reply, hoping that she knew I liked the name and new home.

CHAPTER 2

A Very Happy Family

Everyone was right. Squire Gordon's stables were the best home a horse could hope for. For the first time, I had two friends in Merrylegs and Ginger (who turned out to be not so grumpy after all). John and James took excellent care of us. The Squire and Mrs. Gordon were the perfect master and mistress. We were one big happy family.

One day, John hitched me to the dog cart because the Squire needed to go out on business. It had rained all night, and the sky was still dark with clouds. The river raced high and furious, almost touching the planks of the bridge as it flowed away.

"Good day to you, Squire." The man at the tollgate stepped out, pulling his muffler over his chin against the brisk wind. "Don't worry if the water splashes up between the planks. It is normal for this bridge."

I trotted across the bridge on John's command, even though I could see the river rushing beneath us. It was only water, and we had a sturdy bridge to keep us safe.

It was late in the afternoon when we made our way homeward again. It was nearly nightfall when we got to the bridge. The river had risen further, and the water lapped over the middle exactly as the toll man had said it would.

"Come on, Beauty, let's get home," John commanded, as he steered the dog cart toward the bridge.

I had never refused John or disobeyed my master's orders, but the moment my hooves touched the bridge, I knew something was wrong. I pulled up sharply and wouldn't take another step.

"It's only a touch of water," James said and shook the reins as the sign for me to go on, but I flatly refused to move.

"Stop!" A voice called out from the other side of the bridge. "The bridge has broken." The toll man swayed his lantern back and forward. "Turn back!"

The light from his lantern lit up the bridge. The side rail upriver was still in place, but I couldn't see the other rail at all. The river was angry and powerful as it crashed into the broken planks we had driven over this morning. The middle of the bridge had been swept clean away.

John jumped down and took my harness to lead me around to the road that ran beside the riverbank.

"Thank you, Beauty," Squire Gordon said, as we pulled into the stable at home. "You saved our lives today. We would have been swept away if we had tried to cross the bridge. John, make sure you take special care of this horse tonight."

"I will do, sir." John patted my neck and gave me some crushed beans with my oats. We were safely home, and I'd never been so pleased to see my stable. I was lucky to be alive.

If my master had business farther away from home, Ginger and I would take him together in the bigger carriage. Sometimes, we would spend the night at a different stable. John or James went with us and worked with the local stable hands to make sure we were well cared for.

One night, when James was settling us into a strange stable, he asked the local stable hand to help him.

"Run up the ladder, and drop some hay into the horse's rack, will you?" James asked the young man. "But leave your pipe down here, please."

It was a common thing for men to smoke pipes, but Squire Gordon had a strict ban on smoking in the stables.

I heard the boy step on the beams above my head, and he put the hay into my rack as he was asked.

James looked in at us last thing at night, and then the stable yard fell silent for the night.

I slept for a while but woke up feeling uncomfortable. The air was thick, and I could hardly breathe. There was a strange rushing, crackling sound in the barn above us. I'd never heard that noise before, and it made me tremble with terror.

The other horses were awake, too, and some pulled at their halters while others stamped nervously. We didn't know what was happening, but we were all afraid.

At last, I heard some steps outside, and the door flew open. A strange groomsman came in and untied us all. I could smell the fear on him, and even though we should have all followed him obediently, we were too afraid. We were surrounded by an unknown danger, and we didn't trust this man.

The rushing sound overhead grew louder, and a red light flickered on the wall.

"Fire!" A cry went up outside, and at that moment, the flames turned into a raging furnace above us. Next thing I knew, James was right beside me.

"Come along, Beauty." He spoke cheerily in my ear as if nothing was wrong. "Time to be out of here." He slipped my bridle on and wrapped a scarf over my eyes. I couldn't see anything, but I trusted James, so I let him guide me into the fresh air.

Once out in the yard, he threw my reins to someone else and dashed back into the fire.

Ginger was still in the stable with the flames. Smoke poured out thicker than ever, and I heard a crash of something falling inside. I let out a shrill whinny calling to James and Ginger.

Next moment, they were at the door. James's face was dirty with soot, and Ginger choked violently, her eyes white with terror.

James led us safely to the other side of the market square just as the fire engine arrived.

"Thank you," Ginger coughed when her voice returned.

"Me?" I said.

"Yes, Black Beauty. I wouldn't have come out of that stable if I hadn't heard your call. You saved my life."

"Why, that's what friends are for," I said.

CHAPTER 3

A Midnight Emergency

The Squire and Mrs. Gordon were very impressed with James's bravery that night.

"Most horses would freeze in terror," the Squire said to James the next morning. "You have a real skill with horses, and I am going to recommend you to Lord Wilson, who is looking for a new head groom."

"Thank you, sir, I'm very grateful to you," James blushed as if he was embarrassed, but he didn't need to be. He had saved both me and Ginger that night.

We were all pleased for him when he was offered the job, but we were also sad because we would never see him again.

"Who will take my job here?" James asked John.

"Joe Green, who lives at the lodge."

"That kid?" James said. "He knows nothing about horses."

"He knows nothing now, but he'll learn. Beauty and I will teach him." John patted me gently as he walked past. It was good that John would always look after me, even if James was working far away.

The next day, little Joe Green started work. He was too short to groom me and Ginger, so he began brushing Merrylegs.

"He keeps mauling me about," Merrylegs complained after the first time Joe tried to groom him, but after another week, Merrylegs admitted that Joe was already getting better at caring for him.

Eventually, James had to say goodbye. He patted each of us and thanked us for being such great horses to work with. Of course, we couldn't tell him how grateful we were to be cared for by him, but I think he knew. As he walked away, he dragged his feet and dipped his head low with his carpetbag thrown across his shoulders.

John now had to train Joe Green to be a good stable hand.

*

A few days later, I was settling down for the night, when a cry went up, and I heard feet running outside. John rushed into my stable.

"Quick, Beauty, Mrs. Gordon has taken ill, and we must fetch the doctor before it is too late."

John saddled me, and we started off in the darkness.

He didn't need to use his whip or spurs. I sensed the urgency. Mrs. Gordon was my lovely mistress who had given me the name "Black Beauty" and now she was in danger. I wanted to help her.

The air was frosty, and the moon bright, which meant there was nothing stopping me from galloping at full speed. John pulled me up when we reached the bridge, and I'm sure he would have taken the second half of the journey at a steadier pace, but I didn't want to slow down. My mistress needed the doctor right away, so I galloped on until we arrived in the town.

John thumped on the doctor's front door. The doctor poked his head out the window in his nightcap and gown.

"Mrs. Gordon is very ill, sir," John called up. "Please come quickly."

"Just a moment, I'll be right down." The doctor shut the window and soon came downstairs, tucking his nightgown into his breeches. "But I don't have a horse. Mine has been out all day. Can I take yours?"

"I was supposed to rest him and ride him home in the morning," John said. "He has galloped the whole way here." I sensed the edginess in John's voice.

I felt my heart pounding and my skin burning hot, but still, I willed John to agree. My mistress needed the doctor, and I was the horse to take him to her.

"Okay," John said. "But take care. He's a fine, loyal horse, and we care about him a great deal."

The doctor nodded, and we rode back home. The journey took longer than on the outward run because the doctor was heavier and not such a good horseman as John, but we arrived at last and the doctor rushed inside to my mistress.

I was glad to be home. My legs shook, and I could barely stand. Since John was still in the town, the only person to care for me was little Joe Green. No one had taught him how to care for an overheated horse, but he did the best he could.

"You're too hot," he said as he rubbed me down. "I'm not going to give you a blanket, so that you can cool down." He gave me a bucket of ice cold water, which I gulped down immediately. Then, he left me alone thinking that he had done everything right.

Soon, I began to shake, and my body felt deadly cold. My legs and chest ached, and I felt sore all over. I needed that warm blanket, and I needed John, but I was all alone. I lay down in my straw and tried to sleep.

Later, I remember John being with me. I couldn't tell him how bad I was feeling, but he knew anyway. He covered me with three snug cloths and fed me some warm gruel. Eventually, I fell asleep.

I was now very ill.

John nursed me night and day. He slept in my stable, so that he could check on me during the night. He didn't speak to Joe Green the whole time.

"My poor Beauty," my master cried when he came to see me. "You saved your mistress's life, but look what it has done to you."

I don't know how long I was sick. Merrylegs and Ginger were moved to a different part of the stable because any sound startled me.

It was a lonely time.

Young Joe Green was terribly upset. He'd done his best but didn't know how to care for horses back then.

I lay ill in the stable, and my mistress lay ill in the house.

After a few weeks, my fever passed, and I started getting better. Eventually, I was fit enough to go out for a steady ride. Joe Green rode me as he was the lightest groom, and he treated me respectfully.

My mistress didn't make such a good recovery. The doctor said she needed to be moved to a warmer country.

The house was to be shut up while she and the master were away. That meant that Merrylegs, Ginger, and I needed new homes, and John and Joe had to leave us to find new jobs.

The day Mrs. Gordon left the house, she had to be carried to the carriage because she was too weak to walk. Ginger and I drove her to the train station.

Everyone cried as she said goodbye, and it was a sad party that returned to the house for the last time.

The next day, Merrylegs went to live at the vicarage, and Ginger and I left for our new home at Earlshall, uncertain what lay ahead of us.

CHAPTER 4

Problems at Earlshall

I wasn't looking forward to changing homes, but Ginger was coming with me. We were given bright stables next to each other, and the other horses were pleasant enough, but things started to go wrong as soon as we were hitched to the carriage for the first time. At Earlshall, they used the check rein, which was a horrible thing that I'd heard about but never experienced myself.

The check rein was an extra strap that fitted from the bit in my mouth, over my head, and attached to the harness across my back. It stopped me from lowering my head. It was the fashion to have horses' heads held high, but it was terribly painful, especially if we had to pull the carriage uphill.

Squire Gordon had never used the check rein, but Ginger knew exactly what it was and how badly it hurt.

check rein

To begin with, Ginger didn't complain. York, the coachman, knew we weren't used to this rein, so he didn't tighten it too much, but her ladyship wasn't happy.

"For goodness' sake, York, tighten that rein. I will not have the horses with their heads so low," she complained bitterly. I could feel Ginger's temper brewing as she stood beside me.

She fidgeted and shook her head, knowing what was coming next. The moment York released her rein to shorten it, Ginger reared up. She was still harnessed to the carriage, but that didn't stop her bucking and kicking like a mad thing. Somehow, she managed to jump over the carriage pole. She ended up lying on the floor with York lying on her head to stop her rearing again.

In a mad frenzy, the grooms unbuckled me to release me from the carriage, and they led me back to the stable. I was still trussed up in the check rein, and I wanted to kick out just like Ginger, but I knew that good horses didn't behave like that. Eventually, Ginger was led back into her box. She looked rather shocked. York came over to me, his face red with anger.

"I hate these check reins," he said, as he released me at last. "But I have to do what her ladyship tells me."

Ginger was never put in the carriage again. She was used as a hunter instead, which is a different sort of hardship. Meanwhile, I had to wear the check rein every time I took out the carriage. I always returned to my stable with a sore tongue and aching back, and Ginger came back every night exhausted because she had been ridden hard across the fields.

When York went to London with his lordship, Reuben Smith was in charge. He was a first-rate driver and knew how to care for us if we were ill because he used to work for a veterinarian. He should have been head coachman, but unfortunately, he had a weakness for alcohol. Mostly, he avoided it, but sometimes he got tempted. He would drink too much and behave very badly.

*

One day, Reuben took me for a ride. We stopped at the White Lion, and I was cared for by the inn's own stable hand while Reuben went inside. When he came out, he was in a foul temper and could hardly walk straight.

"Excuse me, but I think your horse has a loose shoe," the stable hand said.

"It'll be all right. Out of my way." Reuben pushed the man aside and mounted me roughly. He rode me just as carelessly, digging his heels in and giving me a sharp swipe with the whip, even though I was going as fast as I could.

The roads were stony. My shoe loosened as we rode, until suddenly, it flew off. Any sensible horseman would have noticed, but Reuben Smith was too drunk to notice. We continued at a wild pace, and my shoeless foot became more and more painful as the sharp stones dug into it.

In the end, the pain was too great. I stumbled suddenly and fell to my knees. Reuben was flung off my back and landed heavily by the side of the road.

I pulled myself to my feet, but my knees were bleeding, and my foot was so sore I couldn't put it down.

Reuben Smith didn't move.

After a while, I heard another horse approaching. It was Ginger pulling the dog cart. I neighed loudly, and soon she was by my side. Two men jumped down to help Reuben Smith, but sadly, it was too late for him.

"This horse has thrown him," one of the men said rudely.

His words cut as painfully as the whip. I had never thrown a rider in my life. Robert, a groom, came over, and the moment he saw my wounds, he knew that something was wrong.

"It's not Black Beauty's fault. There is a stone wedged in his foot. No wonder he went down, and look at the state of his knees."

They put poor Reuben in the cart, and I limped home with Robert.

Next morning, the farrier patched me up as best he could.

"His joints are okay," he said. "But he'll be scarred for life."

He was right. The wounds did heal, but now that I had ugly, scarred knees, my lord and lady didn't want me any longer.

And that is how I ended up in my first-ever horse fair.

CHAPTER 5

A Change of Fortune

There is a lot to see at a horse fair, and I'm sorry to say that not all of it is pleasant.

There were droves of shaggy Welsh ponies and many heavy horses in every shade and condition. There were fine horses showing off their paces in high style with their grooms running by their side and young colts newly broken in.

In the background were a number of poor nags, sadly broken down from hard work. Their knees collapsed under them, and their back legs swung at every step. There were a number of horses like me, highbred but now fallen to a lower class because of an accident or blemish.

The horse dealers bragged and bargained all day. I was put together with some other useful-looking horses, and we had plenty of people examining us. First, they pulled my mouth open and looked into my eyes. Then, they felt my legs all the way down. Lastly, they'd ask me to walk around so they could see how I moved.

Many of these potential owners handled me carelessly, but one chap was different.

He wasn't a gentleman, but he spoke gently, and his quick eyes had a cheery look. After a hard bargain, he bought me, and I was very pleased to leave the fair with my new owner.

We rode a fair way through pleasant lanes and country roads and then came into London. The gas lamps were already lit. Streets went off to the right and to the left, all crossing each other for mile upon mile. I thought we'd never come to the end of it, and I kept thinking what a long way I'd come since I was a young foal running with my mother in the fields.

At last, we pulled up at one of the houses, and a woman and two children ran out to greet us.

"Is he gentle, Father?" the girl asked.

"As gentle as a kitten. Give him a pat."

My owner's wife gave me a lovely bran mash, and for the first time in a long time, I felt happy to call a place my home.

My new master's name was Gerry, and he was a London cab driver, or cabbie. His morning horse was called Captain, and I drove the cab in the afternoon. We all had Sunday off.

I certainly needed one rest day a week because my life as a cab horse was hard work. There were too many people, too many carriages and carts on the road, and too much noise. Luckily, I was in safe hands and soon learned to trust Gerry because he knew where we were going.

All afternoon, we went from one place to another, picking up passengers and taking them where they wanted to go. It was never-ending, but Gerry treated me and Captain well. We had plenty to eat, and I could have a cooling drink whenever I needed it.

His family were delightful. They petted me and groomed me every day, and I felt well loved again. So, the weeks sped by. There were six days of hard work; followed by one day's rest.

Christmas was a very busy time for cabbies. In the daytime, everyone was busy going from shop to shop buying presents; then they needed a cab to get home with their parcels. In the evenings, there were late parties.

Although it was an opportunity for Gerry to earn plenty, Christmas also coincided with the worst of the winter weather, which was not good for his health.

One night, we took some young gentlemen to a party and were instructed to wait outside, so that we could drive them home after the party. It was a cold night, and I could see my breath in the frosty air every time I breathed out. Gerry walked up and down swinging his arms to try and keep warm, but soon he was coughing. He wrapped himself in rugs and sat on his box because cab drivers were not allowed to sit inside. His cough was so bad, the cab rattled with the force of it.

Eventually, the gentleman reappeared, and we drove them home. They paid Gerry a good fare, but it wasn't enough. My poor master could hardly talk. His wife took him inside, and his son, Harry, gave me a bran mash.

Gerry's chest was so bad, he couldn't get out of bed, and he certainly couldn't go back to work. Luckily, Harry knew how to care for me, and I was grateful for the rest because maybe if I had gone out cabbing in that weather, I would have become sick like Gerry.

My master did get better, but he decided to give up cab driving. He found a job in the countryside, but there was no position for me. I was to be sold again, and I couldn't help wondering who would want an old horse with scarred knees like me.

CHAPTER 6

Another Life

At the sale, I was put in with all the old horses. The buyers and sellers didn't look much better off than the horses. Some of the buyers were hard-bitten, but there were others I would have been willing to serve, even if they were poor and shabby.

A gentleman farmer with a young boy

wandered over to look at us. I saw his eye rest on me, and I gave my tail a swish so he could see what a fine beast I used to be.

"He must have been a smart fellow in his day, Willie," the old man said to the boy. "Look at his nostrils and ears. And the shape of his neck. You're a well-bred old fellow." The old man patted my neck, and I put my nose out to him in answer to his kindness. The boy stroked my face.

"Could you buy him, Grandpapa? And make him well again?"

"I don't know, Willie. He might be past fixing."

But the young lad didn't give up. His grandfather asked for me to be walked around, and I did my very best to pick up my feet smartly and toss my head to show I still had a little spirit.

"I'll give you five pounds for him," the farmer said to the dealer.

I was so happy to be led away from the horse market. I made a silent wish for the other poor creatures I left behind and followed my new master home.

The master released me into a large meadow with a dry stable. Young Willie came and visited me every day with a generous helping of oats and hay. I soon grew stronger.

In the spring, my new master took me out in the light carriage, and I showed him exactly the horse I used to be. I trotted on, tossing my mane and tail as if I was still a colt.

"He's growing young again," the old man said, "thanks to you, Willie."

One day, the groom came to tend to me. He cleaned and dressed me with care. I guessed I was to be sold again. I didn't want to leave my lovely field, but I hoped that my master would ensure that I went to a good home.

I was taken to a village a couple of miles away, and we stopped outside a pretty house with nodding daffodils by the door.

Three ladies came out to look at me. One was wrapped in a white shawl that matched her hair. Her name was Miss Bloomfield. The other ladies, Miss Laura and Miss Emily, were younger but clearly gentle and kind.

"Are you sure he's safe?" Miss Bloomfield said. "His knees are scarred. If he's been down once, he might go down again and drag my carriage with him."

"I don't know what happened to him. It may have been an accident. He's never given me any trouble," my master told the ladies.

"I think we should ask Joseph," Miss Laura said.

A servant fetched their groom. He ran his hands over my back and legs like a true horseman. For a moment, I thought I was back at Squire Gordon's again with John and James because this groom treated me just as kindly.

The groom came around and examined my head. I looked in his eyes and could see a question there.

"You look like a horse I knew once– Black Beauty," he said. "He was a fine creature. I wonder where he is now."

"Black Beauty is a fine name," Miss Bloomfield said.

"He had a star on his forehead and one white foot just like this old fellow. He was the same height, too." The groom stood back and scratched his head. "I wonder if this could be the same horse."

He stepped forward and parted the hair on my back as if he was looking for something.

"Why, it is him! Look, that little spot of white hair. John used to call it Beauty's secret penny. This must be the horse I knew when I was a boy. Black Beauty, do you remember me? I am Joe Green. Have you forgiven me for nearly killing you all those years ago?"

I wouldn't have recognized his face because this Joe Green was a man with whiskers, but I recognized his smile.

"Do you know this horse?" Miss Bloomfield asked.

"Yes, miss, and a finer, more loyal horse you could never hope for. He fetched the doctor when the mistress nearly died. Galloped all night and saved her life." He smiled, but I saw a hint of sadness in his eyes as he thought of our mistress. "Black Beauty, I am so glad to see you again."

"I like a horse with a good history and a good name. It would be my pleasure to buy this horse from you. Welcome, Black Beauty," Miss Bloomfield said.

The other two ladies broke into a round of applause. Joe patted my neck, and Willie hugged his Grandpapa.

And me? I whinnied and tossed my head a little at the joy of finding a place I could call home. I served Miss Bloomfield and the younger ladies loyally until the end of my days, and in return, Joe Green looked after me as carefully as John and James had done all those years ago.

The Call of the Wild

Retold by
Stewart Ross

Illustrated by
Vince Reid

ARCTURUS

For Zac Ross, with love—SR.

For Bob, my Dad—VR.

Arcturus

This edition published in 2018 by Arcturus Publishing Limited
26/27 Bickels Yard, 151–153 Bermondsey Street,
London SE1 3HA

Copyright © Arcturus Holdings Limited

All rights reserved. No part of this publication may be reproduced, stored in a retrieval system, or transmitted, in any form or by any means, electronic, mechanical, photocopying, recording or otherwise, without written permission in accordance with the provisions of the Copyright Act 1956 (as amended). Any person or persons who do any unauthorised act in relation to this publication may be liable to criminal prosecution and civil claims for damages.

Writer: Stewart Ross
Illustrator: Vince Reid
Designer: Jeni Child
Editor: Sebastian Rydberg
Art Director: Jessica Crass

ISBN: 978-1-78828-690-9
CH006284NT
Supplier 24, Date 0618, Print run 7516

Printed in Malaysia

Contents

CHAPTER 1
Kidnapped! 4

CHAPTER 2
The Law of Club and Fang 14

CHAPTER 3
The New Leader 24

CHAPTER 4
Rescue 34

CHAPTER 5
John Thornton 44

CHAPTER 6
Return to the Wild 54

CHAPTER 1

Kidnapped!

Buck was like no other dog. His huge size came from his father, a St. Bernard. His mother, a clever sheepdog, had given him his brains. His many adventures began with the men who owned him. But in the end, Buck ran wild and free.

Our story opens in the warm and sunny state of California. Buck was born there into the wealthy household of Judge Miller. His early days were comfortable and easy.

The judge's large house was approached through wide gates down broad drives. His lawns were neat, his gardens tidy, and his fields rich. All this, Buck enjoyed.

He played on the grass and went hunting with the judge's sons. In the evenings, he lay before a roaring fire and dreamed.

The judge's other dogs respected Buck. As well as being bigger and stronger than them, he was also more intelligent. He was their lord, the king of the judge's estate. He understood things, almost like a human.

Almost—but not exactly. He could not, for example, read the newspapers. Had he done so, he would have known trouble was brewing. In the far north, in the land of ice and snow, men had discovered gold.

The only way to travel over the snow of the distant gold fields was by sled. There were no trucks or tractors, and horses could not survive in the cold. Only teams of dogs could manage the heavy loads.

But tie a terrier or a poodle to a sled, and nothing happens. They are too small and weak; besides, they cannot stand freezing temperatures. Sled drivers need heavy dogs with strong muscles and thick, furry coats that keep out the cold.

Buck was one of these dogs. Manuel, one of the judge's gardeners, realized this, and a wicked thought entered his head.

Manuel had a large family and earned just about enough to feed them all. But he needed more. He was a gambler, and every time he played cards, he lost money.

He grew desperate. "Come on, Buck," he called one evening, when no one was around. "We're going for a walk."

Buck trusted Manuel and set off at his side through the orchard. At a small train station, they met another man who paid Manuel money.

Only now, when a rope was slipped around his neck, did Buck sense that something was wrong.

He bared his teeth and growled.

Buck had always trusted humans. But when Manuel handed the rope to the other man, Buck rebelled. Deep inside him, a voice whispered, *This is not right! Danger!*

He leaped up at the stranger, aiming to grasp him by the throat. The man was waiting for him. In the air, the rope tightened around Buck's neck as the man spun him around. He smashed Buck to the ground.

Half choked, Buck was lifted into a train wagon. He was furious! Never in all his life had he been treated so badly. When one of the men guarding him came close, his anger exploded.

With a furious snarl, he sank his teeth into the man's hand. The fellow yelled with pain, but Buck let go only when the rope around his neck was so tight, he couldn't breathe.

To stop him from attacking again, the guards locked him in a wooden cage. In vain, he snapped and charged at the bars. For two days, as the train rattled north, he had neither food nor water.

Buck's eyes grew as red as the anger within him. Gone was the house dog. In his place stood a savage beast that even the judge would not have recognized.

When the train stopped, the wagon door opened, and four men climbed in.

"That's some dog," said one of them when he saw Buck.

"Sure is," said another. Buck, crimson-eyed and full of wrath, snarled. "And looks pretty dangerous, too," added the man.

They lifted Buck's cage and carried it to a small yard. High walls surrounded it on all sides—there was no way out. The men placed the crate on the ground and sat on the top of the wall to see what would happen.

A large man in a sloppy red sweater came in and shut the gate behind him. In one hand, he held a hatchet, in the other a stout wooden club. He smiled and walked over to the cage.

Buck threw himself against the bars. *Another cruel man come to mock me,* he thought. *I'll show him!*

The man in the sloppy sweater chopped open the cage with his hatchet. "Right, you red-eyed devil," he muttered, "come on out!" As he spoke, he dropped his hatchet and took the club in his right hand.

Buck stepped out of the broken cage and sprang. All one hundred and forty pounds of him flew straight toward the man's neck.

Crash! When Buck's jaws were inches from the throat of the man in the red sweater, something cracked into his head. It was the club.

Buck landed heavily on his side. No one had ever hit him like that before, and he didn't know what was happening. He rose and launched himself at the man a second time.

Crash! Once more, the club smashed into Buck's head. He fell to the ground, rose, and attacked again. And again. Each time, he was hammered down, until finally, he passed out.

He was beaten, and he accepted it. He was not broken, but he was too intelligent to attack when he knew he couldn't win. Later, he saw a dog who didn't understand this. The dog was brave but foolish—and he was killed.

Buck had learned his first lesson in a world where only power mattered: A man with a club would always be his master.

Now that the man in the red sweater had shown who was boss, he patted Buck's head and gave him water and meat.

"You've learned your place, Buck," he said in a friendly voice. "So, be a good boy, and everything will be all right."

CHAPTER 2
The Law of Club and Fang

Now that he had learned the law of the club, Buck was ready for work. He was bought by two tough Canadians, Perrault and François. Their job was delivering letters to the gold fields.

Buck hadn't met men like them before. They were as hard as the ice over which they journeyed, but they were fair. If the dogs behaved and worked hard, they were fed and looked after. But woe betide the weak or lazy ones!

Perrault and François carried the letters hundreds of miles by sled. They'd come south to Seattle to buy new dogs for their team. As well as Buck, they bought a gentle Newfoundland dog named Curly.

They trekked back to Alaska by sea. On the boat, Buck met two huskies of the sled team: Spitz, the leader, and the miserable Dave. Buck quickly learned to ignore Dave—and to watch out for the leader. Spitz was clever, crafty, and merciless.

Buck learned something else. The moment his feet touched the ground in Alaska, he leaped into the air. What was this strange, cold white stuff on the ground? It was his first snow.

Life in Alaska was merciless. Among dogs, the law of the fang said only the tough survived, and Buck grasped it immediately. Gentle Curly did not.

They were camped near a store when Curly approached a husky to say hello. The savage beast turned in a flash and struck with its fangs. Curly's face was torn open from eye to jaw.

Immediately, thirty or forty other huskies gathered. They formed a silent circle around the two fighting dogs, waiting for one to fall. Wounded and angry, Curly attacked. The husky dodged aside and slashed at her again.

Curly charged a third time. The husky, an experienced fighter, was waiting. As

Curly reached him, he batted against her with his chest, knocking her to the ground.

This was what the pack had been waiting for, and they leaped upon Curly before she could get back her feet. She screamed for help, but none came. Buck watched—and remembered.

He had seen the law of the fang in action: A dog that went down in a fight was finished. Buck also remembered something else. Spitz had watched the scene with a smile on his face. From that moment, Buck despised him.

Perrault and Francois got going at once. They tied their nine dogs into a harness, or "traces." These were fixed to a line attached to the sled. Spitz, the lead dog, was at the front.

Buck hated the idea of traces. How could a king be forced to work like a horse? But he remembered the man in the red sweater and kept quiet.

He learned fast. The command "mush"

meant go, and "ho" meant stop. If he made a mistake, he felt Perrault's whip. And dogs who did not pull their weight felt Spitz's teeth.

They rose at dawn and ran all day. Up mountain passes and over frozen lakes they went, on and on. On good days, they covered forty, fifty, even sixty miles.

On his first night, Buck wandered about looking for somewhere to sleep. The other dogs were in snug burrows that they had dug under the snow. When Buck learned their trick, he curled up and slept like a puppy.

His muscles became iron hard. His mind hardened, too. He forgot the ways of the soft south. Slowly, he was returning to the wild ways of dogs long ago, before humans had tamed them.

At the end of the day, Perrault and François fed the dogs before themselves. This was the custom of the men of the north. Without their dogs, they would die.

But a dog was useful only if it worked. Buck was shown this when Dolly, one of the quieter dogs, went mad. She ran about wildly, refusing to do what the men or Spitz ordered. One blow from Perrault's hatchet ended her life.

Once again, Buck watched and learned. He now knew how to bite ice from between his toes and how to break the ice on a lake to get a drink. He ate anything and everything.

His senses sharpened. At night, he woke at the slightest sound —was that falling snow or a prowling enemy? Whatever happened, he would survive.

Back in the south, Buck had been a chief. All the judge's other animals had recognized that Buck was born to lead.

But now, in the dog team, someone else was leader. Whatever his feelings, Buck had to follow Spitz. Yet, Buck knew—as did Perrault, François, and all the other dogs—that there could not be two leaders in the same team.

One of them had to go.

When Buck and Spitz first fought, Perrault and François forced them apart with clubs. The next time they fought, there were neither men nor clubs. It was a fight to the death.

After supper one evening, a rabbit darted in front of the team. Off they went in pursuit. A pack of huskies joined in, fifty dogs after one small rabbit.

Buck took the lead. To begin with, Spitz followed him. Then, guessing where the rabbit was headed, he moved to ambush it.

Spitz waited, his fangs gleaming ivory white in the moonlight. When Buck and the rabbit appeared, Spitz caught the rabbit and killed it.

Buck did not stop. Into Spitz he crashed, sending both dogs rolling in the snow. They sprang to their feet, and the fight began. In silence, the pack formed a circle around them and watched.

Spitz had experience, but Buck had imagination. After Spitz had withstood his straightforward attacks, he changed tactics. Darting in upright, he dived down at the last moment and bit deep into Spitz's leg.

Crack! The bone snapped. Limping, Spitz fought on. But his time had come. Buck knocked him down, and the pack closed in. Buck was a king once more.

CHAPTER 3
The New Leader

"What did I tell you?" said François the next morning when he saw that Spitz was missing. "That Buck is a devil."

Perrault looked at Buck's many wounds and observed, "But that Spitz sure gave him a fight. Anyway, we now need a new leader."

To Perrault, the obvious choice was the oldest dog. This was the fierce, one-eyed Sol-leks. But when he moved Sol-leks to the front, the dog did not want to go. It was soon clear why: Buck sprang at him and drove him back.

Perrault pulled Buck to one side and tried again. The same thing happened. "Right, Buck," growled Perrault, "I'll teach you a lesson!" He picked up his club.

Buck remembered the man in the red sweater and backed away. When Perrault advanced, Buck retreated, snarling. But once the man's back was turned, Buck moved up again, growling at Sol-leks.

François came to help. It made no difference. Sol-leks would not go into the traces of the lead dog, and Buck would not come near a man with a club. After an hour, the men gave up, threw down their clubs, and gave the position of lead dog to Buck.

Perrault and François knew Buck was intelligent, and they knew he was powerful. But he was young and had not been in the north for long. Moreover, he was not a husky, the usual sled dog.

Nevertheless, what he did was amazing.

In next to no time, he had the whole team obeying him. Even Joe, the fiercest of them, cowed down when Buck snapped at him. They understood that their new leader was a very special dog.

Life became easier for Perrault and François. The team got into their traces without fuss and pulled harder than ever. In the evenings, when the day's work was done, they behaved.

Buck was proud of his dogs. More than that, he felt at home in the frozen wastes. It was as if he had known the snowy mountains and dark pine forests all his life. They seemed to call to him—the call of the wild.

He had a strange dream, too … *He is in a cave. Beside him, a primitive man squats beside a fire. The man and he are friends. Outside, beyond the mouth of the cave, the eyes of dangerous creatures glint in the firelight.*

The team grew better and better. When two new huskies were added, Buck brought them under control at once. On they sped.

"There's never been a dog like that Buck," cried François. "He must be worth one thousand dollars!"

They finished the trip in record time, at an average of forty miles a day. In the bars of the town, Perrault and François stuck out their chests and boasted. "We are the best!" they crowed.

The journey had left the dogs exhausted. When Perrault and François received orders to make another trip at once, they were heartbroken. Buck and his team were in no state to go on, and they had to be sold. When François said goodbye to Buck, he threw his arms around the great dog's neck and cried.

Two Scottish men bought the team. Not long afterward, they set off along the mountain trail that the dogs had just come down. The load was heavy, and the way was rough. There were no records this time.

Snow fell every day, making the sled hard to pull. The drivers grumbled, and the weakened dogs whined in their sleep. Joe and Sol-leks were grumpier than ever. The future looked grim.

Dave was now very sick. The men examined him but could find nothing. Something was wrong inside, they said.

He had no energy and cried out in pain when the sled suddenly stopped or started. After a week, he was falling over while they ran.

The driver couldn't let the other dogs drag Dave with them. He cut him out of the traces and moved Sol-leks into his place. Dave's pride was badly hurt. He felt he had failed, and whimpered and growled with shame.

When the sled started, he tried to run beside Sol-leks and nip his heels. He moaned in agony at the effort. When his strength ran out, he lay in the snow and howled.

Somehow, he made it to the next camp. The following morning, out of pity, the driver put him back in his old traces. It was hopeless. He fell and the heavy sled ran over his leg.

The next day was Dave's last. When he was too weak to move, the sled left without him. After going a little way, the driver stopped, and his companion went back to the camp. A shot rang out. All the dogs knew what had happened.

When they reached their destination, the team could hardly stand. Their feet hurt dreadfully. Buck's weight had fallen drastically. The other dogs were almost skeletons.

For months, they had toiled in the traces. Day after day, they had risen at dawn, heaved a heavy sled all day, and gone to sleep in the snow. They needed good food and a month's rest.

The drivers were exhausted, too. They expected a long break in which to relax and get their strength back. It was not to be.

New orders said a pile of fresh letters had arrived, which had to be delivered immediately. *And if your dogs are too tired, sell them and buy new ones. Delivering letters is more important than dogs.*

The Scotsmen had no choice. Buck

and his team, thin and worn out, were sold for next to nothing. Those who knew the business said it was a scandal.

Buck inspected his new owners carefully. They were Americans from the south, not used to the ways of the icy north. Their clothes were smart, their hands soft, and their eyes watery. Buck did not like the look of them at all.

CHAPTER 4

Rescue

Now began the very worst period of Buck's life. His new owners, the middle-aged Charles and the nineteen-year-old Hal, were hopeless. They knew nothing about sled travel and nothing about dogs.

To make matters worse, Charles and Hal thought they knew about everything. They used the words "mush" and "ho," but they had no idea about feeding the team properly. Hal, the driver, decided all problems could be solved with his whip.

Charles had his wife, Mercedes, with him. She was an empty-headed, vain young woman. She understood the ways of the north even less than the men.

Things went badly from the very start.

The three explorers piled a mountain of luggage high on the sled. Most of it was Mercedes's clothes. "That load's too heavy," one onlooker pointed out.

Hal ignored him. "Come on—mush!"

Buck and his team heaved, but the sled wouldn't move. Hal slashed them with his whip. "I said *mush*!" he yelled.

The dogs tried again, and slowly, the heavy sled started to slide forward.

An old-timer muttered, "Those fools sure won't get far. You watch."

The old-timer was right. The sled moved slowly along the trail until it came to a bend. Here, the track was higher on one side. The sled leaned, wobbled, and crashed right over into the snow.

When they finally got the sled and luggage back to base, Mercedes burst into tears. She couldn't take all those clothes—there was room for only one or two items.

The sled was loaded up once more, but it wasn't much lighter. The reason was Mercedes. Instead of walking beside the sled, like other companions, she demanded to ride on it with the bags.

The exhausted dogs made slow progress. Hal's whipping and swearing didn't help—nor did his feeding.

Experienced drivers knew how long their journey would take. They packed the right amount of food, so the dogs had the correct rations and wouldn't go hungry.

Hal took enough frozen fish for his dogs to have a good meal every day. However, hoping to make them go faster, he increased their daily ration. The idea was a failure. By the halfway point of their journey, all the dog food had gone.

Starved and hardly able to walk, the dogs struggled on. Meeting a stranger, Hal swapped his revolver for dried horse hide and fed it to the team. It was tough and contained very little goodness, but the dogs ate it all the same.

There were now only five of them left. When he had his revolver, Hal had shot those too sick or too tired to work. After the gun was gone, he killed them with his hatchet. Those that remained, he whipped and clubbed.

In this state, more dead than alive, the team stumbled into the camp of John Thornton. John had lived in the wilds for years, and he knew its ways as well as anyone. When he saw the miserable train of dogs collapse before him, he breathed deep and frowned.

"So, where are you folks headed?" he asked.

"Down there," replied Hal, pointing to a frozen lake below them.

John Thornton frowned again. "I wouldn't do that," he advised. "The ice is paper-thin right now. It won't hold your weight."

Hal laughed. "Nonsense! We haven't come all this way to listen to some scare story." He turned to the dogs. "Mush!"

Buck did not move.

The whip flashed out. Thornton pressed his lips together but said nothing. Sol-leks crawled to his feet, followed by Jo and two others. But Buck just lay there.

The whip cut into him. Thornton stood and walked up and down anxiously. Buck neither whined nor moved.

Hal seized his club and rained heavier blows upon Buck's wasted body. He could have risen like the others, but he had decided not to. He had made up his mind—enough was enough.

Perhaps there was something else, too? As the team had crossed a frozen lake earlier in the day, Buck had felt the thin ice cracking. Maybe he understood the peril of going on? As the blows fell, he felt strangely numb.

Suddenly, John Thornton yelled, sprang forward, and knocked Hal over. "If you hit that dog again, I'll kill you," he gasped. Mercedes screamed. Charles did nothing.

"He's my dog," snarled Hal, drawing his knife. "I'll do what I want with him."

Thornton knocked the knife from Hal's hand. Stooping, he picked it up and cut Buck free from the traces. Hal shrugged. Minutes later, the three humans and their pitiful team headed down the trail toward the frozen lake.

Buck and Thornton watched the sled make its way slowly down the slope. The man sighed and shook his head. With his eyes still on the doomed explorers, he began to run his hands over Buck's body.

The poor creature was in a terrible state. Thornton's fingers, rough but skilled, found almost no flesh on the skeleton. There were terrible, swollen bruises and cuts from the whip, but happily, no bones appeared to have been broken.

By the time Thornton had finished his examination, the sled was at the edge of the lake. Man and dog knew what was sure to happen. The team advanced gingerly across the thin ice, then abruptly stopped.

The back end of the sled dipped down, lifting the dogs. Mercedes's scream carried through the clear spring air like a whistle. Charles turned and tried to run back.

It was too late. A whole plate of ice gave way with a crack that echoed off the mountainsides. The men, the woman, the dogs, and the sled disappeared into a wide, dark hole. Nothing rose to the surface.

Thornton and Buck looked at each other. "You poor devil," John said.

Buck licked his hand.

CHAPTER 5
John Thornton

That spring, as the days grew longer and warmer, Thornton nursed Buck back to health. In return, Buck loved the man who had saved his life and liked nothing better than to lie by the fire, hour after hour, watching Thornton's face.

They shared little habits. The man held Buck's head between his hands, rocked him back and forth, and called him special names. Buck took Thornton's hand between his teeth and held it there, tight. It was his way of saying, *I love you, Master.*

Skeet, Thornton's little Irish setter, helped Buck's recovery. Every morning after breakfast, she licked his wounds. It was like a cat licking a kitten.

Thornton had a third dog, half bloodhound, half deerhound. Though huge, he never turned angry with Buck. All three animals were Thornton's children, and his love spread through them all.

When he had recovered, Buck had a chance to show his master how much he cared for him. They were in a bar when a rough bully punched Thornton. With a mighty roar, Buck was on him, grabbing him by the throat. He was pulled off before he killed the man, but he was now famous throughout all the gold-mining country.

That fall, Buck came to Thornton's rescue in quite another way.

Thornton and his partners, Pete and Hans, were taking their boat down a fast-flowing river. Thornton was on board, drifting with the current. Hans, who was on the bank, steadied the boat with a rope.

The line jerked suddenly. The boat lurched and threw Thornton into the water. The current, stronger than any man, carried him swiftly downstream in the direction of deadly rapids.

Buck immediately leaped in and swam to his master. When he felt Thornton seize his tail, he headed back toward the bank. But the current was too strong for him. Grabbing hold of a rock, Thornton ordered him back to the shore.

Thornton was safe for the moment,

but his strength was failing fast. As Buck reached the bank, Hans tied a rope around him and sent him back into the swirling waters. Bravely though he swam, he could not reach his master.

Hans pulled him back and tried again. Battered by rocks and half-drowned, Buck made it to Thornton's side. The man fixed his arms around Bucks's neck, and Hans heaved. More dead than alive, Thornton and Buck finally reached the bank.

Thornton was mighty proud of Buck. One day in a saloon, he met Matthewson, a man with a big mouth and loads of gold.

"My dog," he boasted, "can start a frozen sled of seven hundred pounds in weight and pull it for one hundred yards."

"Bah!" exclaimed Thornton. "My Buck can do that with a thousand pounds."

"Never!" sneered Matthewson.

"What d'you bet?" retorted Thornton.

Matthewson produced a bag of gold worth a thousand dollars. Thornton did not have that kind of money, but he was too proud to back down.

The sled was loaded with a thousand pounds and the course measured. Buck, sensing the excitement, took his place.

"If you love me, Buck ..." whispered Thornton in his ear. Buck understood.

"Gee!" cried Thornton. Buck heaved the sledge to the right.

On the command "Haw!" it went left and was free of the ice.

"Now, mush!" shouted Thornton.

Inch by inch, the sled moved forward. Soon, it was running smoothly. When it reached the hundred-yard mark, the crowd went wild. No one had ever seen anything like it. Thornton embraced his beloved Buck and cried with pride and joy.

The story of Buck and the thousand-pound sled spread far and wide. Thornton was offered huge amounts for his remarkable dog. But Buck wasn't for sale.

Thornton used the money he made from the bet to pay off his debts. He was now free to explore. With his companions, Hans and Pete, he set off into the empty land of lakes and mountains in the east.

Here, it was said, lay a great mine full of purest gold. No one knew exactly where the mine was—*in the east* was all Thornton had heard. But he was determined to find it.

What a time it was for Buck! There was no speeding along frozen trails. Instead, they went where their fancy took them, on and on, through lonely passes and beside still lakes. They hunted for food and camped wherever they wanted.

Once, they found a trail and followed it through the woods. All of a sudden, it stopped. It had come from nowhere and gone nowhere.

Another time, they came across a log cabin. Inside were rotten blankets and an ancient, rusty gun. There no other signs of life. Human beings had not been there for over a hundred years.

For months they journeyed. Summer turned to fall, fall froze to winter, winter melted into spring. Eventually, in a broad valley, they found the gold they were seeking.

It gleamed like butter in the sunshine. The men toiled day after day collecting it into sacks. They had never worked so hard in all their lives.

There was little for Buck to do, though he felt he was back where he belonged. This land, the primitive land of forest and fang, was his land.

At night, he dreamed of himself and the wild man in the cave. By day, he felt a strange call growing within him. *Come away*, it said. *Return to the wild.*

Buck obeyed the call. He went off on his own, loping through woods and beside clear streams that ran down long, empty valleys. And one day, in this wilderness, he met a wolf.

They did not fight. Instead, after a while, they became friends, and the wolf asked Buck to follow him. They ran together for miles until Buck felt another call: his love for John Thornton.

He stopped and turned back. When the wolf saw this, he sat down, raised his head to the stars, and howled.

CHAPTER 6
Return to the Wild

The man in the red sweater had taught Buck the law of the club. Spitz had taught him the law of the fang. After that, he was no longer a pet.

However, Buck loved John Thornton and would have died for him. But not for anyone else. He allowed Thornton's friends to pat his head, but he did not enjoy it.

He was a killer. He had killed Spitz and other dogs because he had had no choice. It was the primitive law: In the wild, it was kill or be killed.

And Buck killed often now. The men had no need to feed him, for he hunted his own food. Rabbits, birds, fish—with stealth and strength, he caught and killed them.

Once, to test his hunting skills, he brought down a giant moose. The beast was many times bigger and stronger than him. One kick of its hooves would have slain him. Each of the fourteen spikes on its antlers was like a spear.

Buck knew this and kept his distance. For four days, he hunted the great beast until it fell to its knees exhausted. Then, Buck went in for the kill.

For a day and a night, feasting and sleeping, Buck stayed beside the body of the moose he had killed. He then set out for home and John Thornton. At first, the journey was easy. But as he got nearer the camp, he sensed something was wrong.

There was a message in the air. The birds spoke of it, the squirrels chattered about it. Finally, three miles from the camp, Buck picked up the scent. Someone else had been this way.

From the valley came the sound of strange singing. Thornton and his men did not sing like that. Buck crept closer.

He passed the bodies of dogs killed by arrows. The singing grew louder until he came to the edge of the clearing where Thornton's cabin stood. It was a wreck.

Nearby, Yeehat warriors were dancing and singing. This was their land. Their families had lived here for thousands of years. Men like John Thornton had no right to be there, and they had been killed. It was the law of the wild.

For the last time in his life, Buck didn't stop to think. Fury seized him. He uttered a terrifying growl and charged upon the Yeehats.

Later, the Yeehats said the Evil Spirit had attacked them. That was how they remembered Buck. To them, he was not a wolf or a dog. He was a roaring, raging monster.

He sprang at the Yeehat chief and tore out his throat. Without a pause, he killed a second man, then a third. Warrior after warrior fell before his terrible fangs.

Packed together, the Yeehats panicked. Buck moved so fast that they could not shoot at him. When they tried, their arrows hit their own men. Those who were left alive fled into the forest.

When tired of chasing them, Buck returned to the camp. He found the bodies of Hans, Pete, and the dogs, but there was no sign of John Thornton.

Buck followed his master's scent to the edge of a pool. The water was dark, cloudy, and deep. In there, Buck knew, lay the body of the man he loved.

Buck sniffed the dead Yeehats. He was proud to have killed the noblest prey of all. From this time forward, men would not frighten him.

Now that Thornton was gone, men would not own him, either. At nightfall, he retired to the edge of the forest.

Buck had left the world of men, but the animal world had yet to accept him.

He stopped in the middle of a clearing and waited. Silently and stealthily, the wolf pack came out of the darkness.

For a moment, the creatures hung back. Facing them, Buck stood huge and magnificent in the moonlight. One of the pack leaders attacked first, leaping straight at Buck. The wolf's neck was broken before he reached the ground.

Three other wolves came forward. All were soon in retreat, blood streaming from deep slashes. Next, with a snarl, the whole pack launched itself at Buck.

He was too intelligent for them and too quick. Left and right, he snapped and clawed. To give himself height, he rose above them on his hind legs. When they threatened to get behind him, he retreated into a corner.

He was now protected on three sides. There, he stood and held off the wolves for half an hour. In the end, they backed away. Buck had won.

Cautiously, an old, lean wolf came forward. Buck recognized him as the wild brother he had met in the forest. The two animals whined softly at each other as their noses touched.

Buck was now accepted by the pack. When the old wolf sat and howled at the moon, the others did the same. So did Buck. And when the leaders ran off into the forest, Buck ran with them.

He had answered the call of the wild.

How long Buck ran at the head of the pack, we will never know. But it was long enough for a legend to be born. Yeehats and hunters speak of a huge Ghost Wolf, bigger than anything ever seen before. It steals from their camps and kills their dogs.

There are stories, too, of hunters who never return. Their bodies are found in the forest. All around are the footprints of an enormous wolf.

Men stay away from the valley where the Yeehats had met with the Evil Spirit.

But one animal still ventures there. Every summer, when the days are long and warm, he returns alone to that empty place.

He stands for a while, thinking. Then, he sits and howls a single, long, mournful howl. It is Buck's farewell to the man he loved, the man he will never forget.

Anne of Green Gables

Retold by
Sally Morgan

Illustrated by
Mel Howells

ARCTURUS

To Lily, Daisy, and the many kindred
spirits in my life—SM.

For Rachel—MH.

ARCTURUS

This edition published in 2018 by Arcturus Publishing Limited
26/27 Bickels Yard, 151–153 Bermondsey Street,
London SE1 3HA

Copyright © Arcturus Holdings Limited

All rights reserved. No part of this publication may be reproduced, stored in a retrieval system, or transmitted, in any form or by any means, electronic, mechanical, photocopying, recording or otherwise, without written permission in accordance with the provisions of the Copyright Act 1956 (as amended). Any person or persons who do any unauthorised act in relation to this publication may be liable to criminal prosecution and civil claims for damages.

Writer: Sally Morgan
Illustrator: Mel Howells
Designer: Jeni Child
Editor: Susannah Bailey
Art Director: Jessica Crass

ISBN: 978-1-78828-682-4
CH006276NT
Supplier 24, Date 0618, Print run 7507

Printed in Malaysia

Contents

CHAPTER 1
An Arrival at Green Gables..................4

CHAPTER 2
A Surprise for Anne..............................14

CHAPTER 3
Friends and Enemies............................20

CHAPTER 4
A Test of Friendship.............................30

CHAPTER 5
New Lessons..38

CHAPTER 6
A Bend in the Road..............................52

CHAPTER 1

An Arrival at Green Gables

One sunny afternoon in June, Mrs. Rachel Lynde was sewing at her kitchen window when she noticed something she thought surprising—her friend, Mr. Matthew Cuthbert, wearing his best suit and driving his buggy over the hill out of Avonlea.

Well, if that isn't Matthew Cuthbert of Green Gables, Mrs. Rachel thought. *What could he be doing leaving Avonlea when he should be sowing his turnip seed like the other farmers?*

It was for events such as these that Mrs. Rachel liked to work at her window, which was in such a position that little went on in Avonlea without her knowing about it. From here, she was able to keep her all-seeing eye on everything going on in and around the town.

I'll walk over to Green Gables and ask Marilla where he's gone and why, she decided. *I won't find a minute's peace until I know what has taken Matthew Cuthbert out of Avonlea today.*

After tea, Rachel stepped into the lane. Green Gables was not far, even though it was at the very edge of town.

"Good evening, Rachel," said Marilla, "Do sit down. How are all you folks?"

"We're all well," said Rachel. "I was afraid you weren't, when I saw your brother Matthew out in the buggy. I thought he'd gone for the doctor."

Marilla had expected this visit. Matthew seldom went visiting, and she knew that the sight of him, out in his best suit, would be too much for her friend's curiosity.

"I'm fine," she said. "Matthew went to the station at Bright River. We're getting a boy from an orphanage to help us at Green Gables."

"An orphan!" exclaimed Mrs. Rachel. "What can you be thinking? Didn't you read about the little orphan girl who poisoned her adoptive family?"

"I did not," replied Marilla. "But we're not getting a girl. And we need help—the farm is a lot of work for an old man."

Mrs. Rachel wanted to stay until Matthew returned, but after realizing he wouldn't be back for hours, she went to tell a friend the important news that an orphan was coming to Green Gables.

When Matthew Cuthbert arrived at Bright River, he walked up to the station.

"I'm here to meet the 5:30 train," said Matthew to the stationmaster.

"You've missed it," the stationmaster replied. "But there's a passenger for you. She's waiting on the platform."

"She?" Matthew scratched his head. "I'm expecting a boy."

"You'd better ask her," smiled the stationmaster. "She'll explain."

Matthew walked onto the platform and approached the thin girl with red hair who was waiting for him.

"You must be Mr. Cuthbert," she said, putting out her hand. "My name is Anne

Shirley. I was hoping you would come soon but decided if you didn't, I would spend the night in one of those beautiful cherry trees. Don't you think it would be wonderful to spend the night in a cherry tree, Mr. Cuthbert?"

"Well, I don't know," answered Matthew, deciding then and there that he could not tell her there had been a mistake. Instead he led Anne to the buggy.

"I can't wait to see Green Gables," said Anne. "I think it's wonderful that I'm going to live with you. The orphanage was worse than any place you can imagine. Mrs. Spencer said it was wicked of me to talk that way. It's so easy to be wicked without even knowing it. I do try to be good. Would you rather be divinely beautiful, dazzlingly clever, or angelically good? I could never be divinely beautiful. Mr. Cuthbert, how would you describe my hair?" Anne held up a thick braid.

"Red?" answered Matthew.

"Exactly," sighed Anne. "I can imagine almost anything away except my red hair. Am I talking too much?"

"Oh, I don't mind," answered Matthew, who was enjoying the girl's chatter.

Anne continued talking until they

arrived at Green Gables, a pretty white house surrounded by trees.

"Who is this? Marilla asked, startled by the girl in her kitchen. "Where is the boy?"

Matthew explained that there was only Anne.

"Well, there has been a mistake," said Marilla. "She can sleep here tonight, but tomorrow I will take her to Mrs. Spencer."

"You don't want me!" cried Anne. "You don't want me because I'm a girl?"

"What is your name, child?" asked Marilla.

"Please could you call me Cordelia?" answered Anne.

"Call you Cordelia? Is that your name?"

Anne explained that as she wasn't going to live at Green Gables, she would like to be called Cordelia while she was there.

"I've got no time for nonsense," said Marilla, sternly. "What is your name?"

"Anne," said Anne, disappointed. "But please could you be sure to spell it with an 'e' when you say it?"

Then, they sat down to dinner, after which Marilla took Anne to a small, neat bedroom. Anne immediately threw herself face first onto the bed and sobbed loudly.

"There, there, child," Marilla said awkwardly. "We will sort this all out first thing tomorrow. Get yourself dressed for bed, and I'll be back in a minute to take out the candle."

The next morning, after breakfast, Marilla and Anne climbed into the buggy to drive back out to Mrs. Spencer.

CHAPTER 2

A Surprise for Anne

"I didn't expect to see you today," said Mrs. Spencer, as Marilla helped Anne down from the buggy. "How are you, Anne?"

"As well as can be expected," Anne answered, before Marilla went on to explain the mistake that had been made.

"Do you think the orphanage will take her back?" Marilla asked.

"Of course," Mrs. Spencer answered. "But I don't think we will have to. Mrs. Blewett was here yesterday saying she wished I had brought her a girl to help with her many children. What good luck—here she is now!" said Mrs. Spencer, as a woman pulled up. "Mrs. Blewett, this is Anne."

"She's skinny," said Mrs. Blewett, "but the

wiry ones can be strong. I'll take her. I need help with my youngest child—she cries a lot."

"Well, I don't know," said Marilla, seeing Anne looking pale. "We hadn't absolutely decided not to keep her. Let me check with Matthew, and I will let you know."

Marilla didn't know Mrs. Blewett well, but she'd heard that she treated workers unkindly. Returning Anne to the orphanage was one thing—handing her to someone like Mrs. Blewett was another!

"Did you mean it?" asked Anne on the drive back. "Might you let me stay with you and Matthew?"

"I said I hadn't made up my mind," said Marilla. "Now, stop talking, and give me some peace."

Later, while helping Matthew with the cows in the barn, Marilla told Matthew what had happened with Mrs. Spencer.

"I wouldn't give a dog to that Blewett woman," said Matthew.

Marilla agreed, but it was either that or let the girl remain at Green Gables.

"I guess she will have to stay with us," sighed Marilla. "We'll tell her tomorrow," she added.

Matthew grinned.

The next day, Anne held her tongue until she could wait no more.

"Please, Miss Cuthbert," Anne asked while washing dishes. "Please will you tell me whether or not you are going to keep me? I really must know!"

"We have decided that we will," Marilla replied, "if you promise to be a good girl and show yourself grateful."

"Oh, Miss Cuthbert!" cried Anne. "I promise I'll do my best to be good."

Anne kept her word and was very well behaved for two weeks. Then, Mrs. Rachel came to visit.

"Why, Marilla," Mrs. Rachel said, looking Anne over. "Her hair is as red as carrots!"

Anne flushed red with anger. "I hate you! I hate you, I hate you!" Anne shouted loudly, stamping her foot.

"Go to your room, Anne," Marilla ordered, before turning to Mrs. Rachel. "You were too hard on her, Rachel."

"Well, I see I will have to be very careful about what I say in this house!" said Mrs. Rachel, sounding hurt. "Good day, Marilla."

When Anne didn't come down for dinner, Matthew went up to speak to her.

"Mrs. Rachel shouldn't have spoken to you that way," Matthew said, "but you were rude, and you should apologize."

"If you say I must," Anne said, "I will. But I can't promise that I will mean it."

The next morning, Anne and Marilla went to see Mrs. Rachel, and Anne made a very thorough, if slightly overdone, apology. Mrs. Rachel took pity on her and told Anne that she knew a girl who had hair redder than hers, which had turned a beautiful auburn. From that moment on, they became friends.

CHAPTER 3

Friends and Enemies

A week or so later over breakfast, Marilla told Anne some good news.

"I was talking to Mrs. Barrie after church," Marilla said, "and she thought you might want to meet her daughter, Diana. I could take you over to meet her this afternoon, if you'd like."

"I've always wanted a best friend!" said Anne, almost knocking over her milk. "I had an imaginary friend named Katie at the orphanage but never a real one!"

Marilla had tea with Mrs. Barrie that afternoon, leaving Anne and Diana to get to know each other in the rose garden.

Diana liked Anne very much, and the two girls found they had a lot to talk about.

"Let us swear to be best friends forever," said Anne, before she was about to leave.

"It's wicked to swear," said Diana, looking worried. "Though, I would like to be friends."

"This is a good kind of swearing," said Anne. "It's a promise—it's not wicked at all."

So, the girls held hands over the path in Diana's rose garden and promised to be best friends until the end of time.

Anne and Diana played together all around Avonlea every day that summer. When September came, the girls walked to the school house arm in arm, and Diana introduced Anne to all of her friends.

"That's Gilbert Blythe," Diana said, pointing to a dark-haired boy who was grinning from the other side of the yard. "Don't you think he's handsome?"

Anne didn't get a chance to answer as their teacher, Mr. Phillips, rang the bell.

Anne did her best to concentrate on the lesson, but Gilbert Blythe was determined to get her attention.

"Hey, Anne," he whispered, "Anne!"

When Anne pretended she couldn't hear, Gilbert reached out and pulled one of Anne's braids.

"Carrots!" he whispered, grinning.

"How dare you call me 'carrots'!" Anne yelled as whole class stared.

Gilbert had begun to apologize, when Anne picked up the slate and smashed it hard over his head.

"Anne Shirley!" Mr. Phillips shouted. "Stand in front of the board for the rest of the day." He took a piece of chalk and, spelling her name in the way Anne hated, wrote, "Ann Shirley has a very bad temper" in large letters above her head.

When Mr. Phillips let the class out for the day, Anne raced out of the door with Diana trailing behind.

"I'm sorry, Anne!" Gilbert called after them. "I didn't mean to hurt your feelings."

Anne ignored him and marched home with her head held high.

"Oh, Anne. Gilbert teases all the girls. He always calls me 'Crow Head,'" Diana explained, holding out a lock of her own dark hair. "But I've never heard him apologize before."

"Gilbert has hurt my feelings immeasurably, and I will never forgive him," said Anne.

At home, Anne ran into the kitchen and told Marilla that she would not be returning to school and that nothing Marilla said would change her mind. Mrs. Rachel visited before dinner, having heard what had happened to Anne.

"Give her time," Mrs. Rachel said. "She's a bright girl and will go back to school when she's ready. No sense forcing her." Mrs. Rachel had had many children, and so Marilla took her friend's advice.

The next morning, Diana made the walk to school alone, leaving Anne at home with Marilla.

Anne did not return to class. She busied herself with helping around the farm and played with Diana in the evenings. Diana told her all the news from school, without making any mention of Gilbert Blythe.

One Saturday morning in the winter, Marilla told Anne that she would be out for the evening and wondered if she would like to invite Diana over for tea. "You can serve some of my raspberry cordial, if you would like," Marilla added.

"Yes, please!" Anne cried.

Anne baked a cake. Then, even though Marilla said they would make a mess, she brought in flowers from the garden. She wanted to be the perfect hostess.

After Diana arrived, the pair chatted for a while before Anne remembered the cordial. She poured Diana a large glass.

"It's delicious," said Diana. "Much better than Mrs. Lynde's."

Anne smiled and quickly poured her friend another glass—and then another. Diana drank two more large glasses.

"Why, Diana," Anne said, noticing that her friend looked unwell, "are you okay?"

"No," Diana slurred. "Must. Go. Home."

Anne watched in dismay as her friend stumbled toward the door and left!

"Your Anne got my Diana drunk, Marilla," Mrs. Barrie said, when she called by the next morning. "I have forbidden Diana from playing with her. I was worried about my Diana being friends with an orphan, and I was right!"

"Drunk?" Marilla said. "That's impossible. All they had was tea and raspberry cordial."

Marilla fetched the bottle to show Mrs. Barrie, but when she looked more closely at it, she saw that Anne had mistakenly picked up an old bottle of redcurrant wine!

Marilla pleaded with Mrs. Barrie, pointing out that it had been her mistake and not Anne's, but Mrs. Barrie had made up her mind. Anne was a bad influence on her Diana and they were not to play together any longer.

When Marilla told Anne what Mrs. Barrie had said, Anne ran straight to her room and cried until she thought her heart would break.

The next morning was Monday, and Marilla was surprised to see Anne at the breakfast table with her textbooks sitting next to her.

"I have decided that I will go back to school," Anne said to an astonished Marilla.

CHAPTER 4

A Test of Friendship

Winter brought a thick layer of snow to Avonlea, and Anne and Diana had to make the cold trudge to school alone.

At school, Anne and Diana no longer sat together and shared secrets as they had before, and though Anne got along well with the other girls in Mr. Phillips's class, she wanted her old friend back.

One person who did want to make friends was Gilbert Blythe. Gilbert tried to make it up to Anne by giving her a sugar heart, but Anne was stubborn. She placed the candy under her shoe and ground it into powder.

Without Diana, Anne worked hard at her studies. She was smart and caught up with the rest of the class quickly. She often found herself in a tie with Gilbert for the best marks. Sometimes, Gilbert would come first in spelling, then Anne. Whenever Gilbert did come first, Anne would study even harder that night to make sure she beat him the next day.

Anne missed her best friend dearly, but she tried hard to keep herself busy and hoped that one day soon they would be reunited.

Anne had to wait until January before Diana made an unexpected visit. All was calm at Green Gables, as a blanket of snow fell. Marilla had gone out of Avonlea with Mrs. Rachel and many other townsfolk to hear the prime minister speak. Anne and Matthew were enjoying an evening by the fire, when an upset Diana appeared.

"Do come quick, Anne!" Diana begged. "Minnie May is sick—she's got croup and can hardly breathe. Father and Mother are out of town. Anne, I am so frightened she will die."

Without a word, Matthew put on his coat and hat and slipped out the door to get the doctor.

Anne ran to gather medicine from the pantry. "Please don't cry, Diana. I know exactly what to do for croup. You'll see. Minnie May will be better in no time."

Anne wasn't so sure when she saw how sick Diana's little sister was. Anne cradled Minnie May on the sofa and gave her some medicine as she had done for the children at the orphanage before she came to Green Gables. She prayed the doctor would come soon.

The two friends nursed a very sick Minnie May through the night, using up all of the medicine Anne had brought. Anne wasn't sure that Minnie May would make it, until the little girl gave a mighty cough and was able to breathe easily again. By the time Matthew arrived with the doctor in the morning, Minnie May was sleeping soundly in Anne's arms.

The doctor examined Minnie May and was sure the two young nursemaids had saved her life.

Anne went to bed and slept well into the afternoon. When she did come down, Marilla had returned and told her that Mrs. Barrie had stopped by to ask Anne if she would be so kind as to call on her when she woke up.

"Please can I go right away?" Anne

asked, hoping Mrs. Barrie had forgiven her.

Anne didn't wait for an answer but ran out into the snow without her coat.

At Diana's house, Anne was invited into the living room. Mrs. Barrie cried and told Anne how grateful she was to her. She also added how sorry she was that she ever believed Anne had made Diana drunk on purpose.

So, Anne and Diana were friends once more, happy to be able to walk through the wintry woods to school. As they walked, they made up stories and planned adventures to go on when the weather got warmer.

When summer arrived and school was coming to an end, Mr. Philips told their class he would not be returning to teach them in September and that they would be getting a new teacher instead.

Anne and Diana were so beside themselves with sadness that they cried all the way home on his last day.

"I can't say that I particularly loved Mr. Philips," Anne said, before blowing her nose into her handkerchief and remembering her horrible first day, "but I do so hate to say goodbye to anybody."

"Me, too!" Diana sobbed. "I am sure we won't like the new teacher as much as Mr. Phillips. But at least we have a nice, long summer to look forward to."

And then, the two girls quickly forgot their sadness over Mr. Philips as the talk turned to picnics, boat rides on the pond, and apple picking.

CHAPTER 5

New Lessons

When the new teacher, Miss Stacy, did arrive in Avonlea, people dutifully took turns inviting her over for tea before the next school year began.

"Please, may I bake a cake, Marilla?" Anne begged, excited to meet her new teacher. "I'm much better at baking now."

Anne followed the recipe faithfully and almost wore a hole in the rug as she paced up and down in the kitchen, waiting to see how it would turn out.

"Why, Anne," said Miss Stacy, smiling as Marilla poured the tea, "if you made the cake, be sure to cut me a nice, big piece."

Marilla, however, looked horrified when she took a bite of her slice. The cake didn't taste good at all. Anne had mistaken a bottle of antiseptic ointment for vanilla!

"How could you be so careless, Anne?" Marilla tutted, gathering up the plates. "It's time you got serious and stopped daydreaming."

"I am so sorry, Miss Stacy!" Anne cried. "I wanted to make a good impression, and for you to like me!"

"You did make a good impression," Miss Stacy laughed. "In fact, I am here because Mr. Philips recommended that I ask Mr. and Miss Cuthbert if you could join a special class that would help you study to become a teacher."

Miss Stacy explained this special class to Marilla and Matthew. Anne and the other students selected to be in the class would stay behind after school each day and study for the entrance exam to Queen's Academy. If Anne did well and passed, she would be able to attend the academy and study to be a teacher—just like Mr. Phillips and Miss Stacy!

Matthew and Marilla agreed Anne should join the class. They thought it was important for Anne, who had no family of her own, to be able to make her own way in the world. Anne was thrilled. She thought she would like being a teacher very much and promised to work hard.

Anne was less excited to discover that Diana would not be in the class. Mrs. Barrie did not want Diana to become a teacher but preferred that she learn how to keep a nice home instead.

So, the two girls still walked to school together, but when the day was over, Diana left Anne with the rest of the Queen's class—a class that included Gilbert Blythe ...

Anne did well with Miss Stacy as her teacher and found that she enjoyed her studies in a way she never had with Mr. Phillips. Miss Stacy encouraged the class to ask questions, exercise outdoors, and recite poetry—all things that Anne adored.

"I love Miss Stacy with my whole heart, Marilla," Anne said, when she came home from school one day. "She is so sweet. I feel instinctively that when she says my name, she is spelling it with an 'e.'"

Things got even more exciting for the class in November, when Miss Stacy announced that they were to put on a concert to raise money for a new flag for the school. Diana was to sing a solo, and Anne was to recite two poems. Anne couldn't wait for the performance.

"Can you imagine, Marilla," Anne said over dinner, "your Anne standing up in front of all those people? I only wish I had a dress with puffed sleeves like the other girls. Don't you hope I will do well?"

"I just hope that you behave yourself," replied Marilla, who didn't believe children should be running around putting on concerts when they should be studying. "And as for puffed sleeves, your Sunday dress will do well enough."

After dinner, Matthew thought about what Anne had said. He had seen her with her friends, and Anne looked different. He hadn't been sure what it was, but now he knew—it was the puffed sleeves! Marilla had made all Anne's clothes in the same plain style as her own, whereas her friends wore frills, puffs, and bows.

Matthew wanted to do something, and so, the next evening, he drove to town.

"What can I get for you, Mr. Cuthbert?" asked the assistant in the store.

Matthew froze. He was not used to talking to women who weren't his sister, Anne, or Mrs. Rachel.

"Um," he stumbled, "do you have any garden rakes?"

The assistant said she would have to check, since they didn't sell many in

November. Nor did they have hayseed, which Matthew asked for next.

Matthew left with a rake and twenty pounds of brown sugar—but no dress.

On the way home, he stopped in on Mrs. Rachel.

"Please let me choose a dress for Anne," said Mrs. Rachel, when Matthew told her what he wanted. "It will be lovely to see her wearing something decent for once!"

Mrs. Rachel bought a pretty brown dress for Anne and took it to Green Gables the night before the concert. Marilla, who had known Matthew was up to something, did not approve.

"She'll be as vain as a peacock now, Matthew," Marilla said, thinking of the simple dresses she had just made for Anne. "You could make a whole dress from just one of those sleeves!"

Anne, however, did approve. So much so, that for once, she was speechless as her eyes filled with tears.

"Don't you like it?" Matthew asked.

"Like it?" Anne said in wonder. "It's perfect!"

The concert was a triumph. All of Anne's friends told her her speech had been a huge success, but Anne wasn't so sure, and had to be convinced.

"I thought for a moment that I wouldn't be able to begin," Anne explained. "Then, I thought of my lovely puffed sleeves and took courage. I knew that I must live up to those sleeves."

Gilbert Blythe had also read his piece well, and though Anne claimed she hadn't noticed, he had certainly taken notice of her and clapped wildly when she took her bow.

Avonlea's cold winter melted into spring. This was when the real work of the Queen's class began, and when June finally came, Anne took the entrance exam.

Anne thought she would rather fail than not come high on the list, and by high, she meant higher than Gilbert.

However, she was determined not to worry about the results and to enjoy her summer. So, this was how one afternoon, Anne and her friends ended up playing "The Lily Maid" on the Barries' pond.

Anne was to be the dead Lily Maid and lie under a blanket strewn with flowers at the bottom of Mr. Barrie's boat. Her friends, the mourners, were to push the boat into the water, so that it drifted to the little beach, where Anne could get out.

All went well until, not long after setting sail, Anne felt water beneath her. She was sinking! As she floated toward the bridge, Anne climbed out and clung to a post, wondering what to do next.

Anne didn't have to wonder long, because also enjoying the pond that day was Gilbert Blythe, who rowed over and helped her into his boat.

"I do hope this means we can be friends now, Anne," Gilbert said, pulling up onto the beach.

"It does not," Anne said. "Now, if you will excuse me, I must go find Diana and tell her that I am alive."

When Anne's boat hadn't arrived at the little beach, Diana had run to Green Gables in search of Matthew.

"I thought you had drowned!" Diana cried, embracing her friend.

"I'm quite alright, Diana," Anne said, still dripping wet. "The boat sank, but Gilbert was on the pond and rowed me back."

"How romantic of him!" Diana sighed. "Surely you must forgive him now?"

"I will not," Anne said. "And I don't want any talk of romance. Romantic ideas are what had me thinking I could be the Lily Maid in the first place!"

Just then, Mrs. Rachel came walking up the path with Matthew and Marilla.

"You might want to take a look at this, Anne," Mrs. Rachel said, smiling and handing Anne the results paper.

Anne took it, but was too scared to read what was written.

"Please will you look?" Anne begged.

Diana studied the list.

"You passed, Anne!" she cried, hugging her friend. "You can go to Queen's Academy! And you tied for first out of a list of two hundred! With Gilbert!"

"You've done pretty well, Anne," Marilla said.

"She's done very well, Marilla!" Mrs. Rachel corrected. "Very well indeed, Anne!"

CHAPTER 6

A Bend in the Road

The summer passed by too fast for Anne. The final weeks were spent getting everything ready to go to the Academy. There was sewing to be done and arrangements to be made. Anne needed new dresses, and Marilla even bought her a beautiful green one, complete with as many frills and puffs as Anne could ever have wished for.

"I thought you might want something fancy to wear if you were asked out in the evening," she said, as she gave it to Anne.

Anne tried it on and recited a poem for her and Matthew. When she finished, Marilla was crying.

Once everything was packed, Anne

said her goodbyes around Avonlea before stopping at Diana's for the hardest goodbye of all ...

When she got back to Green Gables, Matthew was resting at the gate. He'd become a lot older over the years, and now every day seemed to make him more tired.

"I do wish that I had been that boy you had sent for," Anne said, walking him into the house, "so that I could have helped you more."

"I'd rather have you than a dozen boys," Matthew said, smiling. "You're our girl, Anne."

The next morning, Matthew drove Anne to the station where she was to meet the other Avonlea students, so that they could travel together to Queen's.

The first days were a whirl of excitement, as they were all arranged into classes. Anne and Gilbert found that they were to be in the same class, since they were both to study the two-year course in a single year. Anne wasn't sure what she would have done without him as her rival.

As the term wore on, Anne made new friends, though none were as dear to her as Diana. And she never stopped missing her beloved Green Gables.

To distract from her loneliness, Anne threw herself into her studies. She was determined to win one of the prizes awarded to the very best students. One of the prizes was a scholarship to the university.

Anne took her exams at the end of the year and once again found herself waiting impatiently to find out how she had done.

But when the big day came, she was again too frightened to read the results!

"I can't look," Anne said to her classmate, Jane, as they walked to where the results were posted. "You must read the announcement and then come and tell me. If I have failed, just say so."

Jane promised, but she needn't have, because as they approached the steps, they saw a crowd of boys carrying none other than Gilbert Blythe on their shoulders.

"Hurrah for Gilbert Blythe!" a voice cried. "Winner of the gold medal!"

Anne's heart sank for a moment. She thought that Gilbert had won a prize and she had not.

But then she heard … "Three cheers for Anne Shirley! Winner of the scholarship!"

Anne couldn't believe her ears. She had won, and more than that, she would be going to study at a real university!

With Queen's Academy over, Anne was delighted to return home and enjoy the summer at Green Gables. She had not been back since April, and she longed to see the blossom in the apple orchard and all the delights of Avonlea.

"Oh, Diana, it's so good to be here," she said, as they picked armfuls of flowers along the path. "I will be so sad to leave when college starts."

"Did you hear that Gilbert's not going?" Diana said, "His father can't afford to send him this year, so he is going to teach at Avonlea."

"I didn't," Anne said, dismayed. She had hoped to resume their old rivalry.

When Anne got back to Green Gables, she took her flowers into the kitchen and was looking for something to put them in when she heard a shout.

"Matthew ... Matthew!" Marilla cried. "Matthew, are you sick?"

Anne dropped the flowers and ran to Marilla. She found her with Matthew, who had fallen and looked very pale.

"He's fainted! Run and send Martin to fetch Mr. Barrie," Marilla shouted in a panic, trying to bring Matthew around.

Anne sent Martin, the farmhand, to fetch Mr. Barrie and met Mrs. Rachel on her way back to Marilla.

On the porch, Mrs. Rachel gently pushed Marilla aside and laid her head over his heart to check for his pulse.

"I don't think ... I don't think we can do anything for him," Mrs. Rachel said gravely.

"Mrs. Lynde," Anne started. "You don't mean ... Matthew is ..."

"I'm afraid so," Mrs. Rachel replied, tears in her eyes. "Matthew is dead."

That night in her bed, Anne wept, thinking of her dear Matthew who had been so proud of his girl. Marilla heard and crept in to comfort her.

"How will we go on without him?" Anne sobbed.

"We've got each other," Marilla said. "You may think I have been strict with you, Anne, but you mustn't think I loved you any less than Matthew. You've been my joy since you came to Green Gables."

Two days later at the funeral, they carried Matthew away from Green Gables, away from the fields he had tilled and the trees he had planted.

Avonlea returned to normal, although Anne found it strange that things could continue as before without Matthew.

But not everything had settled back to how it was. Marilla's eyesight was failing, and as an old woman, she would not be able to manage Green Gables. Marilla felt she had no choice but to sell it.

"You absolutely mustn't sell Green Gables," Anne said decisively.

"I wish I didn't have to," Marilla said. "But I can't stay here alone."

"You won't be alone," Anne told Marilla and Mrs. Rachel, who had come to call. "I'm not going to go to the university. I'm going to stay and teach at the school in Carmody. I can travel home each day and help you."

"You will do so no such thing," Mrs. Rachel corrected. "You're going to stay and teach in Avonlea. Gilbert is going to take the Carmody school."

Mrs. Rachel explained that when Gilbert had heard about the situation, he insisted the closer Avonlea school be given to Anne.

"How will I ever thank him?" Anne wondered, amazed.

"You better think of something, Anne." Marilla smiled. "He's coming down the road right now."

Anne rushed after Gilbert.

"Gilbert," Anne gasped when she caught up with him. "I want to thank you for giving up the school for me."

Anne offered him her hand, and Gilbert took it, saying he hoped they could be friends now. Anne nodded, happy to have forgiven him.

Gilbert walked Anne back to Green Gables, where they stood at the gate in the warm evening, catching up on their lost years of friendship and promising to share many more in Avonlea.

The Secret Garden

Retold by
Annabel Savery

Illustrated by
Mel Howells

ARCTURUS

For my A-Team—AS.

For The Crouch Enders—MH.

ARCTURUS

This edition published in 2018 by Arcturus Publishing Limited
26/27 Bickels Yard, 151–153 Bermondsey Street,
London SE1 3HA

Copyright © Arcturus Holdings Limited

All rights reserved. No part of this publication may be reproduced, stored in a retrieval system, or transmitted, in any form or by any means, electronic, mechanical, photocopying, recording or otherwise, without written permission in accordance with the provisions of the Copyright Act 1956 (as amended). Any person or persons who do any unauthorised act in relation to this publication may be liable to criminal prosecution and civil claims for damages.

Writer: Annabel Savery
Illustrator: Mel Howells
Designer: Jeni Child
Editor: Becca Clunes
Art Director: Jessica Crass

ISBN: 978-1-78828-693-0
CH006180NT
Supplier 24, Date 0618, Print run 7518

Printed in Malaysia

Contents

CHAPTER 1
"That's th' moor" 4

CHAPTER 2
"There was someone crying!" 11

CHAPTER 3
"How still it is!" 18

CHAPTER 4
"Might I have a bit of earth?" 24

CHAPTER 5
"Are you a ghost?" 32

CHAPTER 6
"I want to see it!" 43

CHAPTER 7
"I am well" 52

CHAPTER 8
"In the garden" 58

CHAPTER 1

"That's th' moor"

When Mary Lennox was sent to to live with her uncle, everybody said she was a most disagreeable-looking child. She had a pale face, a little thin body, and a sour expression. Mary had been born in India to parents who were too taken up with work and parties to be bothered with a troublesome child. She was left in the care of a nurse, her Ayah, who gave the child her every wish. By the time Mary was six years old, she was as tyrannical and selfish a little girl as ever lived.

When she was nine years old, the cholera struck the small army compound they lived on. The few who survived soon fled, and Mary found herself quite alone in the world. She was sent to Misselthwaite Manor in England to live with her mother's brother, Mr. Archibald Craven.

Through boats, trains, and carriages, Mary listened to people talking and heard that her uncle was a misery-ridden hunchback, and the house was great and gloomy. Eventually, she arrived and met the housekeeper, Mrs. Medlock.

"You needn't expect people to talk to you. You'll have to play by yourself, and you're not to go poking about."

"I shall not want to go poking about," said sour little Mary.

She was led up a broad staircase, down a long corridor, and around a great many corners, until she found herself in a room with a fire and a supper on a table.

"This is your room, and make sure you keep to it," Mrs. Medlock said.

*

When Mary woke up the next morning, she saw Martha, a young housemaid, lighting the fire. Out of the window, Mary could see a great stretch of bare land.

"That's th' moor," Martha said smiling. "I just love it. It's covered wi' growin' things as smells sweet."

She was a strange servant, but Mary was amused at the way she rattled on about her family of twelve living in a small cottage with little to eat and her brother Dickon, who was a great lover of animals. Martha was just as bemused by the little girl from India, who held her arms out expecting to be dressed and refused her good hot porridge.

"Wrap up warm, an' run out an' play, it'll do you good," said Martha, handing her a coat and stout pair of boots. "Mind," she whispered, "one of th' gardens is locked up. Ten year ago, Mr. Craven locked th' door an' buried th' key."

The gardens looked dull and lifeless in the winter sunlight. Mary was curious about the garden that no one had been into for ten years. She wondered whether there were any flowers still alive in it. She turned down a grass walk that led to a door in an old wall, and soon, she came upon an old man digging.

"What is your name?" Mary inquired.

"Ben Weatherstaff," he grumbled, continuing to dig.

"What is this place?" she asked.

"One o' th' kitchen gardens," he answered shortly.

"There's another on t'other side o' th' wall, an' th' orchard t'other side o' that."

She heard a soft little rushing noise, and a bird with a red breast alighted on the earth near the gardener's foot. He had soft, bright eyes, a tiny plump body, and slender, delicate legs.

"What's that bird?" she whispered.

"He's a robin redbreast. They're th' friendliest, curiousest birds alive. He's always comin' to see what I'm plantin'."

The robin hopped about, busily pecking the soil. His little black eyes gazed at Mary with great curiosity. Then, the next moment, the robin flew away.

Mary went down the path and through the second green door. She found winter vegetables and bare fruit trees. The wall went on past the orchard, and she could see the tops of trees above it. The wall here was covered with ivy growing all over it. Above her head, there was a burst of song, and she looked up to see the robin.

"I believe that bird is in the secret garden," she said. "There is a wall around the place, but there is no door."

CHAPTER 2

"There was someone crying!"

From that first day, the many days that came and went seemed exactly alike to Mary. Every morning, she was woken by Martha, she ate a small breakfast and went out. As she ran along the paths, she was making herself stronger and healthier. The air of the moor filled her lungs, her eyes began to grow bright, and her cheeks began to grow pink.

Each day, she explored the garden, but most days, she came back to the one part of the wall where the ivy was not so neatly trimmed. She saw the robin there, and he chirruped to her. But explore as she might, she couldn't get into the garden where he was.

One day, the rain poured down in torrents, and Mary could not go outside. She thought that there must be a hundred rooms in the great house, and she made up her mind to explore. She slipped out of her room and wandered down the corridors, looking at portraits of little girls in long frocks and little boys in lace collars. Suddenly, the stillness was broken by a strange sound.

"It is crying," thought Mary, her heart beating faster. "And it is quite close."

The next moment, Mrs. Medlock appeared from behind a tapestry that must have concealed a door.

"What are you doing here?" she said, pulling Mary away by the arm.

"I was lost, and I heard someone crying." Mary explained.

"You didn't hear anything of the sort," said the housekeeper. She took Mary by the arm, until she had pushed her through the door of her own room.

"You stay where you're told to, or you'll find yourself locked up!" She slammed the door, leaving Mary pale with rage.

"There was someone crying!" she said to herself.

Two days after this, the rainstorm ended, the wind ceased, and a brilliant, deep-blue sky arched high over the moorland. Never had Mary dreamed of a sky so blue.

"Look at the moor!" she called to Martha when she woke.

"Aye," said Martha cheerfully. "Th' storm's over, an' th' springtime's on its way." Martha stared at her a moment—the small plain face did not look quite so sour this morning.

Mary went out into the garden. She found Ben Weatherstaff working in the kitchen garden.

"Springtime's comin,'" he said. "You'll see bits o' green spikes stickin' out o' th' black earth after a little. You watch."

"I am going to," answered Mary. She wanted to know very much if things might be stirring in the locked-up garden, but she didn't dare ask the grumpy gardener.

Mary went to the long, ivy-covered wall over which she could see the treetops. She heard a chirp and a twitter, and when she looked at the bare flower bed, there was the robin.

"Do you remember me?" she whispered. "You do!"

The robin hopped over a small pile of earth freshly turned up by a dog looking for a mole. It was quite a deep hole, and as Mary looked at it, she saw something almost buried in the newly turned soil. It was a rusty metal ring. She picked it up to find that it was an old key, which looked as if it had been buried for a long time.

"Perhaps it has been buried for ten years," she said in a whisper. "Perhaps it is the key to the garden!"

If it was the key to the locked garden, and she could find out where the door was, she could perhaps open it and see what had happened to the old rose trees. She made up her mind that she would always carry it with her, so that if she ever should find the hidden door, she would be ready.

CHAPTER 3
"How still it is!"

Later that week, Martha went home to visit her mother, and Mary was surprised that she missed the lively housemaid. When Martha returned, she had brought a present for Mary.

"It's a skipping rope," she said. "Look, I'll show you how to use it!"

Mary took the rope out into the garden. She was not very clever at jumping at first, but she liked it so much that she skipped until her cheeks were quite red. As had become her habit, she went to her own special walk, and there was the robin, swaying on a long branch of ivy.

"You showed me where the key was," she said. "You ought to show me the door today!"

Mary had heard a great deal about Magic in Indian stories, and later, she always said that what happened at that moment was Magic. As the robin flew up to the top of the wall, a little gust of wind rushed down the walk. The trailing ivy swayed, and Mary jumped and caught some in her hand. She had seen something underneath it.

Mary pulled the leaves aside, her heart thumping and her hands shaking in her excitement. There was a door. She drew out the key, fitted it in the keyhole. She turned it and looked behind her—no one was coming. She held back the ivy, pushed back the door, and slipped through. She was standing inside the secret garden.

"How still it is!" Mary whispered. "I am the first person here for ten years."

She stood looking around her with excitement and delight. The climbing roses had run all over the walls and trees, but there were neither leaves nor flowers on them now.

"I hope they aren't all completely dead," thought Mary.

She began to walk around the garden. Suddenly, she saw something sticking out of the earth—some little green points.

"Here are tiny growing things," she cried out softly, kneeling down to look at them closely. "Even if the roses are dead, there are other things alive."

She went all around the garden and found there were ever so many more of the sharp, pale green points.

Mary looked at the new shoots. The grass seemed so thick that they did not seem to have room enough to grow. She knelt down and dug, until the shoots had little clear places around them.

"Now they can breathe," she said. "I am going to do ever so many more!"

*

The sun shone down for nearly a week on the secret garden. The bulbs were glad to have space to grow. The sun could warm them, and the rain could reach them, so they began to come alive. Mary dug and pulled up weeds, becoming more pleased with her work every hour.

Then one morning, Mary awoke and knew what it was to be hungry. She took up her spoon and began to eat the hot porridge Martha set before her.

"Why did Mr. Craven hate the garden?" Mary asked curiously.

"It's not to be talked about," Martha began. "It was Mrs. Craven's garden, an' she loved it. Him an' her used to stay there for hours, readin' and talkin'. But one day, she was sittin' on an old branch bent like a seat when it broke an' she fell on th' ground. She was hurt so bad that next day she died. No one's never gone in since."

CHAPTER 4

"Might I have a bit of earth?"

One day, as Mary sat working in the secret garden, she heard a peculiar whistling sound. She followed the sound out of the garden and to a little woodland. A boy was sitting under a tree playing a rough wooden pipe. His cheeks were as red as poppies, and his eyes were as blue as the sky. A brown squirrel and two rabbits sat watching him. When he saw Mary, he slowly rose to his feet, and the creatures scampered away.

"I'm Dickon," the boy said. "I know tha'rt Miss Mary." He stooped to pick up a package. "Martha's told me how tha' loves to be in t'garden, so I've brought thee some garden tools."

Mary was so delighted she could hardly speak. They sat down, and he showed her the fork and spade and some packets of flower seeds. He told her what the flowers would look like and how to plant and tend them.

"Has't tha got a bit o' garden?" he asked. Mary said nothing for a time, and then she spoke in a great rush:

"I've stolen a garden. Nobody wants it, nobody cares for it, nobody ever goes into it. Perhaps everything is dead in it already." She said it with such emotion that tears started to form in her eyes.

"Where is it?" asked Dickon. Mary got up at once and pushed aside the ivy that concealed the door.

"Eh! Martha told me there was a locked-up garden," he whispered. He saw her distress at the dead look that everything had. He quickly took out his knife and showed her the live green wood underneath. There would be roses aplenty in the spring, he explained, and all the birds from the moor would love the quiet garden. Then, he spotted one of Mary's own little clearings around the pale green points.

"Who did that there?"

"I did it," said Mary. "The grass was so thick, and they looked as if they had no room to breathe."

"Tha' was right," he smiled. "They'll grow now like Jack's beanstalk. They're crocuses an' snowdrops, an' here's daffy-down-dillys."

"Will you help me again here?" Mary begged. "Oh, do come, Dickon!"

"Aye, I'll come every day," he answered. "It's the best fun I ever had in my life."

"Whatever happens, you never would tell?" Mary said seriously.

"If tha' was a missel thrush an' showed me where thy nest was, does tha' think I'd tell anyone? Not me," he said. And she was quite sure that her secret was safe.

After that, the clock chimed in the courtyard, and Mary had to run in for her midday meal. But she found Mrs. Medlock waiting at the door.

"Mr. Craven wants to see you," she announced. All the pink left Mary's cheeks. She felt herself become her stiff, silent self again. Mrs. Medlock led her to a door and knocked.

"Come in!" sounded a voice, and Mary was ushered inside.

In a chair by the fire sat a man. He had high, rather crooked shoulders and black hair streaked with white. His eyes sank into his face, and his face was lined with sadness.

"Are you well?" he asked. "Do they take good care of you?"

"Yes," answered Mary.

"What do you do all day?" he asked.

Mary's voice trembled. "I play outdoors. I look around for things growing. I don't do any harm."

"Don't look so frightened," he said in a worried voice. "You could not do any harm, a child like you! I cannot give you time or attention; but I wish you to be happy and comfortable. Is there anything you want?"

"Might I have a little earth?" quavered Mary, and Mr. Craven looked quite startled.

"Earth?!" he repeated.

"To plant seeds in—to make things grow—to see them come alive," Mary faltered. He gazed at her a moment, and his eyes looked far away.

"You remind me of someone else who loved things that grow," he said. "You take a little earth, child, and make it come alive."

"May I take it from anywhere?"

"Anywhere," he answered. "You must go now. I shall be away all summer."

"I can have my garden!" Mary thought with delight. "He is really a nice man, only his face is so miserable."

CHAPTER 5
"Are you a ghost?"

Mary was awakened in the night by the sound of rain beating against her window and wind rushing about the house. Suddenly, something made her sit up in bed and listen, turning her head toward the door.

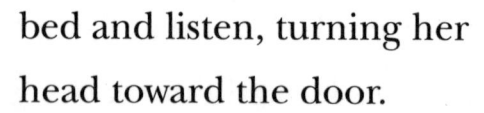

"It isn't the wind, it is crying!" she said in a loud whisper. "I am going to find out what it is."

She picked up her candle and went softly out of the room.

The corridor was long and dark, but faint, far-off crying led her on. At last, she came to the tapestry that concealed a door. She pushed it open.

Mary stared in the darkness. A little candle glowed by the side of a large bed, and on the bed lay a boy, crying. He turned and stared at her. He had a pale white face and wide, pale eyes.

"Are you a ghost?" he said in a frightened whisper.

"No," Mary whispered. "Are you one?"

"No," he replied. "I am Colin. Who are you?"

"I am Mary Lennox. Mr. Craven is my uncle."

"Then, we are cousins! He is my father," said the boy.

"Cousins! Your father!" gasped Mary. "No one told me he had a son!"

"Come closer," he said. "I want to see if you are real."

"I am real. I heard crying and wanted to find out who it was."

"I cry when I can't sleep. Will you come and see me tomorrow? The nurse or Medlock will come any minute. I want to hear more about you, but you shall be a secret—just like they have kept!"

Mary nodded and quickly left the room.

In the morning, Martha appeared, to summon Mary to Colin's room. She was pale and shaking, shocked that he had been discovered. She whispered that he had been ill since he was a baby. He had terrible fits of temper and hysterics, so that the servants were almost terrified of him. His father could not bear to look at him, since his mother had died when he was a baby.

There was a warm fire blazing in Colin's room, and he sat wrapped in a velvet dressing-gown.

"Come in," he commanded. "I want to hear about you."

Colin behaved like a young Indian Rajah, Mary thought, but she sat on a footstool by the bed and told her new cousin about India, the cholera, and her journey to England.

Colin told her about always being ill and how no one believed he would live to grow up. As he spoke, he became more upset and cross.

"Shall I tell you what I've found in the garden?" Mary said, to change the subject.

She talked about green points coming through the earth, about the robin and Ben Weatherstaff, and about Dickon. Colin enjoyed hearing it all, and they talked more than either of them had before. They began to laugh as if they had been two ordinary creatures—instead of a hard, unloving girl and a sickly boy. And in the midst of the fun, the door opened and in walked Dr. Craven and Mrs. Medlock!

"What is this?" said Dr. Craven, astonished.

"This is my cousin, Mary Lennox," Colin said boldly. "She found me, and I like her. She makes me forget about being ill. She must come and talk to me whenever I send for her."

Mrs. Medlock looked furiously at Mary. Dr. Craven gave a puzzled glance at the stiff, sour little girl. However, neither he nor Mrs. Medlock would oppose the young master, and so, Mary remained.

This first meeting was followed by a whole week of rain, and Mary spent every day with Colin in his room, talking about India or gardens or Dickon or the moor. Mary was careful not to mention the secret garden. She wanted to discover whether Colin was the kind of boy who could keep a secret. She thought he might be, and she had the idea that as gardens and fresh air had been good for her, perhaps they would be good for Colin, too.

Finally, the sky became blue again. Mary woke early and found the spring sunshine irresistible. She ran out to the garden and found Dickon already at work, with a tame fox cub and rook beside him.

The two spent the day working in the secret garden. Mary told Dickon about her meeting with Colin, and they agreed that the warm, spring air was sure to do him good.

The sun was beginning to set when they parted. Mary ran joyfully back to the house to see Colin, but the young Rajah was furious at having been left alone. They raged at each other, each shouting that the other was selfish as could be. Mary went back to her room feeling cross and disappointed.

It was the middle of the night when Mary was awakened by such terrible sounds.

"It's Colin," she said. "He's having one of those dreadful tantrums. How awful it sounds." She put her hands over her ears and felt sick and shivering. "He ought to be stopped!"

Mary jumped out of bed and flew along the corridor.

"You stop!" she shouted. Colin had been lying on his face beating his pillow with his hands.

"I felt the lump—I felt it," he choked. "I shall have a hunch on my back, and then I shall die!"

"You didn't feel a lump!" contradicted Mary fiercely. "There's nothing the matter with your horrid back! Turn over, and let me look at it!"

What she saw was a poor, thin back, and every joint of the spine could be counted.

"There's not a single lump there!" Mary said at last. "There's not a lump as big as a pin—except backbone lumps, and I've got backbone lumps myself!"

No one but Colin himself knew what effect those crossly spoken words had on him. He had never spoken about his secret terrors. He had lain and thought of illness for hours and days and months and years.

"Do you ... think ... think ... I could live ... to grow up?" Colin breathed out.

"Of course!" said Mary, indignantly. "But you must stop your hysterics and have a great deal of fresh air." Colin's tantrum had passed, but he was weak and worn out with crying.

"I'll—I'll go out with you, Mary," he said. "I shan't hate fresh air if you are there."

She turned to go, but Colin pulled her hand. "You could tell me about the gardens and spring—I am sure it will make me go to sleep."

"Of course," answered Mary. "Shut your eyes." He closed his eyes and lay quite still. She talked softly until he fell asleep.

CHAPTER 6

"I want to see it!"

The next morning, Mary went out early, then rushed to Colin's room.

"It has come, the spring!" she said, a little breathless. "Dickon says so!"

"Has it?" cried Colin. "Open the window!" Mary threw it open, and Colin drew in great breaths of fresh air.

"Colin," she said seriously, "can you keep a secret? A truly great secret?" Colin nodded, and Mary went on. "Ten years ago, a garden was locked up. No one was allowed into it, and it has been forgotten. But, I found it!"

"Oh! I want to see it!" he cried out with a half sob. She told Colin how the robin had helped her to find the key and then the door—and how she and Dickon had been working to bring the garden to life. The most important thing, they decided, was that the garden must be kept a secret.

Later that day, the head gardener, Mr. Roach, received orders to remove all his staff from the gardens. The strongest footman carried Colin downstairs and put him in his wheeled chair. He was then dismissed, and Dickon began to push Colin along. The wind swept in soft, big breaths down from the moor, and Colin kept lifting his thin chest to draw it in.

"This is it," breathed Mary as they reached the ivy-covered wall. "Here is the door. Dickon, push him in quickly!"

Colin gasped with delight. Dickon pushed the chair slowly around the garden, stopping every moment to let him look at the wonders springing out of the earth.

All over the walls, a green veil of tender leaves had crept. Here and there were splashes of gold and purple and white. The sun shone softly—warming Colin's ivory face and neck and hands.

"I shall get well! I shall get well!" he cried out.

Mary was a great believer in Magic. Secretly, she believed that Dickon worked Magic and that was why wild creatures liked him so much. She felt that Magic was working and making Colin look like an entirely different boy.

"I don't want this afternoon to end, and I'm going to get fresh air every day," he announced. "I shall get well."

"That tha' will," said Dickon. "Tha's got legs, same as other folks. Us'll have thee walkin' an' diggin' afore long."

They had been quiet for a little while, when Colin half-lifted his head and pointed to the high wall.

"Who is that man?" he whispered. Dickon and Mary scrambled to their feet. Ben Weatherstaff's indignant face was glaring at them over the wall! He shook his fist at Mary but stopped the very next moment as he saw Colin.

"Do you know who I am?" demanded Colin imperiously.

"Aye, that I do—wi' tha' mother's eyes starin' at me. But tha'rt th' poor cripple, with a crooked back," he said. Colin flushed scarlet, and he sat bolt upright.

"I'm not a cripple!" he cried out furiously. There was a fierce scramble, the rugs were tossed on the ground, Dickon held Colin's arm, the thin legs were out, the thin feet were on the grass.

Poor Ben Weatherstaff choked, and tears ran down his weather-wrinkled cheeks. Dickon held Colin's arm strongly, but the boy stood straighter and straighter.

"I am your master when my father is

away," he said. "This is my garden. Don't dare to say a word about it! Come around to the door, be quick!"

Ben Weatherstaff's crabbed old face obediently disappeared, and when his head was out of sight, Colin turned to Mary and Dickon.

"I can stand!" And as he said it he looked as strong and straight as any other boy.

*

When Ben Weatherstaff came through the door in the wall, Colin was still standing.

"Look at me!" he commanded Ben Weatherstaff. "Am I a hunchback? Have I got crooked legs?"

"Not tha'," said Ben. "What did tha' shut thysel' up for?"

"Everyone thought I was going to die," said Colin shortly.

"Tha' die!" he said. "Nowt o' th' sort! Tha's got too much pluck in thee. Sit thee down on th' rug a bit, young Mester, an' give me thy orders."

Colin allowed Mary and Dickon to help him sit on a rug under the tree.

"What work do you do in the gardens, Weatherstaff?" he inquired. Ben, they found, had been a gardener to Mrs. Craven. Ben had done his best to tend the locked garden as the years passed, and he would keep their secret.

"How'd tha' like to plant a bit o' somethin'?" said Ben, at last.

"Oh, yes," said Colin, grasping a trowel and turning over some fresh earth. Ben Weatherstaff hobbled out and soon returned, handing a rose in a pot to Colin.

"Here, lad," Ben said. "Set it in the

earth thysel', same as th' king does when he goes to a new place."

The thin white hands shook a little as Colin set the rose in the hole and held it while old Ben made the earth firm.

"It's planted!" said Colin at last. "Help me up, Dickon. The sun is just setting, and I want to be standing when it does. That's part of the Magic."

CHAPTER 7
"I am well"

Dr. Craven continued his visits, but at each, he was dismissed by Colin, who wanted to hear no more of illness and warnings. Each day, the children went into the garden. The seeds Dickon and Mary had planted grew: first showing buds, then opening up into sweet-smelling flowers. The roses climbed up the walls and burst into bloom. Colin watched each change as it took place.

"I am sure there is Magic in

everything," Colin explained one morning. "When Mary found this garden, it looked quite dead. Then, something began pushing things up out of the soil. The Magic in this garden has made me stand up and know that I am going to live to be a man. I am going to make a scientific experiment."

Dickon and Mary were delighted with the idea, and the three sat in a circle beneath the canopy of the plum tree. Dickon's rabbit, crow, fox, squirrels, and the lamb slowly drew near. It all seemed majestic and mysterious as Colin began:

*"The sun is shining—that is the Magic.
The flowers are growing—that is the Magic.
Being alive is the Magic—being strong
is the Magic.
The Magic is in me—the Magic is in me.
Magic! Come and help!"*

He said it a great many times, and Mary listened entranced.

"Now, I am going to walk around the garden," he announced at last, and so, a procession was formed. Colin was in the middle, with Dickon on one side and Mary on the other.

"The Magic is in me!" Colin kept saying. "The Magic is making me strong!"

Once or twice, he sat down on the grass, and several times he paused in the path and leaned on Dickon, but he would not give up until he had gone all around the garden.

"I did it! The Magic worked!" he cried. "This is to be the biggest secret of all. No one is to know I have grown so strong, until I can walk and run like any other boy. I won't let my father hear about it. Then, I shall just walk into his study and say: 'Here I am; I am quite well, and I shall live to be a man.'"

"Your father will think he is in a dream," cried Mary.

Every beautiful morning, the Magic was worked by the mystic circle under the plum tree. After the ceremony, Colin did his walking exercise. At first, he needed to sit and rest a lot, but he was determined. After a while, he began to move around as the others did, walking and running and digging and weeding. And each day, his belief in the Magic grew stronger.

With their gain in strength and spirit, Mary and Colin had both begun to worry that their secret would be discovered. They soon made a plan to keep up an appearance of illness and crossness, and to send away all the food that they could bear to. This was a great struggle, until Dickon had a wonderful thought.

Each morning, he brought a tin pail of rich new milk to the garden with him, along with a napkin of fresh rolls from his mother. Poor Dr. Craven and Mrs. Medlock were mystified. The children ate next to nothing, and yet, their faces were rosy and full of life.

"You see, the scientific experiment has succeeded," Colin announced to Ben on his next visit, and all at once, he realized something completely.

"I'm well!" he cried out.

CHAPTER 8

"In the garden"

While the secret garden was coming alive, and two children were coming alive with it, Archibald Craven wandered the beautiful places of Europe. He was filled with sorrow, believing nothing could free him from it.

At the very moment that Colin called out, "I'm well," his father's eyes began to see things he had not seen for years—the tiniest of flowers. Gradually, their beauty filled his mind and softly pushed the darkness aside.

"What is it?" he whispered. "I almost feel as if—I were alive!"

From that moment, his body and his soul began to grow stronger. One night, while in a deep sleep, a voice sounded in his ears. "Archie! Archie!"

"Lilias!" he answered. "Where are you?"

"In the garden," the voice came back, sweet and clear.

"In the garden!" he said, when he awoke. "I must go home at once!"

In a few days, he was in Yorkshire again. On his long journey, he found himself thinking of the past. He remembered the black days when he had raged because the child was alive and the mother was dead. He had not meant to be a bad father. He had supplied doctors and nurses for Colin, but he could not bear to look at his son.

"Ten years is a long time," he thought. "It may be too late to do anything. I will try to find the key," he said. "I will try to open the door. I must—though I don't know why."

He did not go into the house but went straight to the garden. The ivy hung thick over the door that no human being had passed through for ten lonely years—and yet, inside the garden there were sounds: running, scuffling feet and smothered joyous cries.

And then, the feet ran faster and faster, the ivy swung back, the door was flung wide open, and a boy burst through it. Without seeing the outsider, he dashed straight into his arms.

He was a tall boy, and he was glowing with life. He threw the thick hair back from his forehead and lifted a pair of strange pale eyes—full of boyish laughter and rimmed with black lashes. It was the eyes that made Mr. Craven gasp.

"Who—what? Who!" he stammered.

This was not what Colin planned. But to come dashing out—perhaps it was even better. He drew himself up to his very tallest.

"Father," he said, "I'm Colin. I'm well."

Mr. Craven held the boy's shoulders and stared into his face. His very soul shook with unbelieving joy.

"In the garden! In the garden!" was all that he could whisper.

"Yes," said Colin. "It was the garden!"

They led Mr. Craven into their garden, blooming with bright flowers. Mr. Craven remembered when they had been planted.

"I thought it would be dead," he said.

"Mary thought so at first," said Colin. "But it came alive."

Then, they sat down under their tree—all but Colin, who wanted to stand while he told the story.

It was the strangest thing Archibald Craven had ever heard; mystery and Magic and wild creatures, the midnight meeting, the coming of the spring—and the great secret so carefully kept.

"Now," Colin finished, "it need not be a secret any longer. I am never going to get into the chair again. I shall walk back with you, Father— to the house."

*

Mrs. Medlock had seen the master's carriage arrive, but not the master.

"Did you see Mr. Craven, Weatherstaff?" she asked, when Ben came into the kitchen.

"Aye," he answered slowly. "There's been things goin' on outside as you house people knows nowt about." And it was not two minutes before he waved solemnly toward the window.

"Look there," he said.

Across the lawn came the Master of Misselthwaite. And by his side was a young boy, head up in the air and his eyes full of laughter, walking as strongly and steadily as any boy in Yorkshire—Master Colin.

Robinson Crusoe

Retold by
Stewart Ross

Illustrated by
Vince Reid

ARCTURUS

For Max Macdonald, with love—SR.

For Patricia, my Mum—VR.

ARCTURUS

This edition published in 2018 by Arcturus Publishing Limited
26/27 Bickels Yard, 151–153 Bermondsey Street,
London SE1 3HA

Copyright © Arcturus Holdings Limited

All rights reserved. No part of this publication may be reproduced, stored in a retrieval system, or transmitted, in any form or by any means, electronic, mechanical, photocopying, recording or otherwise, without written permission in accordance with the provisions of the Copyright Act 1956 (as amended). Any person or persons who do any unauthorised act in relation to this publication may be liable to criminal prosecution and civil claims for damages.

Writer: Stewart Ross
Illustrator: Vince Reid
Designer: Jeni Child
Editor: Sebastian Rydberg
Art Director: Jessica Crass

ISBN: 978-1-78828-689-3
CH006283NT
Supplier 24, Date 0618, Print run 7515

Printed in Malaysia

Contents

CHAPTER 1
Leaving Home..4

CHAPTER 2
Slavery and Shipwreck 14

CHAPTER 3
Marooned!...24

CHAPTER 4
My Island Kingdom 34

CHAPTER 5
Cannibals!...44

CHAPTER 6
Home at Last...54

CHAPTER 1

Leaving Home

My name is Robinson Crusoe, and this is the true story of my life and adventures. First, I'll explain my name. My mother's family name was "Robinson." My father came from Germany, and his family name was "Kreutznaer." To help his English friends, he changed it to "Crusoe."

I was born in York, England, in 1632, the youngest of three brothers. The eldest was killed in the wars, and my other brother just disappeared. We were clearly not a lucky family.

Because of this, my parents told me not to do anything

foolish. "Don't go on adventures," my father advised. "Stay in York, and get a good, sensible job as a lawyer."

But you know what young people are like, don't you? I did the opposite of what my parents told me.

In 1651, when I was just nineteen, I went to the port of Hull. There, I met a friend who was about to sail to London in his father's ship. "Come on, Robinson," he urged, "join me! It'll be really exciting!"

The temptation was too great to resist. Without even telling my parents what I was doing, I boarded ship on the first of September, and set sail for London.

My friend said the voyage would be exciting—and he was certainly right! No sooner had we left Hull than the wind began to blow hard, and the sea rose in waves as tall as the Yorkshire hills.

I was terrified. *This is a punishment from God for disobeying my parents*, I thought. I promised myself that, if I survived, I would go straight home and never venture to sea again.

How foolish I was! The wind died down, the sun came out, and I quickly forgot my promise. I had great fun laughing and singing with the sailors.

You can never, ever trust the sea. After a period of calm, the wind rose once more. This time it was much, much stronger. Our ship pitched and rolled in the storm, and started to leak.

I worked frantically at the pumps, trying to keep us from sinking.

We had almost given up hope when another vessel came in sight. Desperately, we waved for help. They launched a small boat, and we managed to scramble into it.

Safe on board the rescue ship, we watched in horror as the sea smashed our vessel to pieces, and it sank beneath the angry waves.

I was pretty shaken and scared when we finally made it to Yarmouth. Seeing me in this state, my friend's father came up and gave me a stern look.

"Young Master Robinson Crusoe," he said, "one thing is clear to me."

"Yes, sir," I answered, "and what is it?"

"You are not a seafaring man," he explained. "You should never go to sea again. If you do, I prophesy you will meet with nothing but disasters and disappointments."

In my heart of hearts, I knew he was right. The sensible thing would be to go home. But once more, I didn't do the sensible thing. Having a bit of money in my pocket, I decided to go to London.

To be honest, I was too ashamed to return to my parents. It would mean admitting they'd been right. I couldn't face that and set out on the high road.

Once I got to the great city, all thoughts of going back to York vanished from my mind. London was a wonderful place, full of interest and excitement, and I soon made new friends. I also had a chance to make money.

One of my new London friends was an honest sea captain. He was an amiable man, and we got along really well.

One day, as we drank a beer together, he said, "I have a proposal, Robinson. Next week, I'm going trading in Africa. Fancy coming with me?"

I remembered my last voyage and hesitated.

"Come on," said the captain. "You can trade, too. You might even get rich!"

That settled it. With the forty pounds I had, I bought goods the captain told me would be popular in Africa. With everything safely on board, we set sail for Guinea. To my relief, though I was horribly seasick, we arrived without meeting a single storm.

In the markets of Guinea, I found I had

a knack for trading. The local people loved the things I brought. I swapped them for a pile of gold dust.

The return trip went well. As soon as we had tied up in the London docks, I hurried to a merchant with my gold. What was it worth? I asked eagerly.

The goldsmith weighed it and said it was worth three hundred pounds: I had turned forty pounds into three hundred in just a few months!

Shortly after our return to London, to my great sorrow, the captain died. However, I decided to continue trading. I gave two hundred pounds to the captain's widow and asked her to invest it for me. The other hundred pounds I took with me on another trip to Guinea.

This time, my luck ran out. Near the Canary Islands, we were chased by a large pirate ship. The enemy was faster than us, and we had to fight.

The battle was between our twelve cannon and the pirates' eighteen. At first, we held them off. But they came alongside with a crafty move, and sixty pirates swarmed aboard.

They immediately cut down our sails so we couldn't escape. A furious battle followed. Twice, we drove them back from our bloodstained decks. In the end, though, their greater numbers won the day.

Three of our crew were killed and eight wounded. The rest of us, myself included, laid down our arms and surrendered. I had heard dreadful stories of what happened to those captured by the pirates of Morocco, and my heart was full of dread as I entered the port of Salé in chains.

CHAPTER 2
Slavery and Shipwreck

I was now a slave. Because I was young and strong, the pirate captain kept me for himself. The rest of the crew were sent to the court of the Emperor, far inland. There they were beaten, starved, and given the most dreadful work to do.

I was more fortunate. My master was a fair man and treated me well—as long as I did as I was told. I tried hard to please him, though this was not always easy at first because I did not speak his language.

With no one to talk to, I grew miserable. Once again, I realized how foolish I had been to ignore my father's advice. *How good it would be to be safe in a lawyer's office in York,* I thought, *instead of lying here, a slave in a foreign land!*

Somehow, I had to escape. My best chance would be to sail on the pirate ship and hope it was captured by an English, French, Spanish, or Portuguese vessel. But whenever my master went to sea, he left me at home to watch over his house.

Then, after two years as a prisoner, an opportunity finally came.

My master liked fishing. Once a week, he went out in a small boat to see what he could catch. He always took me and a boy named Xury with him.

One day, my master decided to serve his dinner guests with fresh fish. Since he was too busy to go himself, he ordered Xury and myself and a strong guard to do the fishing for him. I persuaded the guard to put food and weapons on board, in case we got lost in fog or were attacked by bandits.

When we were out at sea, I threw the guard overboard and ordered him to swim for the shore. I told Xury that

I'd put him overboard, too, unless he accepted me as his master. He gave a broad grin—and the deal was done.

Xury and I sailed together for three weeks. From time to time, we went ashore for food and fresh water. Once, we were attacked by a huge lion, which I shot dead.

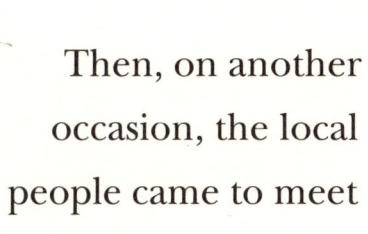

Then, on another occasion, the local people came to meet us with food and presents.

After many adventures, we found ourselves near the Cape Verde islands. Here, we were rescued by a Portuguese ship. I was free at last!

During all my adventures, I have been helped by some very kind people. One of these was the friendly captain of the Portuguese ship that rescued us. He was going to Brazil, and I offered him all I had to take us with him.

The good captain refused my money. In fact, he paid *me*! He gave me eighty gold coins for the boat I had stolen from the pirate captain. He offered sixty more coins if I would sell him Xury.

Of course, I refused. But when the boy said he didn't mind because it would help me, I sadly let him go. I also sold the skin of the lion I had shot.

In Brazil, I bought as much land as I could afford. It became known as Crusoe's Farm, or "Plantation." For the next three years, I lived as a "planter." I grew corn, tobacco, and sugarcane, and I became quite well off.

Looking back, these years proved very useful. First, I learned how to grow crops. Second, because my plantation was far from any town, I became used to living on my own.

As you will see, these turned out to be very valuable lessons.

You've probably guessed that something terrible was about to happen to me. You're right—and this is how it began …

After four years in Brazil, my plantation had become very successful. Before I sailed from England, all those years ago, you may remember that I left two hundred pounds with the widow of my first captain. I now got a Portuguese friend to bring half of that money to Brazil.

I used it to buy servants and workers, and my plantation flourished even more.

Crusoe's tobacco fetched the highest prices in the market. *Ah-ha, father!* I said to myself. *If I had followed your advice, I'd be stuck in an office in York. Instead, look at me now! I'm a wealthy landowner.*

I was proud of what I had achieved. And pride, they rightly say, comes before a fall.

Not content with my fortune, I wanted more. Many of the plantations in Brazil used slave workers. These poor men and women were bought in Africa and shipped to South America. Because I had been to Guinea, in Africa, my friends suggested I go there, buy slaves, and bring them back to Brazil.

I would, they said, make a lot of money.

On the first of September, 1659, I boarded a ship sailing for Guinea. It was precisely eight years since I'd left my poor parents. I still felt guilty, and someone—maybe God—was about to punish me.

The voyage was all storms. The first lasted for twelve long days. Our ship was tossed around like a cork. One sailor was killed, and our young cabin boy was washed overboard and drowned.

The vessel was so badly damaged that we decided to get it repaired in Barbados. After that, we would sail on to Guinea. Tragically, we did not even reach Barbados.

The second storm was much fiercer than the first. It ripped the sails from the masts and snapped the masts themselves. Vast waves thundered over the ship's sides, filling it with water. We were unable to steer, and the roaring tempest drove us on to a foaming bar of sand.

Certain that the ship would break up, we launched the lifeboat. What a mistake! A gigantic wave, as big as a mountain, caught our little craft and swallowed it up.

I struggled to the surface. After a long battle, more dead than alive, I reached the shore and collapsed.

CHAPTER 3

Marooned!

When I came to, I thanked God for saving me. The rest of the crew had all drowned. I was stranded in a strange place with only the clothes I was wearing. Terrified, I climbed into a tree and fell asleep.

The morning broke calm and clear. I saw that our ship had not broken up but was stuck on a sandbank a little way from the shore. If the crew had stayed on board, they would have been saved!

I pulled myself together, swam out to the vessel, and climbed aboard. I collected food and other things I needed, and ferried them back to dry land on a raft. Over the next few days, I made eleven more trips to the ship.

As well as tools, guns, and ammunition, I saved the captain's dog and two cats. They were the only company I had. I laughed when I found gold and silver coins—what use was money to me now?

After my twelfth trip, another great storm blew up during the night. I went down to the shore the next morning and looked out to sea. The wreck had disappeared. I had no choice but to make the best of my new situation.

When I first came ashore, I climbed a tall hill and looked around. Two things became clear. First, I was on an island. Second, as I could see no sign of other human beings, it was a desert island. I was marooned!

Right, I thought, *I'd better make myself safe.* I moved the tent I'd made to a site higher up, and dug a cave into the hillside behind it. It made an excellent storage area.

I circled my little settlement with a high fence. The only way in was by a ladder, which I pulled up after me. I camouflaged the fence, too, so from the outside it looked like a small wood.

I went hunting every morning. To my delight, I found there were goats on the island. I shot some for food and tried, unsuccessfully, to tame a kid. Nevertheless, I still hoped to set up a small farm on the island one day.

To keep track of time, I kept a diary. When I saw how the days, weeks, and months passed, I felt very miserable. *Come on, Crusoe,* I said to myself. *You're the fortunate one— think of what happened to the rest of the crew!*

I had never been very religious. But now, thinking about how I had been saved, I began to pray more. It made me feel good. I set up a wooden cross and carved a notch on it for each of my days on the island.

It's remarkable what you can do if you have to. I carved tools from hard wood and learned how to make storage barrels.

My best invention was a lamp. I put goat fat in a dish, stuck in a piece of string as a wick—and lit it. It worked! My nights were now not so dark and scary.

As time went by, my diet became more varied. I discovered which birds and animals were good to eat. I also killed and ate a turtle, and I cooked its eggs. They were delicious.

The biscuits I brought from the ship did not last long. I couldn't make more because rats had been in my corn. I had to throw it out. Imagine my amazement, therefore, when I found that the grains had planted themselves and were starting to grow!

I now had the farm I had dreamed of, with small fields of wheat and rice.

My island had wet and dry seasons. Starting in June, heavy rain fell daily. It sometimes kept me indoors from dawn to dusk.

It was during one of these days that I suddenly felt cold. *That's strange,* I thought. *I'm in the tropics where the temperature is always high. Even the rain is warm.*

I then realized the truth: I was seriously ill. Fever hit me like the wave that had swamped our boat. I shivered, agonizing pains gripping my arms and legs. Sweat poured from me like the rain off the roof of my tent.

I had neither doctor nor medicine. For days, I lay groaning on my rough bed, unable to move.

Fortunately, I gradually recovered, and for a while, I felt fine. But the fever came sweeping back, worse than before. This time, I had terrible nightmares, always with my parents in them. *Oh, what an ungrateful fool I am!* I cried to myself.

I was surely going to die.

But, through God's mercy, I survived. When able to move, I mixed rum and tobacco into a kind of medicine. I have no idea why, but it made me stronger and helped me return to my usual life.

When I was well, I decided to get to know my island better. I call it "my" island because I saw myself as a sort of king. My dog and the cats were my subjects.

The number of my subjects grew when the cats had kittens. Looking after my animals, hunting, and tending to the crops in my fields, I was kept a busy man.

Exploring parts of the island I hadn't visited before, I came across many new fruits. There were oranges, lemons, grapes, and juicy melons. By drying the grapes, I produced delicious raisins. I also found some wild sugarcane. I chopped it down, took out the juicy sap—and enjoyed sweet drinks with my meals.

The best thing I brought home from my travels was a bird. I managed to capture a young parrot. It was a most beautiful creature with feathers of blue, green, and gleaming gold.

When I got back to my house (as I called it), I fashioned a birdcage out of sticks and put my parrot inside. Slowly, one step at a time, I taught it how to speak. What a joy it was to hear words not spoken by myself!

CHAPTER 4
My Island Kingdom

Two years had now passed since my shipwreck. On one of my trips around my kingdom, I had climbed a hill and spied land in the distance. It was between fifty and sixty miles away.

I wondered about what I had seen. Who lived there? If they were Spaniards, I was safe. But I had heard sailors tell of other people living in this part of the world. Cannibals! I shuddered at the idea of meeting those who ate human flesh.

Nevertheless, I thought, *there's only one way of finding out who lives over there. I'll pay them a visit.*

To cross the sea, I needed a large boat. I chose a suitable tree and chopped it down. It took five months to cut off the branches, smooth down the trunk, and hollow out the inside. In the end, I had a fine boat.

What an idiot! I hadn't worked out how to get it into the water. It was far too big to move on my own. I tried digging a canal to the sea, but it was impossible.

Furious with myself for being so stupid, I gave up. I had to leave my lovely boat rotting in the forest.

By my fifth year on the island, my clothes were in tatters. They hardly covered me. I got wet in the rain and burned by the sun. I needed new ones.

The shirts and trousers I had rescued from the wreck fitted quite well. But my only hat had fallen to pieces. I looked at the materials around me. Goat skin.

Whenever I killed a goat, I took off the skin and left it to dry. Now, having cut out a suitable shape, I sewed it into a neat cap. In fact, it was better than my old hat because it was completely waterproof.

If a goat skin hat can keep the rain out, I reasoned, *why not a complete suit?* I set to work with scissors, needle, and thread. The result might not have been the height of fashion, but it was just what I needed. Who was there to care what I looked like?

My wardrobe lacked just one item: an umbrella. It took me ages to make one like those I had seen in South America. But using goat skin and pieces of wood, I eventually made a perfect sunshade that also kept off the rain.

Five more years passed. My life continued as before, caring for my animals, growing crops, and repairing my furniture and tools. But the image of the distant land remained at the back of my mind.

I needed a new boat.

This time, I made it small enough to get into the water. I fitted it with a mast and sail, and attached my umbrella at the stern. All was ready for a voyage of exploration.

On the first two days, I didn't go far, as I needed to learn how to handle my little craft. By the third day, I was ready to sail out to sea. This was a big mistake.

A powerful current gripped the boat and carried it far from the shore. I wrestled with the sails and prayed for a good wind. Only after struggling for hours did I manage to return safely to the island.

I was utterly exhausted. I tied up my boat, lay down, and fell asleep. I was woken by a voice crying in my ear: "Robin, Robin Crusoe! Poor Robin Crusoe! Where have you been?"

Petrified, I sprang to my feet and looked round. It was just Pol, my parrot, welcoming me home!

Months passed. I was so frightened by my boat trip that I did not go sailing again for a long time. Instead, I stayed at home and worked on my house and farm.

I learned to weave baskets. On one of my trips, I had found tobacco plants. I cut the leaves, dried them in the sun, and in the evenings, smoked them in a handmade pipe. At such moments, I dreamed I was back in England.

Because my gunpowder was running low, I stopped shooting and took up trapping. Gradually, I built up a big herd of goats. It provided me with all the milk, butter, and cheese I needed.

After a year, I plucked up the courage to take my boat out again. I was extremely careful to avoid currents and dangerous rocks. I had had enough of shipwrecks!

Sailing around my tiny kingdom, a thought came to me. As king, I ought to know precisely what I owned. So, when I got home, I made a list of all my possessions.

It was a silly thing to do—but it comforted me when I was about to receive a terrible shock.

When you live on your own for fifteen years, as I had, your mind plays tricks on you. You imagine things that are not there. That's why what happened to me one fine day almost drove me crazy.

I was walking along the beach, not thinking about anything very important. Suddenly, I stopped. There was something on the ground before me.

One pace away, clear as daylight, was a human footprint in the sand—not a track made by someone walking, just one single print. I stood frozen to the spot and stared in terror.

The foot was bigger than mine, so it couldn't have been made by me. Then, by whom? A one-legged monster? The devil, haunting me for behaving so badly toward my parents all those years ago?

I had no answer. I rushed back to my camp and pulled up the ladder. That night, I didn't sleep a wink. After fifteen years of solitude, I was no longer alone.

My only thought was to defend myself. I built a second fence around my home and looked behind me nervously whenever I went out. All I could do was wait.

CHAPTER 5

Cannibals!

The footprint in the sand changed my life on the island forever. But if the print was bad, what I next saw was much worse.

Every day, I climbed the hill near my home to look for boats. Two years after I had seen the footprint, I spied a canoe disappearing into the distance. I hurried to the shore to see if the visitors had left anything behind.

As well as footprints, dreadful remains lay upon the sand. Skulls, bones, and bits of human bodies were scattered near a dark patch where a fire had burned.

My island—my kingdom—was the place where cannibals cooked and ate their poor prisoners!

The sight horrified me. For years afterward, I hardly left my home. I had added new fortifications, making it more like a fortress than a house.

The cannibals never left my mind. I didn't fire a gun in case they heard its noise. I didn't light a fire in case they saw its smoke. I didn't even chop wood in case the sound echoed down to the beach where they held their foul feasts.

My despair deepened when, after a long and faithful friendship, my old dog finally died. These were hard times.

If the cannibals returned, I promised myself that I would attack them. I'd shoot them all dead.

Then I thought again ...

God had created the world and everything in it. Since he had made the cannibals, who was I to condemn them? I hated what they did, but they did not know any better. God himself would judge them, not me.

I did not set eyes on the cannibals until the December of my twenty-third year on the island. Seeing the smoke of their fire, I crept down to the shore and hid to watch their ghastly banquet. I shivered in horror.

*

After that, the savages, as I called them, did not return for a year. In the meantime, a tragedy occurred. A great Spanish ship was wrecked upon the rocks of my island. Not one of the crew survived.

I swam out to the wreck, looking for things that might be of use. There wasn't much, though I did recover bags of money and some gold bars. More welcome was the half-drowned ship's dog that struggled ashore and lay at my feet.

I now had a new companion—even the worst disasters can bring a little comfort.

I dreaded that the cannibals might learn about me and hunt me down. I had to get away. But how? My only hope was to capture a savage who could lead me to safety on the mainland.

As it turned out, I had no need to capture anyone.

Two years after I had watched the grizzly banquet, the cannibals returned. Thirty of them came in five canoes. I armed myself and went down to the shore.

The savages had brought two prisoners to feast upon. As I watched, they killed one and chopped him up for cooking. The other, finding himself unguarded, made a dash for freedom. Half a dozen cannibals set off in pursuit.

To my dismay, I found that the victim was heading toward me! He was a strong runner, and three of his pursuers soon gave up. Another dropped out when the runaway swam across a creek. He was now almost upon me.

I had to save him. Raising my gun, I took aim and fired. The two pursuers dropped to the sand. The man they had been chasing stared in amazement. Then, very slowly, stopping to kneel every few steps, he advanced toward me.

I lowered my gun and smiled.

When the runaway reached me, he knelt and kissed my foot. Later, he explained that this was to say, "Thank you. You have saved my life, and I will be your servant."

I looked up to see that one of the pursuers had only been stunned. He was advancing toward us. Before I could shoot, my new friend grabbed my sword and cut off the attacker's head.

Using sign language, we agreed to cover up the dead bodies to hide them from the other cannibals. That done, I gestured to my friend to follow and then we set out for my fortress home.

Just by chance, I had found the ideal companion. He was tall, good-looking, and intelligent. We got along extremely well. Though he was my servant, I saw him more as a friend.

I called him "Friday," because that was the day of the week on which we had met. He was not used to wearing clothes but liked it when I dressed him in some taken from the wreck. It didn't take him long to pick up a few words of English, either.

One of the first things I told him was that I thought that eating people was wrong. He understood straight away.

At first, Friday slept in a tent outside my main home. However, I quickly realized he loved me, and he was the best and truest friend I ever had. I was happy to share my house with such a man.

I found, to my dismay, that Friday had himself eaten human flesh. Now that he agreed this was wrong, I gave him different meat. I was relieved to find he liked goat and hare.

Friday was terrified of my gun. He had seen what it could do and believed it was magic, like a god! I even found him talking to it, asking it not to kill him. I explained that it was not alive but was only a tool. After I showed him how it worked, he became a good hunter.

Once Friday could speak fluently—which he managed very swiftly—he told me many things. He described the currents of the sea, life with his own people, and how he had been captured. If we had a boat, he said, we could easily get to the mainland.

We talked about religion, too. I explained Christianity to him, and he described his own beliefs to me. I found them very strange, indeed, and I hoped that one day he would become a Christian like me.

CHAPTER 6

Home at Last

Friday and I lived in peace for three years. When he said there were Europeans on the mainland, I was eager to go there. We built a boat big enough to carry us both. But before we set out, six cannibal canoes appeared for another grizzly feast.

Friday wanted to attack them with our guns. I hesitated. But when I saw that one of the prisoners was a European, I changed my mind, and we both opened fire. They screamed and ran about wildly.

I rushed in and rescued the European man, who turned out to be Spanish. In the chaos, four cannibals jumped into a canoe and fled. Friday leaped into another canoe to chase them.

"Master!" he cried. "Come look!"

There, tied up on the bottom of the canoe, was another prisoner. His father!

Friday and I led the rescued men to my fortress home. After a hearty meal, they soon recovered. Friday asked his father whether the cannibals would return with an army to destroy us.

The old man shook his head. No, he said. They were too frightened by our guns ever to return.

For the moment, we were safe.

This was our plan. Friday's father and the Spaniard would use our new boat to collect the other Spaniards from the mainland. Together, we would then build an even bigger boat and sail to safety.

However, before the boat came back from the mainland, my adventures took another strange twist. An English ship anchored close to my island!

But something was not right. In the small boat that came ashore were eight sailors and three prisoners. Friday and I sneaked down to the shore to take a closer look. At midday, the sailors went into the woods for a nap. We crept up to the prisoners and set them free.

You should have seen the looks on their faces! Who was this wild-looking man, and who was his friend, they asked?

I explained about my twenty-seven years on the island, and they told me their story. The ship's crew had mutinied. They had captured the ship's captain and two honest companions, and planned to maroon them on my island. These were the three men we had set free.

"Right," I said. "If we help you, you must do exactly as I say and then take us back to England."

The captain immediately agreed.

Step one was capturing the men asleep in the woods. This was easily done, though one of them was shot dead when he tried to warn the others. The captain said he'd spare those who swore loyalty to him. They all did.

Next, we had to deal with the twenty-six mutineers on the ship. When their mates did not return, ten of them came ashore. After leading them on a wild goose chase, we ambushed them. Two, we shot dead, the rest surrendered.

Finally, with a bit of trickery and bravery, we recaptured the ship. I ordered the leader of the mutiny, Will Atkins, to be hanged. The captain and I reckoned that twelve of the rest of the crew were reliable.

The others, we chose to leave on my island. I explained how to look after the animals and the farm. I also told them that some Spaniards would soon be joining them from the mainland.

One or two of them complained. I reminded them that if they returned with us, they might well be hanged for mutiny. "And anyway," I added, "This island was my home for twenty-seven years. You'll find it's not such a bad place, after all!"

We set sail on the nineteenth of December, 1686. As we were hauling up the anchor, two of the men we had left on the island swam to the ship and begged to be taken aboard. I agreed, though they were whipped for taking part in the mutiny.

By the time we reached England, I had been away for thirty-five years. So much had changed. For a start, we had a new government and a new king.

To my great sadness and regret, I learned that both my parents had died. My father had left me nothing in his will because he assumed I was dead. But I remembered my plantation in Brazil and went to Portugal with Friday to find out what had happened to it.

On arriving in Lisbon, the capital of Portugal, I learned that my plantation had made a small fortune. I was a rich man!

At once, I rewarded everyone who had looked after my business while I was away. That done, I planned how to take my money back to England.

Should I go by sea? No way! I had had more than my fair share of shipwrecks, and I didn't want to risk another.

A group of five of us gathered for the long journey through Spain and France to England. Friday looked about in amazement—the fields, the buildings, the people were all so new and strange to him.

Knowing my luck, you will not be surprised to hear that I had one last adventure. It happened when we reached the lofty Pyrenees mountains. It was winter, and the roads were deep in snow. Poor Friday had never felt so cold in his life. His teeth chattered like castanets, day and night.

The icy weather drove all sorts of wild animals out of the hills, toward the villages. On one lonely road, we were faced by a lumbering bear. Luckily for me, Friday, who had hunted these animals at home with bows and arrows, shot the beast dead.

Later still, we were surrounded by a pack of snarling wolves. I ordered the men to light a ring of fire around us and shoot from behind it. The idea worked, and we were saved.

And so, we reached England at last. There, I settled down, married, and had a lovely family. Friday stayed with me, and when I looked at him, I dreamed of further adventures.

But that is all for the moment. The rest, as they say, is another story.

Little Women

Retold by
Samantha Noonan

Illustrated by
Joëlle Dreidemy

ARCTURUS

To Mum, an original March girl!—SN.

To Lucile, Alice and Mona—JD.

ARCTURUS

This edition published in 2018 by Arcturus Publishing Limited
26/27 Bickels Yard, 151–153 Bermondsey Street,
London SE1 3HA

Copyright © Arcturus Holdings Limited

All rights reserved. No part of this publication may be reproduced, stored in a retrieval system, or transmitted, in any form or by any means, electronic, mechanical, photocopying, recording or otherwise, without written permission in accordance with the provisions of the Copyright Act 1956 (as amended). Any person or persons who do any unauthorised act in relation to this publication may be liable to criminal prosecution and civil claims for damages.

Writer: Samantha Noonan
Illustrator: Joëlle Dreidemy
Designer: Jeni Child
Editor: Becca Clunes
Art Director: Jessica Crass

ISBN: 978-1-78828-685-5
CH006280NT
Supplier 24, Date 0618, Print run 7511

Printed in Malaysia

Contents

CHAPTER 1
A Christmas Gift.....................4

CHAPTER 2
Shyness and Pride...................14

CHAPTER 3
Anger and Vanity....................24

CHAPTER 4
All Play and No Work................34

CHAPTER 5
Dark Days...........................44

CHAPTER 6
A New Dawn..........................54

CHAPTER 1

A Christmas Gift

It was a cold and snowy Christmas Eve. The March sisters were all gathered around the fire, knitting. They didn't feel very festive, since their father was away in the war, and there was no money for presents.

"It would be so lovely to have some pretty things," said Meg, the oldest.

"Who needs pretty things?" scoffed Jo, the second oldest. "I would like a thrilling new book to read."

Little Amy, the youngest, sighed dramatically. "Oh, what I wouldn't give for some new drawing pencils!"

"I would wish for some lovely new piano music," said quiet Beth, "but we mustn't fuss. We must try to be good and kind, like Marmee." Marmee was their pet name for their mother, who was out visiting the poor in their town.

"You're so right, Beth," said Jo. "After all, we have warmth and good company."

"And delicious food," added Amy.

By the time Marmee came home, the sisters were as happy as ever. They all sang carols around Beth's tiny piano and went up to bed, excited for the next day.

When the girls woke on Christmas morning, Marmee was already out visiting the Hummels, a poor family who lived nearby. The girls prepared their Christmas breakfast of warm bread, pancakes, and cream. When Marmee came home, she told them that the Hummels had no food at all.

"We should give the Hummel family our breakfast," said Beth, and the other girls agreed.

"I knew you would say that." Marmee smiled at them. "You are kind girls."

That evening, the sisters performed a Christmas play for all their friends. Jo had written it and played the dashing hero. They had so much fun that they barely thought about all the things their Christmas lacked. When Marmee called them all to dinner, they were surprised to see that it was a feast! There was cake, fruit, bonbons, and even ice cream!

"Did fairies do this?" asked Amy.

Marmee laughed. "No, Mr. Laurence sent it when he heard what you did for the Hummels."

The girls had often glimpsed rich old Mr. Laurence and his young grandson in the big house next door, and thought they looked nice but lonely.

"Maybe now we can make friends with them," Jo said.

On New Year's Eve, Jo and Meg went to a party. Meg was looking forward to dressing up in their prettiest frocks, until she saw that Jo's dress had a big burn mark on the back.

"You always stand too close to the fire," sighed Meg, feeling sad that they couldn't afford new clothes. "You'll just have to keep your back to the wall."

The party was beautiful, and Meg was asked to dance at once. Jo decided to hide in the library, so nobody would see her burnt dress.

She slipped inside—and bumped straight into the Laurence boy!

Jo remembered her manners. "Mr. Laurence, I must thank you for the Christmas feast you sent us," she said.

The boy laughed. "Please, call me

Laurie, and it was all Grandfather's idea."

"In that case, call me Jo, and I bet you told him to," said Jo.

Laurie was just as nice as Jo had hoped. Soon, they were chatting like old pals and doing silly dances where nobody could see.

After the party, Laurie walked Jo and Meg back home, and the sisters hoped that they had made a new friend.

One cold day, Jo was clearing snow outside, when she caught sight of Laurie watching her from an upstairs window. He looked a little sorry for himself.

Jo knew it wasn't ladylike, but she cupped her hands and shouted up anyway. "What's wrong?"

Laurie opened the window. "I've got a cold, so I have to stay inside. It's so dull."

"Well, why don't I come over and cheer you up?" said Jo.

"Would you?" Laurie asked.

"Of course!" said Jo. "I'll just ask Marmee."

A few minutes later, the doorbell rang. Laurie dashed downstairs to find Jo on the doorstep with some strange bundles.

"When I told them you were sick, Marmee sent her love, Meg sent her blancmange, and Beth sent her kittens," Jo said, giggling as one of the kittens tried to wriggle free.

"That's so kind of them," said Laurie. "Do come in."

They played with the kittens for a while, and then Laurie gave Jo a tour of the house. Jo enjoyed seeing where he lived, even though fine things didn't mean much to her. But when they reached the enormous library, she was speechless! There were hundreds of books. Jo spun around, gazing at them dreamily.

Down the hallway, they heard the heavy creak of the front door opening.

Laurie said, "That's the doctor. I'll be back in a minute."

Jo explored the library and stopped in front of a grand painting of an old gentleman. It was Mr. Laurence, Laurie's grandfather.

When she heard Laurie come back in, she said, "Your grandfather isn't as handsome as my grandfather, but he looks kind. I think I like him."

"Thank you, ma'am," said a gruff voice behind her.

Jo turned in horror to see Mr. Laurence standing there. She stammered an apology, but the old man waved it off, smiling.

"Now, what are you doing in my library?" he asked.

"I thought Laurie looked lonely, sir. I came to cheer him up," Jo said nervously, still feeling like she was on thin ice.

Mr. Laurence looked thoughtful. "Lonely, you say? Well, perhaps it wouldn't hurt for him to have a bit of company, and you seem like a nice girl."

To Jo's surprise, he invited her to tea and said that the March girls were welcome to visit whenever they liked.

CHAPTER 2

Shyness and Pride

Jo, Meg, and Amy did as Mr. Laurence said. They were often in and out of the big house, and it became full of life and laughter. However, Beth was too shy to go over, even though she dreamed about the Laurences' grand piano.

Mr. Laurence decided to try to help Beth. He staged a loud chat with Marmee, making sure Beth would overhear.

"It's such a shame. The grand piano sits alone at the far end of the house. Laurie is away upstairs, and I'm shut in my study all day.

Nobody would even hear if it was played. I would be very grateful if one of your girls would. They can just let themselves in and out."

That day, Beth went over to the big house and slipped in through the side door. She found the piano alone, as promised, and started to play. She had a wonderful time, playing for hours. Then, she closed the lid and ran home, absolutely thrilled.

She started to creep over every day, and she had no idea that Mr. Laurence was sitting with his study door open, or that Laurie was sneaking down to the hall to listen to the sweet tunes she played.

Beth made Mr. Laurence some slippers, as a gift to say thank you for letting her play his piano, and left them in his study.

To begin with, Beth heard nothing from him and was worried that he was offended by the small present. Then, one day, when she was coming home from a walk, she saw her sisters waving out of the window like crazy.

"Beth! It's a letter from Mr. Laurence," said Amy, waving a piece of paper. "You'll never guess what he's sent you!"

Beth ran inside to find the whole family standing around a little cabinet piano. Mr. Laurence's letter said that he loved her gift, and he wanted to give her something in return.

Beth sat down on the stool in a daze and touched the keys. It sounded beautiful!

"You'd better go and thank him," joked Jo, knowing that Beth would be too shy.

But to everyone's surprise, Beth jumped straight up. "Yes, I suppose I should."

She marched next door, ran in, and gave Mr. Laurence a big hug.

Her sisters were shocked when they heard this.

"I do declare the world is coming to an end!" said Meg.

Amy was the only sister who still went to school. Beth was too shy and did her lessons at home. Meg and Jo had both finished school and had jobs. Meg was a governess for a rich family. Jo went to read for their Great Aunt March and keep her company.

"Oh, dear me, it is so terrible to be in debt," Amy sighed as she, Jo, and Meg left the house one morning.

"Debt? What do you mean?" Meg asked.

"I owe at least a dozen pickled limes at school," Amy said, in a weary voice. "And I have no money to buy any. Jenny Snow is calling me mean behind my back."

Meg nodded seriously. She remembered how she had always wanted to join in on the latest fashions at school herself. "How much money do you need?"

"A quarter," said Amy.

Meg pulled one out of her purse. "Just make this last as long as you can. We don't have a lot of money," she warned.

Amy was late to school that day, but word quickly went around the class that she had twenty-four delicious limes. Amy promised to share them with everyone, except for nasty Jenny Snow.

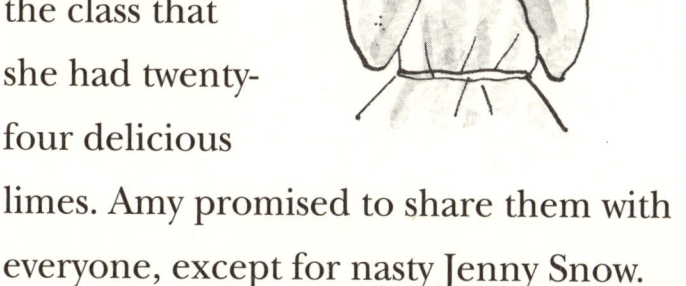

What Amy hadn't told Meg was that Mr. Davis, her teacher, had banned pickled limes from school. So, when Jenny Snow raised her hand and told him that Amy had a bag of them in her desk, he was furious.

He ordered Amy to throw the limes out of the window. Slowly and sadly, Amy did as he said. Next, he made her stand at the front of the classroom and hold out her hands. Mr. Davis struck her hands three times with a leather strap, then ordered her to stand on the platform until recess. Her hands stung a lot, but Amy was determined not to cry. She stood there silently.

When the bell rang, she ran to the cloakroom. She gathered her things and ran out of school, vowing never to go back.

When she got home and told her family what had happened, they were furious that she had been struck. Marmee said it was wrong to have broken the rules, but she didn't believe in hitting children. She wrote a letter to Mr. Davis, telling him that Amy would do her lessons at home with Beth from now on.

One evening, Jo, Meg, and Laurie were going to see a play. Amy had been stuck inside with a cold for the past few days and was bored.

"Please, can I come, too?" she asked as the older two got ready.

"Marmee says you aren't well enough yet," said Meg. "You can go next week with Beth."

Amy pouted. "But it won't be nearly as fun with Beth. Please, Meg, I'm dying for some fun."

Meg looked thoughtfully at Jo. "I suppose if we bundle her up …"

"No," said Jo firmly. "She wasn't invited."

"But Meg says I can, and I'll pay for myself," Amy said. She started to pull on her boots, happy that she was going to get her way.

"No," said Jo. "We already have tickets, so your seat will be somewhere else. You know that Laurie will give you his seat, and he will sit alone. So, you will be ruining his evening and mine. You aren't coming, and that's that!"

Laurie called from downstairs, and Meg and Jo dashed down.

Just as they were on their way out of the door, Amy yelled over the banisters, "You'll be sorry for this, Jo March!"

CHAPTER 3

Anger and Vanity

Jo returned from the evening out and ran straight upstairs to write. She had been working on a little book of fairy tales for the last year that she hoped to finish before Father got home.

But the book wasn't where she had left it. She went downstairs and asked if anyone had seen it.

A guilty look passed over Amy's face.

"Give it back, Amy," Jo demanded.

"I can't. You'll never see your silly book again," said Amy.

"Why not?"

"I burned it up,"

Amy said. "I told you you would be sorry for leaving me behind!"

Jo burst into tears and shook Amy hard. "You are a wicked girl. I'll never forgive you for as long as I live!"

She raced from the room, sobbing, ran upstairs, and hurled herself down on her bed.

If Amy had expected the rest of the family to side with her, she was disappointed. They all agreed it had been a terrible thing to do.

Amy crept up to Jo's room later that night. "Jo, I'm sorry. Please forgive me."

Jo didn't even look at her. "I will never forgive you. You don't deserve it."

Jo was in a bad mood for days. Nothing could make her feel better, because nothing could bring her book back. Amy tried to show Jo that she was sorry, but it was no use. Eventually, Jo decided to get out of the house and go ice skating with Laurie.

Amy heard the clash of skates as Jo was getting ready to leave. She turned to Meg. "Jo promised me that the next time she went ice skating, I could come, too. I bet she'll go back on that promise now."

"You did do a dreadful thing, Amy. I'm not surprised that Jo finds it hard to forgive you," Meg said. "But I think she might, if you wait until the right moment. Why don't you follow her and wait until Laurie has put her in a good mood? Then, you can sneak up to her and give her a kiss. I'm sure all will be forgotten."

Amy thought that was an excellent idea and hurried to get ready.

Out on the icy river, Jo heard Amy following and rolled her eyes. Laurie glanced back, but before he could say anything, Jo muttered, "Ignore her. She just wants attention, and she won't have mine."

Laurie skated ahead, around the river bend. "The ice is getting a little thin in the middle here, Jo," he called back. "Better keep to the edge to be safe."

Jo skated to the edge of the river. She thought briefly about calling back to Amy but then shrugged. "She came by herself, so she can look out for herself."

A moment after Jo rounded the bend, she heard a great crack, a scream, and a splash. She and Laurie raced back to see Amy gasping and thrashing in a hole in the ice.

All of Jo's anger disappeared like a melting snowflake. She shot toward her little sister. She and Laurie pulled Amy out and rushed her home, wrapped in their coats.

At home, Amy warmed up again and was no worse for wear.

While she slept in front of the fire, Jo admitted what she did to Marmee and began to sob. "How can I control my terrible temper, Marmee?" she cried. "Amy could have died, and it would have been my fault!"

Marmee hugged her. "It's something you need to work on, dear, and there's no shame in it. Many people need to work on it their entire lives."

One spring day, the house was full of excitement. Meg had been invited to stay with her friend, Annie Moffat. The Moffat family were going to throw a party while Meg was there, so all the March sisters were helping Meg mend and pack her best things. They knew they were poor, but they didn't want Meg to feel ashamed of her clothes. Marmee even opened her "treasure chest," which was where she kept her few nice things left from before they were poor. She gave Meg silk stockings, a new sash, and a pretty fan.

Meg left in high spirits, but when she arrived at the party, she felt dowdy next to the other girls. Annie and her sisters were kind, even if they thought too much about what they looked like, and they offered to lend Meg a brand-new party dress.

When Meg accepted, they decided to transform her looks too. They crimped and curled her hair, brushed her skin with powder, and painted her lips. Then, they added necklaces, bracelets, gloves, and even silk boots.

When they were finished, Meg did look very pretty but like a doll instead of her own natural self.

At the party, everyone admired Meg, especially the men. Meg knew she was too young for boys, but she couldn't help enjoying the attention. She flirted and drank champagne, until she saw Laurie over on the other side of the room.

Meg glided over. "Laurie! I didn't know you were going to be here! Shall we dance?"

Laurie frowned a little as he looked at her. "You look … odd."

It was Meg's turn to frown. "Don't you mean I look nice?"

Laurie shook his head. "I don't mean to be rude, Meg, but you don't look like you. You look like one of those silly girls who only care about their looks."

Meg caught a glimpse of herself in a mirror and suddenly felt very ashamed. Laurie was right, she thought. She wasn't behaving like herself at all.

When the party was over, Meg went home to confess to Marmee what she had done.

"Wanting to look nice once in a while is fine," Marmee soothed her. "It's only a problem when it's all you think about."

"Well, I shan't worry about my looks from now on," Meg vowed. "I want to be more than that."

CHAPTER 4

All Play and No Work

The girls had many fun games that they would play together. These helped to fill the evenings after work, lessons, and chores were done for the day. When it was cold and dark outside, the little house was warm, bright, and full of joy.

Once a week, the girls would go up to the attic and dress up as characters from a book called *The Pickwick Papers* by Charles Dickens. All the characters were quaint English gentlemen. As these characters, the girls had formed the Pickwick Club.

"I, Augustus Snodgrass, call this meeting to order!" said Jo, straightening her top hat.

"You can't do that," said Meg, peering over a huge pair of spectacles with no glass in them. "I'm the president! I, Samuel Pickwick, call this meeting to order. Mr. Tupman, do you have the newsletter?"

Beth handed over a bundle of papers. They all wrote pieces for the newsletter each week, which included stories, poems, recipes, news, and anything else they could think to write about.

Meg opened up the paper. "We shall begin with a note from Nathaniel Winkle." She nodded at Amy.

Once all the notices had been read out, Jo bounced to her feet. "I say, girls—I mean, gentlemen—I have an idea. Why don't we add a new member to the club? Someone you all like and who is ever so jolly and fun. Let Laurie join the club!"

There was silence.

Then Meg said, "I don't think that's a good idea, Mr. Snodgrass. Of course we all like Laurie, but he'll think this club is silly and make fun of us."

"Oh, let him join!" Jo pleaded. "He won't make fun of us. He'll join in, I know he will. Besides," she added sheepishly, "he's already here."

She flung open the door of the closet, and Laurie jumped out. Meg, Beth, and Amy all fell off their chairs in surprise.

"I'm sorry to shock you!" Laurie laughed. "I'm afraid it was all my idea, and I persuaded Snodgrass. My name is Samuel Weller."

And so, Laurie joined the Pickwick Club and proved to be an excellent member. He even set up an old birdhouse between their houses, which served as a mailbox so they could exchange letters and small presents. Laurie threw himself into character and wrote lots of funny pieces. Every week, the Marches' attic would ring with laughter late into the evening.

That summer, the girls felt that they had worked so hard, they deserved some time off. Meg and Jo decided not to go to work, while Beth and Amy abandoned their lessons.

"Although, it won't be a complete rest if we still have to do our chores," said Amy to Marmee, hopefully.

"That's true," said Marmee, "but you might find that you will feel bored and unhappy if you have nothing to do."

The girls couldn't possibly believe that was true. So Marmee suggested they spend a whole week doing nothing—with no chores—and see how they felt at the end.

"I think we'll have a fabulous time," said Jo.

The experiment was agreed, and each girl set out to do whatever she pleased.

The week wasn't as enjoyable as the girls had hoped. Meg decided to alter one of her old dresses. But she couldn't resist fiddling with it over and over. By the time she was finished with it, it was ruined.

Jo went out rowing with Laurie in the blazing sun for hours, and her nose got sunburned. Then she gave herself a headache by reading too much.

Meanwhile, Beth decided she would clean out her doll cupboard, tidy all their clothes, and brush their hair. But she got bored halfway through and decided she would rather play piano instead. She left the dolls all over the floor, where everybody tripped over them.

Amy discovered that she didn't have much imagination by herself. She couldn't think of anything fun to do and ended up sitting on the window seat, staring outside.

On the evening of the third day, Marmee asked them how they were all feeling about their experiment.

There was silence for a moment, and then Jo exploded. "It's awful. I hate having nothing to do!"

The other girls agreed.

Marmee smiled at them all. "I knew you would feel that way," she said. "It's only by having work and chores that we truly enjoy our time off to play and dream. And now you have learned that for yourselves."

The girls agreed that they definitely had. They were all ready to throw themselves back into work, and Jo knew just what she was going to work on …

A few days later, Jo was writing in the attic, when she suddenly put down her pen.

"That's it, then," she said to herself.

She shuffled the paper into a stack and tied it with a red ribbon. Then, she slipped on her coat and hat, picked up the paper, and set off into town, without telling anyone where she was going. In town, she disappeared into some offices for an hour. When she came out, Laurie was across the street.

He hurried over. "Hello, Jo. What brings you to town?"

Jo looked flushed but proud as she replied. "I finished my book."

"Jo, that's splendid! Well done!" cried Laurie.

"Thank you," said Jo. "I took it to the newspaper offices. The editor says that they might print a couple of my stories next week. I won't tell the others yet, in case it doesn't happen."

Laurie was so proud of his friend, he felt that he might burst. They were very giggly when they got back from town, and nobody knew why they both took a sudden interest in reading the newspaper …

CHAPTER 5

Dark Days

One day, Jo was looking through the newspaper while her sisters sewed.

"There's a story here," Jo said, casually. "Shall I read it to you?"

"Go on, then," said Meg.

Jo cleared her throat. "The story is called *The Rival Painters.*"

The tale was about two painters who both loved the same woman. They competed for her by each trying to paint the most beautiful picture.

"What a wonderful love story!" Meg exclaimed at the end.

"I thought the painting parts were the best," said Amy.

Beth asked, "Who wrote it?"

Jo paused for a moment and blushed. "I did."

All of her sisters leaped up to hug her, and Marmee couldn't have been prouder.

Jo explained that she wouldn't be paid for this story because she was a beginner, but the newspaper would pay for the next one. One day, she hoped to make enough money to support herself and the girls.

"You have used your talents well," said Marmee. "Father will be pleased, Jo."

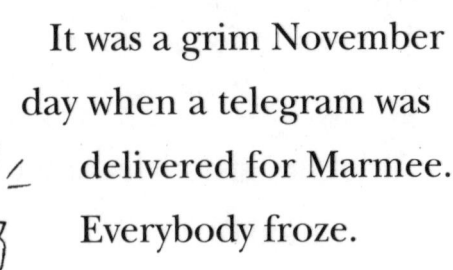

It was a grim November day when a telegram was delivered for Marmee. Everybody froze. Telegrams were only used for emergencies. Marmee opened it and then cried out in shock and sorrow. It read: *Mrs. March. Come at once. Your husband is in a hospital in Washington. He is very ill.*

All the girls broke down in tears, sobbing, and Marmee turned as white as a sheet.

Marmee asked Laurie to send a return telegram, saying she would come at once. She sent Jo to town to buy medicine and asked Meg and Amy to help her pack. She told Beth to go next door and ask

Mr. Laurence if he would watch over the girls while she was gone.

All the girls hurried to obey.

Beth returned from the Laurences' with Mr. Brooke, Laurie's tutor.

"Mr. Laurence has business in Washington that he wants me to see to," Mr. Brooke explained. "So, I thought we could travel together."

Marmee knew that Mr. Laurence didn't really have business in Washington, and Mr. Brooke was just coming to help her.

"Thank you so much," she smiled. "That is very kind of you."

Jo took a very long time to come back from town and Marmee was starting to worry when she walked in, still wearing her bonnet and cape.

Jo went straight to Marmee and put down a small roll of dollar bills. "Here, Marmee, this is for making Father better and bringing him home."

Mrs. March picked up the money. "This is twenty-five dollars, Jo! Wherever did you get such money?"

Jo's voice wobbled a little. "It's all mine. I didn't beg, borrow, or steal it, and I don't think you can be cross with me, for I sold something that was all mine."

As she spoke, she pulled off her bonnet. All of her beautiful long hair had been chopped off!

"JO!" her family cried. They all crowded

around asking why she had done such a thing. Jo's hair was beautiful, and she had been so proud of it.

"I wanted to do something to help Father," said Jo stoutly. "I was walking past the barbershop in town, and I saw that they bought hair, so I knew that was it. I don't regret it at all, if it helps Father."

Marmee hugged Jo. "You are a good girl," she whispered.

The next morning, the girls were tired and pale as they got up. They had all been too worried about Father to sleep much. When Marmee appeared from her room, it was obvious that she hadn't slept at all.

"We mustn't cry in front of Marmee," Meg whispered to her sisters. "We must be brave."

But it was hard. Amy's lips wobbled a few times during breakfast, and Jo had to leave the room.

Nobody was really eating anything anyway.

Soon, it was time for Marmee to leave. She hugged each of her daughters in turn, reminding them to be good and to visit the Hummel family for her while she was gone. Mr. Laurence had agreed to watch over the girls while Marmee was away. He and Laurie came out to wave as she left.

The girls gave Marmee their messages of love for Father. Then, Marmee climbed into the carriage with Mr. Brooke and set off. She turned back to wave at her girls and blow one last kiss.

The girls managed weak smiles until the carriage had rounded the corner, and then they all burst into tears and hugged each other for comfort.

The girls did their best to be good, like Marmee asked, but it was difficult when they were so worried about Father. They all did their chores, but Meg, Jo, and Amy didn't go to visit the Hummels once.

Faithful Beth visited every day, taking food. But she grew worried; the Hummels' baby was sick, and she didn't know what to do for it. Still, she would put on her little cape every day and trudge down the lane, trying to help.

One evening, Jo found her curled up on the floor next to Marmee's medicine cabinet, shivering.

"Why, Beth, what is the matter?" Jo cried.

"The baby had scarlet fever," Beth whimpered. "I think I have it too. I've taken some medicine. You and Meg both had it already, didn't you?"

"Yes," Jo said. "We had scarlet fever as children, so we won't get it again, but Amy hasn't had it. We'll have to send her to Aunt March's. Oh, this is all my fault! I should have gone to the Hummels, but I was too lazy! Well, I won't be too lazy to nurse you. Come on, Beth. Let's get you to bed."

CHAPTER 6

A New Dawn

Jo had hoped that Beth wouldn't have the fever badly, but she was bitterly disappointed. Beth got very sick. She couldn't eat or drink and drifted in and out of bad dreams. Half the time, she didn't even seem to know who Jo was.

To begin with, Jo was determined not to tell Marmee. She had to take care of Father, and it would be no good worrying her, when Beth would be better by the time she was home anyway. But Beth did not improve. If anything, she got worse.

One day, Jo slipped out of the darkened bedroom, with tears running down her face. Meg and Laurie were in the hall.

Jo took a deep breath. "I think we should send a message to Marmee. She needs to come back home because poor Beth is so sick. Laurie, could you go to town and send a message?"

Laurie blushed. "Actually, I already sent a telegram this morning. I talked to Grandfather, and he agreed that it was the right thing to do. I hope you don't mind."

Jo stared at him for a moment in disbelief. Then, she threw her arms around him. "Oh, thank you, Laurie, thank you! Marmee will know what to do."

Beth got worse and worse that night. In the dark, moonlit hours she lay so still, it almost looked like she was dead, except for the sweat on her face.

Jo never left her bedside. "Beth, please don't die," she whispered over and over again as she held Beth's hot little hand.

Nobody in the family slept that night. Not Meg, pacing up and down in the hallway. Not Amy, kneeling at the window at Aunt March's. Not Marmee, racing back home through the darkness. Not Father, left behind in Washington, getting better but still fragile. None of them could believe that the sweetest and kindest of them all might be taken so soon.

A lamp blazed all night in the Laurence house, too, as Laurie and his grandfather prayed for Beth.

Around dawn, Beth's fever seemed to break. Her face relaxed, and she breathed easily. The doctor arrived and said that she was getting better. Jo knelt down by the bed and said a prayer of thanks. The morning light shone through the window and down onto Beth. As Jo looked up, Marmee appeared in the doorway, and she knew all would be well.

Beth's recovery put everyone in the best mood for Christmas. She was still weak and had to be wrapped in blankets, carried from place to place. But she was talking and smiling again, bearing her illness with a cheerfulness that only she could have.

The morning of Christmas Day dawned bright and sunny. There had been fresh snow overnight, so everything gleamed pure white.

Marmee's present to Beth was a red dressing gown made of the softest wool. Beth immediately asked for it to be put on, and she looked like a festive elf! Then, Marmee carried her over to the

window to see
the rest of
her presents.

In the white
garden outside
stood a beautiful
snow sculpture
of a lady. She
was wearing a crown of holly and had
a bright new blanket draped around
her shoulders. In one hand, she held a
basket full of beautiful fruit and flowers.
In the other, she held a roll of piano
music. She looked so funny that Beth
laughed out loud!

Jo and Laurie sang Christmas carols
through the window. Then, they
presented Beth with each of their gifts,
and her laughter turned to tears of joy.

"I'm so full of happiness, if Father was here, I couldn't hold one drop more," said Beth, gazing around at all her beautiful gifts.

The other girls all agreed and knew that they were very lucky to have such wonderful presents and to spend a lovely day together.

Shortly after that, when Beth had gone to have her nap, Laurie stuck his head around the door. "Here's another present for the March family."

He stepped aside to reveal Mr. Brooke leading a tall man who was muffled up in scarves and overcoats.

"FATHER!"

There was a stampede as the entire family seemed to lose their minds at once and rushed toward Mr. March. He was invisible under all the hugs. Jo almost fainted from shock and happiness, while

Amy tripped over a footstool in her mad dash and ended up hugging Father's legs.

A little too late, Marmee said, "Hush now, we'll wake Beth."

But as she spoke, the study door was flung open, and they heard a shriek of excitement. Beth appeared in her little red dressing gown. With a strength she hadn't had in months, she ran straight into her father's arms.

Christmas dinner was the merriest anybody could ever remember. The Laurences and Mr. Brooke joined them, and Father and Beth sat in armchairs at the head of the table together. There was a delicious golden-brown turkey with all the trimmings and a plum pudding afterward.

They drank to each other's health, sang songs, and shared stories of their year. The girls and Laurie had planned to go on a sleigh ride, but they called it off. None of the March girls wanted to leave their father's side.

As dusk fell, the Laurences and Mr. Brooke went home, leaving the March family sitting by the fire.

"Do you remember, girls, a year ago we were all gathered around feeling miserable about Christmas without Father?" asked Jo.

"I do," said Meg, "but I think it's been quite a nice year overall."

"It's been a difficult one," said Amy.

"Yes, but now Father is home," said Beth, nuzzling into him.

Mr. March smiled around at his family. "It has been a difficult year at times for all of us, but I'm so proud of my girls. You are growing into fine young women."

The girls all sat up, their eyes shining.

"Really, Father?" Meg asked.

"Yes, my dear," he replied. "I see that you are not vain anymore, that Jo is becoming more ladylike, that Beth has been brave, and that Amy is not so proud. Nobody is perfect, but we must all work toward being better every day, and that is what you do." He smiled around at them all.

In that moment, the March sisters felt that their world was perfect. They gathered around the piano together and sang carols of joy far into the night.

Heidi

Retold by
Lisa Regan

Illustrated by
Joëlle Dreidemy

ARCTURUS

To my wonderful parents.
I love you so much.—LR.

To my dearest friend Aurore—JD.

ARCTURUS

This edition published in 2018 by Arcturus Publishing Limited
26/27 Bickels Yard, 151–153 Bermondsey Street,
London SE1 3HA

Copyright © Arcturus Holdings Limited

All rights reserved. No part of this publication may be reproduced, stored in a retrieval system, or transmitted, in any form or by any means, electronic, mechanical, photocopying, recording or otherwise, without written permission in accordance with the provisions of the Copyright Act 1956 (as amended). Any person or persons who do any unauthorised act in relation to this publication may be liable to criminal prosecution and civil claims for damages.

Writer: Lisa Regan
Illustrator: Joëlle Dreidemy
Designer: Jeni Child
Editor: Becca Clunes
Art Director: Jessica Crass

ISBN: 978-1-78828-684-8
CH006281NT
Supplier 24, Date 0618, Print run 7510

Printed in Malaysia

Contents

CHAPTER 1
Up the Mountain........................... page 4

CHAPTER 2
Several Visits................................ page 16

CHAPTER 3
New Things.................................. page 27

CHAPTER 4
A Ghost in the House.................. page 37

CHAPTER 5
Peter Goes to School..................... page 48

CHAPTER 6
Distant Friends............................ page 56

CHAPTER 1
Up the Mountain

There is a path at the foot of the mountains that winds through green meadows, past tall trees, and eventually leads the climber high into the summits, if he or she has enough breath in their lungs and energy in their legs to carry them so far.

It is on this path on a sunny morning in June that we find two figures. The first, a tall, strong-looking girl, leads the second by the hand. This character is no more than five years old, with dark curls and sunburnt skin, yet it is clear that her rosy cheeks are aglow.

It is no surprise her cheeks are alight, for this is Heidi, and she has been dressed in all the clothes she owns, despite the summer sun. The older girl is Dete, Heidi's aunt. She strides up the mountain path, barely pausing as a good-natured woman falls in step beside them.

"Is this the orphan child your sister left?"

"Yes," replied Dete. "I am taking her to stay with Uncle."

"Are you out of your senses, Dete? He will send you and your niece packing at once! He speaks to no one and will never agree to have someone live with him!"

"Nevertheless," huffed Dete, "he is her grandfather, and he must do his duty." And so, they carried on, up and up, until the little girl thought she might touch the clouds, they were so high. She ran ahead and watched for Dete to catch her up, and played happily with the goats that jumped and bleated in the grass.

As Heidi waited, she was startled by a shrill whistle. Looking about her, she spotted a thin, wiry boy marching through the mountain plants with a stick in his hand. Upon his call, the goats went hurtling in his direction, bumping and nudging his legs when they found him.

Heidi was just too hot for words. She perched on a rock and removed her clothes, until she stood only in her slip. Peter the goatherd smiled as he saw her fold the extra garments neatly, and then she climbed up next to him and asked him a thousand questions about the goats and the mountains.

Finally, Dete huffed alongside them. "Why are you undressed?" she shrieked.

"I don't want so many clothes," answered Heidi. "But I have kept them safe for you." And she pointed to the pile. Dete scooped them up and then pulled the little girl behind her.

They climbed for fifty minutes more. Eventually, they reached a small hut that stood on a rock, exposed to the winds and the sun. Behind it, the mountain rose steeply, and three old fir trees spread their shade over the roof of the dwelling.

The man that all the village called "Uncle" was sitting outside a hut, quietly looking out across the valley. Heidi walked up to him, smiling, and put out her hand. "Good evening, Grandfather," she said politely.

"Well, well," he said gruffly. "What is the meaning of all this?" and he gazed at Heidi from beneath long, bushy eyebrows. Heidi stared back at his overgrown beard and weathered face, unable to take her eyes off him.

Dete placed a hand on Heidi's back and began to explain why she needed his help. She had looked after the girl, she said, since Heidi's parents had both passed away, but she had recently been offered an excellent job in Germany, and she must take it. Now, it was Heidi's grandfather's time to take his turn, for she had surely done more than her share in caring for the little girl.

The old man seemed to grow more angry with every word Dete said. Eventually, he shooed her back down the mountainside, where the villagers were shocked that she had left a little girl with such a grumpy old man.

Meanwhile, Heidi had begun to explore her new home. She found a lean-to shed where the goats lived when they weren't out with Peter. She listened to the sound of the breeze in the fir trees and tipped her face to the sun. Then, she retraced her steps to where the old man sat by the front door of his hut.

"What is it you want?" he asked, not unkindly.

"I want to see inside," she replied, so he stood and ducked inside the small doorway.

"Bring your clothes," he reminded her.

"I shan't need them," she said. "I want to be like the goats, with their short coats and their thin, light legs."

Grandfather studied this peculiar little girl, then smiled. He placed her clothes in a neat bundle inside a cupboard. "You may need them in the winter," he explained. The cupboard contained almost everything he owned: a change of shirt, clean underclothes, and a few plates and glasses.

"You must be hungry?" he asked. Heidi had not begun to think of food, but the question made her aware that her stomach was very empty. Grandfather laid out bread and cheese, and pulled up a stool for Heidi to sit on. Before she sat, though, she helped him set the table.

Grandfather was happy with this bright, young thing. He poured her a bowl of fresh goat's milk, which she downed thirstily. "Why, that was the tastiest milk I ever drank!" she sighed, and she tucked in to her food.

"Grandfather," she asked, when both their plates were clean. "Where shall I sleep?" His eyes flicked around the tiny hut. "Where would you like to sleep?" he asked. At once, Heidi began to explore every nook and cranny.

She climbed up a tiny ladder to the hayloft. "This would be perfect!" she declared, "I will be able to look out of the window as I fall asleep." And so, the two of them smoothed out the hay and laid a blanket on top. Heidi piled up more hay for a pillow. It looked so enticing, she could hardly wait for night to come.

And so, Heidi began her new life with Grandfather in the mountains. Every day, she would drink goat's milk for breakfast and wait for Peter to trudge up the mountainside to add their goats to his grazing herd. She drank in the fresh, pine-scented air and the smell of the wild flowers. She petted the goats and laughed when they butted their small horns against her. Soon, she knew all their names, but Grandfather's two, called Little Bear and Little Swan, were the ones she loved the best. Before long, Grandfather trusted her enough to let her roam the mountains with Peter each day.

Heidi and Peter led the goats to the best places for them to eat fresh grasss. Heidi showed Peter how to use tasty herbs to lead the goats away from the rocky edges, where they might fall and harm their delicate bones. Grandfather always packed a large lunch for Heidi, which she shared with Peter, for she could never eat so much herself. Peter enjoyed the human company—and the lunch—and Heidi was happier than she could imagine. As the sun set each night, she gazed upon its fiery glory and then slept soundly in her little bed made of fresh hay.

CHAPTER 2
Several Visits

Summer began to fade, and the wind grew stronger, and Grandfather kept Heidi by his side on the gustiest days. He was afraid that such a tiny girl might be blown off the rocks. Instead, she stayed home and helped him make cheese, and she watched in awe as he fixed and mended and carved new furniture with all his carpenter's tools.

As winter crept in and the green of the mountains turned to white, Peter came less often. The goats huddled in their shed, and Heidi watched in excitement as thick flakes of snow drifted past the window.

On one such day, Heidi was startled by a thump at the door. Peter came in, covered in white, and Grandfather laughed as the heat began to thaw him out, and his clothing trickled like a waterfall.

"So, young General," said Grandfather. "Now that you have lost your army of goats, you must turn to your pen and pencil." Heidi was intrigued, and Grandfather explained. "During the winter, he must go to school. He needs to learn how to read and write, but it is tricky sometimes, am I right?"

Peter merely grunted, for he hated school. His face cheered, however, when Grandfather served him some food, for Peter's family was poor, and he was always hungry. As he finished chewing, he remembered a message.

"My grandmother would love for you to visit," he told Heidi. "As soon as the snow clears, of course," he added, seeing that Grandfather looked concerned. Heidi clapped her hands. "I cannot wait to meet your family!" she smiled.

Every day, Heidi pestered to be allowed to go down the mountain to Peter's home. Eventually, Grandfather gave in. He made Heidi dress in her warmest clothes and bundled up the little girl in a blanket. Then, they climbed onto a great wooden sleigh and set off down the mountain.

Heidi squealed with delight as they sped faster and faster down the slope. She felt as if she was flying like a bird! In no time at all, they were outside Peter's hut. Grandfather unloaded his wriggling cargo and reminded her that he would come back for her before darkness fell.

Heidi stepped from the bright sunlight into a room that seemed very dark. A woman sat at a table, mending a coat that belonged to Peter. "You must be Heidi," she said. "I am Brigitta, Peter's mother. And this is Grandmother."

Heidi walked slowly to where an old woman sat at a spinning wheel. The woman put out her hands and grasped for Heidi's smaller ones, and then she ran her fingers over Heidi's face and hair. "You take after your mother, dear girl," she said, and she patted for Heidi to sit down beside her.

Heidi's gaze fell on a window shutter that was broken and flapping in the wind. "Why, Grandfather could fix that in no time!" she exclaimed. "And any other things that need mending. He is so kind and so clever!"

The adults exchanged glances of surprise. No one ever spoke about Uncle in that way! "Ah, my child," said the old woman. "I can hear the shutter banging and loose pieces flapping on the roof, but I cannot see them, and Peter is unable to fix such things."

Heidi could not understand how Grandmother could not see them. "Maybe if you had more light in the house, you could see?" she asked. But Grandmother sighed and said it was always dark in her eyes, no matter how bright the sun or the snow on the ground.

"But surely you can see the fire when the sun goes down?" Heidi asked, and then she burst into tears when she found out that Grandmother would never witness another glorious sunset.

A thump outside the door announced Peter's arrival home. "How was school?" asked his mother, and Peter replied sullenly, "Fine."

Grandmother gave a sigh. "Still no breakthrough with your reading, then?" she queried, and Peter grunted. Heidi wondered aloud why Peter needed to learn to read.

Grandmother took Heidi's hand again. "I have an old book of prayers and hymns," she explained, "that used to give me such pleasure. But it is so long since I heard them that I can hardly remember them. I hoped that Peter would help, but it seems to be too difficult for him."

Another thump at the door told Heidi that it was time to go. She kissed the old lady and ran out to meet her grandfather, who scooped her up and carried her home. That night, Heidi made him promise to go back to Peter's hut and repair the things that were broken. She told herself that she would visit Grandmother as often as she could.

And so, the winter passed, and Heidi made an old lady very happy. The family told the villagers all of the tasks that Uncle had done for them, and gossip began to spread that maybe he wasn't such an old grump, after all.

As spring arrived, the girl and her grandfather received a visit of their own. It was the Pastor, a serious man dressed in black. He gave Heidi such a shock when he appeared outside, while she enjoyed feeling the faint sun on her skin and the new grass on her bare feet.

But Grandfather was not pleased to see him. It was the Pastor's view that Heidi herself was now old enough to go to school and should certainly go when the next winter came. He said that Grandfather was being neglectful by not allowing her to learn.

"She learns plenty that is useful here on the mountains with me!" Grandfather told him. "And besides, she will freeze if she has to trek to the village every day through the winter. Her mother was a sickly girl, and a sleepwalker besides. Who knows what it might do to the girl if she becomes unwell?"

"You are right," said the Pastor, "The walk to the school is too far from your mountain house. Why don't you move down into the village for the winter?"

Grandfather frowned. "No. I don't like people, and they don't like me."

And that was the end of it, as far as Grandfather was concerned. He loved Heidi but would care for her as he knew best. And that did not involve classrooms or books or reading and writing.

CHAPTER 3

New Things

Yet another visitor came to their door during that spring. Dete returned to take Heidi with her to Frankfurt. She had promised a rich family that Heidi would live with them as a companion to their sick daughter. Grandfather was not at all happy about the arrangement.

But Dete would not listen. "You will have everything you could wish for in their grand house!" she coaxed. But Heidi only wished for the mountains and the goats, the sunshine, and the chance to see Peter and Grandmother all the time.

Tears flowed down Heidi's cheeks as Dete led her down the mountainside. "Don't cry," said her aunt. "You will soon be able to come home and bring presents. Wouldn't Grandmother love some soft, white bread?"

Heidi knew that the hard, black bread was too tough for Grandmother, so she agreed that this was a good idea. She dried her eyes and hurried her steps, thinking that the sooner they arrived, the sooner she could find white bread and bring it back as a treat. And so, the little girl left her beloved mountain home and journeyed into the big city.

Heidi was shocked to see the house in Frankfurt. It was large, with many windows and a high roof, packed in between lots of other houses that looked much the same. Dete knocked on the grand front door, and a servant opened it. His name was Sebastian, and Heidi thought he looked very unfriendly.

He begrudgingly showed them into the hallway and left them alone. Heidi gazed at the ornate ceiling high above her. Then, a female servant, Tinette, appeared. "You had better follow me," she said curtly.

Heidi was shown into an elegant room, and Dete disappeared. A sickly looking girl lay there on the couch, covered in a blanket. She was some years older but so pale and thin that she hardly seemed any bigger than Heidi.

She introduced herself as Clara and smiled weakly at Heidi's presence. Then, her gaze crossed the room to where a strict, cross-looking woman sat. "That is our housekeeper, Miss Rottenmeier," said Clara. The lady, who was dressed all in black, looked at Heidi from head to toe.

"So," spoke Miss Rottenmeier, "you are Heidi, are you? What kind of a name is that?" Heidi began to speak, but the lady held up a hand to stop her. "How well can you read and write? What books did you have?"

"Oh, I cannot read or write," replied Heidi. "I never had a single book. And Peter says it is very difficult to learn," she added. Clara looked at her in surprise. She had never heard anyone talk like that to Miss Rottenmeier! She smiled to herself. She was very much looking forward to having Heidi as a friend.

Heidi was given her own bedroom, and she thanked Sebastian for showing her the way. "You look so much like Peter!" she exclaimed, and the shadow of a smile crossed his face. "Child!" scolded Miss Rottenmeier. "Do not talk to the servants as if they were your friends!"

The housekeeper listed a whole host of rules that Heidi could hardly understand, let alone remember. Eventually, she left Heidi alone on her new bed. It was much less comfortable than her hay bed back at home. The bedroom windows were large but covered by blinds. Heidi felt like a bird that had been plucked from the skies and locked into a cage.

Life in the great house was an adventure, with all sorts of new things to understand. Clara's tutor arrived each morning to teach Heidi her ABCs, despite Heidi's fear of such things. But Heidi was easily distracted by the ways of the city, jumping up each time she heard a carriage go past or a market trader shout in the distance.

Clara was having great fun watching her new companion. Her pale cheeks gained a rosy tint, and she laughed daily at Heidi's antics. Sebastian was cheered to see his little mistress look so well, and he seldom scowled at Heidi any longer.

Heidi left the house on several occasions, and each time, Miss Rottenmeier had to send out Tinette to find her. Once, Heidi thought she heard the sound of the fir trees and ran down the road to find them. Another day, she made friends with a ragged beggar boy who took her high up in the church tower to try and see the view. Tinette had to pay him, as Heidi had promised he would receive all the coins she could find if he would only help her.

Heidi's table manners were improving, for she was quick to learn. But one night, as they ate their soup, the silence was broken by a small "Meow!" from under Heidi's chair. "What on earth is that noise?" gasped Miss Rottenmeier. Heidi lifted her new pet onto her lap.

"Get it away! Filthy animal!" cried Miss Rottenmeier. "Meow meow!" they heard again, and Heidi produced six more kittens from beneath the table. "The man was going to get rid of them," she explained, "so I said we would look after them."
Miss Rottenmeier scrambled to her feet and rang the bell for Sebastian to take the kittens away.

Sebastian gave Heidi a hidden wink as he removed the seven kittens. Later, he showed her that he had tucked them safely in the kitchen and promised he would keep them out of sight when Miss Rottenmeier was prowling.

That same fierce lady called Heidi in front of her. "The only punishment I can think of for such a crime," she stated, "is to lock you in the cellar with the rats."

A cellar held no terror for Heidi. She had often gone into Grandfather's cellar, which had fresh milk, good cheese, and no rats. But Clara gasped. "Heidi did not mean to misbehave!" she exclaimed. "I will write to my father if you punish her." And so, Heidi escaped the gloom of the cellar, but it did not endear her to Miss Rottenmeier at all.

CHAPTER 4

A Ghost in the House

Clara's father, Mr. Sesemann, was often away on business, but when he came home, the mood in the house was brighter. He adored his daughter, and he was extremely happy to see the difference it made having Heidi as her friend.

"How are you getting along?" he asked Heidi, for his mind had been troubled by the tales that Miss Rottenmeier told him. Clara jumped in before Heidi could speak. "Oh, it is such fun now that Heidi is here! We have kittens, and games, and I am helping her learn her ABC."

Heidi was not so sure it was going well. She missed Grandfather and Peter, and she had been saving soft white rolls for weeks to take them back for Grandmother. She worried about the goats and missed the sight of the sun dropping behind the mountains each night.

One day, Miss Rottenmeier was putting Heidi's clean clothes in her cupboard, when she came across the bread rolls that Heidi had been setting aside. "What is the meaning of this?" she roared, then sent Tinette to find the girl.

Heidi began to explain, but Miss Rottenmeier cut her short. "I knew it! You are out of your mind!" she said unkindly and threw all of the bread rolls away. Heidi flung herself on the bed crying, until Clara became quite worried.

Eventually, she managed to calm the little girl, promising that she would get new, fresh rolls on the day that Heidi planned to visit her old home.

Miss Rottenmeier spoke to Clara's father. It was the last straw, she felt, hiding bread in the cupboard. The girl clearly had something wrong with her! But Mr. Sesemann felt otherwise.

Clara's father could see how much his daughter cared for Heidi, and he was insistent that she would be staying with them. "What is more," he stated, "I want her to be treated as an equal to Clara and looked after in every way. If she is too much for you alone," he added, "then soon, you will have extra help, for my mother is visiting next week and cannot wait to meet her."

Clara was exceedingly excited at the prospect of her grandmamma coming to stay. She told Heidi how kind and wise she was, and how she would love Heidi as much as Clara did.

Miss Rottenmeier spoke to Heidi about the visit. "You must not call her Grandmamma, but address her as Madam," she instructed. As the old lady walked up the front steps, Heidi remembered to do as she was told.

"Hello, sweet Heidi," said the lady in a very gentle voice.

"Hello, Mrs. Madam," said Heidi, trying to be polite, and everyone smiled.

"You can call me Grandmamma, just like Clara does," the lady said, and took Heidi's hand before they both pushed Clara's wheelchair into the study.

Clara's grandmother had brought presents for them all. Heidi's was a book to help with her reading, but as she turned the pages, tears sprang into her eyes. The pictures were of faraway places, from the high seas to eastern palaces, but a scene with a shepherd and his flock made Heidi feel very homesick.

She knew that Dete had hidden the truth and that she could not visit home whenever she liked. Oh, but she just wanted to see her old friends again!

Grandmother would be getting very old, and Grandfather must miss her help around the house.

Grandmamma stayed for many weeks, and Heidi's reading improved with her patience and help. But the kind lady could sense deep sadness in the little girl. Each morning, Heidi appeared at breakfast with red eyes, as if she had wept during the night.

Both Clara and Grandmamma tried to coax her to say what was wrong. But Heidi could not tell anyone, for she did not want to seem ungrateful. Eventually, Grandmamma's visit came to an end, and a sense of sadness settled over the whole house, which seemed empty without her.

Sadness was not the only emotion inside those walls. The servants muttered fearfully to each other about strange happenings that were spooking them all during the nighttime. Tinette locked her bedroom door each night. Even Miss Rottenmeier checked behind doors and kept away from dark corners and unused, empty rooms.

Each morning, the servants found the front door standing wide open. They all agreed there was a ghost in the house. They promised to keep it from Miss Clara, so that she would not be frightened and become unwell again, but they agreed that someone ought to stay awake one night to keep watch.

Sebastian was chosen to keep guard from the study next to the hall. His head drooped as midnight approached, but he stood and paced to keep himself awake. At last, in the small hours of the morning, he heard the front door creak and peeped outside his own open door.

His blood ran cold as he caught sight of a white figure standing at the top of the steps. He gulped and shook his head, and when he looked again, the figure had disappeared. The decision was made that Mr. Sesemann must be called home at once.

Clara's father returned the very next day, bringing with him his friend, the doctor. They spent some time deciding upon a course of action. That night, the pair of them waited to see what would happen. Yet again, the sound of the front door was their cue to look outside.

It was little surprise to the wise doctor to find Heidi on the doorstep. She stood in her white nightgown, looking up and down the street. Mr. Sesemann gently scooped her up and led her inside for the doctor to examine her. They had found their little ghost!

Heidi knew nothing about her wanderings at night, for she did it in her sleep. The doctor commented how pale and sad she seemed, though. "Are you in pain? Are you happy here in Frankfurt?"

Heidi gave a small sob. Miss Rottenmeier had told her not to cry all the time, but she could not lie and pretend to be happy. "I have no pain, but a heavy feeling here inside me. And I so wish I could see the mountains again." The doctor patted her hair and looked at his friend. They both knew what she needed to be well again.

CHAPTER 5

Peter Goes to School

It was quickly decided that the doctor would take Heidi home. Heidi's parting with Clara was full of mixed emotions. Heidi loved her friend and hated to leave her, but she needed to go. They hugged each other tightly, and Mr. Sesemann promised that he and Clara would visit when Clara was well enough.

Clara made sure that Heidi had a bag of soft, white rolls for Grandmother and sweet cakes for Peter and Grandfather. She waved goodbye with a heavy heart. She would miss her friend.

A change had come over Grandfather while Heidi was away. He had retreated into his hermit lifestyle and no longer saw anyone in the village. But his face lit up when the girl, now grown much bigger than when he last saw her, raced toward him and flung her arms around him.

Peter's family, too, had missed her terribly. Heidi was happy to give Grandmother the bread rolls and Peter's mother the fine hat she had worn in Frankfurt.

The doctor stayed in the village for just long enough to assure himself that Heidi was happy and recovering. He checked with her Grandfather that the sleepwalking had stopped.

The doctor, however, would not leave before he extracted a promise. "Spend the worst of the winter in the village," he warned. "For the cold in that hut will surely make Heidi ill. She is still quite frail," he advised.

Then, he said his goodbyes and left them, but not without sadness of his own. In the short time he had been there, he himself had fallen in love with the fresh mountain air and the sound of the songbirds. He could not wait to return with Clara and her father the following summer.

Heidi soon settled into her old ways, eating simply, sleeping soundly, and sharing her laughter with her dearest friends. Peter often gazed at her outline as she sped ahead of him into the sunshine, leading the goats to the best grazing ground.

Gradually, as nature would have it, the seasons changed, and the days grew colder. When the first snows fell and the ice froze in patterns like leaves on the windows, Grandfather packed up their belongings, and the pair of them moved down into the village.

Now Peter was not alone at school. Heidi dragged him to the classroom every day. He still did not think he could learn. "But Peter," she said. "If I can do it, so can you. And besides," she added naughtily, "I will tell Clara to stop sending cakes, if you do not begin to read soon."

Grandmother still loved to see Heidi, especially now that the girl could read to her from her hymn book. Her glassy eyes filled with tears as the words from her past flooded back. She squeezed Heidi's hands. "This is even better than white bread," she smiled gratefully.

Grandfather also loved to hear Heidi read, and they often sat in front of the fire together. He had patched up an old house in the village, which was too full of holes for anyone else to live in. The goats sheltered in a wooden shed, and Grandfather had even carried down Heidi's bed of hay and tucked it into a corner near the stove.

On some mornings, Heidi awoke and forgot where she was. A troubled feeling washed over her as she struggled out of bed to see if her windows had blinds again. And then, she heard the bleating of the goats and was happy once more.

The winter was long and hard, and Grandmother got sick. Heidi struggled through the snow to see her. She sent word to Clara for extra blankets and pillows to keep Grandmother warm and comfortable when she had to stay in bed.

The whole time, Grandmother did not complain. She thanked Heidi for her kindness and for keeping her soul strong with the readings from the hymn book. Heidi worried, though, for she could not visit when the weather was at its worst, and then Grandmother would not be able to hear the words she loved so much.

One evening, as Heidi sat on Grandmother's bed, and Brigitta sewed in the poor light by the fire, Peter burst into their home. "I can do it!" he cried.

"Do what?" asked his mother.

"Read," he answered, simply. And he picked up Grandmother's book and nervously began to say the words out loud. He made it through a whole hymn, and then Heidi jumped up and danced him around the room.

"Now, Grandmother can have a hymn every day, no matter whether I can come here or not!"

CHAPTER 6

Distant Friends

May had arrived, bringing its clear, warm days that tempted the flowers to show their faces. Heidi was back in her mountain home, singing happily and watching the insects as they hummed along with her.

Grandfather was extremely busy in his shed. He was making new chairs, for they were expecting important guests. "They look amazing!" exclaimed Heidi. "I can tell that one is for Grandmamma, and this one is for Clara. Oh," her face fell. "Is that one for Miss Rottenmeier? Do you think she will come?"

Peter called at that very moment, dropping the goats on his way home. He looked at the chairs and scowled.

"Oh, Peter," coaxed Heidi. "Don't worry, they are lovely people! They will love you as much as I do!" She did not tell him about Miss Rottenmeier, for she was secretly hoping that a mountain trip might be too much for the housekeeper.

But Peter and his Grandmother had secret thoughts of their own. Both were just a little bit afraid that the visitors might want to take Heidi back to the city with them when they left.

The family from Frankfurt made a strange procession when they arrived. First came two men carrying Clara in a chair. Then, another man pushed her empty wheelchair. Grandmamma rode behind them on a horse. Heidi nervously looked to see if Miss Rottenmeier was there but could not see her. Instead, she glimpsed the doctor, striding out at the back.

"Here they come!" she yelled, "and the doctor, too!" She hugged her friend, whose eyes flitted all around her, trying to take in the many sights that spread before them.

Heidi was now strong enough to push Clara around in her wheelchair, although Grandfather had other ideas. He and Peter helped Clara to her feet for a minute. At first, it hurt her legs, but gradually, she managed a little longer each day.

Clara's health improved in every aspect. Her appetite grew, her cheeks glowed, and she slept more soundly than she had ever slept in her big Frankfurt bed. She no longer trekked back down the mountain each evening, for Grandfather had convinced the doctor to let her stay in a bed that he made himself, beneath Heidi's hayloft.

Heidi took good care of her dear friend and would not leave her side. Peter tried to tempt her to the highest pastures with the goats, but Heidi said she could not. Instead, she spoke to Peter every evening, when he returned with Little Swan and Little Bear. She and Clara asked him about his days, but he barely replied. He mostly muttered, "Good evening," and continued quickly on his way.

Heidi dearly wanted to go to the highest ground, for she wanted to show Clara how beautiful it was. "Soon, you will see it for yourself," she promised.

Clara's legs grew stronger day by day, and the girls persuaded Grandfather that she was well enough to leave the hut. The old man lifted her gently from her wheelchair and strode up the mountainside as if she weighed no more than Little Swan. She beamed the whole way, until Grandfather set her down on a ledge with a view all around.

Peter was much less happy. As he strode past the hut, wishing that Clara had never come to stay, he noticed the wheelchair outside. Before he even knew what he was doing, he gave it a hard shove and sent it rocketing down the slope.

The party returned to the hut to find the chair gone and the shed door blowing in the wind. "If the chair has blown down the mountain, it will be in a hundred pieces by now," said Grandfather. He looked across to where Peter stood with the goats, hanging his head. "We must tell Mr. Sesemann what has happened."

Clara's father was planning to visit, and so they sent a message that he should bring a new chair with him. As it happened, the message did not reach him. Clara's father and grandmamma were already in the village below. It had always been their plan to visit early.

Poor Peter was certain that Grandfather knew what he had done. So, when Mr. Sesemann came striding up the mountain, the guilty boy hid behind the hut.

Of course, everyone was shocked to see them. But Clara had a surprise of her own. As her father finished greeting them all, she stood and took a few steps toward him. His eyes filled with tears, and then he turned to Grandfather. "I have heard how well you treat these girls," he said. "I am indebted to you."

"Well, Peter played his part, too," said Grandfather, with a wry smile.

Grandmamma had arrived in time to see Clara walk. She beckoned to the goatherd. "We owe you all so much," she said. "First, we took your beloved Heidi away from you. Now, you have helped our darling Clara to get well again. I know you do not want riches and city life, but will you accept our help for your families, in return for everything you have done for us?"

Peter did not know what to say, so Heidi spoke on his behalf. "As long as the help includes bread and cake, I think that will make everyone happy!"

Peter Pan

Retold by
Saviour Pirotta

Illustrated by
Mel Howells

ARCTURUS

For Jessie Paton—SP.

For Von, Boo & Sylvia—MH.

ARCTURUS

This edition published in 2018 by Arcturus Publishing Limited
26/27 Bickels Yard, 151–153 Bermondsey Street,
London SE1 3HA

Copyright © Arcturus Holdings Limited

All rights reserved. No part of this publication may be reproduced, stored in a retrieval system, or transmitted, in any form or by any means, electronic, mechanical, photocopying, recording or otherwise, without written permission in accordance with the provisions of the Copyright Act 1956 (as amended). Any person or persons who do any unauthorised act in relation to this publication may be liable to criminal prosecution and civil claims for damages.

Writer: Saviour Pirotta
Illustrator: Mel Howells
Designer: Jeni Child
Editor: Sebastian Rydberg
Art Director: Jessica Crass

ISBN: 978-1-78828-687-9
CH006278NT
Supplier 24, Date 0618, Print run 7513

Printed in Malaysia

Contents

CHAPTER 1
Peter Pan and the Shadow 4

CHAPTER 2
Off to Neverland 14

CHAPTER 3
Mermaids in the Sea 24

CHAPTER 4
You're a Codfish! 34

CHAPTER 5
I Believe in Fairies 44

CHAPTER 6
The Journey Home 54

CHAPTER 1

Peter Pan and the Shadow

The Darlings lived in London. There was Wendy, the eldest, then John, and youngest of all, Michael. Their nanny was a Newfoundland dog named Nana. She was just as good a nanny as a human one, but Mr. Darling, the children's father, worried about what other people might think. He worked in a bank, and people who work in banks worry about what people think of them.

Mrs. Darling was very good at reading bedtime stories. One night, she was reading Wendy and the boys an adventure, when Wendy pointed to the window.

"Oh, look, there's Peter Pan! He's come to listen to the story."

"Who is Peter Pan?" asked Mrs. Darling.

"He's a boy who never grew up," replied Wendy.

"He can fly," said John.

"He doesn't have a mother to read him stories," added Michael.

Mrs. Darling looked at the window but could see no one. She remembered believing in a boy who could fly, too, when she was Wendy's age. He lived with the fairies in a place called Neverland.

Now that she was a grown-up, Mrs. Darling did not believe in Peter Pan any longer. Fairy tales are only for children, after all.

After the children went to bed, Mrs. Darling stayed in the nursery, darning socks.

Suddenly, the nursery window blew open. A boy dropped on the carpet. A bright light followed him, zipping around the room.

Mrs. Darling knew at once that the boy was Peter Pan. He had a coat made of autumn leaves. His eyes were bright and full of mischief.

Nana rushed into the room, growling. The boy sprang back to the window. He managed to get out, but Nana slammed the window shut, trapping his shadow inside.

Mrs. Darling rolled it up and put it in a drawer. A few days later, Mr. and Mrs. Darling went out to a party. The children were asleep. Once again, the nursery window flew open. Peter Pan swooped in. "Well, Tink, have you found my shadow?"

The bright light Mrs. Darling had seen flew into the room. It was really a fairy named Tinker Bell. She looked around the room, then pointed to a drawer. Peter Pan opened it. "Ha, here's my shadow. Now, all I have to do is stick it back on again. But how shall I do that?"

"I'll sew it on for you," offered Wendy. Tinker Bell's bright light had woken her up. She fetched the sewing box.

Wendy carefully stitched the shadow onto Peter's heels. "There, it's done!"

"What is your name?" asked Peter.

"I'm Wendy Darling."

"Thank you very much for sewing my shadow on, Wendy," said Peter. "Here's a gift as a thank you." He pulled an acorn button off his coat and gave it to her.

"It's very pretty. Thank you," said Wendy. She threaded the acorn on a chain and hung it around her neck. "I ought to give you a kiss in return."

"A kiss?" said Peter. "What's that?"

Wendy gave him a thimble out of the sewing box. "This is a kiss. May I know your name?"

Of course, Wendy knew already who the boy was. She just thought it polite to ask.

"My name is Peter Pan," said the boy.

There was a tinkle behind him. Peter had accidentally trapped Tinker Bell in the drawer when he found his shadow. He opened it, and Tinker Bell shot straight out. Her light changed from yellow to red as she hovered in the air. She was very angry. She was Peter's best friend, but he had never given her a present.

"This is Tinker Bell," said Peter. Tinker Bell folded her hands across her chest to show that she didn't want to shake hands with Wendy.

"Tink and I live in Neverland with all the Lost Boys," said Peter. "They are children who fell out of their buggies when they were babies. They have no mother to look after them, so they came to live in Neverland. I am their captain."

"They don't have a mother?"

"None of the boys in Neverland do. Not even me. There's no one to tell us bedtime stories."

"Oh, the wonderful stories I could tell you!" cried Wendy.

"Come to Neverland," said Peter Pan. "You could be our mother."

"I'd love to, but I can't leave John and Michael," said Wendy.

"We'll take them with us," said Peter.

Wendy woke up John and Michael, who were delighted to see Peter.

"But none of us can fly," said Wendy.

"All you have to do is think happy thoughts," said Peter. "They'll make you fly."

Tinker Bell shook her wings and stuck out her tongue rudely. "She's saying you need fairy dust to fly, too," said Peter.

He opened a little bag and sprinkled the fairy dust on the children's feet. They flapped their arms and rose in the air. "Follow me," said Peter. And the three of them swooped out the window after him.

It was wonderful flying through the air like birds.

"I can see the street below," said Wendy.

"And the street lamp," said John.

"And look, there's Nana tidying up her kennel," cried Michael. "Hello, Nana. Goodbye, Nana."

Nana looked up and saw the children darting around overhead. For a moment, she thought she was dreaming. Then, she spotted Tinker Bell's light leaping out of the window behind the children's.

Peter's shadow fell across her face. Then, she knew that she was awake.

Nana barked fiercely. She bounded down the street to find Mr. and Mrs. Darling. Mrs. Darling heard her at once. She and Mr. Darling left the party. They raced down the street and up the stairs to the nursery.

But it was too late. The children's beds were empty. Peter's shadow was gone from the drawer. Mrs. Darling looked out of the window. She could see her children tumbling in the sky after Peter.

"Come back at once," called Mr. Darling. "Come back, or I shall be very cross."

"It's useless shouting, George dear. They are too far off to hear us already," cried Mrs. Darling. "Oh, George. We've lost them! Peter Pan has taken them away to Neverland."

CHAPTER 2
Off to Neverland

"How do we get to Neverland?" Wendy asked Peter, as they flew through the night sky.

Peter nodded at the stars. "Second to the right and straight on till morning."

The children followed Peter, delighted to be so high up in the sky. They could see London far below them, then countryside. Soon, they were flying over the sea. When they got hungry, Peter snatched crusts of bread from the beaks of passing birds.

After what seemed like ages, they spotted an island far below them. It shimmered like a diamond in the morning light.

"That's Neverland," said Peter proudly.

The children saw a blue lagoon. A pirate ship was in another bay across the island.

On a headland, they could see wigwams.

"The Natives live there," explained Peter.

The nearby woods was full of wild animals. John spied a tiger, Michael a bear.

"They're dangerous," warned Peter, "but not as dangerous as Captain Hook. He and his crew are always looking for me. He's never forgiven me for chopping off his hand. He wears a hook now. I daresay he'll want to capture you, too. You must keep away from him. If we ever run into him, let me deal with him."

Tinker Bell caught up with Peter, her wings flashing. She tinkled loudly.

"She's saying Captain Hook is getting Long Tom ready," said Peter. "He's spotted Tinker Bell's golden light. Captain Hook hates fairies."

"Long Tom?" said John.

"That's what he calls the ship's cannon," replied Peter.

"Tink had better put out her light," said Wendy.

Tinker Bell tinkled angrily and shook her head.

"She can't put out her light unless she goes to sleep," explained Peter, "and she can't fly while she's sleeping."

"Tink can hide inside my top hat," said John. "Wendy will carry it.'

Everyone thought that was a good idea except Tinker Bell. Still, the others made her get in. Not that it made much difference. There was a loud boom, and a cannonball came hurtling at the children.

The blast carried Peter Pan out to sea. John and Michael were sent spinning through the air. Wendy, still carrying Tinker Bell in the top hat, was blown high up into the clouds.

Tinker Bell laughed inside the top hat. At last, Wendy had become separated from the others. Now, Tinker Bell had her to herself. And she knew exactly what to do to get rid of her.

Far below, Neverland was teeming with a flurry of activity.

The Lost Boys had seen the cannonball blasting Peter out of the sky. They tramped through the jungle to see where he landed. There were six Lost Boys: Tootles, Nibs, Slightly, Curly, and the twins.

The pirates were also on the move. They were looking for the Lost Boys, hoping they would lead them to Peter. What a fierce-looking bunch they were!

Cecco the Italian, Bill Jukes, who was covered in tattoos, Cookson, Gentleman Starkey, Skylights, and Smee, the bosun. Captain Hook came last of all. He was dressed like a king, except he had a pirate hat instead of a crown. Hook was afraid of nothing except his own blood, which was a disgusting muddy brown. He smoked two cigars at the same time and would kick anyone who spoke to him without permission.

Following the pirates through the long grass were the Natives. Friends of Peter, they wanted to stop the pirates from getting the Lost Boys. Their chief was a proud man named Great Big Little Panther. His daughter, Tiger Lily, was a true princess. She was fearless and a great friend of Peter's.

"Have you seen Peter?" asked Great Big Little Panther.

"No," said Tiger Lily. "We must press on!"

Tick-tick-tick! Following the Natives was a crocodile. You could hear it ticking because it had once swallowed a clock. It had also swallowed Captain Hook's hand when Peter chopped it off. Now, it wanted the rest of the captain.

The Lost Boys came to their home, a secret underground cave. They decided to have a rest before continuing their search. The pirates stopped for a rest, too. Hook sat on a giant mushroom.

"Smee," he yelled, jumping up. "This mushroom is HOT. It singed my bottom."

Hook had sat on the Lost Boys'

chimney, which the boys stopped up with a mushroom whenever they went out. Smee kicked it aside. Now, he and Hook could hear the Lost Boys chatting in the cave.

"Ha," grinned Hook. "We've got the rascals at last."

But just then, he heard an awful noise. Tick. Tick. Tick.

"It's that dastardly crocodile," he cried. And he dashed away into the forest.

The Lost Boys heard Smee kicking the mushroom aside. They came out to investigate. There was no sign of Hook and the pirates. They had all run away in the blink of an eye.

All the boys could see was Tinker Bell swooping down from the sky. She was followed by a girl carrying a top hat.

"It's not a girl," called Tinker Bell, "it's a dangerous Wendybird. Shoot it, quick. Peter would want you to."

Tootles fitted an arrow in his bow. "Out of the way, Tink," he said. He fired, and Wendy fluttered to the ground.

Tootle's arrow had shot her straight in the heart.

The Lost Boys crowded around the Wendybird.

"Why, she's not a bird," gasped Curly. "She's a lady."

Tootles went as white as a sheet.

"A woman," whispered Nibs. "And we've killed her."

"Peter was bringing her to look after us," said the twins. "She was going to be our mother."

Tootles started shaking with fear. What would Peter say when he found out that he, Tootles, had killed the Lost Boys' new mother? He started edging away into the forest. Peter was sure to be angry with him.

Suddenly, the Lost Boys heard a whooping call up in the air. Peter had arrived. He dropped to the ground in one neat movement.

"No welcome home for me, then, boys?" he said. "Don't look so glum. I have brought you a mother."

CHAPTER 3

Mermaids in the Sea

"Tootles shot the lady!" cried Nibs. "Shot her straight through her mother-heart."

"It wasn't my fault. Tink told me to do it," called Tootles from the edge of the trees. "She said it was a dangerous Wendybird, Peter. You'd be pleased if we shot it."

Tinker Bell was hovering in the air above the Lost Boys. She stuck her tongue out at Tootles. "Traitor…"

"Hey, look everyone," cried Nibs. "The dead lady moved her arm."

"Then she isn't dead," said Peter. "She's still alive. Look, Tootles's arrow got stuck in the acorn button I gave her. What a piece of good luck she wore it around her neck."

There was a mournful tinkle in the air. Tinker Bell was annoyed because Wendy was not dead. "You should be ashamed of yourself, Tink," said Peter. "I told you not to be jealous. Now, go away. I never want to see you again."

Wendy fluttered her hand.

"Wendy forgives you, Tink," said Peter. "Don't go away forever. Just a week."

Now that the Lost Boys knew Wendy was alive, they were eager to get her indoors. But they were afraid the damp in the cave would not make her get better.

Wendy started singing without opening her eyes:

I wish I had a pretty house,
The littlest ever seen.
With funny little red walls
And roof of mossy green.

"You heard her!" said Peter. "She wants her very own house. Quick, let's get to it."

The boys chopped wood and fetched moss and branches they found on the jungle floor. They built the house around Wendy. As they worked, they sang too:

Oh, really, next, I think I'll have
Gay windows all about,
With roses peeping in, you know,
And babies peeping out.

Before long, the little house was finished. Soon, Wendy opened her eyes and cried out in delight. She was snug inside the house of her dreams. The walls were a rusty red, just like she wanted. The carpet was green moss.

"It's a mighty fine house," cheered Tootles.

"There's only one thing missing," replied Peter. "The house needs a chimney."

He found John's top hat, which Wendy had dropped. With a blow of his fist, he knocked the top off. And that made the perfect chimney.

Just then, John and Michael arrived. They saw a smiling Wendy peeping through the door.

John and Michael were given bunks
in the Lost Boys' cave. It was very snug in
there. Wendy loved telling them all bedtime
stories. She cooked them tasty meals and
darned their socks while they were asleep.

While she worked alone, she often
thought of home. She knew her parents
were missing her and John and Michael.
Mother would leave the window open for
the day the children got back.

Wendy knew she must return home one day. She would grow up and become a real mother in the real world. But for now, she had to look after Peter and the Lost Boys.

One morning, Peter took Wendy and all the boys swimming in Mermaid Lagoon. A lot of mermaids lived there. They were very rude and refused to talk to anyone except Peter. They sat on a large, dark rock and combed their hair with beautiful combs made from seashells.

"That rock is called Marooners' Rock," Peter said to Wendy, John, and Michael. "The pirates maroon their victims on it. They tie them up so they cannot swim away. When the tide rises, the poor victims drown."

A huge bird floated past the children on a twiggy nest. It was humming gently to itself.

"That's the Neverbird," said Peter. "It built its nest in a tree, but the wind blew it into the sea. Now, the Neverbird floats around on her nest. She won't let go of her eggs."

"She is a good mother," said Wendy.

After their swim, the boys had a picnic on Marooners' Rock. They roasted a wild boar. Tootles and Curly offered some to the mermaids, but they turned away in disgust.

Mermaids eat only fish and seaweed.

The boys had a story and then fell asleep in the sun. Wendy started to knit. She was making scarves for when the winter came.

While she knitted, the sky grew dark. Waves rippled across the lagoon. It became cold.

Wendy heard the splashing of oars. "Peter," she whispered.

Peter sat up at once. "It's a pirate boat," he whispered.

He woke up the other boys, and they all dived into the sea to hide. The mermaids followed them.

By the time the pirates arrived in their boat, there was no one left on Marooners' Rock. Smee and Starkey clambered ashore. They had a prisoner with them. It was Tiger Lily!

The pirates lashed Tiger Lily to a wooden post. "This will teach you to try and board our ship," tittered Smee.

"You Natives will never catch Hook," added Starkey.

"They sure won't," boomed out a voice. "HA-HA-HA!" It sounded just like Hook.

"It's the captain," said Smee, peering around. "But I can't see him. Where is he?"

"He must be hiding to eavesdrop on us," whispered Starkey. "He wants to make sure that we do our job properly."

"Set the Native free. At once!" ordered Hook's voice.

"But—" said Smee. His knees were knocking together, and his teeth were rattling in his mouth.

"RIGHT AWAY, I tell you," repeated Hook.

The pirates cut Tiger Lily free. She dived into the water at once and swam away.

"Well done, lubbers," boomed Hook's voice. "Ha-ha-ha!"

It wasn't really Hook, of course. It was Peter, hiding with Wendy behind a nearby rock in the water, pretending to be Hook.

"You are so clever, Peter," said Wendy.

Then, she spotted someone in the water—someone in a pirate hat. It was the real Captain Hook. He was swimming toward Marooners' Rock.

CHAPTER 4

You're a Codfish!

Hook clambered ashore. He looked very glum. "I've been thinking, men. The game is up. We'll never catch the Lost Boys, now that they have a mother."

"What's a mother?" asked Smee.

Hook pointed to the Neverbird on her nest. "It's someone who never deserts you."

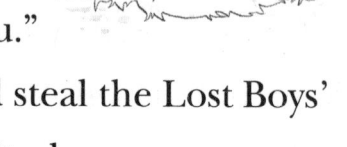

"Perhaps we could steal the Lost Boys' mother," suggested Starkey.

"A capital idea," exclaimed Hook. "We'll catch the Lost Boys and make them walk the plank. Then, we'll keep that Wendy girl for a mother."

These last words made Wendy gasp.

"What was that?" snapped Smee.

The pirates listened, but they heard nothing else. "It must have been a fish."

Suddenly, Hook looked around him. "Men, where is Tiger Lily?"

"You told us to let her go," said Starkey.

"By the point of my hook, I did no such thing," roared the captain.

"But you did," insisted Smee. "We heard your voice loud and clear."

Hook's face turned purple with rage. "Brimstone and gall, I gave no such order."

"This lagoon must be haunted," said Starkey. "Because we heard a voice from the water."

"Spirit that haunts this dark lagoon," Hook cried, "do you hear me?"

Hook sounded scared, which pleased Peter. "Odds, bobs, hammer and tongs, I hear you," Peter called in a spooky voice.

Smee and Starkey grabbed each other in fright.

"Who are you, stranger?" called out Hook, trying to sound brave.

"Captain James Hook," came the reply.

Hook turned pale. "You are not."

"Brimstone and gall," repeated the ghostly voice, "Argue with me again, and I'll put my anchor through you."

Hook was shaking now. "If you are Captain James Hook, then who am I?"

There was silence for a moment. "Why—you're a … codfish."

Hook's fear turned to anger. Someone was playing a trick on him. And he knew exactly who it might be …

"Spirit," he called. "Are you a man?"

"No ..."

"Are you a clever, wonderful boy?"

"Yes, I am clever. I am Peter Pan."

Hook leaped to his feet. "Get him, men!"

Peter shouted out across the water.

"Attack!" The Lost Boys pounced on Smee and Starkey. They soon had them tied up. Peter climbed ashore to face Hook. He whipped out his wooden sword. Just then, Hook slipped on some seaweed. Without thinking, Peter leaned over to help him.

The pirate sank his sharp hook into Peter's shoulder.

"Ouch!" Peter fell to the ground, clutching his shoulder. Hook leaped to his feet. The tide was rising, so the pirate struck out back to his ship. He could see the other children and Wendy swimming toward the shores of Mermaid Lagoon.

But he knew he would never see Peter Pan alive again. The boy was too wounded to swim. He would drown.

The tide rose higher and higher. Soon, there was hardly any of Marooners' Rock above the water. Peter looked up at the stars. He was trying very hard not to be scared. "Death will be an awfully big adventure," he thought.

Then, he felt something brushing against his leg. The Neverbird's nest, floating on the water. He climbed aboard.

There was a lot of cheering when Peter stumbled into the secret cave that night. Even Tiger Lily and the Natives came around to celebrate with them.

"You saved my daughter's life," said Chief Little Big White Panther. "We shall call you Peter the Great."

"And we promise to protect you from the pirates forever," added Tiger Lily. Peter's wounded shoulder healed. He was soon up and about, helping the Lost Boys to hunt for nuts in the woods.

Wendy told the Lost Boys about the afternoon teas she used to have at home. The boys were very taken with the idea. They started having make-believe teas.

Wendy would tell them stories while they pretended to sip tea out of gourds. Peter never joined in this game. He thought it was a bit too much like the real world.

"Tells us a story about your family," the boys asked Wendy one day.

"Once there was a girl," began Wendy,

"who lived with her family in London. One night, she and her brothers flew away to a place called Neverland. The parents were very sad, but the mother knew that they would come back one day. She kept the window open to welcome them home. You see, mothers always keep a window open should their children fly away."

Suddenly, there was a voice at the door. "Not all mothers." It was Peter. He had come back home. "Once there was a boy who thought his mother would always keep a window open for him, too. So, he flew away and had a grand old time for moons and moons. But when he returned home, the window was shut."

"There was another boy in his bed."

"Oh, Peter," cried Wendy. "I hope it wasn't you! *Was* the boy you?"

Peter nodded.

John and Michael both turned to Wendy at once. "Oh, what if Mother forgets us, Wendy? What if she closes the window? Oh, do let's go back home!"

"Yes, we must," said Wendy. "At once! And we'll take the Lost Boys with us. Mother and Father will adopt them. We'll live as one big happy family, and they'll have a grown-up mother at last."

She turned to Peter. "Won't you come with us, Peter? Our mother tells wonderful stories."

"Never," replied Peter firmly. "Your folks will make me grow up. I want to be a boy forever. But I shall not keep you in Neverland against your will. I shall ask the Natives to show you the way through the jungle. And Tinker Bell will guide you home when you are flying. I'm sure she'll be happy to have me all to herself again."

Just then, they heard whoops and screams above the cave. John and Michael grabbed Peter.

"It's Captain Hook and the pirates," they cried. "They've attacked the Natives on guard outside our cave. Oh, Peter, save us!"

CHAPTER 5

I Believe in Fairies

"Hush," said Curly. "I can hear the Natives whooping a war cry and the pirates calling out to each other."

Above the cave, a fierce battle was taking place. The pirates had crept up on the Natives unawares. But the Natives were a fierce people. They fought back bravely, twirling their tomahawks and leaping from one pirate to another. Tiger

Lily was especially brave. Peter Pan had saved her from certain death. Now, she was determined to save him. Her father fought beside her, growling fiercely.

Below in their cave, Wendy and the Lost Boys heard the sounds of the battle grow fainter and fainter.

At last, there was the sound of beating tom-toms. John and Michael heard loud whooping sounds.

They looked at Peter with joy in their eyes. "That means the Natives won, didn't they?" said John. "They've chased Hook and his men away. We're saved."

But the Natives hadn't won. The pirates had taken them all prisoner. The sounds of Native victory were only a dirty trick. Smee was beating the tom-toms. Captain Hook was whooping to fool the Lost Boys.

One by one, the boys climbed out of the cave. And one by one, they were captured. The pirates trussed them up like chickens, so they couldn't run away.

Captain Hook grabbed John, Michael, and Wendy himself.

"Bundle them into that stupid Wendy house," he roared.

Smee and three of the men pushed the children into the Wendy house and tied them up. It was a tight squeeze in there, and the children could hardly breathe.

"Peter will get you for this," cried John.

"Yes," shouted Michael. "He will feed you to the crocodile."

"Alas, Peter Pan is no more," said Hook. "I left him to die on Marooners' Rock. No one can save you now, boys."

Hook frowned at the pirates. "Take them to the ship. Make them walk the plank!"

Four of the pirates raised the Wendy house to their shoulders and set off. The other pirates followed with the Lost Boys.

Hook was about to follow when he heard a familiar sound. It sounded like someone snoring. It sounded like Peter Pan snoring. But that couldn't be. Hook thought his ears were playing tricks on him. Peter Pan was dead.

Hook slipped down the tunnel to the Lost Boys' cave. He couldn't get into the cave itself because there was a gate at the bottom of the tunnel. It was locked.

He peered through the bars to see Peter Pan lying on a bed. Hook was furious. How had the boy escaped death?

Then, Hook spied a medicine bottle on a table nearby. Carefully, he reached through the bars and picked it up with his hook. When it was close enough, he took a small vial from his pocket. Carefully, he poured three drops of poison in Peter's medicine bottle.

Then, he put it back in place.

Hook rubbed his hands with glee as he hurried out of the tunnel. "Drink, my boy," he sniggered. "Drink your medicine and die."

In the cave, Peter was woken up by a bright light zipping around his head. "Tink, what's the matter?"

"The pirates have captured Wendy and the boys."

Peter leaped out of bed at once. "Then we must rescue them."

He sneezed loudly and spied the medicine bottle on the table. "Wendy was right. I am getting a cold. I should drink some of this before we go."

"Don't!" shouted Tinker Bell. "I heard Hook talking to himself in the jungle. He put poison in your medicine."

"Nonsense," laughed Peter. "Hook couldn't reach the bottle. The gate was locked." He raised the bottle to his lips.

"Please, don't." Suddenly, Tinker Bell swooped between Peter and his cup. She swallowed the poison herself. Instantly, her bright light started to fade. She clutched her tummy.

"Tink, what's the matter?" cried Peter.

"I told you," whispered the fairy. "The medicine was poisoned. Now, I am going to die."

"Oh, Tinker Bell," said Peter. "You saved my life."

The fairy did not reply. Her light grew even fainter. Her wings fluttered weakly, and she plummeted onto Peter's bed.

"Tink," cried Peter. "What can I do to save you?"

"If more children believed in fairies," mumbled Tinker Bell, "I might get better." And then she lay quite still.

Peter thought of all the children dreaming of Neverland. He spoke to them in their dreams. "If you believe in fairies, clap your hands."

There was a silence that seemed to last forever. Then, Peter heard the faint sound of clapping, coming all the way from the real world. It got stronger and louder till the cave was echoing with the noise.

Tinker Bell moved and opened her eyes. Children still believed in fairies, after all. She was saved.

"Time to rescue Wendy," cried Peter. "But first, I must find that crocodile …"

Aboard the *Jolly Roger*, the pirates had tied the children to the mast.

"Join my crew, boys," roared Hook. "All you have to do is say, 'Down with the king!'"

"We'd rather stay loyal to the king," said Michael. "Is that right, boys?" He looked around, and everyone nodded.

Hook sniggered. "Then you shall walk the plank."

"Be brave, boys," called Wendy.

Smee and Starkey dragged Michael toward the plank. "Say your prayers, boy. You will be the first to go."

Just then, they heard that awful sound.

Tick-tick-tick. "It's that crocodile." Captain Hook fell to his knees. "It's coming on board."

Michael, standing on the edge of the plank, tried not to laugh. He could see right down into the water. It wasn't the crocodile making that ticking sound. It was Peter pretending to be the crocodile.

He was climbing up the side of the ship. The real crocodile was in the water behind him, not making a sound. The clock in its tummy had run down at last!

CHAPTER 6
The Journey Home

Peter slipped like a shadow into Hook's cabin. He picked the lock on the weapons cupboard. Then, he blew out the lamp …

Now that the ticking had stopped, Hook found his courage again. "I shall teach these rude boys to laugh at me," he growled. "Jukes, fetch the whip from my cabin."

Jukes ran below deck. Almost at once, there was a blood-curdling scream. Jukes tottered back on deck and collapsed. He'd been run through with a sword.

Hook sent two more pirates to the cabin. They, too, returned clutching their bellies.

"Captain, there must be a monster down there," whispered Smee.

"Send the boys to deal with it!"

The pirates cut the boys free and pushed them into the cabin. But this time, there was no howling, just a loud cock-a-doodle-do. It was Peter crowing with joy.

"This ship is cursed," groaned Starkey.

"It's because we have a woman on board," said Smee.

"To the plank," snapped Hook.

Smee untied her, and Hook forced her away with the tip of his sword. "Into the brink you go! No one can save you now."

"There's one who can save her," replied a loud voice. "Peter Pan, the avenger."

He leaped at Wendy and pulled her to safety. A moment later, the deck was full of boys with swords from the weapons cupboard. A terrible battle followed—a battle that the boys won hands down, driving the pirates into the sea.

Soon, only Hook was left. He swung his sword around him, keeping the boys at bay.

"Leave him to me," hissed Peter.

The two great enemies circled each other. Their swords rang against each other. Peter was a great swordsman, but Hook was just as good. And he could hit out with his hook as well as his sword.

For a long time, no one seemed to be winning. Then, Peter sprang forward, and his sword drew blood from Hook's stomach. Hook stared at it in horror.

This gave Peter his chance. He kicked out, sending Hook flying toward the sea— and straight into the jaws of the waiting crocodile. There was a loud snap as the crocodile's mouth closed over the pirate. And that was the end of Captain Hook.

The Lost Boys cheered. Now that the pirates were gone, they could sail home on the *Jolly Roger*. They all voted for Peter to be their captain.

"I shall take you all to London myself," he said.

The boys scrubbed the decks clean. They filled the ship's hold with food and the barrels with drinking water. Peter settled in the captain's cabin, and the other boys slung hammocks below deck.

When all was shipshape, Michael and John unfurled the sails. The other boys pulled up anchor, and the journey started.

For months, the *Jolly Roger* sailed across seas and oceans. It sailed past islands and volcanones. Then one day, Curly shouted from the lookout.

"Land ahoy! Land ahoy!"

Tinker Bell blew some fairy dust in the air, and Wendy, John, and Michael rose up. Peter and the fairy went with them.

They flew through the clouds, first past the white cliffs of Dover, then over fields and farms. At last, they could see the tall spires of London and the glowing, round face of Big Ben.

"We're nearly home!" shouted Michael.

At last, their street came into view, their house and the nursery window. It was open …

Mrs. Darling was playing piano in the music room. She always felt sad when she played the piano nowadays. There were no children to sing along. "I'll go up to the nursery," she said to Mr. Darling. "I want to make sure that the window is open."

"It's been such a long time since the children flew away," said Mr. Darling gently. "Shut the window, darling."

"Never," said Mrs. Darling fiercely. She hurried upstairs and let herself into the nursery. For a moment, she thought she was dreaming. There were John and Michael lying in their cots and Wendy in her bed.

Mrs. Darling stared in disbelief. Were her eyes playing tricks on her?

Then, Michael reached out and took her hand.

"Mother!"

Mrs. Darling could hardly speak for joy. "Wendy. Michael. John. You have come home."

Nana heard from downstairs and came tearing up. She was followed by Mr. Darling. There was much joy as the family hugged.

"We have brought the Lost Boys with us, Mother," said Wendy. "Will you be their mother, too?"

"Oh, yes," said Mrs. Darling. "We shall adopt them all. We shall be one big, happy family."

"We must adopt Peter, too," said John.

Wendy went to the window. "Oh, Peter, come in. Be part of our family."

"Would they send me to school?" asked Peter.

"Yes," replied Wendy. "It will be fun learning new things."

"And then to work in an office?"

"Yes."

"I would be a grown-up, then."

"We all have to grow up, Peter."

"Not me," said Peter. "Goodbye, Wendy. Be a good mother to the boys. Please don't cry, we shall meet again. Goodbye."

Peter and Tinker Bell rose high up in the sky. Wendy watched them disappear. Then, she came away from the window. But she didn't close it. She left it open for when Peter Pan would come back.

And Peter did come back. Once every spring, he took Wendy with him to Neverland. She helped tidy up the house and read him stories. When Wendy grew up, she had a daughter named Jane. She had stopped going to Neverland because she was all grown up.

Peter Pan came for Jane one day. Wendy let her go to Neverland with him. She knew she would come back. And the story of Neverland would go on forever ... as long as there are children who are brave and innocent and believe in Peter Pan.

The Wizard of Oz

Retold by
Samantha Noonan

Illustrated by
Alex Paterson

ARCTURUS

For Fred Randall—SN.

For George and Sticky—AP.

ARCTURUS

This edition published in 2018 by Arcturus Publishing Limited
26/27 Bickels Yard, 151–153 Bermondsey Street,
London SE1 3HA

Copyright © Arcturus Holdings Limited

All rights reserved. No part of this publication may be reproduced, stored in a retrieval system, or transmitted, in any form or by any means, electronic, mechanical, photocopying, recording or otherwise, without written permission in accordance with the provisions of the Copyright Act 1956 (as amended). Any person or persons who do any unauthorised act in relation to this publication may be liable to criminal prosecution and civil claims for damages.

Writer: Samantha Noonan
Illustrator: Alex Paterson
Designer: Jeni Child
Editor: Susannah Bailey
Art Director: Jessica Crass

ISBN: 978-1-78828-697-8
CH006117NT
Supplier 24, Date 0618, Print run 7520

Printed in Malaysia

Contents

CHAPTER 1
Whisked Away..4

CHAPTER 2
Finding Friends 14

CHAPTER 3
Panic and Peril..26

CHAPTER 4
A Dangerous Deal 36

CHAPTER 5
Return to the Emerald City.................46

CHAPTER 6
Glinda the Good Witch 56

CHAPTER 1
Whisked Away

There once was a little girl named Dorothy, who lived with her Aunt Em and Uncle Henry in the middle of the Kansas prairie. The prairie was a huge plain of grass that stretched as far as Dorothy could see. It wasn't a very cheerful place—the hot sun and the wind dried everything out and made it dull, and Aunt Em and Uncle Henry seemed worn out by their struggle to make a living from their farm.

The only thing that kept Dorothy from being as miserable as everything around her was Toto, her little dog. He had long, silky black fur, twinkling eyes, and a funny little nose. He played all day long and made Dorothy laugh a lot.

One day, the wind on the prairie blew more strongly than usual, and black clouds appeared in the sky. Uncle Henry squinted across the land. "There's a tornado coming! Quick, hide in the storm cellar! I'll get the sheep!"

A little trapdoor outside the house led to the storm cellar. Aunt Em ran straight to it. "Quick, Dorothy! Get in!" she screamed.

Dorothy was in her bedroom. She was about to run for the cellar, when Toto wriggled out of her arms and hid under the bed. The wind started to howl, and Dorothy could see farm tools and bales of hay flying past the window.

"Come on, Dorothy!" Aunt Em screeched, as she climbed down the ladder.

Dorothy caught Toto, but then the house shook, and she was knocked to the floor.

The wind blew so hard that the house started to spin. Then, with a great gust of wind, it was lifted up into the air! Up and up, Dorothy and Toto flew, away from the prairie and Aunt Em and Uncle Henry.

Dorothy was scared—she hugged Toto close as the house flew on for hours.

Eventually, it fell back to earth with a bang, and bright sunlight shone through the window. Dorothy ran to the door and opened it to see the most beautiful land! There was green grass, tall trees filled with singing birds, bright flowers, and a crystal-clear stream. She gasped. This was not the dry and dusty prairie that she knew. She was sure she must be very far from home ...

Dorothy spotted three men and a lady approaching her house. They were about her height, but they looked much older.

The lady bowed and said, "Welcome, sorceress, to the Land of the Munchkins. Thank you for killing the Wicked Witch of the East and setting our people free."

"But I haven't killed anyone!" said Dorothy, confused.

"Well, your house did, and that's the same thing." The lady pointed to where a pair of feet wearing silver shoes stuck out from beneath the house.

Dorothy was horrified.

"Oh, it's a good thing," the lady assured her. "She was very evil, you see. Here in the land of Oz, there are two good witches and two evil witches. Now that you have killed the Wicked Witch of the East, there is only the Wicked Witch of the West left. I am the Good Witch of the North."

One of the men added, "And now we Munchkins are free again! Thank you!"

Another handed Dorothy the silver shoes. "These belong to you now. They have a magic spell on them, but we don't know what it is."

"So, this is the land of Oz?" said Dorothy. "Please could you tell me how to get back to Kansas?"

"I'm afraid I've never heard of Kansas," said the Good Witch, "so I can't help you. But I know someone who could."

"The Wizard of Oz!" cried one of the munchkins.

"He lives in the Emerald City," said the Witch. "It's a long journey through many different places. Some of them are nice, but some of them are horrid. All you have to do is follow this yellow brick road." She pointed, and Dorothy saw that there was a paved road made of gleaming yellow bricks leading away into the trees.

"Oz is a great and powerful wizard," said one of the munchkins. "If anyone knows how to get to Kansas, it will be him."

"Could you please come with me?" Dorothy asked.

The witch shook her head and said, "I am afraid not, but I will give you this." She kissed Dorothy on the forehead, leaving a silver mark. "Nobody will dare hurt someone I have kissed."

Dorothy thanked her and prepared to set off. She took a liking to the pretty silver shoes and put them on for the journey.

Dorothy and Toto started walking down the yellow brick road. Soon, they passed a field in which a scarecrow stood, tied high on a pole.

"Good day," said the scarecrow.

Dorothy jumped in surprise. She'd never met a talking scarecrow before! "Good day," she replied, nervously. "How are you?"

"I'm not very well," the scarecrow said. "I have this big pole stuck up my back. Could you get me down? I'd be very grateful to you."

Dorothy climbed into the field and helped the scarecrow from the pole.

"Oh, thank you!" said the scarecrow.

Now that he was off the pole he could walk as well as talk. "I'm lucky that you were passing. Not many people walk this way."

"I'm going to the Emerald City to ask the Wizard of Oz to send me back to Kansas," Dorothy explained.

"What's the Emerald City? Who is Oz?" the scarecrow asked.

"You don't know?" said Dorothy.

"I don't know anything," said Scarecrow. "I've got no brains. Do you think if I came with you, Oz would give me some brains?"

"Well, it couldn't hurt to ask," said Dorothy.

So, they set off together.

CHAPTER 2
Finding Friends

As they walked, Dorothy and Scarecrow told each other more about themselves. Dorothy described the huge, dull prairie in Kansas.

Scarecrow frowned. "But why would you want to leave such a beautiful land as Oz to go back to such a dreary one?"

Dorothy shrugged. "There's no place like home. I'd rather be there than anywhere else, no matter how beautiful it is."

"I suppose I would understand that if I had brains," said Scarecrow.

They walked past lots of fields, farms, and gardens. Then, ahead of them, the dark woods loomed.

Dorothy felt nervous, but she knew she

had to go through them if she wanted to get to the Emerald City. She held on tight to Toto as they went into the woods. Once they were inside, she found that it wasn't very scary at all—until dusk began to fall …

It got too dark for Dorothy to see where she was going, so Scarecrow found an empty cottage for them to rest in. Dorothy and Toto curled up on the floor and went to sleep. Scarecrow didn't need sleep, so he stayed up all night, watching over them.

The next day, as they walked through a small woodland, they heard a groaning noise. Dorothy peered off the road and saw a man made of tin standing in a strange position. He was holding a weapon above his head.

"Was that you we heard groaning?" Dorothy asked.

"Yes," said Tin Man. "I'm rusted, stuck like this! I need my oilcan. It's by that tree."

Dorothy picked up the can and poured oil on all his joints—first his neck, then his shoulders and arms, and finally, his legs.

"Oh, thank you," said Tin Man. He made lots of squeaking noises as he started to move. "I've been stuck that way for a whole year! It feels so good to move. It's lucky you were passing by. Not many people come this way."

"We're on the way to the Emerald City," Scarecrow told him. "Dorothy is going to ask the Wizard of Oz to send her back to Kansas, and I'm going to ask him for some brains."

"Oh, do you think he could give me a heart if I asked?" cried Tin Man. "My dearest wish is to have a heart."

"Why don't you come with us and see?" said Dorothy.

So they kept going through the woods.

Suddenly, a great big lion jumped out from the trees, roaring and snarling! He started chasing Toto, scaring the little dog.

Barely thinking about what she was doing, Dorothy rushed forward and smacked the lion on the nose. "What do you think you're doing, attacking a little dog like that?" she cried.

The lion clutched at his nose and looked tearful. "Well, a little dog is the only thing I could attack," he sniffed. "Because I'm so big and look scary, everyone expects me to be fearsome and brave. But really, I'm afraid of everything. I'm just a big coward. Now you know my secret, so I'm sure everyone else in the forest will soon."

"We're just passing through," said Dorothy.

"We're off to the Emerald City to see the Wizard of Oz," added Scarecrow.

"Dorothy is asking him to send her home to Kansas, Scarecrow is asking for some brains, and I'm asking for a heart," Tin Man explained.

The Cowardly Lion's eyes widened. "Do you think the Wizard could give me some courage?"

"I don't see why not," said Dorothy. "Why don't you come with us?"

Lion beamed and decided he would.

The new friends and Toto all continued walking down the yellow brick road.

"Dorothy, now that you've made so many friends in Oz, do you still want to leave to go back to Kansas?" Scarecrow asked.

Dorothy felt a pang as she thought about leaving dear Scarecrow, lovely Tin Man, and sweet Lion behind. But then she thought about Aunt Em and Uncle

Henry. "I'll be very sad to be away from all of you," she admitted, "But I must go home to my family."

The journey was very long. The Emerald City was nowhere in sight, and Dorothy had run out of food. She had packed some bread in her basket before leaving the cottage, but she and Toto had eaten it all.

As dusk fell, they sheltered under a large tree. Tin Man chopped some wood to start a splendid fire, and Scarecrow discovered lots of nuts in the forest. He gathered them all up in Dorothy's basket for her to eat. Lion went into the forest to find his own dinner. Then, he curled up with Dorothy and Toto to sleep while Tin Man and Scarecrow watched over them.

The next day, the yellow brick road brought them to a ditch that ran all the way across the land, as far as their eyes could see. It was too wide to step over, and it was so deep that Dorothy couldn't see the bottom, even when she bent down and peered in.

"What are we going to do?" she asked the others, as she squinted into the distance. "It seems to go on forever, so we can't go around it."

Scarecrow looked thoughtful. "I think we're going to have to jump over it," he said.

Dorothy was doubtful. The gap looked much farther than she could jump.

Lion measured the distance with his

eyes and said, "I think I could do it."

"Perhaps you could take us on your back?" Scarecrow suggested. "I could come first, because if I fall off, it won't hurt me."

Lion agreed, so Scarecrow climbed up on his back. Lion took a run up and then leaped over the big ditch, landing safely on the other side. They all cheered. Scarecrow climbed off, and Lion jumped back over. Dorothy was next, carrying Toto in her arms, and finally, Tin Man went!

Then they found themselves in a very gloomy forest, and there were horrible growls and snarls coming from the trees.

"It's the Kalidahs!" said Lion, fearfully. "They are horrible beasts, with heads like tigers and bodies like bears. They'll kill us all! Run!"

They all started to run away, but then they came to another ditch that stretched as far as they could see. This one was so wide, it was impossible to jump over. The growling of the Kalidahs was coming closer and closer.

"Quick, Tin Man, you can chop down that tree," said Scarecrow, pointing to a tree next to the ditch. "It will fall across the gap and make a bridge for us."

Tin Man hurried to do as he said. Just as the tree fell, two Kalidahs ran out of the forest and onto their path. They were the most terrifying beasts!

Lion managed to leap in front of his friends and roar at the Kalidahs. They stopped for a minute, and the friends ran across the tree bridge. However, the Kalidahs started to cross the bridge, too.

Things were starting to look bad, until Tin Man quickly chopped the tree from the other side! It fell down into the opening, taking the Kalidahs with it.

CHAPTER 3

Panic and Peril

Soon, the friends came to a rushing river, with a gap too wide for any tree to make a bridge across it.

"I know," said Scarecrow. "Tin Man can chop wood to make us a raft. We can float across!"

Tin Man chopped the wood and made a fine raft. They all climbed on, and Tin Man and Scarecrow pushed the raft through the water with long poles. However, they struggled against the strong current and were in danger of being swept downstream, into the land of the Wicked Witch of the West ...

Then, Scarecrow pushed so hard on his pole that it got stuck in the mud. The raft was swept away, and he was left clinging to the pole in the middle of the river!

Tin Man couldn't fight the current alone, and the raft began to rush out of control downstream.

Lion leaped into the river. He called to Dorothy and Tin Man. "Hold on to my tail! I'm going to swim to the bank!"

They did as he said, and Lion towed them safely to shore. But Scarecrow was still stranded in the water!

"Help!" shouted Scarecrow.

"What are we going to do?" Dorothy cried in a frightened voice.

Lion was too tired to swim again, Tin Man would rust in the water, and Dorothy couldn't swim.

"Help, somebody help me!" Scarecrow wailed pitifully.

Just then, a stork flew by and landed next to Dorothy.

"Hmm," said the stork. "If he wasn't so big and heavy, I would rescue him."

"Oh, but he isn't heavy!" Dorothy said eagerly. "He's only made of straw, and he's ever so light. Please could you try?"

"I will," the stork agreed. "But if he does turn out to be heavy, I'll have to drop him in the water."

She spread her big wings and flew over

the river. She picked up Scarecrow easily and swooped back to land, dropping him next to his friends.

"Oh, thank you, thank you!" they shouted up to the stork.

"You're most welcome," she squawked in reply, flying back to her nest.

Now that Scarecrow was safe again, they had a chance to look around at the new land they had come to, and Dorothy gasped. They were standing on the edge of a meadow filled with the most beautiful poppies!

The yellow brick road cut through the poppy meadow, and Dorothy skipped down it, enjoying the pretty flowers. After a short while, she started to feel quite sleepy and decided to sit down.

"Oh, no, you mustn't!" Tin Man warned. "These poppies are poisonous. If you rest here, you will lie down and sleep forever."

However, Dorothy was just too tired to stop herself. She yawned and quickly fell to the ground, fast asleep. Tin Man carried her to the edge of the meadow and laid her next to a stream, hoping that the fresh air would wake her up.

But when he went back to Lion and Scarecrow, Lion had fallen asleep, too!

"What are we going to do?" Scarecrow cried. "He's far too heavy for us to lift."

Just then, he heard a little squeak from

down by his feet. He looked down to see a little mouse sitting there. "We can help," she said. "I am the Mouse Queen, and these are my subjects."

Hundreds of mice appeared in the meadow. They all scurried around Lion, and together, they pushed and pulled him all the way out of the meadow on a sled that Tin Man had made from wood.

"Call on me whenever you need help," the Queen said, as she scampered off.

A little while later, Dorothy and Lion woke up, feeling confused. Scarecrow and Tin Man told them what had happened, but Dorothy didn't understand why they were smiling so much.

"Because we're almost there!" said Scarecrow. "Look!"

He pointed down the yellow brick road. It sloped down a hill, and there, in the distance, was the Emerald City! The green buildings gleamed in the sunshine.

"Hurrah!"

Dorothy and Lion leaped to their feet, and they all started to trot quickly down the road.

Along the way, they met a man and a woman who were the same size as the Munchkins back in the East. "Where are you going in such a hurry?" the man asked.

"We're going to see the Wizard of Oz," said Dorothy.

"But the Wizard never sees anyone!" the lady said, looking surprised.

Dorothy's heart sank. "So, you don't think he can help us?"

"I'm sure he can," said the man. "He is all-powerful. If you can persuade him to see you, I'm sure he will grant your wishes."

"We'll just have to make him see us, then," Dorothy said firmly, smiling around at her friends.

The Emerald City was dazzling up close. The walls were bright green, and the green gates had hundreds of emeralds set in them. A little man dressed all in green was standing next to the gates.

"Greetings," said the man, "I am the Guardian of the Gates. What is your business in the Emerald City?"

"We are here to see the Wizard of Oz," said Dorothy.

The man looked shocked. "Why, nobody has asked to see the Wizard in many, many years!"

"Are we allowed to?" Lion asked nervously.

"Yes, I suppose you are," said the Guardian. "But first, you must all put on these spectacles, so that you will not be blinded by the brightness of the city."

He pulled out some strange-looking glasses that fastened around the back of the head with a lock. Once the friends were locked in, he pulled out a much bigger key and opened the gates.

The friends gasped as they stepped inside. The buildings, the streets, everything in the shops, and even the people were tinged with green! And everybody seemed so happy.

CHAPTER 4

A Dangerous Deal

They were taken straight to the Emerald Palace and were each shown to a beautiful bedroom. Dorothy was also given a gorgeous green silk dress. Then, they were taken to the throne room.

When they went in, Lion started quaking, Toto whimpered, and the other three gasped in surprise. The Wizard of Oz was a giant floating head that took up nearly the whole room!

"What do you want from Oz, the great and powerful?" boomed the head.

Dorothy steeled herself and spoke up. "My name is Dorothy, and this is Toto, Scarecrow, Tin Man, and Lion. I'm here because I'd like to go home to Kansas."

One by one, the other three stammered their wishes.

Oz considered for a moment. "I will grant your requests," he roared, "only if you do something for me first. You must kill the Wicked Witch of the West."

Dorothy gasped. "But how?"

Oz looked furious. "That's for you to figure out!"

Dorothy hated the idea of killing anyone—even a witch—but she couldn't see another option. "We'll do it," she said.

The Guardian took the friends back to the gate and unlocked their spectacles. Dorothy was surprised to see that her silk dress was now white.

"Which way is it?" Scarecrow asked.

The Guardian pointed up into a vast and hilly country. "That way," he said, trembling a little. "That's the Land of the Winkies. The Wicked Witch of the West took it over and made the Winkies her slaves many years ago. Nobody dares go near that land."

Dorothy felt Lion start to shake next to her again and took his paw in her hand. "We'll be all right," she said firmly. "After all, I already killed one witch in Oz without even trying."

They started to walk, and soon they had crossed into the witch's country.

But little did the friends know that the witch was already watching them from her tower, far away. She had only one eye, but it was very powerful.

"Who are these fools who dare to enter my lands?" she muttered. "Wolf pack—attack!"

At her command, a pack of forty vicious wolves left the tower and raced toward the friends.

"What is that strange noise?" Dorothy asked her friends as they trudged up a rocky hillside. "It sounds like dogs or wild coyotes."

"*Wolves!*" cried Scarecrow as he squinted ahead. "They'll tear us all into lots of pieces!"

"No, they won't," said Tin Man grimly, as he lifted his weapon.

The wolves reached them, snarling and howling. Tin Man met them all and fought them off until all forty wolves were dead.

"Well done, Tin Man!" the other three cried.

Far away in her tower, the witch drummed her heels and cursed. "How dare they kill my precious wolves! Well, I'll show them. Winkies, come here!"

Her slaves, the Winkies, were gentle folk

who had once been peaceful tinsmiths. They all wore yellow and had yellow-tinted skin. They were terrified of the Witch.

They bowed before her. "Yes, Mistress. What will you have us do?"

"Find the party of idiots who have wandered into my land, and kill them all!"

The Winkies bowed and went to do as she said. When they drew close to the friends, however, Lion roared at them so loudly that they were scared out of their wits and ran away.

The Wicked Witch then went to her cupboard and put on her golden cap. It was an enchanted cap. The wearer of it could call the winged monkeys of Oz to do their bidding three times. The Witch had already used it twice—once to capture the Winkies and once to cast the Wizard out from her lands.

The monkeys appeared and bowed before her.

"Go to that little group that dares to enter my lands!" the Witch shrieked. "Kill them all except the lion. I shall put him to work in my castle."

The monkeys flew off sadly. They did not like hurting anyone, but they had to do what the Witch told them to do.

They soared over the hillside and grabbed Tin Man and Scarecrow. They dropped Tin Man on some rocks, so that he was all dented, then they tore Scarecrow apart and left his body up on some tall trees.

They were about to swoop down for Dorothy when they saw the mark of the Good Witch on her forehead, and they dared not harm her. Instead, they captured her and Lion, tied them up with ropes, and took them to the Wicked Witch's castle.

The Wicked Witch saw the Good Witch's kiss on Dorothy's forehead and knew that she couldn't hurt the child.

"You shall be my cleaning servant," she snapped at Dorothy. "Start on the kitchen and scrub my cauldrons well, or I will change my mind and kill you after all."

Dorothy scurried to obey, terrified.

"And you, lion, will pull me around in my cart," said the Witch. She dragged Lion out to the courtyard and tried to harness him to the cart.

Lion summoned all his strength and *roared* at her! The Witch was so scared that she fell over. She knew she couldn't make Lion pull the cart; he was much stronger than her and seemed so fierce. She decided to starve him until he obeyed her demands.

She shut Lion in a cage in the kitchen and didn't feed him for days and days. Every time she went close, Lion roared again and again.

What the witch didn't know was that Dorothy was secretly sneaking down every night to bring Lion food, and then she would curl up with him, nestling in his soft mane. Together, they dreamed of being free.

CHAPTER 5

Return to the Emerald City

Now, the Wicked Witch knew that Dorothy's silver shoes were very powerful indeed, and she wanted them for herself.

Dorothy had no idea of their strength, but she loved them anyway and took them off only to sleep and to wash. The Wicked Witch was afraid of the dark and water, so she couldn't steal them. Instead she laid an iron bar across the floor of the kitchen and used a spell to make it invisible. Cackling, she hid in the corner of the kitchen and waited. When Dorothy walked through, she tripped right over the bar, and one of her shoes flew off. The

Witch snatched it up and put it on.

"Hey, give that back!"
Dorothy cried. She
was so cross that
she snatched
her bucket of
cleaning water
and threw it all
over the Wicked Witch.

Instantly, the witch began to melt.

"How did you know my secret weakness?" she cried.

"I didn't!" gasped Dorothy.

Screaming, the witch melted away completely into a puddle.

"We did it," Dorothy whispered to herself. Then, she started calling as she ran outside: "Lion, we did it! The Wicked Witch is dead, and we're free!"

Dorothy, Lion, and the Winkies all cheered. At last, they could leave!

"But now we must save Tin Man and Scarecrow. Winkies, can you help us find them?" Dorothy asked.

The Winkies bowed. "Anything for the one who set us free," they chorused.

First, they found Tin Man all bashed up and broken on the rocks, where the monkeys had dropped him. Luckily, the Winkies were tinsmiths. They had never met a tin man before, and they were fascinated as they fixed him. When they were done, Tin Man was as good as new!

Next, they found where the monkeys had thrown Scarecrow, high in a tree. Quickly, Tin Man managed to chop it down. Then, the Winkies brought new stuffing for him, and soon Scarecrow was back to his old self.

"Thank you so much!" Dorothy cried.

Dorothy packed some food for the journey from the Witch's supplies. While she was in there, she found the magic golden cap. She didn't know that it was powerful, but she thought it looked lovely, so she put it on.

All the Winkies came out to wave to them as they went back to the Emerald City.

However, since they had been taken to the Wicked Witch's castle by flying monkeys, they didn't know the way back, and soon, they were lost.

"Wait," said Scarecrow. "I know who we can call!" He cupped his hands and called. "Your Majesty, we need help!"

The Mouse Queen appeared, followed by her subjects. "Yes?" she squeaked.

"We're trying to find our way back to the Emerald City," Dorothy explained. "But we're lost. Do you know the way?"

The Queen's face fell. "I don't know the way from here." Then, she brightened. "But you are wearing the golden cap! The owner of the cap can command the winged monkeys to do their bidding three times. The monkeys can take you back to the Emerald City."

Dorothy was shocked. "I didn't know it was an enchanted cap! I just thought it looked nice!"

"How do we know we can trust the monkeys?" Tin Man said, frowning. "They hurt us last time."

"They used to do the bidding of the Wicked Witch," said the Queen. "But now, they will be bound to do what Dorothy says. They won't hurt you. Just call them!"

The mice scuttled away.

Dorothy did as the Queen told her and summoned the monkeys.

They waited a moment, and then the sky around them was filled with monkeys, all hooting and flapping their wings.

Their leader landed in front of Dorothy. "What would you like us to do?"

"We would like you to carry us—gently—to the Emerald City, please," said Dorothy.

The monkey bowed low. "As you wish, Mistress. We are sorry about before. We monkeys are bound to serve the wearer of the golden cap, so if the wearer is evil, we must do evil deeds. It is not something we enjoy." He looked around at each of them in turn, looking apologetic.

"We forgive you," said Dorothy.

Dorothy, Scarecrow, and Tin Man

were each picked up under their armpits by a monkey. Lion was carried by two monkeys holding ropes. Toto sat on his back. They took off into the air. Dorothy enjoyed flying over Oz—it looked like a pretty patchwork quilt, and there, up ahead, gleamed the Emerald City.

When the friends arrived, the monkeys set them down carefully, and Dorothy thanked them for their help.

"What are you all doing back here?" boomed the Wizard's giant head, as the friends walked back into the throne room.

"We killed the Wicked Witch, like you asked," Dorothy replied. "So we've come back for our wishes."

"No," said the Wizard.

Dorothy stamped her foot. "You mean to say that you made us go all the way to that horrible witch and risk our lives, and now you won't grant our wishes?"

Lion roared, hoping it would scare the Wizard the same way it had scared the Wicked Witch. It made everybody jump, but it terrified Toto, who leaped backward with fright and crashed into a screen.

The screen toppled over to reveal a man speaking into a microphone. "I can't grant your—oh."

The man saw them staring and stopped.

"*You're* the Wizard of Oz?" Dorothy asked, confused.

The man's face fell. "Well ... yes ... and no. I'm just a simple showman from Ohio. I used to take my hot-air balloon out, but one day, I got blown far away, and I landed here. The Ozians thought I was a wizard, and I never corrected them. Really, I have no magical powers. Please don't tell anyone my secret!"

CHAPTER 6

Glinda the Good Witch

Now, the Wizard did not have a bad heart, and he hated to disappoint Dorothy and her friends by not granting their wishes.

He was sure that Scarecrow did have brains—he just didn't know it yet. And Tin Man had heart and Lion had courage, they just didn't feel it. If he could find a way to make them realize, then their wishes would be granted.

"Come to think about it, I can grant your wishes," the Wizard said. "Scarecrow, here are your brains." He made a little cut in the top of Scarecrow's head and poured in lots of pins and needles before sewing it back up.

"I feel so sharp all of a sudden!" Scarecrow said.

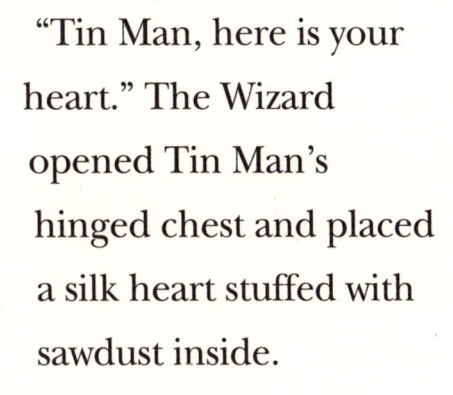

"Tin Man, here is your heart." The Wizard opened Tin Man's hinged chest and placed a silk heart stuffed with sawdust inside.

"I'm full of love!" gasped Tin Man.

Finally, the Wizard held up a small dish. "Lion, this contains liquid courage. If you drink it, you will be the bravest creature in the land."

Lion did as he was told and felt full of fire. "I'm not scared of anything!" he declared.

They all thanked the Wizard for his gifts.

The Wizard looked sadly at Dorothy. He knew that no amount of trickery would get her back to Kansas. Then, the Wizard had the most wonderful idea.

"Dorothy, I think it's high time I went back home, too. Ohio and Kansas aren't so very far apart. We can fly there together."

"Fly?" Dorothy asked.

"In my hot-air balloon!" said the Wizard. "I'll tell the Ozians that I am going to visit my brother wizard, who lives in the clouds."

The Wizard pulled out his old hot-air balloon, made some repairs, and fired it up. However, just as Dorothy was about to climb into the basket, Toto wriggled out of her arms to chase a kitten!

Dorothy couldn't bear to leave Toto

behind in Oz, so she ran after him.

"Dorothy, we can't wait!" the Wizard called, as it started to lift up into the air. "Dorothy! Dorothy!"

Dorothy caught Toto and ran back to the balloon, but it was too late. The balloon was high up in the sky and being whisked away by the wind.

"Oh, no!" cried Dorothy, with tears in her eyes. "Now I'm stuck here forever!"

"You could stay here with us," Tin Man suggested. "Surely that wouldn't be so bad? We love you."

"I love you too," Dorothy sobbed. "But I also love my Aunt Em and Uncle Henry, and I can't bear the thought of never seeing them or Kansas again."

"Glinda!" Scarecrow exclaimed. "She's the Good Witch of the South and I've heard she's very powerful. Maybe she can help?"

"I'll try anything," said Dorothy, wiping her tears.

"And we'll be right by your side," Lion assured her.

So, the friends set out on another long, hard journey south. They climbed over a huge wall to reach the country of the Quadlings, where Glinda lived in a beautiful castle.

Three young Quadling girls in red-and-gold coats stood guard outside the castle. "Why are you here?" one asked.

"We are here to see Glinda and ask for her help," said Dorothy.

They were let in at once. Glinda was the most beautiful person any of them had ever seen. She had bright red hair that tumbled around her shoulders in ringlets, piercing blue eyes, and pale skin. She wore a dress of pure white and sat on a throne of rubies.

"What can I do for you, my dear?" Glinda asked Dorothy.

"I need to find a way to get back to Kansas," Dorothy answered. "You are my last hope. Please, can you help me?"

Glinda smiled kindly at her. "You sweet child. You don't even need my help! Those silver shoes on your feet have all the power you need to get home. All you have to do is click your heels three times and say where you wish to go. You will be whisked straight there."

"Oh, thank you!" Dorothy cried. "How can I ever repay you?"

"Well, I wonder if I might have your golden cap," asked Glinda, "since its magic only works in Oz?"

"Of course!" Dorothy gave her the cap.

Glinda summoned the flying monkeys right away. "Please take Scarecrow to the Emerald City to rule there. Tin Man shall go and rule over the Winkies, and Lion shall be the king of the forest," she said.

The monkeys bowed, and then it was time for the friends to say goodbye. Dorothy hugged them all and promised she would never forget them.

Finally, she picked up Toto, took a deep breath, clicked her heels three times, and said, "Aunt Em and Uncle Henry's house, Kansas."

Dorothy was whirled through the air, as if she was back in the middle of the twister. She landed with a bump and looked around. She was back on the prairie! The storm was over, and there was her house, the same as it had ever been.

"Toto, we're here!" she said, joyfully.

Then she saw Aunt Em stepping out of the house, and Dorothy ran to hug her.

Dorothy knew she would miss her friends and Oz, but she was so happy to be home again!

Oliver Twist

Retold by
Stewart Ross

Illustrated by
Alex Paterson

ARCTURUS

For Evie Ross, with much love—SR.

For Arthur—AP.

ARCTURUS

This edition published in 2018 by Arcturus Publishing Limited
26/27 Bickels Yard, 151–153 Bermondsey Street,
London SE1 3HA

Copyright © Arcturus Holdings Limited

All rights reserved. No part of this publication may be reproduced, stored in a retrieval system, or transmitted, in any form or by any means, electronic, mechanical, photocopying, recording or otherwise, without written permission in accordance with the provisions of the Copyright Act 1956 (as amended). Any person or persons who do any unauthorised act in relation to this publication may be liable to criminal prosecution and civil claims for damages.

Writer: Stewart Ross
Illustrator: Alex Paterson
Designer: Jeni Child
Editor: Sebastian Rydberg
Art Director: Jessica Crass

ISBN: 978-1-78828-686-2
CH006279NT
Supplier 24, Date 0618, Print run 7512

Printed in Malaysia

Contents

CHAPTER 1
The Workhouse Boy..................4

CHAPTER 2
Into the Den of Thieves..................14

CHAPTER 3
Escape and Recapture..................24

CHAPTER 4
The Mystery of Oliver Twist..................34

CHAPTER 5
Murder!..................44

CHAPTER 6
Happiness!..................54

CHAPTER 1

The Workhouse Boy

At the beginning of our story, almost two hundred years ago, a young woman is lying in the street. She is very pretty but also very poor and very sick. She is expecting a baby.

No one knows her name.

She is carried into a workhouse, the ugly building for poor people without a home. That night, she gives birth to a baby boy—and dies. Her only jewels, a ring and locket, are stolen.

Poor little baby boy! His father had disappeared, and now he has no mother. In other words, he is an orphan. It is not a very happy start to life.

Mr. Bumble, the fat, bossy man running the workhouse, names the orphans born there. He does this in alphabetical order. Since he named the last baby "Swubble," beginning with S, the next has to begin with T—so he chooses "Twist." Oliver Twist.

For the first nine miserable years of his life, Oliver is cared for by a matron. To be honest, she doesn't care for him at all. He sleeps in a coal cellar, and she gives him just enough food to stay alive.

✼

On his ninth birthday, Oliver was returned to the workhouse. There, he lived with other poor and wretched boys. Mr. Bumble did not send them to school. Instead, he gave them hard, boring work to do.

All day long, the boys sat taking apart old rope. Their fingers were red and raw. If they made mistakes or didn't work hard enough, Mr. Bumble beat them.

At mealtimes, the boys were given a bowl of thin porridge, known as "gruel." They grew thinner and thinner, hungrier and hungrier. Oliver feared that one of the bigger boys was hungry enough to eat *him*!

They decided they must do something or starve to death. One of them would tell the cook what they all wanted. They drew lots and the boy chosen to do this was Oliver.

That evening, when every bowl of gruel had been scraped empty, Oliver got up nervously to his feet. All eyes were on him.

Very slowly, he walked to where the cook stood before a huge tub of gruel. Quietly, in his most polite voice, Oliver asked, "Please, sir, I want some more."

The greasy cook turned pale. "What?" he gasped.

"Please, sir," repeated Oliver, "I want some more."

The workhouse staff couldn't believe it. Ask for *more*? How rude! How ungrateful!

The men shouted, the women screamed, and Mr. Bumble hurried into the room. *More*?! He'd never heard anything so ridiculous in all his life. The boy had to go.

Oliver was thrashed and locked in a room for a week. The only sound was his own crying. Outside, Mr. Bumble put up a notice asking someone to take Oliver away and teach him a skill. He offered five pounds to whoever did this.

A cruel chimney sweep saw the notice and grinned. His last three workhouse boys had died, and he needed a new one.

He made a deal with
Mr. Bumble.

A group of
important men,
the magistrates,
had to approve
this deal. They
didn't like the
way the chimney sweep behaved—he sent
boys up the inside of chimneys to clean
them. If they got stuck, he lit a fire to
drive them out!

Did Oliver want to be a chimney
sweep, they asked. "No!" he wept,
unable to lie. "Please starve me or even
kill me—but don't send me with that
dreadful man!"

Oliver did not become a chimney
sweep, but Mr. Bumble did beat him again.

Can you imagine poor Oliver? He was small, thin, and pale, with such a sad look on his little face! Who would want a boy like that? Well, there was one person—Mr. Sowerberry.

Mr. Sowerberry was an undertaker. He collected the bodies of people who had died. He then made their coffins and arranged their funerals. He needed someone to walk beside children's coffins. This person had to be small and look truly sad.

When Mr. Bumble showed Oliver to Mr. Sowerberry, the undertaker rubbed his hands. Just the boy he needed!

The two men had a chat, and Oliver left the workhouse to live with Mr. and Mrs. Sowerberry and their daughter Charlotte.

Mr. Bumble was delighted to get rid of Oliver. The Sowerberrys were delighted to find such a miserable-looking boy. Only Oliver was unhappy. He had been sold, like a carpet or a kettle. Nobody loved him; nobody had ever loved him.

Mr. Sowerberry was quite kind to Oliver, but Mrs. Sowerberry grumbled at him for eating too much. Charlotte's boyfriend, Noah Claypole, was worse. Every time he saw Oliver, he bullied him. One day, he went too far.

At dinner time, Noah pulled Oliver's hair and twisted his ears. Oliver, who had a heart of gold, did nothing, which annoyed Noah. "Hey, workhouse boy," he said, "how's your mother?"

"She's dead," replied Oliver. "Don't you dare say anything bad about her!"

"What did she die of, workhouse boy?"

"She died of a broken heart," replied Oliver quietly. A tear rolled down his cheek.

"Oh, dear," sneered Noah. "I'll tell you what, she was a right bad one!"

"What did you say?" whispered Oliver.

"I said she was a right bad one!"

Oliver exploded with anger and punched Noah with all his strength. The bully fell flat on the floor, crying. Mrs. Sowerberry hurried in, and she and Charlotte attacked Oliver.

As the two women scratched and punched the poor boy, Noah ran to fetch Mr. Bumble. "Oliver Twist tried to murder me!" he lied.

Mr. Bumble hurried to the Sowerberrys'. The problem was meat, he said. They should never have given Oliver meat.

When he heard this, Mr. Sowerberry beat Oliver soundly. Mr. Bumble did the same. Finally, battered and bruised, the orphan boy was sent to his lonely bed.

CHAPTER 2

Into the Den of Thieves

Oliver was very brave while Mr. Bumble and the Sowerberrys were hurting him. He didn't cry once. But now, all alone, the bruised and unhappy little boy fell to his knees and wept.

Around the middle of the night, Oliver rose and looked outside. The night was cold and clear. *Yes*, he thought, *I will run away!*

At first light, he opened the Sowerberrys' front door and stepped outside into the fresh air. His path took him beside the workhouse. He shuddered when he saw the grim building. A young boy named Dick was already at work in the garden.

"Hello, Dick," said Oliver quietly. "Please don't tell anyone you saw me.

I'm running away."

Dick looked pale and sad. "I wish I could come with you, Oliver," he said with a sob. "But the doctor says I'm dying."

Oliver came up to the iron bars of the garden fence. Dick stretched out his thin arms and held on to him. "Don't stop, dear Oliver," he said kindly. "Goodbye, and God bless you!"

This was the first time anyone had said that to Oliver, and he never once forgot it.

Oliver was terrified that Mr. Bumble would come after him, and he ran until he could run no more. After that, he struggled on, step after step, for twenty miles.

Beside the road, he saw a stone with "London 70 miles" carved into it. *London—what a great place!* he thought. *No one will ever find me there. That's where I will go.*

Seventy miles is a long, long way for a small boy with no food and nothing to drink. Oliver was about to collapse on the road, like his dear mother, when a kindly old couple took pity on him. They invited him in and gave him a large meal.

Refreshed, Oliver struggled on to the town of Barnet. He had now been walking for seven days, and his feet were terribly sore. He was starving hungry again, too. He sat down in despair.

"Hello!" said a voice.

Oliver looked up at the strangest person he had ever seen. He was about Oliver's age, but he behaved and spoke like an adult. He wore a man's coat, with the sleeves rolled up. On his head sat a top hat, always about to fall off.

"Hello," repeated the stranger. "What are you up to, then?"

"I'm tired and starving hungry," replied Oliver. He was trying hard not to cry. "I've been walking for seven days."

"Running away from the beak, I suppose?" said the stranger. He looked closely at Oliver. "Know what a beak is?"

"Yes," said Oliver. "It's a bird's mouth."

The stranger laughed. "Maybe. But in my world a 'beak' is a magistrate." He put his hands in his pockets, and asked, "Got any money?"

"No," replied Oliver.

"Anything to eat? Anywhere to live?"

"No!"

"Then I'm your man!" The stranger introduced himself: Jack Dawkins, known to his friends as the Artful Dodger. He gave Oliver a hearty meal at an inn. Dodger then invited Oliver to come to

London with him and his friend, Charley.

"Shall we go now?" Oliver asked.

"Best go after dark," he replied, winking at his friend Charley.

"And where shall we stay?"

"I've a friend," said Dodger, "a very kind old gentleman who'd love to give you accommodation. Free."

"How kind of him!" smiled Oliver.

"Oh, yeah!" said Dodger and Charley together. "He's so kind."

After dark, the three boys entered London. They avoided the nice areas and tramped down muddy lanes between ugly houses. Foul smells hung in the filthy air.

Oliver was thinking of running away again, when Dodger grabbed his arm and led him down broken steps into a grimy hovel full of grubby boys. At the end of the room, cooking sausages over an open fire, stood the "very kind old gentleman."

Tangled red hair hung down over the man's thin and ugly face. He wore no shirt, only a greasy gown that reached to his dirty ankles. His name, said Dodger, was Fagin.

Fagin looked Oliver up and down. "Very glad to see you, Oliver. Very," he said. "We need good-looking lads like you, don't we, boys?"

"Yeah!" grinned the others in the room.

Oliver looked at the precious silk handkerchiefs hanging from a line. "Very pretty, aren't they, Oliver dear?" said Fagin.

Oliver nodded. The boys laughed.

Early the next morning, when he thought no one was looking, Fagin took out a box stuffed with watches, rings, and other valuables. Oliver, who was awake, stared in amazement. *How could poor people afford such beautiful things?* he wondered.

I think you know what was going on, don't you? Fagin was a thief, and his boys were a gang of pickpockets. They had stolen all those beautiful things from other people.

As we know, Oliver saw only the good in people. Dodger and Fagin had rescued him and had given him food and shelter. For this, he was most grateful. He was too innocent to notice that he was in a den of thieves—but he would soon learn the horrible truth.

When Fagin taught Oliver how to pickpocket, he thought it was a game. After a couple of weeks, Dodger and Charley took him out "to work" with them. He was delighted to get out of Fagin's smoky den.

They wandered through the London streets, looking for a target. Dodger pointed to a kindly looking gentleman in a green coat outside a bookshop. Oliver watched, horrified, as Dodger snatched a bright silk handkerchief from the man's pocket.

The man reached into his pocket … No handkerchief!

"Stop, thief!" he cried.

Dodger and Charley had already run away. When all eyes turned on Oliver, he, too, ran. He did not get far. A huge fist crashed into his face, and all went black.

CHAPTER 3

Escape and Recapture

Oliver didn't know why he had run when Dodger stole the silk handkerchief. Maybe because he was shocked and frightened? Whatever the reason, everyone thought he was the thief.

A policeman took Oliver before a magistrate, Mr. Fang. The terrified boy turned very pale. He was clearly sick. He couldn't even open his mouth to tell Fang his name. Moments later, he fainted.

"He's pretending," snapped Fang. "He won't get pity from me. Instead, he'll spend three months in prison doing hard work."

All this time, the gentleman in the green coat had been looking closely at Oliver. He felt sorry for the boy. What was more,

Oliver's face reminded him of someone.

"My name is Mr. Brownlow," he said to Fang. "I believe this boy isn't the thief!"

The man who owned the bookshop spoke up. He had seen everything. Two other boys had stolen the handkerchief!

At this, Mr. Brownlow asked to take Oliver home and look after him.

"All right," said Fang. "Case over!"

Just by chance, for the first time in his life, Oliver was about to discover the meaning of happiness.

Oliver was extremely unwell. He lay tucked up in bed in Mr. Brownlow's home for many days. All the while, Mrs. Bedwin, Mr. Brownlow's kindly housekeeper, nursed him like an angel.

Mr. Brownlow was very fond of Oliver— and fascinated by him. *The boy looks like the portrait of the pretty young woman which hangs in my house,* he thought. *When he's stronger, I must ask about his family.*

Oliver also noticed the portrait. "It's strange, dear Mrs. Bedwin," he said. "I feel so close to that lovely lady. It's as if she were my mo…" He did not finish the sentence because it sounded foolish.

What a happy time Oliver spent at Mr. Brownlow's! He was well fed, slept in a clean, comfortable bed, and was taught to read and write. Above all, everyone around him was warm and kind.

*

In Fagin's den, nothing was warm or kind. The old crook was furious when he heard about Oliver. "You fools!" he hissed at Dodger and Charley. "How could you lose him? He'll now tell the police all about us—who we are and where we live."

Fagin paced around his filthy room. "We must get him back," he muttered.

Oliver was enormously grateful to Mr. Brownlow and Mrs. Bedwin. Their kindness did not spoil him because he remembered the misery of his old life. He was sad only because he couldn't repay them.

"Is there anything I can do for you?" he asked every day. The answer was always the same: "No, but thank you for asking, Oliver."

One evening, the answer was different. "Yes, there is something, Oliver," said Mr. Brownlow. "Please run down to the bookshop and return these books, and pay the man what I owe him."

Oliver was delighted. He put Mr. Brownlow's five-pound note

in his pocket, tucked the books under his arm, and went out.

Fagin had plotted with the thug Bill Sykes to recapture Oliver. Sykes got his girlfriend, Nancy, to play a cruel trick.

"Oh, my dear brother!" Nancy sobbed when she saw Oliver. "Please come home!" She threw her arms around him.

"Don't!" cried Oliver. "Who are you?"

Bystanders sided with Nancy and called Oliver an "ungrateful brute."

Bill Sykes strode up. "Books?" he shouted, grabbing those Oliver was carrying. "I told you not to steal books!"

Oliver's cries echoed into the darkness as he was dragged back to Fagin's den.

The thieves took Oliver's fine clothes. Sykes ripped up his books, and Fagin grabbed his five-pound note. Sykes snatched it from him, saying it was his pay for recapturing the boy.

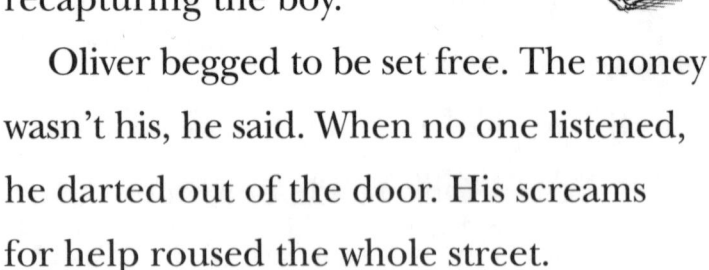

Oliver begged to be set free. The money wasn't his, he said. When no one listened, he darted out of the door. His screams for help roused the whole street.

Dodger and Charley dragged Oliver back into the dark room. Fagin raised a heavy club.

"So, you wanted to get away, my dear, did you?" he said.

Oliver did not reply.

"Called for the police, did you?" sneered Fagin. "Well, take that!" He crashed the club onto Oliver's shoulders.

Before he could strike again, Nancy threw herself forward. "Stop! You got the boy, Fagin. Isn't that enough?"

Fagin and Sykes told her to be quiet, but she refused. Yes, she lived a life of crime, she said. But she knew good from evil. For once, she would do the right thing: She'd defend innocent Oliver against them all.

Oliver was not beaten any longer, just locked in a dark room. As he lay down to sleep, he knew that, even in Fagin's foul den, he had found one good person: Nancy.

While Oliver was Fagin's prisoner, Mr. Bumble came to London. There he saw a notice put up by Mr. Brownlow. It offered a reward for information about a boy named Oliver Twist.

Mr. Bumble wanted the money. He told Mr. Brownlow and Mrs. Bedwin that Oliver was a lying, low-born rascal. Since they loved Oliver, they didn't believe him.

Meanwhile, a mysterious man named Monks was also looking for Oliver. After finding him, Monks offered Fagin money to turn Oliver into a criminal.

Fagin set to work. Every day, he told Oliver that robbing was an amusing game. In the end, Oliver began to believe this.

Monks's plot was now ready. Bill Sykes needed a boy to help him rob a house. He had to be small enough to squeeze through a tiny window, open the front door, and let in the robbers. Oliver was just the right size.

Nancy had to bring Oliver to Bill Sykes. She didn't want to, because she loved Oliver and knew he had a good heart. But, terrified of her brutal boyfriend, she did as she was ordered.

Thus, one dark and gloomy night, poor little Oliver Twist became a thief.

CHAPTER 4

The Mystery of Oliver Twist

Sykes pushed Oliver through the tiny window in the house he was robbing.

"Now, open the front door, and let me in," growled the thug. "And remember my pistol. One false step, and I'll shoot!"

Sykes didn't shoot Oliver, but someone in the house did. Hearing a noise downstairs, they grabbed a gun. Bang! Oliver staggered, blood pouring from his arm. Sykes grabbed him by the collar and heaved him back through the window. He carried Oliver until he heard men coming after him. To get away quicker, he dropped Oliver into a ditch and ran off.

More dead than alive, Oliver crawled toward the nearest light. It came from the house where he had been shot! On the doorstep, he collapsed, and passed out.

In the house lived a pretty girl named Rose and her good-hearted guardian, Mrs. Maylie. When they that saw Oliver was badly wounded and likely to die, they took pity on him. They paid for a doctor to treat him and informed the police the boy had nothing to do with the break-in.

In the care of these good people, Oliver recovered. Once again, he enjoyed the comfort of a loving, peaceful home.

When Oliver didn't return, Fagin visited Nancy. She said Sykes was still gone, too.

"It's my fault," she wailed. "Poor little Oliver! I should never have helped make him into a robber."

"Pah!" sneered Fagin. "He's only a boy. But it's a shame. His robbing could have earned me money!"

Nancy called him a hard-hearted monster. He called her a soft-hearted fool and left.

Oliver knew nothing of his parents, but

Monks did. That's why he'd struck the bargain with Fagin.

When Fagin called on Monks, he found him furious that the robbery had gone wrong. He hated Oliver, he muttered, and needed him out of the way. Once again, he explained his plan to Fagin.

"I pay you to make Oliver a criminal, right?" Monks began. "The boy commits a crime, and the police arrest him. The judge sends him to Australia, where criminals go these days. And Oliver Twist disappears forever!"

Why did he want this? Because he and Oliver were brothers! Their father had left them money. With Oliver gone, he would have it all to himself!

Do you remember, at the beginning of our story, how a locket and a ring were stolen from Oliver's mother? It happened in the workhouse, moments after she died.

Oliver believed his mother had left him nothing. If he found the stolen jewels, he would learn who his mother was. But Monks didn't want Oliver to know about his parents. He was determined to find the ring and the locket and destroy them.

Widow Corney, a nurse at the workhouse, knew about the things stolen from Oliver's mother. She also liked the fat and important Mr. Bumble. And he liked the well-off Widow Corney.

After smiling at each other for a time, the pair were married.

It was not a happy marriage. Widow Corney wanted everything her own way. If Mr. Bumble disagreed, she screamed at him. After a while, he wished he had never married.

After one of his fights with his wife, Mr. Bumble went to the pub. Monks was waiting for him.

"I think you can get something for me," whispered Monks. "I will pay good money for it."

Mr. Bumble asked what Monks wanted. When Monks said he wanted the stolen locket and ring, Mr. Bumble smiled.

Monks met with Mr. Bumble and Widow Corney at night, in a building resting on poles over a black, muddy river.

"We're here," announced Mr. Bumble. He didn't know which he was more afraid of, his wife or Monks.

"Give me the things," snarled Monks.

"Money first!" said Mr. Bumble.

"Twenty pounds," snapped Monks.

"Twenty-five," replied Mr. Bumble.

Monks agreed. He handed over the money, and Widow Corney gave him a small bag containing the jewels stolen from Oliver's mother.

Monks tore it open. Inside was the locket holding two strands of hair. The name "Agnes" was engraved on the gold wedding ring. Here, at last, was the name of Oliver's mother!

"What will you do with them?" asked Widow Corney.

"You'll see," said Monks. With these words, he opened a hatch in the floor of the room. Below them, the river swirled and gurgled. For a moment, Mr. Bumble feared Monks was going to push *him* down there. Instead, he dropped the bag into the water. It fell with a tiny splash and was carried away by the current.

Now the jewels were gone, Monks needed Oliver to be caught stealing. That's why Fagin had Sykes use the boy in his robbery. But it had gone wrong, and Oliver was living with Rose and Mrs. Maylie. Monks went to see Fagin to plan their next step.

The pair met in Fagin's den. He sent the boys out and told Nancy to stay where she was. Fagin and Monks then went into the next room. When they were alone, Monks told Fagin about the locket and the ring.

"The last link to Oliver's mother has gone," he chortled. "The money will all be mine. But first we must get Oliver back."

Nancy was secretly listening at the door. She heard about the locket and the ring, about Monks being Oliver's brother, and about the plan to get Oliver sent to Australia as a criminal!

What could she do? She ought to tell Oliver's new friends the truth. But if she did, she would be in danger from the murderous Bill Sykes.

Nancy chose the path of goodness and honesty. Knowing that Rose and Mrs. Maylie were in London, she went to see them to pass on what she had heard.

CHAPTER 5

Murder!

Nancy rang the doorbell of the house where Rose was staying. "We don't want girls like you in here!" said the servants.

Nancy pleaded, and eventually a kind maid showed her into Rose's sitting room. Nancy expected Rose to be snobbish like the servants. But she wasn't at all. She felt sorry for Nancy and listened carefully to her story.

"Thank you so much," she exclaimed when Nancy had finished. "You have been very kind—and very brave."

"I am only doing the right thing for little Oliver," explained Nancy.

Rose smiled at her. "Of course. And you have put yourself in danger. Why not stay here? We'll protect you from Sykes."

When Nancy said she had to get back, Rose sighed. They agreed to meet again by London Bridge. In the meantime, Rose would tell Mr. Brownlow Nancy's news.

When Rose and Oliver called on Mr. Brownlow and Mrs. Bedwin, the room was filled with hugs and kisses and tears of joy.

Afterward, Rose told Mr. Brownlow about Monks's plot. They must get hold of Oliver's wicked brother, they agreed. Nancy had promised to help.

Rose was right when she said it was dangerous for Nancy to visit her. As Nancy was getting ready for the secret meeting at London Bridge, Sykes got angry.

He frowned when she put on her hat and asked sharply, "Where are you going, Nance?"

"Nowhere important," she replied, twisting her fingers anxiously.

Sykes swore. "Then, you're not going," he ordered.

Nancy was very upset to miss the meeting. She cried and stamped her feet. Fagin noticed her mood and thought, *Aha! This girl is up to something!*

Fagin needed someone to spy on

Nancy. The boys would be too young. He wondered if he could trust the new member of his gang. In the end, he decided he could.

And who was this person? Noah Claypole! The same cruel oaf who had bullied Oliver when he worked for Mr. Sowerberry. Noah had stolen money, run away to London, and joined Fagin's gang.

"Want to do a little job for me, Noah?" Fagin asked.

"Anything you wish, Mr. Fagin, sir," replied Noah with a bow.

Fagin nodded. "You any good at spying?"

"It's what I'm best at," grinned Noah.

"Good. Then listen carefully …"

While Noah Claypole was preparing to spy on Nancy, something extraordinary happened. The Dodger was arrested!

He was not caught for stealing something valuable, but for taking a small box worth two and a half pennies! He was furious. In the law court, he made a great scene. He was a "victim," he said. The police had taken away his "privileges"!

The judge took no notice of Dodger's nonsense and ordered him to be sent to Australia. Fagin's gang was falling apart. It wouldn't be long before the police caught up with Fagin himself.

Meanwhile, Noah had set out after Nancy when she sneaked off on her own one night. He followed her through the dark streets to London Bridge. There, he hid where he could hear her conversation with Rose and Mr. Brownlow.

Nancy agreed to tell them where Monks lived. So, thought Noah, *Nancy's love for Oliver is greater than her friendship with Fagin. She is a traitor to the gang!*

Noah went straight back to Fagin and reported what he had heard. An evil look came into the old man's eyes, a look that said he would teach Nancy a lesson she would never forget!

"Bill, your Nancy is a good girl," said Fagin when he next met Bill Sykes.

The thug nodded. "Yeah, she's all right, I suppose."

"Pity she likes Oliver Twist more than us," said Fagin casually.

"What do you mean?" cried Sykes. "Speak up, you old skeleton!"

Fagin told him what Noah had overheard. He twisted the story, suggesting that Nancy would turn Sykes over to the police.

Sykes gave a terrible scowl. He frowned and ground his teeth. Swearing dreadfully, he stormed out of the room and ran to his own house.

Nancy smiled when she heard him come in. Her look changed to one of terror when she saw his face.

"Please, Bill," she begged, grabbing hold of him. "I've done you no harm!"

"No harm?" roared Sykes. "Liar!"

Nancy's face was streaked with tears. "I love you, Bill," she gasped, clinging tightly to him.

"Get off me, traitor!" he shouted, pushing her away.

He raised his pistol above his head …

*

When Sykes saw what he had done, he was filled with shame and horror. He had done many wicked things, but this was the worst. There could be no forgiveness, no mercy for a man who had killed an innocent girl.

Sykes could not stay in London, where everyone would guess who had killed Nancy. He fled into the countryside, where he hoped to be safe.

But there was no escape. When he tried to rest, Nancy's ghost floated before his eyes. She haunted him—and would haunt him to the end.

Wherever Sykes went, all the talk was of the cruel murder of a young woman. He felt all eyes were on him. He had nowhere to hide.

In desperation, he returned to London. He knew of a dark and dirty building where he wouldn't be found. He was wrong.

A man recognized him, and a large crowd gathered outside. "Murderer!" the mob cried. "Come out, you monster!"

The only escape was across the roof.

Sykes found a rope. On one end, he made a loop to go around his body. The other end he tied to the chimney.

Carefully, he climbed out of the window and edged along the roof.

Below, the mob bellowed and shrieked. Above, Sykes stared at the ghost of Nancy, slipped—and fell.

The rope that was supposed to go around his body went only around his neck. And that was the end of Bill Sykes.

CHAPTER 6

Happiness!

Nancy had told Rose and Mr. Brownlow what Monks looked like and where he could be found. Mr. Brownlow went there with two strong men and forced Monks to return home with him.

"Now," he said, when the two men were alone, "tell me the truth."

At first, Monks said he didn't know what Mr. Brownlow was talking about.

But when he heard what Nancy had said about him and Fagin, Monks confessed.

Monks's real name was Edward Leeford. His father, Edwin Leeford, was Mr. Brownlow's best friend. Edwin had been forced to marry a woman he didn't love, and after the birth of Edward, the couple separated. Years later, Mrs. Leeford died.

How does Oliver Twist fit into all this? Read on, and you will see …

Free from his unhappy marriage, Edwin Leeford fell in love. The girl he adored was named Agnes. One day, he told Mr. Brownlow all about the lovely Agnes, and he gave him a portrait of her. This portrait still hung in Mr. Brownlow's house.

Before marrying Agnes, Edwin tragically died. Agnes, who was expecting a baby, was left by herself with nothing.

I expect you've guessed what comes next, haven't you?

Agnes was the poor young woman who died in Mr. Bumble's workhouse at the beginning of our story. Her baby was Oliver Twist.

No wonder Mr. Brownlow thought Oliver looked like the picture hanging on his wall! Agnes was Oliver's mother. It's not surprising Oliver also loved the picture.

"Well, Edward Leeford," said Mr. Brownlow. "What did you do when you learned you had a brother?"

"I was furious," muttered Leeford. "Half my father's money would go to this wretched Oliver Twist. I wanted it all for myself—I had to get rid of him."

Mr. Brownlow looked shocked. "Get rid of him?"

"Not kill him! I wanted Fagin to make him a criminal, so he'd be sent to Australia. Like the Artful Dodger."

"And your wicked plan failed," said Mr. Brownlow, shaking his head. "Oliver has a heart of gold, and he could never be a criminal."

When Oliver heard his brother's story, he gave him a second chance. After all, Oliver said, Mr. Brownlow and Rose had both given *him* a second chance. He shared the family money between himself and his half-brother.

Edward Leeford was grateful to Oliver for sharing the family money and for his second chance. He stopped using the name "Monks." From now on, he promised, he would lead an honest life.

Promises are easier to make than keep. Edward went to America. There, he said, everyone could make money. True, he did make money, but he made it as a criminal.

He was caught and sent to prison. The man who had tried to get his hands on everything, ended up with nothing.

*

The police caught up with Fagin, too. He was found guilty of many crimes. The worst was training boys, such as Dodger and Charley Bates, to be thieves. The judge said execution was the only suitable punishment for such crimes.

Oliver and Mr. Brownlow went to see Fagin on his last evening. They found him sitting on the stone bed in his cell. He was filthier than ever. His clothes were torn, his long red hair hung over his face, his eyes stared at things that were not there.

When Oliver asked him if he wanted to say a prayer, Fagin mumbled nonsense. His mind had already gone. In the morning, his body would be gone, too.

Fagin's gang was no more. His boys were horrified to learn that Bill Sykes had murdered Nancy, and most of them gave up thieving.

The Artful Dodger's friend, Charley Bates, left London altogether. He decided to move to the countryside, where the air was cleaner and criminals did not hang about on every street corner. Charley's honest, hard work as a cattle farmer paid off, and in the end it made him a very wealthy man.

*

That leaves just two more rogues for us to learn about: Mr. Bumble and the Widow Corney. The magistrates got to hear how the locket and the ring had been stolen from Oliver's mother. They learned, too, how Mr. Bumble and the Widow Corney had sold these jewels to Monks.

For these disgraceful actions, Mr. Bumble and the Widow Corney lost their jobs. What could they do now? Mr. Bumble knew only how to eat and drink and be a bully. Widow Corney knew only how to scream, lie, and cheat. No one wanted good-for-nothings like that working for them. With no jobs, they grew poorer and poorer.

The wicked pair became so poor, in fact, that they were sent to a workhouse—the very same one where Mr. Bumble had once been the big bully. A lot of people said it served them right.

*

Oliver's story has one more surprise. The beautiful Rose, the young woman who had been so kind to him, turned out to be his mother's sister. She was his aunt!

The two of them spent many happy

hours together. Aunt and nephew walked in the countryside and chatted by the fireside. In time, Rose married her boyfriend, Harry. He was as fond of Oliver as she was. And when the couple had children, they also loved Oliver dearly.

When not visiting Rose and Harry, Oliver lived with Mr. Brownlow and Mrs. Bedwin. Because Mr. Brownlow had been such a good friend of Oliver's father, he adopted the boy. The wise and good-hearted old man did all he could for his adopted son. He gave him a good education and, most important of all, a secure and loving home.

Oliver Twist, the orphan child with a heart of gold, had entered life all alone. Though wicked people did their worst to harm him, he never gave up.

Now, Rose has taken the place of his mother, and Mr. Brownlow has taken the place of his father. And so our story, which started with tears, ends with smiles and happy laughter.

Alice in Wonderland

Retold by
Lisa Regan

Illustrated by
Mel Howells

ARCTURUS

To my gorgeous husband and boys.
I love you so much—LR.

For Evie—MH.

ARCTURUS

This edition published in 2018 by Arcturus Publishing Limited
26/27 Bickels Yard, 151–153 Bermondsey Street,
London SE1 3HA

Copyright © Arcturus Holdings Limited

All rights reserved. No part of this publication may be reproduced, stored in a retrieval system, or transmitted, in any form or by any means, electronic, mechanical, photocopying, recording or otherwise, without written permission in accordance with the provisions of the Copyright Act 1956 (as amended). Any person or persons who do any unauthorised act in relation to this publication may be liable to criminal prosecution and civil claims for damages.

Writer: Lisa Regan
Illustrator: Mel Howells
Designer: Jeni Child
Editor: Becca Clunes
Art Director: Jessica Crass

ISBN: 978-1-78828-681-7
CH006097NT
Supplier 24, Date 0618, Print run 7508

Printed in Malaysia

Contents

CHAPTER 1
Down the Rabbit Hole 4

CHAPTER 2
A Long Tale 16

CHAPTER 3
Advice from a Caterpillar 26

CHAPTER 4
A Mad Tea Party 36

CHAPTER 5
The Mock Turtle 47

CHAPTER 6
Who Stole the Tarts? 56

CHAPTER 1

Down the Rabbit Hole

It was a sunny day, and Alice was sitting on the bank of the river with her sister. The heat made her feel quite tired, and it was getting rather boring with nothing to do. Alice was just wondering if she could muster the energy to pick daisies for a daisy chain, when a White Rabbit with pink eyes dashed past.

Alice didn't think much about it, until she heard it mutter to itself, "Oh dear, oh dear! I shall be late!" And then, when it took a watch out of its jacket pocket, Alice really did sit up and take notice.

Alice followed the rabbit across the field and watched it disappear down a rabbit hole. Without a thought about the consequences, Alice climbed down after it. The hole began as a tunnel but soon became steeper, until Alice was falling, falling, falling, as if she were in a well.

It seemed that she was falling very slowly, for Alice had plenty of time to look around her. The sides of the well were filled with cupboards and shelves; Alice managed to reach a jar that said ORANGE MARMALADE on it but found that it was empty. *I have fallen so far that I may reach the other side of the earth,* Alice thought to herself. *Wouldn't that be fun?*

Alice fell for so long that she was starting to doze off, when suddenly she hit the ground with a bump. A long, dark passage stretched ahead, and the White Rabbit scurried along, still fretting about being late. Alice followed, but the rabbit rushed off, and she was left alone in a long hallway with doors along each side.

A little three-legged table made of glass stood before her with a key on the top. Alice tried the key in all of the locks, but none of the doors opened. What was she to do? Then, she noticed a low curtain with a small door behind it. The key was the perfect fit, and the little door swung open.

The door was too small to climb through, so Alice knelt down to have a look. A passage led to the loveliest garden with bright flowers and sparkling fountains. How she longed to be there, away from this dark hallway! *If only I could close up like a telescope,* thought Alice. *Perhaps I could, if I think hard enough? So many strange things are happening today!*

Alice clambered to her feet and noticed something new. A little bottle stood on the table ("which I'm sure was not here before," she said). The bottle had a label on it that said DRINK ME in large letters.

Alice was not so stupid. The bottle might contain poison, and Alice did not want to become a warning to other children. But the bottle was not marked "poison," so she took a tiny sip. It tasted delicious, and soon, she had drunk it all.

"How very curious!" said Alice. "I feel like I'm closing up like a telescope!" Sure enough, she had shrunk to the size of a doll. The table leg was now vast beside her, but at least she could fit through the door and reach the lovely garden.

Alice waited to check that she wasn't still shrinking ("for that might end in me going out altogether, like the flame of a candle") and then skipped to the door. But—oh!—she had left the key on the glass table and was now much too small to reach it. Poor Alice began to cry.

After a minute, Alice shook herself hard and pulled herself together— what was left of her, for she was extremely small. She noticed a little glass box beneath the table. It contained a very small cake with the words EAT ME written on the top.

Well, here goes nothing, thought Alice and nibbled at the cake. She held her hand to her head to see if she was growing again and was surprised that nothing happened. Of course, that is usually the case when you eat cake, but Alice's day had been most peculiar so far, and she was beginning to expect the unexpected.

Soon, Alice had polished off the whole cake. "Oh!" she cried, as she began to feel a peculiar feeling. "Oh, oh! Curiouser and curiouser!" (Her grasp of good English had gone with the shock of it all.)

Alice was growing again at an alarming rate. "Goodbye feet!" she called down to her shoes far below her. "It's been nice knowing you!" As her head banged on the ceiling, Alice grabbed at the key on the table and made her way back to the door.

Now she was so tall that not only was she unable to fit through, she also had to lie down even to see into the garden. She began to cry again and cried so many tears that she made a pool all around her.

The sound of footsteps made Alice stop and dry her eyes. It was the White Rabbit once again, dressed in his finest clothes and carrying a large fan and a pair of gloves. "The Duchess will be so angry," he fussed, and then he gave a start when he saw Alice. He dropped his things and ran in the opposite direction.

Alice picked up the fan and wafted it in front of her as she pondered. Things were so strange today. Had something happened to her overnight? Was she actually even Alice any longer? *Well, I can't be Lucy, for she has dark hair, and I can't be Emily, for she is not very clever at all. Oh, who am I?*

Alice waved the fan as she tried to think clearly. "Let me see how much I know," she mused. "Four times six is thirteen, and London is the capital of Paris. Oh, that's not right!" she wailed and then looked down at her lap. The glove seemed the right size, and she saw that she had shrunk by fanning herself.

She dropped the fan hastily, just in time to prevent herself from disappearing altogether. That was lucky, but other things were not—the key was still on the table, and she was once again too small to reach it.

She was about to burst into tears once more, but as she stepped back in dismay, her foot slipped.

SPLASH! Somehow, she was up to her chin in salty water. She thought she'd fallen into the sea, but then she made out she was in a pool of her own tears, cried when she was tall enough to fill the room.

As she swam and wondered what would happen next, a creature splashed past close by. Was it a walrus or a hippo? But no, she was now so small that it was only a mouse doing the crawl to reach the edge of the pool. Alice swam alongside and wondered if the mouse could talk.

The mouse could indeed speak, and they chatted as they swam together. "I do wish I hadn't cried so much," said Alice, as swimming was becoming very tiring.

Alice and the mouse swam past the other creatures that had fallen into the pool. Among them were a duck and a dodo, an owl and a parrot, and finally they all reached the shore. They clambered onto the bank and sat there for a while, their fur and feathers and Alice's clothes dripping, and they wondered how they might get dry before they all caught cold.

"The best thing to get us warm and dry," offered the dodo, "would be to hold a Caucus-race."

CHAPTER 2
A Long Tale

No one else knew what a Caucus-race was, so the dodo offered to show them. First, it marked out the racecourse in a wobbly sort of a circle. Then, the whole party of creatures were placed along the course, here and there in no particular order.

Alice waited for someone to say *Go!* but nobody did, so they all began running when they felt like it. Nobody said *Stop*, either, so they gradually finished running when they wanted. But after about half an hour, they were all quite dry, and the dodo announced that the race was over.

"But who has won?" they panted. The dodo took a long time to think about this. Eventually, he announced, "*Everybody* has

won! And we must all receive a prize."
And he nominated Alice to find prizes for
everyone. Panicked, Alice felt in her pocket
and pulled out a box of raisins. Luckily,
there were just enough to go around.

The animals insisted that Alice also
had a prize and seized the empty box as
a trophy. "We beg your acceptance of this
precious prize," said the dodo, and Alice
did her best not to laugh as all the other
animals cheered.

"Now," said Alice to the mouse. "Tell me your tale as you promised while we swam."

"Ah," said the mouse, "it is a long and sad tale."

It is a long tail, certainly, she thought, but she wasn't sure why it was sad. She puzzled about it so much that the mouse stopped talking and glared at her. "You aren't concentrating!" he scolded, and got up and stomped away.

The other animals gradually wandered off as well, and soon, Alice was left by herself. She felt very lonely and out of sorts, and she began to wonder if she should have followed the rabbit after all.

As she was thinking about the White Rabbit, he reappeared in front of her.

"Oh, my dear paws! Oh, my fur and whiskers!" he muttered, "Where *can* I have dropped them?"

He was searching for his gloves and his fan, so Alice scrambled to her feet and began to help. It was most peculiar; they were nowhere to be seen, nor were the glass table or the great hall or the little door. Everything had vanished.

Very soon, the rabbit noticed Alice.

"Mary Ann, what are you doing here? Fetch me my gloves and fan! Quick, now!"

Why, he mistook me for his housemaid! thought Alice, but she ran to fetch them.

Rabbit had a neat little house, with W. RABBIT engraved on a brass plate by the front door. Inside, Alice found the items she needed, but a little bottle caught her eye.

This one did not have a label saying DRINK ME, but Alice put it to her lips anyway and took a sip. She hoped it would make her grow large again, for she had had enough of being so very small.

Sure enough, before she had drunk half the bottle, her head was pressing against the ceiling, and she had to stoop to stop her neck from breaking. She put down the bottle and looked at the little doorway out of the house. She was stuck!

"I wish I hadn't drunk so much!" she exclaimed, but it was too late for that. She kept on growing until she filled the whole room and had to poke one foot up the chimney and stick an arm out of a window.

It was much pleasanter at home, thought poor Alice, *when one wasn't always growing larger and smaller!*

As Alice lay squeezed against the door,

she heard the White Rabbit come huffing and puffing up the front path. "Bill! Bill!" he called, as he caught sight of the giant hand poking out of the window. "You must remove that at once!"

"You shall do no such thing!" shouted Alice, who didn't know who Bill was but didn't want him coming just the same. The White Rabbit called out again, and a lizard came running up. Together, they set a ladder against the roof, and Alice heard scrambling up and then scrambling back down again, this time inside the chimney.

"You won't get in that way!" said Alice, and gave as big a kick as she could, considering the great size of her foot and the narrow width of the chimney. Poor Bill hurtled high in the air, and all Alice then heard was, "Quick, catch him by the hedge!"

Alice gave a start as a shower of pebbles flew in at the window. Even more surprising, they turned into little cakes before her very eyes. *Here we go again,* she thought. *I may as well take a bite to try to change my size. It cannot possibly make me larger, so I suppose it must make me smaller.*

Sure enough, Alice began to shrink once more. As soon as she was small enough, she ran out of the door and away from the house as fast as she could. She stopped running only when she heard a bark and nearly crashed into an enormous puppy with large, round eyes.

Of course, I am still small, she thought, as she threw a stick for the puppy to play with. *How must I get big, and will I ever make it to that lovely garden? I suppose I must eat or*

drink something again, but what should it be this time?

There was nothing but flowers and grass all around her. There was certainly no food or drink. Then, Alice caught sight of a giant mushroom. She walked all around it, hopefully. She decided to take a look on the very top and pulled herself up on tiptoe.

Imagine her surprise when she was suddenly faced with a very large caterpillar! Its eyes were closed and it appeared to be meditating. It was not even aware that Alice was there.

CHAPTER 3

Advice from a Caterpillar

The caterpillar opened its eyes. "Who are YOU?" it asked, rather grumpily. "Well, I don't really know," Alice sighed. "I seem to have changed several times already today. I'm ever so confused. And I can't remember the things I used to know. I try to repeat them, but they all come out different from how they should."

The caterpillar closed its eyes again and then said, "Repeat the poem 'Father William' to me, and then we'll see how confused you are." Alice took a deep breath and began.

"'You are old, Father William,'
   the young man said,
'And your hair has become very white.
And yet you incessantly stand on your head:
Do you think, at your age, it is right?'

"'In my youth,' Father William replied to his son,
'I feared it might injure the brain.
But now that I'm perfectly sure I have none,
Why, I do it again and again.'"

"Quite wrong from beginning to end," said the caterpillar and there was silence for some minutes. Alice waited patiently until the caterpillar shook itself and asked suddenly, "What size?"

"Pardon?" said Alice.

"What size do you want to be? The mushroom can help."

The caterpillar crawled down from its perch and wriggled away, saying, "One side will make you taller, and the other side will make you shorter." Alice stretched out her arms and broke off a piece of mushroom with each hand. Nervously, she nibbled at the left-hand piece. Her chin nearly hit the floor!

Alice ate a little from her right hand. Oh, dear! Now, her head reached high into the clouds, and her neck stretched like a snake. She frightened a passing pigeon before looping her head down to the mushroom and taking a bite. In time, she managed to balance things out until she felt her proper size again.

The next place Alice came upon was a tiny house, no taller than she was. "Not again!" sighed Alice, and she nibbled more mushroom until she was small enough to look in the kitchen window. She didn't want to frighten the owners half to death.

It was Alice herself who was startled when she noticed two servants in uniform at the door of the house. One was a frog, and the other one looked remarkably like a fish. The fish gave the frog an invitation.

"The Queen invites the Duchess to play croquet." Then, he bowed low and went on his way.

Alice was about to approach the frog when a large plate hurtled out of the doorway, just grazing the frog's nose as it flew past. Through the door was a kitchen in chaos. Smoke billowed from the fireplace, and a cook stirred soup in a giant pot. Pepper filled the air and made Alice sneeze.

A well-dressed lady—*the Duchess*, thought Alice—sat in the middle with a baby in her lap. Both of them sneezed constantly. "Too much pepper in the soup!" shouted the Duchess, between sneezes. The only ones in the kitchen not sneezing were the cook and a large cat.

The cat sat by the fireplace, grinning from ear to ear. "Excuse me," said Alice politely. "But why does your cat grin like that?"

"Because it is a Cheshire Cat," said the Duchess as if that explained everything. "All Cheshire Cats can grin, and most of them do," she continued. Then, very abruptly, she shouted, "Pig!"

Alice was quite taken aback at this rudeness, and then she saw that the Duchess was speaking not to her but to the baby. As she pondered what to say next, the cook stopped stirring the soup and began throwing plates around the room.

The Duchess stood up, narrowly avoiding a saucer that whizzed past the baby's little face, and handed the bundle to Alice. "Here, you look after this," she said. "I have to play croquet with the Queen." And off she went.

The baby grunted, and Alice rocked it in her arms and carried it out into the garden. When it grunted again, she looked more closely at its face to see what was the matter with it. Surely that wasn't … but it was! The baby had a snout and tiny, piggy little eyes. Alice set it down on the floor, and it trotted into the trees.

Alice was startled to see the Cheshire Cat sitting on the branch of a nearby tree. It was grinning at her in a friendly way. Still, it did have sharp claws and a great many teeth, so she thought she ought to treat it with respect.

"Cheshire Puss," she said, and it grinned a little wider. "Would you tell me, please, which way I should go from here?"

"That depends on where you want to get to," replied the Cat.

"I don't care where I go to, as long as I get somewhere."

"Oh, you're bound to do that," said the Cat, "if you walk for long enough."

Alice tried another question. "What sort of people live around here?"

"In that direction lives the Hatter," said the Cat, with a wave of its paw. "And in that direction lives the March Hare. Visit either of them. They're both mad."

"I don't want to visit mad people," declared Alice.

"Well, I have to go," said the Cat. "Are you playing croquet with the Queen today? If so, I'll see you there." And with that, it vanished.

Then, it appeared again, asking, "What happened to the baby?"

"It turned into a pig," replied Alice.

"I thought it would," said the Cat, and it vanished again.

After reassuring herself that the Cheshire Cat was completely gone, Alice began to walk in the direction of the March Hare's house. She looked up to see the Cat in front of her once more. "Did you say pig or fig?" it asked. "Pig," replied Alice. "And your vanishing act is making me dizzy."

"Sorry," said the Cat, and it slowly disappeared, bit by bit, beginning with the end of its tail. Eventually, all that was left was its grin, and that hung around for quite some time. *I have often seen a cat without a grin,* thought Alice, *but never a grin without a cat!*

CHAPTER 4
A Mad Tea Party

Alice soon came to the March Hare's house, where a tea party was set out on a large table in front. Only three guests were present, but they saw Alice and began to shout, "No room! No room!" in quite a puzzling way.

"There's PLENTY of room," said Alice. She sat down opposite the March Hare and the Hatter, who were both leaning on a dormouse that slept with its head on the table. The pair of them were drinking tea. "Have some wine," offered the March Hare. Alice looked, but there was nothing to drink except tea. "There isn't any wine," she commented. "It isn't very polite to offer something you don't have."

"It isn't very polite to sit down without being invited," said the March Hare.

"The dormouse is asleep again," said the Hatter, and he poured a little hot tea upon its nose. It didn't even open its eyes.

"How Time flies!" said the Hatter thoughtfully. "Do you know, the last time I was on speaking terms with Time" (at this, Alice raised her eyebrows), "was when I sang at the concert given by the Queen of Hearts. I sang 'Twinkle, Twinkle.'"

He began to sing mournfully.

"Twinkle, twinkle, little bat!
How I wonder what you're at!
Up above the world you fly,
Like a tea tray in the sky ... "

Here the dormouse began singing in its sleep, until they pinched it to make it stop.

"I'd hardly finished the first verse," said the Hatter, "when the Queen shouted, 'He's murdering time! Off with his head!' and that's the last time Time did a single thing I asked. It's always six o'clock now, you know." An idea dawned on Alice.

"Is that why you have so many tea things at one table?" she asked.

The Hatter nodded. "It's forever teatime. We never have a chance to tidy up, so we just keep moving around the table. Have some more cake, by the way."

"I've had nothing yet," said Alice, "so I can't take more."

"You mean you can't take less," said the Hatter. "Of course, you can take more than nothing. Foolish girl."

This was too rude for Alice, so she got up and walked away. The dormouse snored, and the others took no notice of her leaving. The last time she looked back, they were trying to put the dormouse into the teapot. *That's the stupidest party I've ever been to,* thought Alice, as she noticed a door in a tree trunk. Passing through cautiously, she found herself back in the hall with the key and the little door to the lovely garden. *Now I know how to handle this better,* she thought and took hold of the key before nibbling the mushroom pieces to change her height.

Finally, Alice found herself standing among the flowers next to a babbling fountain. She watched as three curious-looking gardeners busied themselves painting the white roses red.

"Ahem," coughed Alice, "could you tell me why you are doing that?" The gardener on the left, who looked very much like the Five of Spades, explained. "It was supposed to be a red rose tree, miss, but we planted a white one by mistake. If we don't put it right, the Queen will chop off our heads."

At that moment, a voice shouted, "The Queen! The Queen!" and the three gardeners threw themselves flat on the floor. Alice watched in fascination as a procession of cards marched past.

First came ten soldiers, carrying clubs, then ten courtiers who were richly decorated with diamonds. They all marched in, two by two. After them were the ten royal children, all ornamented with hearts and holding hands with each other. Finally, in paraded the guests: a rich party of kings and queens, with the White Rabbit scuttling at the back.

The King and the Queen were the last to arrive, and as they walked past Alice, they stopped. Alice wondered if she should lie face down like the gardeners but decided against it.

Instead, she stood still and waited. *After all,* she thought, *what is the use of a procession if nobody can see it?*

"Who is this?" the Queen asked the Knave of Hearts, standing next to her.

"My name is Alice, so please your Majesty," she said and dropped a curtsey in front of the Queen.

"Impertinent child! I was not asking you! Off with her head!" she screeched, turning crimson with anger.

The White Rabbit crept up to Alice and led her away. "Where is the Duchess?" she whispered. "She is due to be executed, too," he replied. Alice wasn't particularly sorry, but the Queen's voice cut through their conversation. "Get to your places! Let the croquet begin!"

It was the most curious game Alice had ever seen. The balls were live hedgehogs, and the mallets were flamingos. The soldiers folded themselves over to make the croquet hoops. They kept getting up and walking off, and Alice soon decided it was a very difficult game indeed.

Alice's hedgehog constantly unrolled itself and moved to a new place, and none of the players waited their turn. The flamingo would not keep straight and still, and twisted itself around to look at

Alice with a puzzled expression that made Alice giggle. The Queen worked herself into a fury and stamped about shouting "Off with his head!" every minute.

"It's a wonder that anyone is still alive," said Alice, at which point the Cheshire Cat reappeared. Alice waited until the Cat's whole head was in front of her (*for it is no use speaking until its ears have come*) and then began to complain about the game.

"Who ARE you talking to?" asked the King, as he strolled past with his flamingo under his arm.

"A friend of mine," said Alice. "Let me introduce you."

"I don't like the look of it at all," responded the King, and the Queen walked past and shouted, "Off with its head!"

The executioner looked at the cat's head without a body. "I cannot see how that can be done," he exclaimed. "For how can you cut off a head with no body to cut it from?" At which point, the Cat began to fade away slowly, and the argument became pointless.

CHAPTER 5

The Mock Turtle

The Queen called for the Duchess to be fetched from her prison. When she appeared, the Duchess tucked her arm into Alice's in a most friendly way, and they walked off together.

The Duchess was in a much better mood, and Alice wondered if the lack of pepper and sneezing had cheered her up. *Maybe pepper makes people hot-tempered,* thought Alice. *And vinegar makes them sour, and sugar makes them sweet.* She was quite pleased with herself for having thought of this rule. They talked most pleasantly until the Queen arrived and the Duchess scurried away.

The game of croquet had been abandoned. All the players had been put in prison, and all the soldiers were guarding them, so there were no hoops left. Now the Queen turned her attention to Alice.

"Come and meet the Gryphon," she said. "It will take you to meet the Mock Turtle. You DO know about the Mock Turtle, don't you? It's the thing Mock Turtle soup is made of. Follow me, and he shall tell you his story." Alice was quite perplexed by all these new creatures.

The Gryphon had been sleeping soundly in the sun, but it woke at the sound of voices and rubbed its eyes. "Up, lazy thing!" said the Queen, "And take this young lady to see the Mock Turtle. I have some executions to oversee." The Gryphon watched as the Queen retreated and then said simply, "What fun!"

"I'm not sure about fun," said Alice. "Everyone is being executed!"

"Don't you worry about that," said the Gryphon. "It's fun for the Queen to make the orders, but nobody ever really gets their head chopped off. Come with me."

Alice was pleased to hear this, but she was getting a little fed up with being bossed around. Still, she followed the Gryphon, and soon, they came upon the Mock Turtle sitting sad and lonely on a rock.

The Mock Turtle sighed as if its heart would break. "What on earth makes him so sad?" Alice asked.

"Oh, it's all his imagination," whispered the Gryphon. "He hasn't got any sorrow, really." The Mock Turtle's eyes brimmed with tears while the Gryphon explained that Alice wanted to hear its history.

The Mock Turtle sighed and stayed silent for an awfully long time. Then, it began to speak. "Once," it sobbed, "I was a real Turtle."

Then it was silent again, and Alice wondered if that was both the beginning and end of its story. But she sat patiently and said nothing. "When we were little," the Mock Turtle finally resumed, "we went to school in the sea. The teacher was a Turtle, and we used to call him Tortoise."

"Why did you call him Tortoise if he wasn't one?" queried Alice.

"We called him Tortoise because he taught us," said the Mock Turtle angrily. "Are you very stupid?"

"We were taught Reeling and Writhing, of course, and all the branches of Arithmetic," he continued. "Ambition, Distraction, Uglification, and Derision." Alice was confused but didn't dare ask any other questions.

The Mock Turtle counted off more subjects on his flippers. "We took Mystery, ancient and modern, and Seaography. We had a conger eel for Drawling, and an old crab was the Classics master. He taught Laughing and Grief, but I never studied those."

Alice felt she needed to move things along a little. "And how long did you attend school each day?" she asked, thinking that was a safe question with a straightforward answer.

"Our lessons began with ten hours per day, and then nine on the next day, and eight on the next, and so on."

"What a curious plan!" exclaimed Alice.

"That's the reason they're called lessons," added the Gryphon. "Because they lessen each day, you see. But enough of that. Let's sing and dance."

Alice watched as the two creatures stood and began to move slowly around. "Usually, we have lobsters for this," said the Mock Turtle. "But we shall have to do without. Shall I sing?" The Gryphon nodded, and the Mock Turtle began to wail.

*"'Will you walk a little faster?' said a whiting
to a snail.
'There's a porpoise close behind us, and he's
treading on my tail.
See how eagerly the lobsters and the turtles
all advance!
They are waiting on the shingle—will you
come and join the dance?*

*"'Will you, won't you, will you, won't you,
will you join the dance?
Will you, won't you, will you, won't you,
won't you join the dance?
You can really have no notion how delightful
it will be
When they take us up and throw us, with
the lobsters, out to sea!'"*

Alice clapped, and the Mock Turtle

actually smiled. "Would you like to hear another song?" Alice nodded, and the Mock Turtle started again.

"Beautiful soup, so rich and green,
Waiting in a hot tureen!
Beau—ooootiful Soo—oop!
Beau—ooootiful Soo—oop!"

Alice didn't know whether to applaud or if there were more verses, but the decision was soon taken out of her hands. There was a loud cry of, "The trial's beginning!"

CHAPTER 6
Who Stole the Tarts?

The King and Queen of Hearts were on their thrones with a great crowd around them. There was a gaggle of birds and beasts and a whole pack of cards. The Knave stood in front, guarded by two soldiers. In the middle of the court was a table with a plate of very delicious-looking tarts on it.

Alice was hungry and hoped they would serve the refreshments quickly. In the meantime, she studied the jury box (*What an assortment of creatures!* she noticed) and then looked up when the White Rabbit shouted, "Silence in court!"

The White Rabbit continued by declaring the accusation.

*"The Queen of Hearts, she made some tarts,
All on a summer day.
The Knave of Hearts, he stole those tarts
And took them quite away!"*

"Consider your verdict!" the King said to the jury.

"Not yet, not yet!" interrupted the White Rabbit hastily.

"Call the first witness!" said the King.

First was the Hatter, who came in with a teacup in one hand and a piece of bread and butter in the other. Teatime was a never-ending process for him.

The Hatter looked nervous, and Alice felt a little twitchy on his behalf. Then, she had a horrible thought. That twitchy feeling meant that she was growing again. She felt herself pressing against the dormouse next to her, who got up grumpily and moved across the room.

The Hatter had no real evidence to offer and was soon replaced by the Duchess's cook. Before she arrived at the witness stand, people all around began to sneeze violently. "Give your evidence," said the King.

"Shan't!" said the cook. The King looked anxiously at the White Rabbit and then said, "What are tarts made of?"

"Pepper, mostly," said the cook.

"Treacle!" said the dormouse sleepily, and the guards seized him and carried him away. The King called the court to order and then announced the third witness to replace the cook. Imagine Alice's shock when her name was called!

Alice jumped up, quite forgetting how large she had grown, and tipped over the jury box with the edge of her skirt. Hastily, she straightened it and gathered up the jurors. She accidentally put Bill, the lizard, in head first and quickly corrected her mistake.

At this moment, the King shouted out, "Silence! Rule Forty-two. All persons more than a mile high to leave this court." Everybody looked at Alice.

"I'm not a mile high!" she said.

"You are nearly two miles," interjected the Queen.

"That isn't a proper rule," said Alice. "You just made it up."

"It's the oldest rule in the book," said the King.

"Well, in that case, it should be Rule Number One," Alice reasoned.

The King turned pale and hastily closed up his rule book. "Anyway, let us reach a verdict!" he said, turning to the jury.

"Sentence him first, and then we'll hear the verdict!" declared the Queen.

Alice was now so big that she wasn't scared to speak up. "That's ridiculous! He can't have stolen the tarts," she suggested, "because they are right there." and pointed to the table.

"Off with her head!" shouted the Queen, unsurprisingly. Nobody in the courtroom moved.

"What a lot of nonsense!" said Alice. "Why, you're nothing but a pack of cards!"

At this point, the whole pack rose up against Alice and came flying down upon her. She gave a little scream, half out of fright and half out of anger, and tried to beat them off. She found herself lying on the bank of the river with her head in her sister's lap.

Her sister was gently brushing some dead leaves away from Alice's face. "Wake up, Alice dear," she said. "Why, what a long sleep you've had!"

"Oh, I've had such a curious dream!" said Alice, and she told her sister, as well as she could remember, all about the strange adventures she had down the rabbit hole. Her sister agreed that it was most curious and sent Alice indoors to have tea.

Then, she sat with her head on her hand and pondered what Alice had told her. She drifted into a dream herself, where the grass rustled as the White Rabbit rushed by, and the Queen shouted and hollered, and the court was filled with excited voices.

And then, she brought herself back to reality, where the grass simply moved in the breeze, and the shepherd boy called to his sheep, and the farmyard buzzed with all sorts of noises.

Alice's sister smiled at Alice's tale and rejoiced in her ability to make faces light up with her stories. She thanked the skies above for their happy summer days, full of joy and sunshine, and hoped that they would never end.

Tom Sawyer

Retold by
Saviour Pirotta

Illustrated by
Vince Reid

ARCTURUS

For Albie Paton—SP.

For Pat and Mary—VR.

ARCTURUS

This edition published in 2018 by Arcturus Publishing Limited
26/27 Bickels Yard, 151–153 Bermondsey Street,
London SE1 3HA

Copyright © Arcturus Holdings Limited

All rights reserved. No part of this publication may be reproduced, stored in a retrieval system, or transmitted, in any form or by any means, electronic, mechanical, photocopying, recording or otherwise, without written permission in accordance with the provisions of the Copyright Act 1956 (as amended). Any person or persons who do any unauthorised act in relation to this publication may be liable to criminal prosecution and civil claims for damages.

Writer: Saviour Pirotta
Illustrator: Vince Reid
Designer: Jeni Child
Editor: Sebastian Rydberg
Art Director: Jessica Crass

ISBN: 978-1-78828-694-7
CH006285NT
Supplier 24, Date 0618, Print run 7521

Printed in Malaysia

Contents

CHAPTER 1
Painting the Fence 4

CHAPTER 2
Ghosts in the Graveyard 14

CHAPTER 3
An Island and a Funeral 24

CHAPTER 4
Under the Cross 34

CHAPTER 5
Danger in the Cave 46

CHAPTER 6
Treasure! 56

CHAPTER 1

Painting the Fence

"It's not fair," groaned Tom Sawyer, coming out of the house with a paintbrush. His aunt Polly followed with a bucket of whitewash.

"That'll teach you to skip school, Tom," she said.

"And to lie," added Tom's cousin Mary. She had come out behind Aunt Polly.

"I promised your mother before she died that I'd look after you and your brother, Sid," said Aunt Polly. "And that includes teaching you to obey your elders."

"And to tell the truth," giggled Mary.

It was a mighty warm Saturday. All the children in St. Petersburg would be going down to the river to swim. But not Tom. He had to paint the garden fence as punishment for skipping school.

The front door banged shut behind Aunt Polly and Cousin Mary. Tom's heart sank. The fence was big. He would never finish painting it by the end of the day, let alone in time for a swim.

He'd have to get help. Perhaps he could pay some of his friends to do some whitewashing. Tom emptied his pockets to see what he could pay them with. He had only a couple of marbles and a few bits of string.

The situation seemed hopeless, until he had the best idea ever! The first boy to come past the house was his friend Ben Rogers, pretending to be a grand steamboat. He was taking bites out of a big, juicy apple in between the tooting.

"You coming along for a swim, Tom?"

Tom picked up the brush and started painting. "Who'd want to go swimming when they have a lovely fence to whitewash?"

"You mean you choose to stay home and work?" cried Ben.

"It's only work if you don't want to do it!"

Ben stared at the fence. "Please, Tom, could I have a go?"

Tom sloshed more whitewash on the

fence. "Not sure you'll do a good job, Ben."

"I'll give you what's left of my apple," pleaded Ben.

"Alright," said Tom at last. He sat down on the grass and took a big bite out of Ben's apple. His trick had worked. Here he was, resting in the sun while Ben did all the hard work. Another friend, Johnny Miller, came along. He, too, wanted to have a go at painting. Tom wouldn't let him till he handed over his kite.

Before long, there was a long line of children wanting to help paint the fence. By the time it was finished, Tom had a collection of goodies, including marbles, toys, and even a dead rat swinging on a piece of string.

Tom learned a great lesson that warm, sunny day. If you want to sell something to people, make it hard to get. Then everyone will want it.

He went in to ask Aunt Polly if he could go swimming. She was so astonished to see the fence all painted, she gave him another apple.

Coming home from the river later that evening, Tom spotted a girl in Judge Thatcher's garden across the street. She was picking flowers. He'd never seen her before.

"Hello," called Tom.

The girl ignored him. Tom did some cartwheels to impress her. She still didn't look his way. Instead, she threw a pansy over her shoulder and went indoors. Tom's heart beat like a drum. That girl was the prettiest he'd ever seen. She was even prettier than Amy Lawrence at school. Tom was in love with Amy. Or had been till now. Now, Tom's heart belonged only to this mysterious girl.

He pounced on the pansy and held it close. He would keep it till the day he died.

Next morning, Tom got to school late.

"Thomas Sawyer," cried Mr. Dobbins, the schoolmaster. "What kept you?"

Tom was about to make an excuse involving Aunt Polly. Then, he spotted the mysterious girl. She was sitting with the other girls on their side of the schoolroom, an empty chair at her desk. Tom saw an opportunity …

"I got held up chatting to Huckleberry Finn, sir," he replied.

Mr. Dobbin's face turned a bright purple. "You did what, Thomas Sawyer?"

Huckleberry Finn was a street urchin, the son of a drunk. He slept outdoors and had been caught stealing. All adults considered him a very bad example.

"You were told not to talk to Master Finn," growled Mr. Dobbins, reaching for his cane. "Take off your jacket, Thomas."

Later, Tom sat down with his bottom stinging. His friends tittered, but he ignored them. His plan had worked. He'd been made to sit on the girls' side, right next to the mysterious girl. She seemed to feel sorry for Tom. "Hello," she said.

Tom's heart leaped for joy. She'd spoken to him!

He placed a peach in front of her.
"Pleese, tejk it," he scrawled on his slate.

"I'm Becky," she whispered. "My father's Judge Thatcher. I've just moved here."

Tom scrawled *I love you* on his slate.

"You bad thing," giggled Becky.

At dinner time, Tom and Becky sat on the grass. "Do you like ice cream, Becky?"

"I love it so," answered Becky.

Tom fished a brass paperweight from his pocket. "I don't have money for ice cream," he said. "But I will one day, I promise.

Meanwhile, here's a gift for you."

He watched Becky admiring it. "Becky, was you ever engaged?"

"Engaged?" said Becky.

"You know, to be married," said Tom. "Do you love me enough to marry me?"

"I do! But how do you get engaged?"

"Why, you just kiss."

"Well, I'll close my eyes, and we'll kiss," said Becky, and they kissed. "Now you must never marry anyone but me, Tom."

"And you must never choose anyone for games at parties but me," said Tom. "Why, when Amy and I were engaged ..."

Becky's eyes grew wide with horror. "You've been engaged before?"

"I don't love Amy any longer," said Tom hurriedly. "I only love you, Becky." But it was too late. Becky had stomped off.

CHAPTER 2
Ghosts in the Graveyard

Tom decided to skip school for the afternoon. He wandered down to the river, where he ran into Huckleberry Finn carrying a dead cat by the tail.

"I'm using it to get rid of the warts on my hand," he explained.

"Say," Tom said. "How do you do that?"

"Why, you takes it to the graveyard at night," explained Huck. "You stand close to a grave where someone wicked has just been buried. At night, the devil will come to fetch the wicked man's soul to hell. You throws the cat after the devil and say: 'Devil follow corpse, cat follow devil, warts follow cat, I'm done with ye.' And the warts will leap straight off you and follow the devil to hell. I'm going to the graveyard tonight. Old Hoss Williams has just been buried, and I reckons he was a very wicked man. Wanna come with me?"

Tom could not possibly say no. He might never get the chance to see warts jumping off someone again.

"I'll fetch ye tonight," Huck promised.

Time passed very slowly as Tom waited for Huck in his room.

At last, he heard a loud howling on the street below. It sounded like a cat, but Tom knew it wasn't. It was Huckleberry Finn, sending a signal.

Tom howled back to show he'd heard. Then, he climbed out of the window. Soon, the two boys were in the graveyard.

The wind moaned in the trees. It sounded like a ghost, looking for its grave.

"I reckons the devil is about tonight," whispered Huck.

Tom spotted a faint light hovering at the other end of the graveyard. "Huck," he gasped. "The devil is about. Look, he's coming."

Both boys dived behind a tree, their hearts beating loudly. "Think the devil'll get us?" cried Huck, "Pray, Tom, pray."

Tom began to pray. But then he

stopped. A muffled voice carried on the wind. And he recognized it.

"Why, Huck, that ain't no devil. That's old, drunk Muff Potter with the lantern. And there's two more fellas with him."

Tom and Huck watched from behind the tree as Muff and his two pals came closer. They stopped by Hoss's grave, only a few feet away from the boys. Muff put down the lantern.

"I know the other two," muttered Huck. "One's that old crook, Injun Joe. The other's Dr. Robinson, the doctor."

Muff and Injun Joe started digging. Soon, they had uncovered Hoss's coffin.

"Bring up the corpse, hurry!" barked Dr. Robinson.

"Not so fast, doctor," replied Muff. "Injun Jo and I want another five each."

"Muff's right," growled Injun Joe. "If you want this body for your experiments, you're going to have to pay more, Doctor."

"No, I've paid you enough," said Dr. Robinson firmly.

"Why …" hissed Injun Jo, grabbing Dr. Robinson by the collar. "Five years ago, I came to your house begging for bread. You had me thrown in jail for breaking into your garden. I swore then

I'd have my revenge. So pay up, or I'll crush your head with my bare hands."

Dr. Robinson kicked out with his leg and sent Injun Jo flying.

"Hey," said Muff, clambering out of the grave. "You leave my friend alone." He tried to grab Dr. Robinson, too, but the doctor pushed over the gravestone. It landed on Muff's head with a loud thud. The drunk was knocked out cold. "Why, you …" roared Injun Joe. He spotted Muff's knife sticking out from under his belt. He snatched it and plunged it in Dr. Robinson's chest.

Just then, the moon slid behind a cloud. When it came out again, Dr. Robinson was lying on the ground in a pool of blood. Muff was sitting up. He looked dazed. The knife was in his hands.

"Muff, you shouldn't drink so much," said Injun Joe. "Now, see—you've gone and killed Dr. Robinson. Let's get away from here, quick."

The two men hurried away. Tom and Huck stared at Dr. Robinson's corpse. Their hair stood on end. Then, they stood up and ran away as fast as they could.

"We got to tell Judge Thatcher what we saw," said Tom. "Injun Joe is pinning the murder on poor Muff Potter."

"We cain't do that," said Huck. "Injun Joe'll be after us. We have to swear never to say anything about this to anyone."

"Alright," said Tom. "I swear."

"That ain't enough for this kind of promise," said Huck. "We have to write an oath. We have to seal the deal with blood."

They found a flat stone by the roadside. Tom took a piece of chalk from his pocket and started writing:

Huck Finn and Tom Sawyer swears they will keep mum about this, and they wish they may drop down dead in their tracks if they ever tell and rot.

Then, they both pricked their thumb with a pin from Tom's pocket and signed their name in blood. They buried the flat stone deep in the ground, where no one would ever find it.

In the morning, as Tom was getting dressed, something came flying through the window. It landed on the carpet with a thud. Becky had returned the brass paperweight he had given her as a gift!

Tom went down to breakfast with a heavy heart. Nothing in his life seemed to be working.

"Tom, something awful happened," said Cousin Mary. "Poor old Muff Potter has been arrested for the murder of Dr. Robinson."

CHAPTER 3

An Island and a Funeral

Tom's heart was broken over Becky returning the paperweight. He was scared Injun Jo might find out he and Huck had seen his crime. There was nothing for it. Tom decided to run away. He would go that very night, while everyone was sleeping.

On his way to school, Tom met his friend, Joe Harper. He looked sad, too. "My ma's accused me of eating the cream," said Joe. "I'm planning on running away."

"Me, too," cried Tom. "No one loves me. I might turn pirate or soldier."

"I had my mind set on becoming a hermit," said Joe, "but I'll go with you instead, Tom."

"I'll ask Huckleberry Finn to come with us," added Tom. "He's the best person I know at running away."

At midnight, the three boys met at a secret spot on the riverbank. Tom brought a large ham. Joe had an enormous side of bacon. Huck had stolen a frying pan to cook the meat on. They found an old raft and sailed to an island in the middle of the river.

It was called Jackson's Island, and it was full of trees. No one lived on it. It was the perfect hiding place.

"We shall live here til we die," said Tom.

"Yeah," agreed Joe, "I shall never return to civilization."

They fried some delicious ham and bacon. Then, they stretched out on the grass to sleep. Tom looked up at the stars, feeling very contented. There was no Aunt Polly to tell him off now. No Becky to break his heart. And no Injun Joe to try and murder him. He fell asleep and had wonderful dreams.

In the morning, the boys discovered that the raft had floated away. Not that it mattered. They didn't need it anymore.

They spent the morning fishing and swimming. Coming back to their camp at lunchtime, they spied a ferryboat moored across the river. There were people on the deck, scurrying about.

Little fishing boats were sailing around it.

"Whatever is going on?" wondered Tom, peeping through a bush.

"They're looking for something," said Tom, craning his neck.

Suddenly, there was a loud puff of smoke on the ferry. It was followed by a loud "boom," and a cannonball shot across the water.

"Why," cried Huck. "I believes they're looking for a drowned body."

"How does a cannonball find a drowned body?" Joe wanted to know.

"It churns up the water so the body floats to the surface," replied Huck. "I seen it happen when old Bill Turner got drowned last year."

"Wonder who drowned this year."

Tom grinned from ear to ear. "Us, Joe. Someone must have found our raft and think we drowned."

Suddenly, Tom felt a lump in his throat. People did love him if they were looking for him. He wondered how Aunt Polly, Sid, and Mary were taking the news.

That night, after Huck and Joe had gone to sleep, Tom swam across the river. Soon, he was crouching outside Aunt

Polly's living room. He took a peep inside. Aunt Polly sat with Sid, Mary, and Joe's mother. They were all dressed in black.

"Those poor children," wailed Aunt Polly. "Tom was such a lovely boy. He was naughty, but he had a heart of gold. He was my rock. I depended on him."

My rock! Tom had never heard Aunt Polly call him that before. His chest swelled with pride.

"We shall give all three boys a splendid funeral service on Sunday," howled Aunt Polly.

"And a mighty fine funeral it will be, even if the coffins are empty," sobbed Joe's mother.

"Amen," sobbed Mary and Sid.

When Aunt Polly blew out the lamp, Tom hurried back to Jackson's Island. In the morning, he told Joe and Huck all about the wonderful funeral they were to have.

"I didn't know we were so loved," said Joe. "It almost makes me wish I could go back there."

On Sunday, everyone in St. Petersburg was crammed into church. Three small coffins lay in front of the altar. The air was full of sobbing and the rustling of mourning clothes.

Mr. Sprague, the minister, began the sermon. He talked about Tom and Joe and Huck. He told stories that showed how brave and kind they were.

"Yes, sir, they were wonderful boys," cried Mr. Dobbins.

"Always kind to old ladies," bawled Widow Douglas, the richest woman in the whole town.

Suddenly, there was the sound of sobbing up in the church gallery. Footsteps echoed down the wooden stairs. Everyone turned to see three boys walking up the aisle. It was Tom and Joe and Huckleberry Finn. They had sneaked into the church to attend their own funeral.

"Ha," bawled Joe. "You're all so kind about us, we're moved to tears."

"Why, my Joe is back from the dead,"

shrieked Mrs. Harper.

"And so is our Tom," cried Mary. "Thank the good Lord."

"And Huck," said Tom, "Don't forget Huck. He's safe and sound, too."

Everyone gathered around the boys. "We're mighty relieved to see you still in the land of the living," said Mr. Dobbins.

Tom thought how nice it was to be back home. To know that he had been missed by everyone in town. Only one person didn't seem glad to see him.

Becky Thatcher was frowning at him from the front pew.

CHAPTER 4
Under the Cross

Tom tried very hard to make friends with Becky again. She would have none of it. "I'll ask you to keep yourself to yourself, Thomas Sawyer," she snapped, when he tried to talk to her in the schoolyard. "I'm never going to be engaged to you again."

The situation seemed hopeless until a few days later.

Mr. Dobbins had a book that he kept locked in his desk. He took it out only once every day to read while the class were doing arithmetic. No one in school had ever looked in it or knew what it was about.

Then one lunchtime, Mr. Dobbins went out for a walk. Becky found herself alone in the schoolroom. Everyone else had gone outside to play. She noticed that Mr. Dobbins had left the key in the desk drawer. Quick as a flash, she took out the book and opened the cover.

"Oh," she cried. "It's a book of anatomy."

She gazed in wonder at a huge picture showing the insides of a human body. Just then, Tom came in looking for her. Becky tried snapping the book shut. She did it in such a hurry, she ripped the picture of the human body in two.

"See what you made me do, Tom, you horrible thing," she cried. "Don't you know you should never sneak up on a girl?" She put the book back in the desk and turned the key.

Later that afternoon, Mr. Dobbins took out his precious book to look at. He gasped when he found the torn picture.

"Who has ripped up my book?" he growled.

"Joe Harper, was it you? Or you, Alfred Temple?"

Tom could see Becky trembling with fear. She was trying to raise her hand, but she couldn't. He leaped instantly to his feet.

"I did it, sir."

"Come here this instant, Thomas Sawyer!" hissed Mr. Dobbins. Tom knew what was coming. A whipping. His bottom was stinging when he left school after a two-hour detention. But the pain didn't matter. He had saved his dear Becky from a severe punishment. And she was extremely grateful.

"Oh, Tom," she said the next morning. "How could you be so noble? You're a real hero."

With Becky his best friend again, Tom should have been happy. But he wasn't. He was anxious and worried. Muff Potter's trial was coming up. The poor man might be hanged for a crime he did not commit.

And it would be Tom and Huck's fault because they were too scared to tell what they had seen.

The boys went to see Muff in prison. They took him some food.

"You've been mighty good to me, boys," said Muff. "Better than anyone else in this town."

That made Tom feel even more guilty. "Are you sure we can't tell anyone what really happened that night?" he asked Huck.

"Injun Joe or one of his friends will kill us for sure," replied Huck. "We have to keep our secret whatever happens."

The trial started. All of St. Petersburg came to watch, even Injun Joe. Muff Potter was brought to the dock. Judge Thatcher took his seat.

He called one witness after another. One said that he saw Muff sharpening his knife on the day of the murder. Another claimed he had spotted Muff sneaking into the graveyard on the night of the murder. An old woman said she had come across Muff washing himself in a stream the same night. The water around him was red with blood.

Muff looked terrified as the witnesses spoke, but Injun Joe seemed pleased. He kept chuckling to himself. Somehow, he looked even more terrifying when he was smiling. But Tom just couldn't live with his guilt. He leaped off his seat and shouted, "Mr. Judge, sir, Muff Potter is innocent. Injun Joe did it. Huckleberry Finn and I saw everything."

There were screams at the back of the courtroom as Injun Joe jumped to his feet. He pushed his way roughly through the crowds. In a moment, he had crashed through the window.

Muff Potter was saved, and Tom was the hero of St. Petersburg. The local paper even said he might be president of the United States one day.

Once again, Tom should have been happy. But he couldn't stop thinking about Injun Joe. People said they'd seen him leave town on the morning train. But what if they were wrong? What if Injun Joe came back at night to get his revenge on Tom? Tom was so terrified, he couldn't sleep at night.

"There's nothing for it, Huck," Tom said. "We've got to do something to take our mind off things."

"Like what?" said Huck.

"We could look for treasure," Tom said.

"Ha," said Huck. "That's bully. I likes that idea. But where will we dig?"

"Somewhere spooky," said Tom. "That's where robbers always hide their treasure. It stops folk from coming to look for it."

"I knows a spooky place," cried Huck. "The deserted house on Cardiff Hill. It's haunted. Come on, Tom, let's borrow your aunt's shovel."

The two boys made their way to the house on Cardiff Hill. It was indeed very spooky and dark. Enormous cobwebs hung from the ceiling in every room. The floorboards creaked.

"Let's see what's upstairs," said Huck. "Someone might've left some old clothes behind. I could do with a spare shirt."

They were halfway up the stairs when

they heard voices. "Ghosts," gasped Tom.

"Don't be silly," said Huck. "It's people, and they're alive."

They ran up the rest of the stairs and hid in a bedroom. It was dusty, and there was a big hole in the floorboards. Tom and Huck could see right through it to the kitchen below. The voices got louder, and two men came in.

One of them was a Spanish man in a poncho. The other was—Injun Joe. So, he hadn't skipped town after all. Tom felt his blood turn cold.

"You sure there's a treasure in this house?" said the Spanish man.

"That's what I heard," replied Injun Joe. "The Murrel gang buried it here after they robbed a train."

The two men pried up the floorboards to reveal a hole in the floor. They pulled out a wooden chest. Injun Joe smashed the lock with the shovel Huck had left on the floor. The Spanish man threw back the lid.

"Why, there's enough gold here to make us both rich."

"True," agreed Injun Jo. He stared at the shovel in his hands. "But what's this doing here? Someone else must be looking for the treasure."

He peered around the room. Tom's heart nearly stopped beating. What if Injun Joe came up the stairs and found them both?

"Let's get away from here before anyone sees you," said the Spanish man to Injun Joe. "You are a wanted man, after all."

"Yeah," said Injun Joe. "Why don't we take the treasure with us and hide it somewhere else?"

"Where?" asked the Spanish Man.

"In the safest hiding place I know," chuckled Injun Joe. "Under the cross."

CHAPTER 5

Danger in the Cave

Tom and Huck wondered what "under the cross" meant. "They must be burying the treasure in a grave," said Tom. "Graves have crosses on them."

"Or in a disused church," said Huck, as they crept away from the house on Cardiff Hill. "I'll starts shadowing Injun Joe, Tom. He has no idea I knew his secret, too."

Back home, Tom found Aunt Polly baking a cake for the picnic the next day.

Tom had been so worried about Injun Joe, he'd forgotten all about the picnic. It was held every year for the older children in St. Petersburg. No grown-ups were allowed to go except Mr. Dobbins and a few eighteen-year-olds to organize games.

At the crack of dawn, a ferryboat full of merry children sailed down the river. It stopped at a lovely spot full of trees. Much fun was had as the children ate their picnic. Then, they played games. And soon, it was time to explore the famous McDougal's Cave.

The children all crowded around an opening in the cliffs. It was shaped like a giant "A" and it looked very dark.

"There's a guide who will show us around the cave," said Mr. Dobbins.

"You stay close to me at all times," said the guide. "Don't wander off by yourselves. The cave is like a maze, and people have been known to get lost in it. Some have never been found."

He handed out candles. The children followed him, peering in the dark. "You hold my hand, Becky," said Tom. "You don't want to get lost."

McDougal's Cave was really lots of small caves joined together with narrow tunnels. There was graffiti made with candle smoke all over the walls. Some of the children stopped to read them. "Oh, look," said Tom. "This one says, 'Thomas and Gertrude were here.' I wonder who they were?"

Becky held up her candle. "Did you hear that noise, Tom? There's a waterfall in here. Let's go see it."

"Careful! We mustn't get lost in the dark," said Tom.

"We'll leave markers with candle smoke on the walls," replied Becky. "That way, we can find our way back."

They followed the noise, which led them into a small cave. The water was gushing out of a hole in the rocks. Next to it was the entrance to a second tunnel.

"Oooh," said Becky. "A secret passage. Let's see where it leads."

Before Tom could stop her, she dived into the tunnel. Tom followed. "Becky …"

Tom's voice echoed around the walls. Suddenly, there was a loud squeaking, and a flock of bats appeared out of the darkness. In a moment, the air was full of the furry creatures flapping and diving. One of them swooped down over Becky and knocked the candle out of her hands.

Becky screamed. "Let's get back to the others, Tom!"

They raced down the tunnel, chased by the angry bats. But they couldn't find their way back to the waterfall. No matter how hard they tried, they kept finding themselves back where they started.

"We're lost, Becky," said Tom.

The two of them called out over and over again, but no one heard. Hours passed. Tom's candle ran out, and they found themselves in total darkness. "We're done for," cried Becky. "We're going to die in here."

"Let's stop and rest for a while," said Tom. "We don't need to panic. Your father will organize a search party when he discovers we're missing. All we have to do is wait."

Tom had some of Aunt Polly's cake in his pocket. They shared it. Becky sat with her back against a lumpy rock, and before long, she was fast asleep. Tom just sat in the darkness, thinking. Would they really be found if Judge Thatcher sent a rescue party? Would he and Becky get out alive?

Suddenly, Tom heard a noise. Footsteps. "Wake up, Becky!" he cried. "They've found us."

Lamplight glowed at the other end of the cave. Shadows moved on the cave wall. Two figures came out of a tunnel at the other end of the cave. Tom stifled a gasp.

It was Injun Joe and his Spanish friend. They were dragging something behind them, but Tom couldn't see what it was.

"I don't like this cave at night," grumbled the Spanish man. "Can't we come back in the morning?"

"Why?" chuckled Injun Joe. "It's always dark in here no matter what time of day."

"But there are ghosts at night."

Injun Joe laughed. "Well, you go home if you're scared. I'll do this on my own."

"See you tomorrow." The Spanish man hurried off one way. Injun Joe continued the other way, dragging the heavy thing.

Tom wrapped his arms around Becky. He was so glad she hadn't woken up. He didn't want her to know Injun Joe was in the cave, too. That would terrify her.

Now Tom was more determined than ever to find a way out of the cave. He felt in his pocket and found a ball of kite string. He tied one end to a stone, which he left next to the sleeping Becky. Then, he struck out in the darkness, leaving a trail of string behind him. It would help him find Becky again.

Tom wandered around till the string ran out. He was about to return to Becky when he saw a glimmer of light. Sunlight. He let go off the string and stumbled toward it. The light was coming through a hole in the rocks. It was big enough for Tom to stick his head through.

He could see the river below. A ferryboat was chugging past.

"Help," he shouted. "Help!"

People looked up and waved. Tom was so relieved, he passed out and fell back into the darkness.

When he came around again, he was tucked up in his own bed at home, safe and sound.

CHAPTER 6

Treasure!

"How long have I been lying here, Aunt Polly?" asked Tom.

"You've been laid up for near four days," said Aunt Polly.

"And you were lost in the cave for three days," added Mary, who was cooling Tom's brow with a wet handkerchief. "Becky was very weak when we found you two. Her mother is looking after her now."

"No one will get lost in that cave again," said Judge Thatcher, who'd dropped by to check up on Tom. "I've sealed up the entrance."

"Oh, but Injun Joe is in the cave!" cried Tom.

Judge Thatcher sent some men to arrest Injun Joe at once. They found him lying on the ground, his hand stuck under the door. He had died trying to get out of the cave.

"I reckons it's fear what killed him," said Huck, when he was allowed to visit Tom.

"Injun Joe hid his treasure deep inside McDougal's Cave," Tom said to Huck when he came to visit. "I saw him dragging something out of a tunnel, and I reckon it was the treasure chest."

"Pity that the cave has been locked up," sighed Huck. "We'll never find the gold now."

"But I know a way in," replied Tom. "The same way Becky and I got out."

Aunt Polly came in to shoo Huck out of the room. But the two boys had already laid their plans. Tom waited until he heard Aunt Polly opening the door to Widow Douglas, who'd come for tea. Then, he stole out of bed, fetched the coil of rope he always kept hidden in the closet, and climbed out the window.

Huck was waiting at the end of the street. The two of them borrowed a raft and sailed downriver. When they got to McDougal's Cave, Tom found the hole he'd stuck his head through.

Huck tied the end of the rope to a nearby tree, and they lowered themselves in.

Huck lit a lamp that he'd brought with him. He held it up to see.

"What are we looking for, Huck?" asked Tom.

"A trail of Injun Joe's footprints," said Huck. "They'll lead us to the treasure, for sure."

"Here it is!" cried Tom. They followed the footprints till they came to a small cave.

Inside it was a small cot with a threadbare blanket on it. There was an old frying pan close by, still full of bacon rinds.

"This must have been Injun Joe's secret hideout," said Huck. "Hey, Tom, what's that on the cave wall over there?"

Tom looked at where Huck was pointing. "Why, it's a cross made with candle grease."

"Under. The. Cross," whispered Huck.

"Do you think it's the cross Injun Joe was talking about back in the haunted house?" asked Tom.

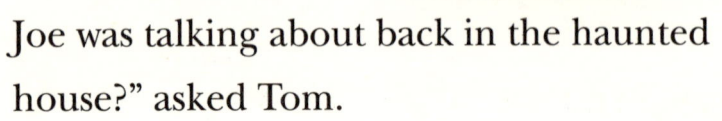

"It must be," said Huck. "We were looking for a gravestone or a church steeple, but the cross is just a marker on a wall."

The two boys approached the cross. The ground below it was rock solid.

"The treasure can't be buried here," said

Huck. "No shovel could cut through stone."

Tom knelt on the ground. "Bring the lamp closer, Huck. Do you see this large round stone? There's footprints on one side of it but not the other. That means someone stood near it and pushed it out of the way. And look, Huck, there's candle wax on the ground, same side as the footprints. Someone set a candle down here, so he could see what he was doing. I reckon the treasure is under this stone."

"Thomas Sawyer, you could be right," laughed Huck.

The two boys started pushing the stone aside. It moved slowly with a grating sound, revealing wooden boards. Tom and Huck lifted them up, and there, dark as the mouth of hell itself, was a hole in the ground.

Huck reached in. "The box is here! Help me lift it out."

They pulled up the box, and Tom threw open the lid. Gold glittered in the lamplight.

"My, but we're rich, Tom," whispered Huck in the dim light.

"Yes, we are," replied Tom. "You never need go hungry again, Huck. And you can buy yourself new clothes."

"I have no use for new clothes," said Huck. "I might be rich now, but I will stay a street boy. I will not be tamed."

The two of them dragged the chest out of the cave. It was late afternoon by the time they got to Aunt Polly's. She was fretting in the parlor. Judge Thatcher, Becky, and a few of her friends were with her. She was frantic with worry.

"I tell you, Judge, Tom's run away again."

"Huck and I went looking for treasure, Aunt Polly," said Tom through the window.

"The boy's still sick," sniffed Sid. "He's imagining things."

"But it's true," said Tom. "Huck and I brought it home in a cart we borrowed from old Benny Taylor!"

"He lives out near McDougal's Cave," added Huck.

The two boys pushed open the door and dragged the treasure chest into the parlor. Tom opened it.

"Good heavens," said Aunt Polly.

"Wow!" gasped Mary and Sid together.

"Oh, my!" Becky looked at Tom with joy in her eyes. "You're a hero, Tom!"

Tom scooped up a handful of gold. "A rich man, too, now, Becky. Come on, everyone. Ice cream is on me."

The Wind in the Willows

Retold by
Samantha Noonan

Illustrated by
Vince Reid

ARCTURUS

To Dad, remembering many happy evenings
reading about the Riverbank—SN.

For Lucia and Ronan—VR.

ARCTURUS

This edition published in 2018 by Arcturus Publishing Limited
26/27 Bickels Yard, 151–153 Bermondsey Street,
London SE1 3HA

Copyright © Arcturus Holdings Limited

All rights reserved. No part of this publication may be reproduced, stored in a retrieval system, or transmitted, in any form or by any means, electronic, mechanical, photocopying, recording or otherwise, without written permission in accordance with the provisions of the Copyright Act 1956 (as amended). Any person or persons who do any unauthorised act in relation to this publication may be liable to criminal prosecution and civil claims for damages.

Writer: Samantha Noonan
Illustrator: Vince Reid
Designer: Jeni Child
Editor: Becca Clunes
Art Director: Jessica Crass

ISBN: 978-1-78828-696-1
CH006286NT
Supplier 24, Date 0618, Print run 7519

Printed in Malaysia

Contents

CHAPTER 1
The Summertime River...........................4

CHAPTER 2
The Wild Wood 14

CHAPTER 3
Toad's Lesson...24

CHAPTER 4
A Grand Escape.......................................34

CHAPTER 5
Homeward Bound 44

CHAPTER 6
The Battle for Toad Hall.........................54

CHAPTER 1

The Summertime River

There once was a mole who lived underground. One day, he was spring-cleaning his house. It was hard work, and when he paused for a moment, he felt something calling to him from above the ground—something light and exciting. It was the call of spring! Mole threw down his duster and started to burrow upward through the earth until his pink nose popped into bright sunlight.

He rolled out into the warm grass of a meadow. It was so golden and pleasant above the ground! Birds were singing, flowers were blooming, and across the meadow was something Mole had never seen before: a river!

As Mole stared at the water, a Water Rat came rowing along in a smart little blue-and-white boat.

"Hello, there!" said the Rat, noticing Mole gazing at him. "Would you like to come aboard?"

"Oh, yes, please!" cried Mole.

Rat rowed over to him, and Mole carefully climbed in. They glided off down the river.

"This is wonderful," said Mole, leaning back, "I've never been in a boat before!"

"What, *never*?" exclaimed Rat. "Why, I think there is nothing better than messing about in boats!"

"I think I like boats already," said Mole, waggling his back paws.

"Well, then, let's spend a day on the river!" replied Rat.

He rowed them downstream, tied the boat up to the bank, and pulled out a picnic basket. Inside was the most wonderful picnic Mole had ever seen! There were cold meats, pickles, egg sandwiches, and salad, with lemonade and ginger ale to wash it all down.

As they began to eat, Rat's friend, Otter, climbed up out of the river. Rat introduced Otter and Mole, and they all had a merry lunch together. Otter and Rat told Mole how lively and fun life on the river was all year round.

Mole spotted a patch of dark woodland beyond the river and asked what it was.

"That's the Wild Wood," said Rat, as Otter shuddered a little.

"Is it a nice place?" Mole asked.

"It's not the place that's the problem; it's the animals," said Otter.

Rat nodded. "We riverbankers avoid the Wild Wood. Of course, our friend Badger lives there, but there are weasels and stoats, too. Nasty creatures, all of them. Stay away from the Wild Wood."

When they had finished eating, Otter said goodbye and dived back into the water. Mole and Rat packed everything up and put it in the boat. Rat began to row down the river once more.

"Rat, can I try rowing?" Mole asked.

Rat chuckled. "It's not as easy as it looks. Better wait until you know the river a little better."

Mole felt annoyed by this. How hard could rowing be? He stood up suddenly and snatched the oars from Rat. Rat was so surprised that he fell off his seat backward. Mole tried to dig the oars into the water and pull, but he missed completely and ended up toppling over. As he tried to scramble up, he slipped and tumbled over the side of the boat, landing in the river with a splash.

Mole couldn't swim, so he sank down in the cold water until a brown paw came down after him and scooped him out. Rat plonked him on the riverbank.

"R-Rat, I'm s-so s-sorry," Mole said, through chattering teeth.

"That's all right," said Rat. "Why don't you come and stay with me, if you like the river? We'll make a rower of you yet!"

One day, when Mole had been staying at Rat's for a while, Rat announced that they were going to visit his friend, Toad.

"I'll warn you, though," said Rat, "Toad's a nice animal, but he's too rich for his own good. He's always taking up expensive hobbies for a week or so and then getting bored with them. He's tried rowing and punting and sailing. I've heard he has a new hobby now, but goodness knows what it is."

They rowed up the river to Toad Hall, a grand old house. Toad was standing outside it, and he looked delighted when he spotted them.

"Hello, hello!" he called. "You're just in time to join me on my trip!"

"Trip?" asked Rat. "Down the river, you mean?"

"Oh, pooh to the river!" Toad bounced ahead of them, leading them to a canary yellow caravan that was hitched to a horse. He flung his arms wide. "I travel by road now! The open road, in my beautiful caravan!"

"So, that's his new hobby," muttered Rat.

"You must come with me," said Toad. "I won't take no for an answer."

"It does sound rather fun," said Mole.

The next morning, they were trundling down a quiet lane. Mole was walking in front of the caravan, chatting to the horse. Toad was telling Rat stories about himself, which he loved doing.

Suddenly, they heard a buzzing noise and then a "Poop-poop!" behind them. A bright red motor car zoomed past like it was on a racetrack. It gave the horse such a fright that he leaped backward. Toad was sent flying, and the caravan fell into the ditch with a crash.

"It's broken, completely broken!" Rat shouted, while shaking his fist at the car. Mole calmed the horse down and unhitched him. Then, they both tried to pull the battered caravan out of the ditch.

"Toad, come and help," said Rat. He looked round to see Toad, sat in the middle of the road where he had landed. Toad looked happy as he gazed after the car. "Poop-poop!" he said.

"What?" asked Mole.

"*That*, my friends, is the only way to travel!" said Toad.

"I think we just discovered Toad's next hobby," Mole whispered to Rat.

Sure enough, the next day, Toad ordered a brand-new motor car.

CHAPTER 2
The Wild Wood

Winter arrived at the river, and it became a quiet place for once. All the animals tucked themselves away from the cold in their snug homes. It was too chilly to mess around on the water.

Rat liked to pass his days in front of the fire, writing poetry and dozing. Mole found it rather boring and longed for something to do. He remembered hearing about Rat's friend, Badger, who lived in the Wild Wood. Every animal spoke very highly of Badger, but he hadn't visited the river all summer.

"Rat, why don't we call on Badger today? I would love to meet him," Mole suggested one crisp morning.

"Not a good idea," yawned Rat, as he poured his tea. "Badger sees people only when he wants to. I'm his friend, and I've never even called on him. Besides, you don't want to go to the Wild Wood at this time of year. It's an awful, dark place."

Mole was disappointed by this. He had left his underground home for excitement, not sitting! That afternoon, when Rat had begun to doze in his armchair, Mole sneaked out. "I'm not scared of any wood," he muttered to himself.

Mole scurried toward the Wild Wood in the chilly air. The bare trees and bushes were rough and tangled. "But there's nothing so scary about them," Mole muttered to himself. Inside the wood, though, the light was much dimmer than outside. The farther he went, the darker it got. The trees loomed closer and closer. Mole began to feel a little scared …

Then, Mole saw a pair of sharp eyes staring at him from a hole. Nervously, he sped up. Another mean face glared out of a small hole, then another and another.

Next, he heard pitter-pattering, as if hundreds of tiny paws were heading toward him. Mole panicked and started to run, tripping over roots in his haste to get away. He found a hollow in an old tree to hide in. Curled up, he listened to all the terrible noises outside and shivered.

"Oh, why didn't I listen to Rat?" Mole whispered sadly to himself.

Meanwhile, Rat had woken up to find Mole gone. When he spotted Mole's paw prints, he raced straight after his friend. He eventually found Mole in his hollow and crawled in. Both friends were so tired that they fell asleep.

They woke up a few hours later to find that a thick, white blanket covered the whole wood. Snow! And it was still falling hard.

"We must try to get home," said Rat, "but this snow makes everything look so different, I can't be sure of the way."

After walking for a long time and not finding the edge of the wood, they started to lose hope of getting home. Suddenly, Mole tumbled forward and squealed.

"Ouch, my leg! I tripped over something—something that was hidden in the snow!"

Rat knelt down to look at Mole's leg. "Hmm, it's a clean cut," he said. "It looks like something sharp did it, not a tree root."

"Well, it hurts, whatever it was," grumbled Mole.

Rat looked thoughtful and started digging through the snow.

"It's a door scraper!" he said.

"How odd!" Mole exclaimed.

Rat kept on digging. Next, a shabby old doormat appeared.

"What on earth?" cried Mole, but Rat hadn't finished. He started scraping at a bank of snow above the doormat. The snow fell away to reveal a green door.

Peering close, Mole could see a brass plaque with a name written on it: Mr. Badger!

Eagerly, Rat and Mole rang the doorbell. After a while, they heard muffled shuffling and grumbling. The door swung open, and Badger peered out grumpily. "Who wants what in this weather?" he snapped.

"Please, Badger, it's us," said Rat, "We got lost in the woods."

Badger's face softened right away. "Rat and Mole! Come in, you poor, cold fellows. It's not a night for small creatures to be out." He ushered them in, and they followed him to a warm and snug kitchen.

Badger urged them to sit as he bustled around, fetching them dry clothes, hanging their wet things in front of the fire, and making a splendid supper.

Once they had eaten and shared their news, Badger asked after Toad. "Keeping out of mischief, I hope?" he said.

"Afraid not," said Rat, "He's smashed up six cars so far."

"Been in hospital three times," Mole put in.

"And has a mountain of fines to pay," Rat finished.

Badger looked very cross indeed. "Somebody needs to tell that Toad off. When the weather is warmer, I am coming over, and we will deal with him together."

Rat and Mole slept very well in Badger's comfy house and awoke only at noon, when Otter came looking for them. Badger grunted at another uninvited guest, but he made them all a delicious lunch of hot soup and fresh bread.

"Thank you for taking such good care of us, Badger, old chap," said Rat, as he wiped his whiskers. "Now, we really must be going before it gets dark again."

"Don't you worry about that," rumbled Badger, "I can take you right to the edge of the wood in my tunnels."

They followed Badger through the dark tunnels. Being underground made Mole miss his own little house for a moment, but then he shook himself. He preferred the river life, of course. Finally, they saw daylight. Badger pulled the undergrowth aside to reveal that they were at the edge of the Wild Wood.

"Run along, now," he said, "I'll see you in the summer, and we'll deal with silly Toad."

"Bye, Badger!" they chorused and set off toward the river.

When Mole glanced back, Badger had already replaced the bushes, and the tunnel had completely disappeared.

CHAPTER 3

Toad's Lesson

Badger was as good as his word. On the first proper day of summer, the sun was shining brightly on the rushing river. Mole and Rat were preparing their boat to go on a fishing trip, when Badger appeared.

"Hello there!" they cried.

Badger's face was grim. "I have heard that Toad is having a new car delivered today," he said. "We must go at once to Toad Hall."

The three friends set off along the riverbank. Sure enough, when they reached Toad Hall, a new car was sitting outside. As they drew close, the front door of Toad Hall flew open, and Toad stepped out, dressed in his driving cap and goggles.

He caught sight of them and beamed. "My good fellows! Do you like my new car? You're just in time to join me on a very jolly trip!" He faltered as he caught sight of their stern faces. "Why, whatever is the matter?"

Badger strode up the steps. "Take Toad back inside," he said to Rat and Mole. Then, he turned to the man who was delivering the car. "I'm afraid Toad does not want this car. Please take it away."

Toad spluttered and struggled as Rat and Mole dragged him through the front door. "What is the meaning of this? Let go of me! I'm going driving, you nincompoops!"

"No, you aren't," growled Badger. "You've been a fool, wasting the money your good father left you and being a danger to yourself and all the other animals. It's time somebody stopped you."

He took Toad by the shoulder and led him into the dining room, closing the door behind them.

They were in there for a long time. Rat and Mole settled into armchairs by the fire. Through the door, they could hear the growl of Badger's voice, scolding, and the squeak of Toad's voice, pleading.

Eventually, the door opened, and Toad appeared, looking very sorry for himself.

"Now," said Badger, "Toad has agreed that he will stop this driving nonsense and be a good animal once more. Haven't you, Toad? Come on, tell them what you told me."

Toad was quiet for a moment, then he burst out laughing. "No, I haven't, and I won't!" he chortled. "I love driving, and I will never stop—never!"

Badger looked furious. "Then you leave us no choice, you very silly animal."

Mole and Rat took Toad to his room and locked him in.

Badger stood behind the door as Toad yelled and beat it with his fists. "It's the only way, Toad. You'll remain there until you give up your dangerous hobbies."

Toad was furious and not very nice to be around, so they all took turns watching him.

One day, when Rat was on watch, Toad turned to him, looking rather pale and wobbly, and said, "Rat, I think I am unwell, and I need a doctor."

Rat had to agree that Toad was looking rather ill, but he didn't know what to do. Badger and Mole were both out, and he knew that he shouldn't leave Toad alone.

"I really think this might be the end," Toad muttered, falling to the floor. "Ah, well, I have lived a good life."

Rat jumped up right away and ran for the doctor.

As soon as he had gone, Toad stopped being wobbly and pale. He watched from the window as Rat hurried down the road. Toad chuckled to himself, jumped up, and dressed as quickly as he could. He filled his pockets with money. Then, he tied all his bed sheets together, threw them out of the window, and climbed down.

Toad skipped down the road, laughing and smirking to himself.

"I am the cleverest of all Toads! They can lock me in a room, but they can't outsmart me, haha! Wonderful Toad! The best actor in the land!"

He walked for a long time, and then decided to reward himself with a fine lunch at a country inn. Before he could take a bite, he heard the noise he had been dreaming of: a loud "Poop-poop!" and the rumble of a car engine. Toad leaned to look out of the window and saw a gleaming green sports car pulling up in front of the inn. The passengers all got out and came inside.

"There would be no harm in looking at it," Toad said to himself, leaving his lunch and heading outside.

"There would be no harm in starting it," Toad reasoned, cranking the handle and making the engine roar once more.

"There would be no harm in sitting in it," Toad muttered, glancing around before slipping into the leather seats.

Before he knew it, he was in the car, racing away at high speed.

"No harm! No harm at all!" Toad shrieked as the wind whooshed past him, "I am *me* again!"

Later that afternoon, Toad was in handcuffs, standing in front of a judge in court. A policeman was holding him still, and Toad kept trying to stamp on his foot.

The judge frowned down at Toad from the bench. "It is rare that we have such a dreadful and bad criminal brought before us. Now I will give you your sentence: one year in prison for stealing a valuable car. Then, I will add three years for dangerous driving. Another *fifteen* years for being rude to a policeman, which all together would be nineteen years. So, why don't we round it up to twenty years, to be on the safe side?"

"Excellent!" said the policeman.

"Absolutely not!" gasped Toad.

"Twenty years in prison it is," said the judge. "Take him away!"

Toad could barely believe what he was hearing. He shrieked and struggled as the policeman hauled him away. Outside, the crowd threw rotten vegetables at him.

The policeman dragged him to the jail, and Toad was thrown in the deepest, darkest dungeon of the most secure prison in all of England. Toad threw himself down in his horrible cell and cried and cried.

CHAPTER 4

A Grand Escape

"Oh, this is the end of Toad! Woe is me! How stupid I have been! Why didn't I listen to wise Badger, stout Mole, and good Rat? Now I shall rot in this hole."

Toad wailed like this day and night and refused all food and drink.

The jailer's daughter was a sweet girl, who loved animals and hated that Toad was so upset. She persuaded her father to let her take Toad his meals and see if she could cheer him up. The jailer was tired of all the noise, so he agreed.

The girl took a stack of hot, buttered toast and two mugs of tea to the dungeon. "Toad, why don't you share supper with me?" she called over his crying.

Toad wanted to ignore her, but then the warm, buttery smell drifted into his nostrils, and he licked his lips.

"Very well, then, I suppose I could have a little piece of toast," he sniffed.

Soon, Toad had gobbled up nearly the entire stack of toast and drunk all the tea. He was almost back to his old self, as he told the girl tales of his life.

The girl visited Toad every day and grew fond of him. She thought it wasn't fair that he was in prison for such a long time.

"Toad," she said to her friend one day. "I think I may have a way for you to escape."

"What is it?" cried Toad, eagerly.

"My aunt is the washerwoman here," said the girl. "She is going to deliver the clean washing tomorrow. I think I could persuade her to lend you some of her clothes, and you could leave the prison disguised as her. You both have very similar figures."

Toad spluttered. "I could not leave the prison as a washerwoman!"

"Well, then, you can stay here as a toad, you ungrateful creature," said the girl.

Toad quickly understood this might be his only chance of escape. "I mean, of course, that is an excellent plan and most kind of you. It would be my pleasure to dress up as your aunt, the washerwoman."

"Wonderful!" said the girl, "I'll ask her."

Her aunt agreed, and the next day, they dressed Toad up in her clothes.

"There, nobody would know the difference!" said the girl, proudly.

Toad felt very silly, but he bit his tongue.

Toad picked up a basket of washing and made his way out of the prison. He was terrified that the guards would see through the disguise. Instead, they held the prison door open for him. They wished him a pleasant afternoon as he stepped into the fresh air.

"I am a cunning and brilliant Toad!" he whispered to himself, as he scurried down the road, completely forgetting that it hadn't been his own plan.

He ran straight to the train station to catch the fastest train home, but when he tried to pay for a ticket, he found he had no money. He'd left it in the pockets of his own clothes back at the prison!

Toad stood on the platform, cursing his bad luck. The kindly train driver spotted him and asked what was the matter.

"Oh, I am a tired, unhappy, old washerwoman, with no money to get home," Toad cried.

"You poor thing!" said the driver, "I can't just leave you here. Tell you what, how about a free ride if you do some of my washing later?"

Toad could hardly believe his luck. "That would be wonderful, kind sir. Thank you!"

The train set off in a great cloud of steam and began to race through the countryside. Toad smiled to himself. He would be home in time for supper.

Then, the train driver frowned as he looked out of the cab. "It looks like we are being followed by another train. A very strange one, packed with policemen, all shouting 'Stop! Stop!'"

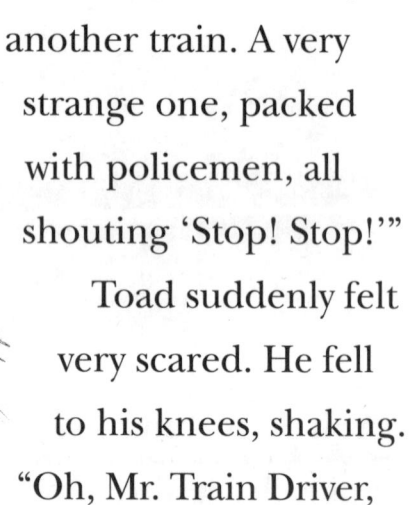

Toad suddenly felt very scared. He fell to his knees, shaking. "Oh, Mr. Train Driver, I am afraid I have not been honest with you. I am not a simple washerwoman. I am the Famous Toad. I just escaped from the horrid dungeon that my enemies threw me in, and now they are trying to catch me again. Please, won't you help me?"

The train driver looked thoughtful. "I think you must be a very bad Toad, but I feel sorry for you. So, I will help."

Together, they scooped coal in the train's stove, so they could pick up speed. But no matter how fast they went, the train of policemen kept catching up with them.

"It's no good!" said the train driver. "They're faster than us."

"Oh, what shall I do?" shrieked Toad.

"Listen," said the driver, "we are about to go through a tunnel." He pointed to it up ahead. "We will come out of the other end while they are still inside. That's your chance. You will have to jump for it before they come out. They won't see you, and they can keep on chasing my train until I run out of coal."

Toad gulped. The train was going so fast, he didn't know how hard his landing would be, but he nodded.

The train shot into the tunnel. Everything went black, and the sound was almost deafening. When they came out the other side, Toad saw that a bank sloped steeply down to a dark wood.

The driver shouted, "JUMP!"

Toad leaped from the train and tumbled down the bank. Luckily, it didn't hurt. He jumped up and ran to the trees. From his hiding place, he saw the policemen's train rattle past, with all of them still shouting, "Stop!"

Toad laughed heartily to himself. He was free! Then, he remembered he was also all alone in a strange, dark wood. Feeling a little scared, he found a hollow tree, curled up inside, and went to sleep.

CHAPTER 5

Homeward Bound

The next morning dawned bright and cheerful. Toad woke up in his hollow. For a moment, he had no idea where he was—or why he was wearing a dress! Then, the story of his daring escape came back to him.

"That's right! I am a free Toad!" he giggled. He leaped out of the hollow and set off to try and find the way home.

Before too long, he came across a pathway by a canal. An old horse was pulling a brightly painted canal barge. There was a stout woman at the back, steering the boat.

She greeted Toad. "Lovely morning, isn't it?"

Toad put on his best washerwoman voice. "Maybe it is for those who aren't in trouble, like me. Here I am, a poor washerwoman, called to help my poor daughter, but now I'm lost, and I've got no money. Goodness knows how I will reach her now. She lives by Toad Hall."

"Well, I'm going that way myself!" said the woman. "This canal joins the river up there, and then it's only a short walk to Toad Hall. Why don't I take you?"

Toad climbed onto the barge, congratulating himself again for being so clever. He settled down next to the barge woman, and they chatted as the boat drifted lazily along.

"Do you enjoy being a washerwoman?" asked the barge woman.

"Enjoy? Why, there's nothing I love more in the world," lied Toad.

"Oh, well then, I have a treat for you!" smiled the barge woman. She pulled out a huge pile of dirty clothes. "I hate washing, and these are terribly dirty. You can wash them. It's my gift to you!"

Toad couldn't see a way out of it, even though he had no idea how to wash clothes. He took them to the tub she pointed to, dunked them in the water, and rubbed them, but nothing seemed to get them clean. Toad got hot, cross, and covered in soapsuds.

"I'm afraid there's something wrong with your washtub," he said.

"I'm afraid there's something wrong with *you*," retorted the barge woman. "You're no washerwoman!"

Toad stood up and kicked the tub. "That is true. I am the world famous Toad."

"Yuck, a toad!" the barge woman squealed. She picked him up and threw him into the river.

Toad landed with a big splash in the chilly water. Brrr, it was cold and full of slimy duckweed. He tried to swim for the shore but was slowed down by his wet dress.

The barge woman was laughing so hard at him that tears were streaming down her face. "Take that, you nasty Toad!" she called, as she sailed off.

Toad was determined to get even. He struggled to the bank and pulled himself up onto dry land. Then, he gathered up his wet skirts and raced after the barge. Catching up with the plodding horse, he jumped on its back. Then, he cut the tow rope and cantered off, leaving the barge far behind.

It was Toad's turn to laugh as the barge woman waved her arms and cursed him.

"Take that!" he yelled back at her.

He rode several miles on the horse before meeting a man who was making a delicious-smelling breakfast. Toad's tummy rumbled, and he gave the horse to the man in return for some food and money.

Toad walked on, feeling very smug with how things had turned out. As he walked, he made up a song about his adventures.

Toad caught sight of a car and clapped his hands in delight.

"Oh, what a stroke of luck!" he cried, "I shall ask them for a lift and that excellent car will take me all the way home. I can't wait to see Badger's face!"

He stepped out into the middle of the road and waved at the car.

But as it drew closer, Toad's glee turned to horror. The car approaching was the very same one that he had stolen from outside the inn!

Toad was certain he would be taken straight back to prison if they saw it was him. He was so scared that his legs felt weak, and he slumped down in the middle of the road.

He heard the car stop and two men getting out.

"Oh, dear, that poor woman must have fainted in the heat," said one of them.

"Let's take her to the nearest village and see if anyone knows her," said the other.

Gently, they picked Toad up and laid him in the back seat. As they drove away, Toad felt the roar of the engine beneath him and his courage came back. He just couldn't help himself ...

Toad sat up and said in a wavering voice, "Good sirs, I think I might feel better if I could sit at the front, next to the driver."

The kind men stopped the car, moved Toad to the front seat, and set off again.

A few minutes later, Toad said, "Why, I should love to try driving this car. I've been watching you, and I believe I could do it."

The men laughed and the driver said, "I like your spirit. Go on, try it."

They shuffled seats again, and Toad slammed his foot down, making the car zoom off.

"Slow down!" cried the driver.

Toad cackled. "Never! 'Tis I, the famous, fearless Toad!"

"It's the wretch who stole our car! Get him!" said the men.

They tried to grab the steering wheel from Toad, but he shoved them back, and the car spun off the road and into a hedge. Toad went flying through the air and landed straight in the river! It was flowing very fast, and Toad was whisked along, spinning and dipping below the surface several times until he drifted up against a bank. There, he found himself looking up at a familiar face. It was Rat!

CHAPTER 6
The Battle for Toad Hall

"My good Rat!" Toad cried, as Rat fished him out of the river. "I have had such an adventure. You will never believe what a clever Toad I have been. It all began with my daring escape from the deepest, darkest dungeon—"

"Oh, do be quiet, Toad," said Rat, looking a bit cross. "Come and change into dry clothes, or you'll catch a cold."

Toad followed Rat to his house and changed. Then, Rat laid out sandwiches for lunch.

"Now," said Toad, "I shall tell you my splendid stories. Where to begin? How about the time I leaped like a daredevil from a speeding train? Or stole a mean old barge woman's horse?"

Rat glared at Toad. "Stop it this minute. Those stories don't sound splendid. They sound ridiculous and embarrassing. Stealing horses? You are an idiot, Toad, and you have been ever since you bought that first car."

Toad was shocked, but he knew there was some truth to what Rat said. After a moment, he replied. "You are right, Rat. I have been a fool. I will go home right away and get rid of all my cars."

"Home?" cried Rat. "You can't go home! Haven't you heard?"

"Heard what?" Toad asked.

"Why, the weasels have taken Toad Hall for themselves!" said Rat.

Toad frowned. "Impossible."

"I tell you, they have," Rat insisted. "When you were arrested, the riverbankers were all on your side and said it was a terrible thing, but the Wild Wood creatures said you deserved it. Mole and Badger decided to move into Toad Hall, to take care of it until you returned."

"They are, indeed, excellent friends," said Toad.

"But one dark, stormy night, the weasels broke in to Toad Hall, beat poor Badger and Mole, and threw them out! Toad,

I'm afraid the weasels have been living in your house ever since."

Toad was almost shaking with fury. He pushed his chair back and said, "Well, it's time I kicked them out again!"

Rat said, "Toad, wait!"

But Toad was already out of the door and marching to Toad Hall. There was a nasty weasel standing guard at the door.

"This is my house!" Toad said to him. "I demand that you all leave immediately!"

The weasel grinned as he pointed a gun at Toad and pulled the trigger.

Toad yelped and dived.

"I tried to tell you," Rat said when Toad returned, a little shaken. "We'll need a proper plan to take it back. Let's wait for Badger and Mole to get home. They've been camping out, watching Toad Hall."

Soon, Badger and Mole appeared, looking tired and dirty. They greeted Toad with weary joy.

"Although it isn't much of a homecoming without a home," said Badger.

"How will we take it back?" Toad asked.

"It's a hopeless situation," moaned Mole. "They have dozens of armed sentries posted at every entrance. When they see us watching, they just laugh."

"Oh, hopeless indeed," murmured Rat.

Toad began to wail at the thought of never getting his home back.

"Silence!" roared Badger. "Toad Hall is thoroughly guarded, it's true. But I know a secret passageway that opens up in the middle of it."

"There is no such thing!" Toad declared.

"Indeed, there is," said Badger, "in the butler's pantry. Your father never told you because he knows you can't keep a secret. The weasels are holding a banquet for the Chief Weasel's birthday tomorrow night. So, they'll be unarmed and distracted. We can sneak through the passageway and take them by surprise."

"Where is Mole?" Rat asked the next morning. Nobody had seen him.

At that moment, Mole trotted up, wearing Toad's old washerwoman dress. "I've just been down to Toad Hall," he giggled. "I pretended to be a washerwoman looking for work. I told the sentries that I'd heard hundreds of badgers, rats, moles, and toads were coming from all directions to attack Toad Hall tonight! They all started panicking!"

"Excellent work, Mole," said Badger, heartily. "They'll be so worried about what's coming from outside, they won't be prepared for anything coming from the inside. You clever creature!"

When night fell, the friends armed themselves with big sticks and set off, with Badger leading. They took the secret passageway and slipped up through the trapdoor. The weasels were all laughing and singing in the next room, enjoying Toad's finest food and wine.

The Chief Weasel stood up on his chair. "I would like to declare a toast to Mr. Toad, our host. Long may he rot in jail, so that we can enjoy his house!"

The weasels all roared with laughter. Badger turned and nodded to the others.

"NOW!"

They burst into the banquet room, yelling. For a moment, the weasels just stared in shock. Then they leaped up, smashing plates and glasses. The huge table was overturned, and chairs went flying.

A great fight began. The weasels had their fists and teeth, but they were no match for the big sticks that the four friends carried.

Toad went straight for the Chief Weasel and gave him a few good whacks with his stick. "Have me rot in jail, would you?" Toad shouted. "Take that and that!"

The Chief Weasel squealed in pain and dived out of the window.

Meanwhile, Badger was picking weasels up and hurling them toward the door. Rat had forgotten his stick and was wrestling with a couple of weasels by the fireplace. Mole was chasing shrieking weasels as they escaped through the doors, the windows, and even up the chimney!

In a few minutes, the room was cleared.

"We've won!" cried Toad.

Through the windows, they could see the weasels racing out so fast that they all ended up falling in the river. Toad was master of the Hall once more!

"I think another banquet would be just the thing to celebrate," Badger suggested, "but with no speeches or songs by Toad."

"Oh," said Toad, crestfallen.

Toad did finally learn his lesson that day. He became humble and did not boast about himself any longer. The other animals liked him all the better for it.

The weasels had learned their lesson, too. They would never hurt the friends of Badger, Mole, Rat, and Toad. All creatures could walk around the Wild Wood safely.